NE

Douglas E. Richards
& Joshua T. Calvert

Paragon Press

This book is a work of fiction. The characters, incidents, and dialogues are products of the authors' imagination and are not to be construed as real. Any resemblance to actual events or persons, living or dead, is entirely coincidental.

Published by Paragon Press, 2026

Email Douglas E. Richards at douglaserichards1@gmail.com

Visit Richards website at www.douglaserichards.com

First Edition

1

Night had settled like a cosmic shroud over the forests of Livingston, Louisiana, while Dr. Lukas Heuer was still sitting in front of the monitors. The bluish light from the screens cast pale shadows on his sleep-deprived face, drawing deep furrows around his eyes—maps of a life devoted to the mysteries of the universe. He now carried 44 years on his shoulders, and in the last few months, each of those years seemed to have doubled in weight.

The control rooms of the LIGO observatory lay deserted. It was Friday evening. The others had hurried home to their families, their loved ones, their warm living rooms, and shared joy over good conversation, baseball, or barbecues—the modern equivalents of campfires.

Home. A concept that was becoming more and more of an abstract equation for Lukas, unsolvable in the many variables of loneliness that his mind had recently been forced to explore. His much-too-large apartment near the campus was no longer a home, but merely a place where memories of Lisa lurked.

Four months had passed since he and his wife had separated. Four months during which he had desperately tried to fill the void of her absence with work.

"You can't be serious, Lukas," she had said shortly before she left, her voice a pattern of disappointment and resignation. "You're like a ghost. Present and yet not there. Your passion for the stars is too great for me to compete with."

He let his gaze wander around his temporary office. Plain white walls, not a single picture. A desk piled high with trade journals like tectonic plates. Three monitors constantly spitting out the same data. The only personal touch was a small German flag stuck to his computer screen—a subtle reminder of his origins amid the fascinating yet often painful strangeness of America.

Nevertheless, this was where he wanted to be—where he *had* to be: the LIGO-Virgo-KAGRA—the global gravitational-wave network.

Lukas rubbed his tired eyes and took a sip of his now cold coffee. He grimaced. At that moment, he missed German coffee, if such a thing existed, and he missed the little cafés in Göttingen where he had grown up, where his father, a mathematics professor, had first introduced him to the secrets of numbers—those universal symbols that represented both the language of science and the cosmic order.

With sluggish movements, Lukas opened a browser to scroll through the news reports. He didn't do this because he was really interested in current events, but to drown out the silence that otherwise threatened to engulf him like a black hole. In the distance, a car rushed by, a fleeting sound in the quiet of the night.

Then a notification popped up, imposing itself pompously over a news article about a trade war. A soft beep sounded from the speakers. Lukas glanced at the short message.

The interferometer had detected something, a cosmic pulse in the digital arteries of the system. He was instantly alert.

His heartbeat quickened almost imperceptibly. Gravitational wave detections were no longer a rarity, but each one was a window into the cosmic abyss, a moment when the boundary between the known and the incomprehensible became permeable for a fraction of a second. He was accordingly excited as he clicked on the notification and opened the data packet.

A 3-dimensional spectrogram appeared on the main screen: the vertical axis represented the frequency of the waves, the horizontal axis represented time, and the color intensity represented the amplitude—the strength of the signal, or the volume of the cosmic whisper, so to speak.

What Lukas saw made him freeze.

The typical signature of a gravitational wave originating from merging black holes or neutron stars resembled a so-called "chirp"—a signal that rose in frequency and amplitude like a cosmic bird singing its short, intense song into the void. But what pulsed on his screen did not follow any known pattern. It was rhythmic, almost structured—a cosmic heartbeat with mathematical precision.

"That can't be," he muttered, hastily typing in a series of commands to check the system's calibration.

The signal strength was enormous, comparable to that of a neutron star in the immediate cosmic vicinity. But the signal oscillated in a precise rhythm that seemed to defy any natural explanation, as if the universe itself were opening a Morse-code channel.

A mistake, he thought instinctively.

It had to be a mistake. Maybe a malfunction in the detector, an earthquake, unusual seismic activity that was interfering with the sensitive instruments, or dirty mirrors. The scientific method demanded skepticism, especially in the face of the extraordinary, and his skepticism grew with every second he stared at the data.

Lukas launched the standard error detection protocols, letting the system search for anomalies in the environmental sensors, for temperature fluctuations, for minimal vibrations that could distort the signal.

The code danced across the screen.

Nothing. The system reported no irregularities.

"Come on," he whispered, running his hand through his uncut hair. "Show me where the mistake is."

He began triangulating the data, using measurements from all the detectors connected to the network to locate the source of the gravitational waves. He even called up the seismic data from the earthquake monitoring stations to see if there could have been any tremors anywhere that might have reached Livingston, however slight.

The hours passed. Midnight came and went. The office air conditioner hummed its monotonous melody as Lukas sank into a whirlpool of calculations and checks.

At around three in the morning, he stared in disbelief at the result of his hours of analysis: the source location did not point to a distant galaxy, not even to a cosmically close event horizon dozens or hundreds of light-years away. It pointed to a spot within the *solar system*.

Which, of course, was outright *impossible*. There were no neutron stars or colliding black holes here. Still, the measurement data was certain: it came from the immediate vicinity. The data pointed to the solar system.

To Mars's orbit, to be precise.

"Impossible!" he said aloud into the empty silence of his office, as if he needed the sound of his own voice to emphasize the absurdity of the result, as if words alone could force reality back into familiar channels.

Gravitational waves of this magnitude could only be generated by massive cosmic events—by the collision of black holes, by neutron stars merging in their final death dance. Objects with the mass of a *million* Earths, compressed to the size of cities. Nothing in the solar system except the Sun had anywhere near the mass or density required to ripple space-time in this way.

And yet the data clearly pointed to Mars's orbit. Not even to a single point, Lukas realized with growing amazement, but to three distinct sources that seemed to be arranged in an exact triangle—a nexus of perfection that, in the chaotic symphony of the cosmos, *screamed* of intelligence.

He leaned back in his chair, feeling his heartbeat hammering uncomfortably against his ribs. If this were real, then he had just discovered something that would shake the very foundations of physics. Something that couldn't be. Something that was *impossible.* An anomaly that called the entire scientific paradigm into question—or something that . . .

He didn't dare finish the thought.

Instead, his hand wandered to the phone, then paused in midair. He curled his fingers until they cracked, then opened them again.

Who should he call? The lab director? NASA? To say what? That he might have discovered three neutron stars in Mars's orbit? They would declare him insane. Or worse, incompetent, a scientific fossil who had lost touch with reality because he was drowning in heartbreak.

Science was a ruthless field, a Darwinian ecosystem of ideas. One false claim, one premature alarm, and the career he had sacrificed his life and marriage for would be destroyed.

No, he needed more data to avoid making a fool of himself. Independent confirmation, a second window to the truth, which he had to open this weekend before everyone returned to the office on

Monday—because in the unlikely event that this wasn't a measurement error, he wasn't so selfless as to be willing to let someone else take full credit for what could well be the greatest discovery in history.

But how?

He thought of Carlos Mendoza—his colleague and friend at the European Southern Observatory in Chile. Carlos worked on the Very Large Telescope, one of the most powerful optical telescopes in the world. If these alleged objects that LIGO claimed to have measured—whatever they were—actually existed, then they should also be visible in the electromagnetic spectrum. That would yield a second face of the cosmic enigma, a second piece of evidence. Lukas glanced at his watch to assess his chances of success in such a short time.

It was early evening in Chile. If he flew there immediately, he could arrive the next day. Saturday. He would have to fly back on Sunday at the latest and be back in the office. No one would go to the observatory or here to LIGO before Monday. No one would notice his absence, and no other researcher was likely to see the data he had seen—unless a recently divorced colleague somewhere in Italy or Japan was also afraid of his own apartment.

With trembling fingers, he booked a flight to Santiago, Chile. The first available connection: 6:30 a.m. via New Orleans. In three hours. Just enough time to drive to his apartment, pack a bag, and rush to the airport. He could just call, but that wouldn't convince Carlos to drive up to the observatory for him. It had to be in person. This was too big a favor—and too crazy—for him to ask over the phone.

When Lukas rose, he noticed that his knees had gone weak, as if the potential weight of his discovery was pressing down on him. Exhaustion left its heavy mark on his already worn features, but his mind was wide awake, electrified by the possibility that he was on the verge of a discovery that could change everything.

He glanced one last time at the monitors, where the mysterious signals were still pulsing, as if trying to convince him that they weren't just his imagination; *look, we are real.*

Lukas shuddered.

In the darkness of his office, only the bluish-shimmering screens remained as he pulled his jacket off the chair and hurried out to his car. Before settling into the driver's seat, he paused briefly and looked up. The sky over Louisiana was clear, the stars twinkling like distant beacons, sparkling beautifully and numerous. Somewhere out there, something was waiting for him, even though he clung to his doubts like a drowning man. This was something that couldn't be. Something that made space and time itself vibrate.

Lukas Heuer got in his car and drove through the dark streets, praying that no one would happen to come into the office until he could prove, or disprove, what he thought he had found.

2

The air in the depths of the Pyramid of Cheops carried the heavy breath of past millennia. Dr. Mira Najafi wiped a bead of sweat from her forehead with the back of her hand as she stepped with her head bowed through the narrow, low passageway that countless archaeologists had traversed before her. But behind these familiar paths lay secrets that had remained undiscovered even after centuries of research.

"Pay attention to the markings in the limestone," she instructed the small group of doctoral students who were close behind her. "Even tiny carvings can be significant. The ancient Egyptians speak to us not only through their hieroglyphs, but also through the language of architecture itself."

Her voice sounded distant even to her own ears, as if it belonged to someone else. At 37, she was one of the youngest project leaders ever to head an expedition to the Pyramid of Cheops, an honor that gave her less pleasure today than she had once imagined. In her right hand, she clutched a small notebook bound in worn brown leather, its pages curled from frequent use.

"But—" she continued, "and this is where the trained eye of experience comes into play—not everything is original. Over the centuries, particularly skilled tomb raiders and looters have been able to cover their tracks extremely well in some cases. Lime-plaster and clay, or lime-plaster and cellulose, are enough to make it look deceptively real and feel the same. What's more, both were readily available very early on. So we always have to check whether we're being fooled by past crooks."

The soft light of their LED lamps revealed the astonishing precision of the stone blocks, whose joints were still only slightly wider than the edge of a credit card, even after thousands of years. Mira stopped and pointed to a series of barely visible markings on the wall.

She gently touched the stone, a fleeting connection between the present and the past. "Also note the discoloration—it may indicate chemical reactions caused by small air pockets or moisture, which in turn may indicate hidden cavities."

Of course, she was thinking of the discovery of the chamber known as *ScanPyramids North Face Corridor*, a breakthrough in 2023 that had changed everything. After a century without the discovery of new chambers, an international team had used muon tomography to finally discover one—a corridor about 30 feet in length, 6.6 feet wide, and 6.6 feet high, hidden behind walls of solid limestone. The news made headlines around the world and opened the door to a new era of pyramid research—as well as the wallets of financial backers.

"Professor Najafi?" A young woman with short, dark hair—Leila, if she remembered correctly—raised her hand tentatively. "Shouldn't we wait until Dr. Abdelrahman is back with the ground-penetrating radar? The preliminary scans have shown unusual density differences in this area."

Mira blinked, suddenly torn from her thoughts. "Of course, Leila. Good point." She forced a smile. "We'll proceed methodically. Science is a game of patience, not a race."

In front of them, the passage opened into one of the side corridors they had already explored, one of many branches in the complex labyrinth of internal structures. As she spoke, her thumb unconsciously stroked the worn leather cover of the notebook like a talisman that gave her security but also kept drawing her attention back to it.

Mira licked her lips and led her group back to the temporary base camp they had set up in the Great Gallery, the impressive, nearly 30-foot-high corridor that led to the King's Chamber. The rest of her team from Yale University, the institution that had been at the forefront of Egyptological research for more than a century, was already waiting there. The camp blended state-of-the-art equipment with the pyramid's ancient grandeur.

Professor David Markowitz, her mentor and sponsor, had handed her the reins of the project two months earlier, fully aware that her motivation went beyond pure science. Yale had provided generous funding after the sensational discoveries of 2023 had electrified the scientific community. The suspicion that dozens of additional chambers and cavities could be hidden in the pyramid had fired the imagination of researchers and financiers alike. But with the leap of faith came an unspoken demand: she had to deliver.

"Let's go through the new data," she said, pointing to the makeshift work tables on which computers and scientific instruments were set up—modern technology in the belly of a 4,500-year-old monument.

Dr. Ahmed Abdelrahman, an Egyptian colleague from the Cairo Museum, nodded to her as she approached. His screen showed a 3-dimensional model of the interior of the pyramid that had been mapped so far, interspersed with colored markings indicating potential anomalies.

"We've scanned the northeast quadrant with ground-penetrating radar," he explained solemnly, looking at the students. "The scans reveal promising anomalies in density here and here."

The students gathered around the screen, excited by the possibility of new discoveries. Mira looked at the displays with professional interest, but her mind kept wandering back to the private notes in the small leather book in her hand.

"At this point," continued Abdelrahman, zooming in on a specific area, "we found an unusual reflection signature. The density doesn't change abruptly like it would in a normal cavity, but gradually. That could indicate a passage that was deliberately filled in.

"In addition," he continued, "we have the latest data from the muon detectors. He called up a new visualization showing the density of muon penetration—brighter areas where more particles passed through, darker areas where the massive stone structure blocked them. "The main cavity from 2023 is clearly visible here." He pointed to a long, bright area above the Grand Gallery. "But these smaller signatures here and here are new and correlate with our radar results."

"Okay, then," said Mira. "Let's split into three groups. Team one will check the anomaly in the northeastern area with me. Team two, led by Dr. Abdelrahman, will investigate the western corridor with the new infrared scanners. Team three will document the hieroglyphs in the newly discovered antechamber. Pay particular attention to repetitions of the ankh symbol in connection with astronomical signs—this was a recurring motif in the previous chambers."

The division of tasks was quick and routine. Mira led her group through the Great Gallery, whose sloping floor seemed like a path to another dimension. The lights of their headlamps danced on the walls like fleeting thoughts as they advanced in silence, each lost in awe of this place that had survived for millennia.

After reaching the area that the radar scans had marked as unusual, the methodical work of investigation began. "The pyramid is more than simply a structure," said Mira after the group had been studying sensor readouts for some time. "It is a repository of knowledge, a stone library whose language we are only just beginning to decipher."

After an hour more of methodical work, she was overcome by the familiar uneasiness that had accompanied her since the beginning of this expedition.

"Keep mapping," she said to her team as the hairs on the back of her neck stood on end. She felt strangely watched. But maybe it was just guilt. "I'll check the eastern side corridor, which showed a slight anomaly on the muon scans. Jason, you take the lead. Document every inch and send the data directly to my tablet."

As soon as she was out of sight, she slowed down. She listened briefly to make sure no one was following her, then pulled a small, homemade device out of her bag. No larger than a smartphone, it was an extremely sensitive anemometer, capable of registering even the slightest air movements. Movements that could indicate hidden openings too narrow for conventional instruments to detect. She had paid a small fortune to fund its development.

She opened the leather book and turned to a page with a hand-drawn map of the pyramid, supplemented by cryptic notes in her father's distinctive handwriting. Dr. Dariush Najafi had disappeared from this very spot 15 years ago, leaving behind his daughter and wife without explanation, without saying goodbye—a man who had dedicated his life to researching ancient Egypt, suddenly wiped out like a footprint in the sand.

He would never have left her voluntarily; she was sure of that.

Mira looked around when she felt herself being watched again, but there was no one else here, and she didn't even hear the muffled echoes of her students.

She looked at the map again and tried for the hundredth time to decipher its secrets.

The official investigation had gotten nowhere, intimating that her father had either met with foul play or had wanted to ditch his family and begin a new life. Mira didn't believe either. Her father had been too experienced, too cautious, to let himself fall into a trap, natural or man-made. And he had loved his family beyond all else. Besides, the way his personal records had disappeared, leaving behind only this one notebook, was highly suspicious.

All of this pointed to something bigger. Somehow, she was sure of it.

The pages of the book were filled with precise drawings, mathematical calculations, and cryptic references to astronomical constellations. Her father had studied the "precession of the equinoxes" in particular, the slow, cyclical process by which the Earth's axis described a complete circle in the sky—a cycle that lasted about 25,920 years, the "Great Cycle," as he called it.

She followed a narrow passageway that led away from the main routes. Here, the air was even thicker, the dust of millennia floating like a fine mist in the light of her headlamp. The anemometer in her hand showed no significant readings as she slowly moved it along the wall, inch by inch, in a ritual she had repeated dozens of times over the past few weeks.

At one point, she stopped and looked at a series of barely visible markings in the stone. To the untrained eye, they might have appeared to be natural irregularities, but Mira recognized a pattern—a stylized star surrounded by three small triangles. She had seen the same symbol in her father's notes, accompanied by complex calculations relating to the hour stars, the celestial bodies that the ancient Egyptians had used to measure time.

Mira leaned her forehead against the cool stone, briefly overcome by exhaustion. After two months of intensive research, she was no closer to finding her father. She had only one month left before her funding ran out and the research time would be handed over to other teams.

Her thoughts wandered back to the last days with her father. He had undoubtedly been different, distant, immersed in ancient texts and astronomical calculations. "It's all connected, Mira," he had said to her one night, his eyes feverish. "The stars, the pyramids, the cycles of time—a pattern just waiting to be deciphered."

At the time, she had dismissed his words as the usual enthusiasm of a passionate scientist. Today, she wondered if he had actually discovered something—something so significant that it had cost him his life.

She sank to the floor, the notebook on her bent knees. The last page her father had written on contained a series of numbers and astronomical symbols, next to a sketch of a constellation she couldn't identify. Below it was a single sentence in Farsi, her mother tongue: "They are not returning, they are still here."

What did he mean by that? *Who* was still here? And what was the connection to the Great Cycle of Precession?

Mira closed her eyes for a moment and stubbornly blocked out the thought that he might have gone mad. In the silence of the pyramid, surrounded by stones that had seen thousands of years of human history, she suddenly felt small and insignificant.

Her father had discovered a secret here, something that had torn him away from his family—or had violently separated him from them.

She remembered his laughter, his warm hand holding hers as she ran through the museums of Boston with him when she was a little girl. He had explained the hieroglyphics to her, taught her to decipher the mysterious symbols, told her stories of pharaohs and gods, of forgotten cities and ancient wisdom. He would never have left her of his own free will—not without a good reason.

She opened her eyes, filled with new determination. Somewhere in this vast stone complex, the answer lay hidden. She would find it, whatever the cost.

As she stood up, her gaze fell on the wall opposite. Something on the surface of the stone caught her attention—not an obvious inscription or mark, but a subtle irregularity in the masonry, barely perceptible in the dim light, so marginal that hardly anyone would have noticed it.

She stepped closer and ran her fingers over the rough limestone. There, almost invisible to the untrained eye—even her own just a moment ago—was a symbol carved into the stone: three small triangles arranged in a specific formation that she recognized from her father's notes.

The small digital pointer of the anemometer in her hand suddenly moved—almost imperceptibly. She didn't feel anything on her fingers or skin, but the sensitive instrument had detected a hint of movement, a tiny stream of air passing through an invisible gap.

Mira held her breath and checked the spot again.

There it was again!

After all this time, all the methodical searching, she had finally discovered a clue. Not a random anomaly in the data, but a *sign*, placed there by human hands—perhaps her own father's. The triangles were located directly beneath the tiny air current.

With trembling fingers, she touched the carved symbol, pressing lightly against the ancient stone as the anemometer continued to register the subtle movement of air—the whispered promise of a hidden truth.

3

The Boeing 787 lifted gently off the runway at Louis Armstrong International Airport in New Orleans. Lukas watched as the lights of the city below him merged into a glowing texture, a web of lights from the bustling civilization that never seemed to rest. He had barely slept in the last 24 hours, and yet he felt a strange clarity in his thoughts.

Almost ten hours flying time to Santiago. Ten hours in which his discovery hung unconfirmed, neither true nor false, like the proverbial cat in Schrödinger's box of uncertainty.

As the plane reached cruising altitude, Lukas leaned his head against the small window.

The ocean below him was a black void, broken only occasionally by the silver glow of moonlight on the waves. The night was cloudless, and above him the stars shone with cold clarity, indifferent to the questions he threw at them. What if he had made a mistake, after all? What if his sleep-deprived eyes had seen patterns where there were none?

A lonely man longing for meaning, for a reason to escape the emptiness of his life.

He closed his eyes, trying to find the sleep he so desperately needed, but his mind kept circling around the data he had seen. Three signal sources on Mars's orbit. Three objects with the gravitational signature of small neutron stars. Not one impossibility, but three.

As the first light of day touched the horizon—after hours of brooding and self-doubt—the plane finally landed in Santiago, nestled among the mighty peaks of the Andes. Lukas felt strangely detached, as if the journey had catapulted him not only across the globe, but out of his own reality.

He had called before he left to arrange for the fastest rental car money could buy to be waiting for him, and just a handful of minutes after landing, he was sitting in a dark blue Audi SQ3, racing out of the Chilean capital toward the Atacama Desert. The European Southern Observatory was located in La Silla, almost 300 miles north of Santiago—a journey through one of the driest and most inhospitable landscapes on Earth, but at least traffic was minimal.

Lukas didn't slow down. The landscape on either side of the road flew past him, a kaleidoscope of golden brown rocks and pale green, sparse vegetation. The sky above him was so intensely blue that it almost hurt to look at it directly—a blue that only existed in regions where the air was so clear that it seemed almost nonexistent.

He streaked over the highway at nearly 100 miles per hour, having arranged to meet with Carlos before he had left. His colleague was one of the few people he would call a friend—a brilliant astronomer with a talent for optical telescoping who had been working at the VLT in Chile for three years.

He had told Carlos that he'd booked a flight to Chile and would be arriving that morning, and convinced his friend to let him access the telescope, given that on the weekend it would normally lie dormant.

Not that Carlos hadn't objected. Vigorously. It was a transgression that could easily get him fired from a job he loved. Lukas had told him he couldn't explain over the phone, but that it was vitally important or he wouldn't have made the request.

Nobel Prize level important. A phrase that had certainly gotten Carlos's attention.

The last few miles to La Silla led along a lonely mountain road that wound its way up the slope in tight curves. The landscape became barren, the air thinner.

As he took the last bend, the observatory appeared before him, a cluster of white domes on the summit of the mountain, glistening in the sunlight like giant mushrooms sprouting from the dry ground. The European Southern Observatory in La Silla was one of the first large observatories to be built in Chile, a pioneer of modern astronomy. Its strategic location in the Atacama Desert, far from light pollution and atmospheric disturbances, and an average of 300 clear nights per year made it one of the best sites for astronomical observations on Earth. Lukas parked the car in front of the main building and got out. The sudden silence after the long drive was almost palpable.

The air was dry and cool, filled with the scent of desert dust. He looked around and saw an old pickup truck parked at the edge of the parking lot. Next to it, Carlos Mendoza was leaning against the hood, his arms crossed in front of his chest, sunglasses on his nose.

"You look like you've seen the devil, my friend," said Carlos as Lukas approached him. Carlos shook his friend's hand warmly and then pulled him in for a quick hug. "What the hell is going on?" he said, arching an eyebrow. "Since your call, I've been super stressed out about letting you in. But also highly . . . *intrigued*. Given you've flown halfway around the world for this, I tend to take your word that it's important."

Lukas nodded toward the entrance to the telescope and swallowed hard. "I guess we'll find out."

They entered the main building, and Carlos led him through a long, air-conditioned corridor.

"You got lucky," said Carlos with a rolling Spanish accent. "The New Technology Telescope isn't scheduled for observations today. Just being calibrated."

With its main mirror measuring 10 feet in diameter, the NTT was one of the smaller telescopes at the observatory, but it had adaptive optics that could compensate for atmospheric disturbances and was ideal for short-term observations.

They entered the control room, a windowless space filled with monitors and computer terminals. Carlos sank into one of the swivel chairs before booting up the computers. "What are we looking for?"

Lukas took a deep breath. The moment of truth. He took a USB stick out of his pocket, plugged it into the computer, and opened a file with the LIGO coordinates after Carlos gestured that he could go ahead.

"These 3 points," he said, pointing to the screen. "They're near the orbit of Mars."

"Uh, cool. And what exactly do we expect to find there?"

"I don't know. But last night, LIGO recorded gravitational waves from these positions. *Gravitational waves*, Carlos. From Mars's orbit."

Carlos snorted. "Then your equipment is malfunctioning, my friend. Instead of flying here, you should have searched the web for a LIGO repairman. My cousin works on air-conditioners. Do you think he could help?" he said with a wry smile.

"Very funny, Carlos. Because when data shows me that three black holes, or three neutron stars, have suddenly appeared near Mars, I don't question it at all. Just another Friday, right? No need to check the equipment and readings, right?"

Carlos winced. "Okay," he allowed. "I suppose you did check it out."

"You think? Exhaustively. Many, many times. The equipment and the data."

"Which is why you're here."

"Exactly."

Carlos looked at him for a moment, then turned to the computer. "These coordinates are accurate?"

"As accurate as LIGO could determine."

With practiced movements, Carlos entered the coordinates into the telescope's control program.

An image of the telescope dome appeared on one of the side monitors, slowly opening as the massive optics inside aligned with the specified section of the sky.

"It'll take a while," said Carlos. "The NTT uses adaptive optics to correct distortions caused by turbulence in the Earth's atmosphere in real time. It uses tiny actuators to almost microscopically change the shape of the mirror—a technological marvel that has revolutionized the quality of terrestrial telescopes. And it can not only take images, but perform a spectroscopic analysis."

A star map of the target area now appeared on one of the main monitors. The Martian orbit was empty at that moment, as Mars was currently on the opposite side of the Sun.

"If there's anything there, we should be able to see it," said Carlos. "Even relatively small objects reflect sunlight."

Lukas nodded, the tension making it difficult to breathe. The next two hours passed in a state of tense anticipation. Carlos worked on the controls, adjusted the telescope, took the first test images, and refined the alignment.

Lukas stared at the monitors, searching for even the slightest anomaly. His tension grew into an uncomfortable lump in his throat, and he began to pace back and forth like a caged tiger.

Then came the disappointment: the first images showed nothing but the eternal emptiness of space, interspersed with distant stars glittering like diamonds on black velvet.

"We need to increase the exposure time," muttered Carlos. He raised his eyebrows. "On the other hand, if we really are dealing with a black hole—which we're not, because that would be *loco*—we could gather light for eternity and never see it. We'd have to look for gravitational lensing, and so on. You know, in this fantasy reality of yours."

An hour later, Carlos shook his head. "Still nothing. Are you sure the coordinates are right?"

Lukas felt a cold hand wrap around his heart. "Positive. Let's switch to a different spectral range," he suggested, feeling like he might vomit. Either there was a possible anomaly out there that threatened the extinction of humanity, or he had lost his mind. Not two great choices. "Let's look for it in the infrared range."

Carlos nodded and reprogrammed the instrument. Another half hour passed as the telescope gathered new data. Then the computer began processing the images, algorithms filtering out noise, amplifying weak signals, combining different images into a single image.

And then they saw it.

Three faint but unmistakable structures appeared on the main monitor, three seemingly equilateral triangles, at first glance slightly different in size. They reflected hardly any light, were almost black, absorbed almost all the radiation that hit them, but they emitted heat.

"These aren't natural bodies," whispered Carlos, his voice suddenly hoarse. "Dios mío! Lukas, what is that?"

No, not natural bodies. The three objects had a precise triangular shape, with sharp edges and smooth surfaces, as far as the telescope image showed. Geometric perfection where nature had created only chaos and organic irregularity.

Carlos enlarged one of the objects and the image became sharper. The triangle seemed to be made of a material that was blacker than the darkness of the surrounding space, a black that not only barely reflected light, but seemed to swallow it.

"What the hell are those things?" muttered Carlos, his accent now much stronger.

Lukas had no answer. He slumped powerlessly into his chair and rolled back a little. Thoughts raced through his head, desperately trying to squeeze the impossible into a framework of comprehensibility. The triangular objects in Mars's orbit looked like pyramids. Pyramids! Three structures that generated gravitational waves, which could only come from objects with the density of neutron stars. Three obviously artificial constructs, where nothing artificial should be.

Lukas felt a chill run down his spine. It was time to face what he had studiously avoided facing since the start. If these were truly neutron-star-mass objects traveling near Mars's orbit, the consequences would be apocalyptic. The gravitational tug-of-war would have already yanked Mars, Earth and the other planets out of their stable orbits. Tides would be monstrous, earthquakes constant, with the entire inner system spiraling toward chaos.

Lukas wasn't always that observant, but he had to believe that the Earth being yanked from its orbit was something he would have *noticed*.

He quickly shook these thoughts from his head once again. He would take the data as it came and not get mired down in preconceptions—even if dictated by the laws of physics. The presence of these triangular objects was impossible, and it wasn't entirely surprising that one impossibility might lead to others.

He couldn't help thinking of extraterrestrial objects. Spaceships, perhaps? Because what else could it be?

The feeling that this couldn't be reality, that what they were seeing, mere data on a screen, couldn't be real, was the strangest thing he had ever felt.

But it didn't change what they were seeing. At least he now had a confirmation—and a witness. Or perhaps losing one's mind was infectious.

"We need to collect more data," said Carlos, his voice now calm, the scientist in him regaining control. "Spectral analysis, precise movement parameters, everything."

Lukas hardly listened to him. He had stood up, his legs feeling strangely wobbly, his gaze still fixed on the three black pyramids staring back at him from the screen like a cosmic indictment.

The images were generated by the computer and were not live footage in the sense that a camera would have captured them, but the technology was proven.

"I need to make a call," he said, his voice sounding strange to his own ears.

Carlos looked at him, his face a mixture of excitement and confusion. "Who do you want to call?"

Lukas looked at the images on the monitor, at the three perfect pyramids that, cosmically speaking, stood directly in front of humanity's front door like heralds of an unknown power.

"Everyone," he said, swallowing. "Everyone."

4

"I've found something."

Mira's four simple words instantly silenced the conversations in the makeshift base camp. Her team, tired from a long day of meticulous documentation, looked up at her as she returned with a stern expression and an unmistakable gleam in her eyes.

Dr. Abdelrahman rose cautiously from his laptop, as if not wanting to allow himself to show any enthusiasm.

"Found something? What is it?" Hope lay in his voice like a barely audible vibration—suppressed only by the fear of that very hope.

"An anomaly in the eastern corridor." She tried to sound matter-of-fact, even though her heart was racing. "Three engraved triangles and clear signs of a concealed opening."

Mira took out her tablet and showed several close-ups she had taken of the symbol. The images showed three small, equilateral triangles arranged in a perfect formation—a formation they all recognized. "I suspect it could be a previously undiscovered passageway." She didn't mention the homemade anemometer or the barely perceptible air currents it had registered.

This personal method of discovery, based on her father's notes, would remain her secret for now, especially since she would look like an idiot if it proved to be nothing. After all, air currents weren't uncommon in the pyramid, as there were countless ventilation shafts.

What would she tell her colleagues? That her instincts screamed at her that her father had left her a breadcrumb trail. That she couldn't accept that he had left her and her mother without having extraordinary reasons.

Within minutes, the entire 20-person team had gathered around her. Their fatigue was now forgotten, replaced by the excited tension that only real discoveries could trigger.

"We need a complete scan of the area immediately," said Mira. "Jason, bring the portable ground radar. Michael, we need the high-resolution lidar scanner. Leila, prepare the thermal imaging."

The group moved with the efficient precision of a well-coordinated team. Mira led them back to the site of their discovery, hiding her own excitement behind a professional composure. The narrow passageway filled with people and equipment, while headlamps and portable LED lights bathed the old limestone in bright light.

"Here." Mira pointed to the barely visible markings on the wall. "See the triangles? They're carved quite hastily, probably with a copper tool."

Or something much more modern that wasn't intended for that purpose, she added in her mind.

Dr. Abdelrahman stepped closer, his experienced eyes studying the markings intently.

"Definitely man-made. And they differ from the style of the other markings in this corridor. Strange. If I didn't know that no one except accredited archaeologists had access here, I would have thought it was modern graffiti."

Michael had meanwhile set up the lidar scanner, a high-precision device that could create a 3-dimensional model of the wall using laser measurements.

"The scan is running, Professor. I think we'll have a complete surface profile in 5 minutes."

Jason prepared the ground radar, which would send electromagnetic waves through the stone and identify differences in density based on the reflected signals.

The next two hours passed in methodical precision work. Layer by layer, they scanned the wall with various technologies, collecting data and analyzing patterns. Mira monitored the process with rapt attention, while part of her consciousness kept returning to the leather book in her bag—to her father's cryptic notes about three triangles and hidden paths.

"Dr. Najafi, you should take a look at this." Jason's voice broke her train of thought. His tablet displayed a colored depth profile of the wall. "The radar clearly shows a large stone block that differs from the surrounding masonry. It has virtually no mortar in the joints."

"Yes!" Michael nodded excitedly. "The lidar scan confirms that, as far as I can see. The surface shows minimal differences in height along a rectangular shape, about 5 feet high and 3 wide."

"A passageway," whispered Leila, the awe in her voice unmistakable.

"Or a dead end," warned Dr. Abdelrahman, ever the hesitant skeptic. "We shouldn't jump to conclusions."

But Mira knew better. The subtle pulsing of the airflow registered by her anemometer could only mean one thing: behind this wall was a cavity connected to other areas of the pyramid. A hidden room, undiscovered for millennia—or at least until 15 years ago, when her father may have found the same passage. She stubbornly ignored the possibility that it could just be a ventilation shaft.

"The Supreme Council of Antiquities must be informed," said Abdul. "We need official permission from the Egyptian authorities before we can make any structural changes."

Mira felt a pang of impatience, but she knew he was right. The discovery of a new passageway in the Pyramid of Cheops was not a matter to be handled alone. The bureaucratic process was strict, and for good reason: Egypt's archaeological heritage had suffered too often in the past from hasty or improper interventions.

"We'll document everything and prepare an application," she said. "Abdul, could you inform your contact at the SCA? We need an urgent permit, if possible."

"Very well." The Egyptian archaeologist nodded after studying her for a long time. "I'll call Dr. Hawass. He's retired, but he still has considerable influence. If we're lucky, we'll get the green light within 24 hours."

"Until then," added Mira, an unfamiliar commanding tone in her voice, "this discovery remains between us. No one outside the team will be informed or given access to this area."

She noticed the surprised looks exchanged by some of her students. Her usual collegial, rather soft leadership had given way to sudden determination. But perhaps that was why no one objected.

The return to base camp took place in an atmosphere of suppressed excitement. While the team began preparing the application, Mira retired to a quiet corner, opened her father's leather book, and turned to the pages with the triangular symbols. Now that she knew what she was looking for, she saw his notes in a new light—not as cryptic theories, but as precise signposts.

"Everything okay, Dr. Najafi?"

She looked up and saw Jason looking at her with a slightly concerned expression. She hadn't noticed how much her hands were shaking.

"Yes, of course." She closed the book. "Just the usual excitement of a new discovery. A lot depends on this project."

"Are you sure it's nothing more?" The young man hesitated. "Forgive my directness, but you seem . . . more excited than usual."

Mira looked at him for a moment. Jason was one of her best students, sharp and empathetic. She had chosen him because he not only worked methodically, but also understood how to read the subtle human stories behind the archaeological finds without always viewing everything from the macro perspective of ancient Egyptian society.

"My father," she said finally. "He disappeared 15 years ago during an expedition in this pyramid. The official reports say it was an accident, but I've always believed there was more to it than that."

Jason nodded slowly, the realization dawning in his eyes. "And you think this discovery could be connected to his disappearance."

"It's more than a suspicion." She opened the book again and showed him a page. "These are his notes. He drew the same three triangles in the same place we just found."

"That's remarkable." The young archaeologist whistled softly through his teeth. "Have you talked to Professor Markowitz about this?"

"He knows about my personal motivation, but not the specific details." She closed the book again. "I'd prefer to keep it that way, at least for now."

"Of course." Jason hesitated. "But what if there is a connection? If your father found this passageway, then the question arises whether . . ."

"In that case," interrupted Mira, "I want to know what's behind it first." She gave him a sharp look. "And why it might have cost him his life."

The next few hours passed in a whirlwind of activity. The application to the Supreme Council of Antiquities was prepared with meticulous care. Every detail of the discovery, every measurement, every image was documented and accompanied by comprehensive scientific justifications for the necessary investigation.

Mira made several phone calls to her mentor, Professor Markowitz, at Yale, who used his considerable influence to apply additional pressure. She guessed that he was acting as much out of sympathy for her as out of the prospect of finally landing the big scoop. Dr. Abdelrahman also activated his contacts in the Egyptian Antiquities Service, emphasizing the scientific significance and professionalism of the team.

Evening came, night passed, and Mira couldn't sleep. In her Spartan quarters near the pyramid complex, her mind incessantly played through possible scenarios as she gazed out of the window at the illuminated pyramids.

What would they find behind the passageway once the request had been approved? An empty room? Another archaeological sensation? Or perhaps—and this thought made her heart race—a clue to her father's fate?

His body, perhaps?

Early in the morning, her phone rang, rousing her from wakefulness to what had eventually turned into a restless sleep. Abdul Abdelrahman informed her that the Supreme Council had granted preliminary approval, on the condition that the passageway be opened under the supervision of one of their representatives. Dr. Mahmoud Khalil would arrive in two hours.

"That's incredibly fast," said Mira in delight, not bothered by the government watchdog.

"We were lucky," replied Abdelrahman. "The discovery of the three triangles aroused interest, especially in connection with the clear instrumental measurements. In addition, Dr. Hawass personally spoke on our behalf."

"Thank you, Abdul."

When Mira returned to the pyramid, she was the first to arrive. Fifteen minutes later, the rest of her team arrived. Equipment was checked, documentation cameras set up, and protective measures prepared for the fragile passageway and its possible contents.

Dr. Mahmoud Khalil arrived on time, a slender man in his fifties with sharp eyes and a well-groomed gray beard. After a brief greeting, he personally inspected the discovered area, checked the scan data, and listened attentively to Mira's explanations.

"The procedure must be controlled," he emphasized. "No rash actions. We will only open the passage as far as is absolutely necessary to carry out an initial inspection. Only then will we decide on further measures."

Mira nodded in agreement, although she was trembling with impatience inside. "We've taken all the necessary precautions."

The opening of a possible passageway in the Great Pyramid followed a strict protocol. First, tiny fiber optic cameras were inserted into the barely visible joints to get a first look at the possible cavity behind them.

Tension filled the air as Jason carefully inserted the thin probe into one of the fine cracks at the edge of the identified block.

Blurry, dark images appeared on a monitor. Mira held her breath. She had let him go first because her hands were shaking and she wanted to hide it.

"Definitely a cavity," he confirmed. "I can see about a yard in, then it gets too dark."

Encouraged by this confirmation, the team moved on to the next step. Small, precise holes were drilled at strategic points around the stone block—just large enough to test the air quality and insert tiny endoscopes, but small enough not to cause any irreversible damage.

The extended endoscope images confirmed what Mira had hoped; behind the stone block was indeed a passageway extending into the depths of the pyramid.

And no corpse.

"Time for the critical moment," she said, looking at Khalil. "We'll try to move the block without causing structural damage."

The Egyptian nodded.

The method was careful and precise. Special padding was placed around the edges of the block to prevent damage. Then they attached hydraulic lifting devices that had been specially developed for archaeological purposes—strong enough to move stones weighing tons, but with fine control to avoid abrupt movements.

"Are all the cameras running?" asked Mira, receiving nods of confirmation from her students in charge. Every angle was covered, every movement would be documented—for posterity, but also as legal protection.

"Begin," Mira instructed her team.

With agonizing slowness, the technical experts assisting her research team increased the pressure on the hydraulic jacks. Millimeter by millimeter, the massive stone block moved outward. A soft crunching sound could be heard as stone dust came loose and made the air suddenly even drier.

Mira's heart was beating so loudly that she feared the others could hear it. At that moment, she was not only a scientist but also a daughter—a daughter hoping to get one step closer to the truth about her lost father.

After 20 minutes of precise work, the block had moved about a foot from its original position—just enough to create a narrow opening through which a person could slip.

The first rays of light to enter the room in possibly thousands of years—or fifteen years—revealed the beginning of a low, narrow passageway.

The walls were roughly hewn, lacking the careful craftsmanship of the pyramid's familiar corridors.

"A construction worker's passage," Abdul Abdelrahman murmured reverently. "Possibly a way for workers to reach certain areas of the pyramid without using the main corridors."

"Or a deliberately hidden path for ritual purposes," added Dr. Khalil.

"The three triangles could be a clue to a special meaning." Mira stepped forward, her gaze fixed on the dark opening. Something was visible at the threshold of the passageway—a small object that reflected the light from her headlamp.

"There's something there," she said, pointing. "I'm going in."

Mira squeezed through, which was her right as the discoverer. Using a long gripping tool designed for such situations, she carefully retrieved the object. When it came into the light of her headlamp, she heard herself gasp.

It was a thin metal emblem in the shape of a scarab—identical to the one her father had always worn on his field hat. A personal identifier she remembered from her childhood.

Her eyes widened. It was unmistakable.

"I think I found something that belonged to my father," she called back, turning around so the others could see it through the crack. "A scarab emblem. An insignia my father always wore on his hat."

Those present exchanged confused glances, but Jason nodded in understanding. Dr. Khalil looked at her with renewed interest.

"Your father was Dariush Najafi, correct? The archaeologist who disappeared here years ago?"

She nodded, unable to speak, her fingers clutching the metal emblem—proof that her father had indeed found and entered this hidden path.

"In that case," said Dr. Khalil slowly, frowning, "this discovery may have a very special significance that goes beyond pure archaeology. I knew him; he was a good man, and I recognize this emblem."

"I have to keep going." She looked Khalil in the eyes.

"No." He shook his head. "We now have proof of a passageway. Which means we need a whole new set of permits, as you are well aware, Doctor. But I will make sure that it happens with the appropriate urgency."

5

The Alps rose like ancient guardians in the distance as the plane began its descent over the idyllic Swiss landscape. Lukas blinked dazedly as the gentle jolt of the landing gear pulled him from a dreamless sleep. His body had taken the 12-hour flight from Santiago to Geneva as a welcome opportunity to surrender—a vacuum of unconsciousness in which neither the mysterious objects near Mars nor the consequences of their discovery existed.

Next to him, Carlos looked out the small window at the rolling green landscapes passing beneath them. "Your home continent is still photogenic, amigo," he remarked with a smile.

His German friend just nodded, unable to respond to the banality of everyday conversation. The world had changed, and yet it looked unchanged—a paradox that had accompanied Lukas since his discovery had been confirmed in La Silla. Six days had passed; six days of feverish activity, communication, and confirmation from other observatories. Six days in which the initial incredulity of their discovery had condensed into an indisputable certainty, and they had suddenly found themselves at the center of the international scientific community—not to mention the media.

As the plane touched down on the runway, Lukas was struck by a strange feeling—as if none of this was real, as if he were moving through the scenes of a dream. Was it the lack of sleep? The aftereffects of jet lag, which had disrupted his circadian rhythm? Or was it simply the incomprehensibility of what they had discovered?

He shook the thought away. This was not a dream. The black pyramids were real. And whatever they were, they were getting closer.

"Carlos," he said after a few minutes, waiting for his friend to look at him. "Thank you. For everything."

"De nada, amigo."

"No, really. I know it wasn't easy. You're a good friend, and I won't forget that. This is our discovery."

"You're too generous, papa."

For the first time in a month, Lukas grinned. 'Papa' was the Latin American Spanish word for 'potato,' a teasing nickname that dated back to their college days.

The Geneva airport terminal greeted them with the crystalline efficiency for which Switzerland was famous. An inconspicuous man in an immaculate suit was already waiting for them, holding a sign with their names on it.

"Dr. Heuer, Dr. Mendoza?" The man smiled politely. "I'm Jean-Pierre Rousseau from CERN. I'll accompany you to the institute."

They followed him to a waiting vehicle, an inconspicuous black van that would take them across the border into France and then back into Switzerland—a geographical curiosity that reflected the special nature of CERN, the European center for nuclear research, which straddled two nations like a symbol of scientific boundlessness.

"Why CERN, of all places?" asked Carlos as they drove through the autumnal landscape. "I thought our discovery belonged more to the field of astronomy than particle physics."

Rousseau glanced over his shoulder and seemed to think the question was directed at him rather than Lukas.

"I think it was chosen as neutral ground. Switzerland stands for neutrality, and CERN itself embodies international cooperation like few other scientific institutions. We also have the infrastructure to host a conference of this magnitude at short notice—conference rooms, simultaneous interpretation of multiple languages, security measures, and other necessary accommodations."

What the man didn't say, but Lukas understood clearly, was that CERN had experience with discoveries that shook the foundations of physics. It was here that the Higgs boson had been detected, the particle that had finally completed the standard model of physics. Here, people were used to operating at the forefront of human knowledge.

"What's more," added Rousseau as the van drove through a security gate into the outer ring of their destination, "CERN's choice signals that this is a matter that concerns the entire scientific community, not just individual countries or institutions."

The unspoken message echoed in Lukas's mind: whatever these triangular objects were, they concerned all of humanity.

The main CERN building presented itself as a modern functional structure, its architecture a balance of pragmatism and aesthetics befitting a center of rationality. They were guided through several security checks, given visitor passes, and followed Rousseau through long corridors where the buzz of concentrated intellectual activity seemed to intensify.

No sooner had they reached the main corridor than Lukas spotted several familiar faces from the international physics community. Dr. Amelia Wong from the Caltech-LIGO team came toward him with her hand outstretched.

"Lukas! Incredible work! I've seen the data, but I still can't believe it."

"Thanks, Amelia. Actually, all I did was look at a monitor at the right moment." He shook her hand with a smile, feeling the underlying excitement in her grip. "We should talk later. I have to . . ."

He gestured vaguely down the corridor, unsure where their actual destination was.

"Of course, of course. The whole world is waiting for your report."

The whole world. The words echoed in his head as they continued walking and cutting short other encounters in a similar fashion—a nod here, a quick handshake there. The weight of expectation lay heavy on his shoulders, pressing him into the reality of this moment, this gathering of the world's brightest minds waiting for him.

They passed an intersection of corridors when a tall man with silver-streaked hair intercepted them. "Mr. Heuer? I'm Robert Lancaster, head of the American science delegation." His handshake was firm, his gaze searching.

"Very pleased to meet you," said Lukas.

"And I, you," responded the tall American. "There's a call for you in the director's office."

Lukas frowned. "A call? From whom?"

"Follow me," said Lancaster by way of answer.

Carlos glanced questioningly at his friend, who shrugged slightly. "I'll see you in the conference room," said the German before following Lancaster, already striding ahead.

The CERN director's office was at the end of a curved corridor, away from the main traffic of the institute. An elegantly dressed assistant stood up when they entered.

"Dr. Heuer." She nodded politely. "The call will be put through in a few minutes. Please take a seat there." She pointed to an area of the office where a conference phone stood on a small table.

Lancaster remained standing at the door. "I'll leave you alone. See you at the conference."

With a brief nod, he disappeared, leaving Lukas with the assistant, who sat down behind her desk and politely pretended he wasn't there. It was all very strange.

Lukas looked at the simple telephone as if it were an artifact from another time. What was going on here?

Before he could fully process this fact, the phone rang softly. The assistant nodded to him.

With a strangely detached calm, Lukas picked up the receiver.

"Dr. Heuer?" asked a woman with a broad American accent in English.

"Yes?"

"Please hold, I'll connect you to the president," she said, and her words hit him like a hammer blow.

The president? The President of the United States wanted to speak to him, Lukas Heuer, a German physicist at LIGO, who was well known to gravitational wave researchers, but to no one else?

"Lukas! I can call you Lukas, can't I?" The voice on the other end sounded surprisingly ordinary, a little nasal, but unmistakably that of the man he knew from countless television appearances.

"Yes, Mr. President. Of course you can."

"Wonderful! I'm calling to thank you personally for your remarkable discovery and to congratulate you. I was only informed of the full significance yesterday, and I must say—it's indescribable."

"Thank you, Mr. President." Lukas's voice sounded stiff, even to his own ears. "It took a while for the international community to confirm everything."

"The LIGO project is a triumph of American science, and your work there is a testament to the excellent international cooperation that benefits us all."

There was a short pause, and Lukas realized that a response was expected.

"It's an honor for me to be part of this project," he said finally.

"The United States is determined to pursue this matter with all available resources. You have our full support. Whatever you need, you have it."

The formality of the words couldn't hide the underlying tension. What the president was really saying was: this is a threat we take seriously, and you are now on our team—until the end.

"I appreciate that very much, Mr. President. We'll get started right away."

"I owe you one, Lukas. Find out what's out there." A favor from the President of the United States? "I wish you every success at the conference. America is counting on you, Lukas. The world is counting on you."

The connection was interrupted, and Lukas slowly put down the receiver. The assistant smiled professionally. "The conference room is in the west wing, Dr. Heuer. Room W1. Would you like me to call someone to accompany you?"

"No, thank you." He shook his head dazedly. "I've been there before."

The walk to the conference room felt like walking through a dream, the corridors of CERN stretching and distorting in his perception. Reality had taken on a surreal quality—a call from the president, dark triangles in Mars's orbit, a world that suddenly looked at him with different eyes.

When he reached Hall W1, his breath caught in his throat. The room was filled to capacity, an amphitheater of scientific excellence. Nearly 200 people, he estimated—astrophysicists, cosmologists, experts in gravitational waves, quantum physicists, the elite of the international scientific community.

And they were waiting for him. His hands were already getting clammy.

Carlos spotted him and waved him to the podium.

"There you are. It's our turn."

Lukas stepped up to the lectern, Carlos at his side. A microphone stood in front of him, ready to carry his words to his assembled colleagues. The room had fallen silent, a silence that was not just the absence of noise, but an almost palpable presence of expectant attention.

"Hello to all the esteemed scientists here," began Lukas. "It's an honor for us to be with you today." He paused for a brief moment and then launched straight into it. "On August 11 of this year, the LIGO observatory in Livingston, Louisiana, recorded a series of gravitational waves with unprecedented characteristics."

He guided those present through the events of the last few days—the nighttime discovery at LIGO, the hasty trip to Chile, the confirmation by the optical telescope. Carlos took over the part about the astronomical observations, explaining the special features of the images they had taken at La Silla. Of course, everyone here was already aware of the most important details, but the summary still helped set the stage.

The images of the three pyramid-like objects now appeared on the screen behind them—black, geometrically perfect triangles against the backdrop of space.

"The objects are similar in size," explained Carlos. "The exact dimensions are difficult to determine at this distance and due to the low reflectivity in the optical spectrum, but we can say with relative certainty that there are two objects of almost equal size and one significantly smaller object. They are made of a material that reflects or emits virtually no electromagnetic radiation—a kind of perfect black."

Lukas took over again. "What makes these objects particularly . . . *puzzling* . . . is their gravitational signatures." He sighed. "And by puzzling, of course, I mean absolutely *inconceivable*. Impossible by any known science. Absolutely unambiguous evidence of intelligent life in the universe, possibly as far beyond us as we are beyond the *amoeba*."

He paused to let this sink in.

"The objects generate gravitational waves that we normally only see from massive cosmic events," he continued finally. "From the merger of black holes or neutron stars. Each of these objects has a gravitational signature that suggests a mass far beyond what their physical size and shape should allow."

He showed diagrams, gravitational wave profiles, mathematical models. The scientific language offered an anchor in the uncertainty, a familiar structure amid the incomprehensible.

"In the last 6 days," he continued, "a total of 28 observatories worldwide have confirmed our observations. These include the Virgo Observatory in Italy, KAGRA in Japan, the Keck Observatory in Hawaii, and the Very Large Telescope in Chile—all of which have verified the existence of these three objects."

Carlos stepped forward again. "Based on the combined data from all observations," he said, "we can now say with certainty that the three objects are pyramid-shaped." He winced. "And are . . . well . . . are moving in a direct line toward Earth."

A murmur rippled through the hall like a wave rolling across a scientific sea—not everyone present had received this information yet.

"Current calculations," continued Carlos, his voice controlled and neutral, "indicate that in nine months, the objects will reach a specific point in Earth's orbit—the exact point where Earth will be at that time."

Lukas watched the faces in the audience closely. Skeptical looks that turned to concern, and maybe horror, as the implications of these words became clear.

"Another peculiarity we have observed over the last 48 hours," said Lukas, taking a deep breath, "is that the distance between the three objects is continuously decreasing. The formation they are creating is becoming more compact as they approach Earth."

He showed a projection of the expected trajectory and the changing formation. "If this trend continues, the three objects will reach their minimum distance from each other just as they reach our orbit."

Or fly right through us, he thought to himself, trying to push this frightening thought out of his mind. Or stop and say hello. Or consume the entire Earth as a light snack before moving on. With technology this advanced, *anything* was possible.

The silence in the room had now taken on a different quality—no longer tense anticipation, but the deep silence before an approaching storm.

Lukas looked into the faces of his colleagues, the assembled intelligence of humanity, and recognized in them the same mixture of scientific fascination and existential concern that preoccupied him.

"We will now open the discussion for questions," he said, stepping back from the microphone as the first hands shot up in the audience.

6

The "reasonable haste" Dr. Khalil had promised had turned into six days. Six days during which Mira had waited in her room at the base camp and resisted the constant urge to pull her hair out.

It was *maddening*.

But now the time had come. Now she was finally back in the small tunnel inside Cheops where she belonged.

Mira hunched her upper body as she squeezed through the narrow passageway. The rough limestone brushed against her shoulders as she moved forward cautiously, her headlamp the only point of light in the surrounding darkness. The passageway was so narrow that she had to turn her head to the side again and again to move forward.

"Are you sure you want to go alone?" Dr. Khalil had asked, his voice a mixture of professional concern and obvious curiosity. Normally, only one person went in at a time to minimize disturbance to the environment.

"I have experience with confined spaces," she had replied. "And this passageway was not built for men of your stature, Dr. Khalil."

It was a practical truth, but not the real reason. She wanted to—no, she *had* to—see this space alone first. If her father had taken this path, if this was the place where he had disappeared, it was important to be the first to find his traces. She couldn't leave anything to chance.

The passageway led steeply downward, a primitive tunnel that had been carved without the precision of the pyramid's main corridors. This was not a representative passageway for rituals or the transport of the royal corpse—it was a functional shaft, perhaps actually used by workers to reach different levels during construction. Or, as a quiet voice whispered in her head, a deliberately hidden path to something that wasn't meant to be found.

But she couldn't indulge in hasty interpretations. After all, she was no longer a student, but a professor—one of the youngest. That meant that she, of all people, had to be able to explain each of her conclusions precisely.

Her knees ached from walking bent over, her skin was covered with a thin layer of dust and sweat. The air was old and stale, but breathable—a marvel of the ventilation systems that the ancient builders had integrated into the pyramid. Even after thousands of years, enough fresh air still flowed through the tiny gaps between the massive stone blocks to supply the interior of the monument.

The radio on her belt crackled.

"Dr. Najafi, can you hear me? Position and status, please." Abdul's voice sounded distorted, but just about intelligible.

She reached for the device and pressed the transmit button. "I'm moving farther down. The passage is narrow but stable. No apparent risk of collapse. Our connection may soon be lost."

"Understood. Remember to mark every ten meters."

She didn't even bother to respond, as she couldn't help but find this directive a bit insulting. She knew what she was doing.

Mira had already placed three small glow sticks on the walls—modern technology that would ensure she could find her way back. They would remain lit for 48 hours. Not that she could get lost in such a straight, narrow tunnel, but archaeological protocols were strict, especially after several tragic accidents in recent decades.

After about a hundred yards, the structure of the passage changed. The floor became flatter, the walls slightly wider. Mira could now walk almost upright, a welcome relief for her aching back and scraped knees. Then, without warning, the tunnel split.

She stopped, letting the beam of her lamp wander between the two identical-looking passages. There was no indication which was the intended path—no markings, no obvious differences in construction. A classic labyrinth element found in many ancient structures, often as protection against grave robbers or as a symbolic test for those seeking access to sacred areas.

Mira pulled out her father's leather book and hastily leafed through the pages. Had he mentioned this point? Was there any clue as to which path was the right one?

Nothing clear. Just a cryptic note: "I follow the path of sunlight, not that of the Moon."

She frowned. At this depth of the pyramid, there was neither sunlight nor moonlight. What could he have meant?

Instinctively, she pointed her lamp at the floor of both passages. The left tunnel seemed to lead slightly downward, while the right one ran more horizontally. The Sun traveled from east to west during the day, but every new dawn saw it rise in the east again. How was this possible? Egyptian mythology had supplied an explanation. At night it made the return trip through the underworld. So should she go downward? The path the Sun took each night to return to the underworld?

She decided on the left passage, placed a particularly bright marker at the intersection, and informed her team of the change of route, hoping they could still hear her.

Time lost its meaning in the silent darkness. Minutes stretched into what felt like hours as she continued forward, carefully noting every turn, every change in the tunnel structure. The radio on her belt crackled only sporadically—the massive stone blocks of the pyramid had finally blocked the signal.

After what felt like an eternity, the passage suddenly widened. Mira stepped out of the narrow tunnel into a larger room, her beam of light no longer sufficient to grasp its dimensions. She switched on her more powerful secondary lamp and slowly directed it at the walls around her.

The sight made her gasp.

She was standing in a rectangular chamber, about 25-five-feet long and 15 wide, with an unusually high ceiling of perhaps 10 feet. This alone would have been remarkable—but what took her breath away were the walls.

Every inch was covered with hieroglyphs and depictions, in colors that, despite their unimaginable age, were less faded than in comparable chambers such as the King's Chamber. The preservation was exceptional, better than anything she had ever seen in burial chambers or temples. The low-humidity, constant environment deep inside the pyramid had acted as the perfect preservative.

Mira turned slowly, trying to absorb the overwhelming feeling of her discovery. This was no simple construction worker's chamber. This was a carefully designed, deliberately hidden room with obvious ritual significance—perhaps the most important one ever discovered.

Her gaze fell on the north wall—and what she saw made her pause and squint her eyes.

Three pyramids were depicted on a dark blue background, possibly representing the evening sky. Not just any pyramids, but clearly those of Giza in their characteristic arrangement and relative size. What was unusual was their color: they weren't depicted in the typical sandy tones, but in deep black, as if they were swallowing the light itself.

"Black pyramids against a blue sky," she murmured. "Next to the Moon . . ."

Indeed, the depiction showed a large, silvery-white crescent Moon next to the pyramids—an unusual combination in Egyptian iconography, where the Sun typically occupied the dominant position.

Below the pyramids sat a group of seven priests in ceremonial robes, depicted in the characteristic side view of Egyptian art. Their eyes were closed, their hands raised in a gesture of meditation or prayer. Six of the priests were painted in pale, lifeless colors—a typical sign of the deceased in ancient Egyptian wall paintings. The seventh, however, glowed in vivid colors, and a bright beam rose from his chest directly to the black pyramids.

"A connection between priests and pyramids," she whispered to herself as she took photographs. "A kind of contact with the gods? Or a representation of communication between priests and deceased pharaohs?"

On the opposite side of the scene stood a significantly larger figure—a pharaoh wearing the double crown of Egypt, the Pschent, symbolizing Upper and Lower Egypt.

The priest with the beam of light seemed to be speaking to the ruler, one hand raised in a gesture of narration or explanation.

Mira shook her head to be sure she wasn't dreaming. This was *extraordinary*. She methodically photographed every inch of the image. The craftsmanship was remarkable, the color pigments of unusual quality.

The images must have dated from the Fourth Dynasty, she guessed, around the same time as the pyramid itself was built. But the preservation was incredible, and the fact that the finished pyramids were depicted in correct proportions, stunning."

Surely, once published, this depiction would give pre-astronautics fans a boost and make Erich von Däniken rejoice.

She turned her attention to the hieroglyphs framing the image. Her knowledge was sufficient to recognize some recurring symbols—signs for stars, for travel, for time. And again and again, a symbol she had rarely seen before: three small, connected triangles.

"The same markings as at the entrance," she noted aloud. "Was that you, Father?"

The other walls showed similarly fascinating scenes: depictions of star constellations she couldn't immediately identify; processions of priests carrying complex instruments; and, again and again, the three black pyramids, sometimes floating in the sky, sometimes standing on the ground. Strictly speaking, both appeared twice: on the left, the pyramids in the sky; on the right, the pyramids of Giza on the ground; then again, the pyramids in the sky; and then again on the ground. A repetition, which was very strange. To her knowledge, it was the first Egyptian mural that had a direct copy, painted with astonishing accuracy and directly on the wall next to it.

In the middle of the room stood a simple rectangular table made of limestone. Unlike the rest of the room, it was unadorned, its surface rough but even. It seemed functional, perhaps intended for ceremonies or for storing objects—although now there was nothing on or under it except a small symbol carved into the stone. It looked like a kind of lion, but not in the typical Egyptian imagery. Something was different.

She frowned and took a photo.

Mira proceeded methodically, studying every corner, every joint between the stone blocks, every unusual shadow on the wall paintings. After a particularly detailed examination of the stone table, she sighed in frustration. Nothing. No signs of recent presence, no modern traces, no clues as to what might have happened to her father. The chamber was immaculate, untouched—as if no one had been here since the pyramid was sealed 4,500 years ago.

But that couldn't be. Her father's metal hat emblem at the entrance proved that he had taken this path. Had he gone farther? Was there another exit she had overlooked? Had she misinterpreted his path to the sunlight after all?

She checked all the walls again, looking for hidden passages or clues to other rooms. Nothing. The chamber seemed to be a dead end, an isolated room with no further connections.

Finally, she had to admit to herself that she would not find any answers here—at least not the ones she was looking for. She took a few final wide-angle shots and then, with a heavy heart, made her way back through the narrow tunnel. When she reached the fork again, she took the other path, but it soon ended in a small, empty chamber measuring one and a half yards across.

When she returned to base camp, everyone immediately gathered around her and murmured excitedly. The excitement on their faces turned to awe as she showed them the pictures of the chamber on her tablet.

"This is . . . *unprecedented*," whispered Abdul in awe as he scrolled through the photos on the laptop.

"The preservation is perfect, the craftsmanship exquisite. And this depiction of the black pyramids—I've never seen anything like it."

"This is new." Dr. Khalil nodded in agreement, rubbing his chin repeatedly. "This could completely revolutionize our understanding of Fourth Dynasty iconography. Particularly interesting is this depiction of the shining priest in connection with the pyramids, and the repetition of the whole."

"The hieroglyphs seem to speak of ritual communication," added Sarah, looking over Abdul's shoulder. "I recognize symbols for *speak*, *hear*, and, interestingly, both *now* and *before* as a connected hieroglyph. They don't actually exist in that combination."

"No," agreed Mira. "At first I thought it was a mistake by the artist, but it's the same in the copy next to it. The two glyphs seem to form a single new one, which has never previously existed."

The discussion gained momentum as the team analyzed the discovery. Theories were proposed, rejected, modified. A hidden priestly caste with astronomical knowledge? A secret ritual for communicating with cosmic entities? A metaphorical representation of the transition to the afterlife?

"We need to document this thoroughly," said Dr. Khalil. "Dr. Abdelrahman and I will inspect the chamber ourselves as soon as we've prepared the necessary equipment."

Mira nodded mechanically, suddenly overwhelmed by a wave of exhaustion and disappointment. She'd made a remarkable archaeological discovery, perhaps the most significant in the last hundred years—and yet it felt hollow, for which she was secretly ashamed.

As the team bustled about in excited activity, she withdrew unnoticed. She found a quiet corner away from the main camp, sank to the cold stone floor, and buried her face in her hands.

The discovery would make her famous, bring prestige to Yale and Professor Markowitz, inscribe her name in the history books of Egyptology, and give something back to her mentor, who had helped her achieve an incomparable career. It was the kind of find archaeologists dreamed of their whole lives.

And yet she had failed in what had been most important to her.

"Where are you, Father?" she whispered into the silence. "What happened to you?"

The pyramid responded with the same stony indifference with which it had met thousands of years of human questions. The shadows of the past remained silent, the mysteries unsolved.

Mira took the small scarab insignia out of her pocket and examined the familiar object in the dim light. It was the only tangible proof of her father's presence at that time, the only indication that she was on the right track. But the path ended in a dead end, in a chamber full of riddles without answers.

The small emblem felt heavy in her hand, laden with the weight of unfulfilled hopes.

But as she looked through her numerous photos once again, she realized there was one last avenue for her to explore. The strange lion figure. It seemed familiar to her, yet it had never been a part of Egyptian iconography. Moreover, on closer inspection, it had a number of tiny flaws in the details that were uncharacteristic of the artists who had worked in these chambers thousands of years ago.

She had to find out what it was. Her intuition had rarely let her down before, and now it was telling her that this might just be the thread that would unravel it all.

7

After Lukas and Carlos finished their presentation, the participants split up into different working groups as planned. The initial unease caused by the revelations they had made gave way to excited commotion as the experts gathered in specialist teams and made their way to smaller conference rooms. Their excited conversations echoed so loudly through the rooms and corridors that one could have been forgiven for thinking that noisy school classes were being shown around CERN.

Lukas finally entered a small, windowless conference room where ten of the world's leading gravitational wave researchers had gathered. The simple functionality of the room underscored the seriousness of the situation. Here they would analyze the data, think through the implications, and search for answers through their specialized lenses. Dr. Dylan Mercer sat at the head of the table. Mercer was a world-renowned physicist who, for decades, had worked with Kip Thorne, a Nobel Laureate whose theoretical work had laid the foundation for the LIGO project. Mercer's calm eyes behind thick glasses scanned the attendees attentively and quietly.

"Let's summarize the facts," he began in his clear, sober voice. "We have three pyramid-shaped objects on a direct course for Earth. Their gravitational signatures correspond to a mass that is incompatible with their visible size."

Dr. Sana Malik, a Pakistani-born American from MIT, shook her head as a wide grin appeared on her face. "*Incompatible?*" she said in amusement. "If they gave Nobel Prizes for understatement, you'd have my vote, Dr. Mercer."

He returned her smile. "I'm working in the tradition of Watson and Crick, the current holders of the understatement of the millennium award."

Malik raised her eyebrows. "I'm not familiar," she admitted.

"The final sentence of their 1953 paper on the structure of DNA," said Mercer. "They wrote, and I quote: 'It has not escaped our notice that the specific pairing we have postulated immediately suggests a possible copying mechanism for the genetic material.'"

Malik nodded. "Yes. A truly epic understatement. But you still have it beat. Anyway, to continue, the key question is, what danger do these impossible objects pose to Earth?"

"Let's start with the basics," said Dr. Alessandra Romano from the Virgo Observatory.

Lukas had only known her from video conferences and scientific publications. "The gravitational waves from these objects have a similar amplitude to those of a medium-sized neutron star, but their frequency patterns are fundamentally different from anything we know."

She projected a diagram onto the wall—different colored wavy lines forming different patterns. "The blue line shows a typical neutron star binary system shortly before merging. The red line represents our objects. Note the regular oscillations and perfect periodicity. This pattern doesn't correspond to any natural phenomenon we know of—not to mention the geometry."

Dr. Hiroshi Ishiguro, head of the KAGRA project in Japan, looked at the diagram with intense concentration and respectfully raised his hand. Since there was no one to call on him, he cleared his throat and began to speak with a strong accent: "The regularity suggests a controlled process. It seems as if the objects are deliberately generating gravitational waves, or there are processes within them that trigger them."

A brief silence followed this statement. The implication was clear, even if no one had yet stated it directly.

"If these objects actually have the mass suggested by their gravitational signature," said Dr. James Barry, another Nobel laureate, "we're talking about bodies with the density of a neutron star but limited to the volume of a pyramid. A pyramid with an edge length of about 90 by 140 meters."

He shook his head. "Hard to believe I just said that. We all know the textbook examples: a teaspoon of neutron-star material would weigh about as much as Mount Everest. And a small neutron star, since it began bigger than our Sun, collapses down to have a final radius of about ten miles. Ten miles. Not ninety meters. And a *radius*. Because it collapses into a sphere, which is stable. Not a pyramid. It's like these objects are giving us a cosmic stick in the eye. They clearly haven't studied physics."

Dr. Jonas Richter, the third Nobel laureate present, couldn't help but smile. "The cosmos flipping us the bird," he said in amusement. "I wonder if *that* will appear in future textbooks. But let's pretend that most of physics still works. In that case, there has to be some unknown force or technology that's maintaining the pyramidal shape."

"Maybe so," said Barry, "but let's get to the real question. Will there even be future textbooks? Will there even be a future? What do these objects mean for Earth?"

Lukas activated his tablet and projected a series of simulations onto the designated wall using the small projector. "Based on our measurements, the objects are plodding along at about 18,000 miles per hour, or 5 miles per second. One thirty-seven-thousandth of the speed of light. Fast enough to circle the Earth in two minutes, but slow enough that photons treat them like they're standing still. They're currently near Mars and will reach Earth in around nine months if they maintain their speed and course."

He gestured at Dr. Romano. "I believe you've made some calculations as to the effect their gravity will have on us as they approach?"

"I've tried," she replied, opening a detailed model on her laptop and connecting it to a projector. "But there are so many anomalies here that nothing can be certain. The gravitational waves detected imply the objects have a combined weight of two solar masses. But of course they don't. If they did, Mars would have already been destroyed, and so would we. Based on the impact they're having on Mars's orbit, we estimate its effective mass to be about the same as our Moon."

She showed a diagram of Earth and its immediate surroundings, with concentric circles for different distance levels. "At a distance of half a million miles—slightly more than twice the distance to the Moon—the tidal forces will be strong enough to cause measurable changes in the oceans. Nothing catastrophic yet, but clearly detectable.

"At about a quarter-million-miles, basically the same distance as the Moon, the tidal effect will be so strong that we can expect significant seismic activity. Exactly twice as strong as the Moon's tidal effect now. The Earth's crust will also deform under the influence of the gravitational fields. This will lead to tsunamis, volcanic eruptions, and tectonic shifts."

"We don't really need calculations to know what will happen as they get closer than this, do we?" said Dr. Barry, looking as if he might vomit.

Romano blew out a long breath. "No. At 30,000 miles out, tidal forces will be strong enough to break open the Earth's crust. We're talking about global catastrophes—massive faults, changes in the axis of rotation, possibly even partial decompression of the Earth's mantle."

"And direct impact?" said Dr. Barry. "How many times over will that be able to drive us into extinction? I'd say the over/under is . . . uh . . . 70."

Romano showed another simulation. "I don't have that number, but I'd say it's well over. At the current speed and estimated mass, the impact energy would be equivalent to about 500 times all of Earth's nuclear arsenals. I'll leave it to you to figure exactly how much overkill that really is."

"The objects are clearly the result of intelligent design," said Lukas. "And we've already acknowledged there are too many anomalies, too many things we have no understanding of, to count. It's noteworthy that of all possible trajectories, they're headed precisely to our location in space. That isn't an accident. So is it a painfully slow-moving missile that will casually rid this solar system of its pesky third planet? Or something else? Will it veer off in time to spare us?"

"Just to call out one of the anomalies that's been bugging the hell out of me," said Barry, "how and why are they getting closer to each other as they approach Earth? Even more incredibly, how are objects this massive and this close being *kept apart*? Given the force of gravity between two objects increases rapidly as they grow closer, at this tiny separation the force they're exerting on each other is almost incomprehensible. I did an armchair calculation. The weight of four-hundred-trillion pounds should be pressing them together. And yet they remain separated."

Lukas shook his head. "Not exactly how I thought first contact would go," he said. "I really thought the aliens in flying saucers would finally call a press conference to reveal they've been flying around us all along. I never expected three pyramids that defy all reality would pay a house call to destroy us, without even saying hello."

"That remains to be seen," said Dr. Malik. "Maybe they will communicate with us. Maybe this is just a ploy to get our attention before they do."

Barry snorted. "If so, they've succeeded. They have *my* full attention, I can tell you that."

"What if the gravitational *waves* themselves are a form of communication?" said Malik.

"Gravitational waves as language?" Dr. Barry asked with a mixture of skepticism and interest. "An interesting hypothesis."

"Gravitational waves penetrate everything," explained Dr. Malik. "They aren't blocked or reflected by matter like electromagnetic radiation. They travel through the universe virtually unimpeded as direct changes in space-time itself."

Dr. Romano nodded. "An advanced civilization might consider them a universal form of communication. Independent of chemical elements, biological processes, or cultural contexts."

"The question is," said Dr. Mercer, "whether we can decode these signals. And whether we could even respond. Our interferometers can detect gravitational waves. But we can't *generate* them—the theoretical ideas involving superconducting disks or the Gertsenstein effect are highly speculative and beyond our technical capabilities."

"Completely out of the question." Dr. Richter shook his head decisively.

"Practically speaking," said Lukas, "we'd need extremely massive objects that we could accelerate with high precision. Which *far* exceeds our current technical capabilities. But perhaps there are alternatives."

"Perhaps there are, at that," said Dr. Ishiguro. "We are here at CERN, after all. If we use precisely synchronized particle collisions we could—theoretically—generate very weak but specifically modulated gravitational waves."

"Many orders of magnitude too weak for us to even *detect*," noted Barry.

"For *us* to even detect," repeated Lukas. "But what if they have technology that surpasses ours by orders of magnitude? If they really can generate gravitational waves as a byproduct of their movement, why shouldn't they be able to detect waves a million times weaker than we can?"

The group fell silent for a moment as they considered this possibility.

"We should attempt communication," said Dr. Mercer finally. "Yesterday! Every second these pyramids are getting five miles closer to wiping us out."

"Assuming they don't decide to accelerate," noted Romano grimly.

"Thanks," said Barry wryly. "That's super helpful. Because we didn't have enough to worry about already."

"Sorry," said Romano sheepishly.

Dr. Malik nodded. "I suggest we form a team for this task. An interdisciplinary team—with physicists, linguists, mathematicians, and cryptologists."

"At the same time," added. Romano, "we need to develop strategies in case communication fails."

Lukas looked at his assembled colleagues. He saw the same mixture of scientific curiosity and deep concern on every face. They were at a turning point that held both promise and danger.

Aliens, he thought. The idea still felt surreal.

Dr. Mercer stood up, signaling that the discussion had reached a turning point.

"I suggest we split into two groups. One group will work on communication strategies, the other on measures to protect Earth in case this communication fails—although I can't think of how we would do that. Dr. Heuer, would you lead the communications group?"

Lukas's heartbeat quickened. The responsibility offered to him was as frightening as it was honorable—a vote of confidence from a man who had worked arm in arm with Kip Thorne while he had defined the foundations of modern physics. A man who had gone on to accomplish almost as much as his mentor.

Lukas swallowed hard. "Of course," he replied. "I'll give it everything I have."

The others now rose as well, their faces tired and marked by the same confusion Lukas felt. They were clearly thinking hard.

At that moment, Lukas felt the full significance of what lay ahead and what his working group really had in mind. Humanity's first conscious attempt to make contact with extraterrestrial intelligence. A moment that would forever blur the boundaries between science fiction and scientific reality.

As the others left the room, he remained alone for a moment, looking at the diagrams and simulations that were still projected on the wall. No one had thought to turn them off. The regular patterns of gravitational waves suddenly appeared to him like handwriting—cosmic calligraphy written in the curves of space-time.

A thought formed in his consciousness, at first fleeting like a dream, then increasingly clear. What if these patterns were not just a language, but an invitation? An invitation to dialogue with something that existed far beyond the horizon of human experience?

He frowned deeply.

But how could one decipher a language with no ears to hear it? And no vocal cords with which to respond?

8

The screen cast a bluish light on Mira's exhausted face. An almost oppressive silence reigned in her small hotel room on the outskirts of Giza, interrupted only occasionally by the soft whirring of the laptop fan and the occasional honking of a distant car. Outside, night had fallen over the desert landscape, but Mira had no eye for the beauty of the starry sky arching over the ancient monuments.

Her eyes burned from staring at the screen for hours, while her fingers flew restlessly across the keyboard. Since returning from the pyramid she had thrown herself into feverish research, driven by the strange lion that she could not place in any iconography.

It was a stylized lion with a wavy mane and raised paws. At first glance, it might have looked like one of the typical Egyptian lion symbols—but Mira had known immediately that something was wrong. The iconography was wrong, too playful, too . . . strange.

"You don't belong here," she murmured as she enlarged the image for the hundredth time. "You're not an Egyptian lion, that's for sure."

Egyptian depictions of lions were usually stern, powerful, with straight lines emblematic of all art of the ancient civilization. This lion, however, seemed almost to be dancing, with flowing lines and a decorative quality reminiscent of a completely different cultural context.

After hours of research, her suspicion was confirmed. It was most likely a Tibetan snow lion—a mythical creature from Buddhist tradition, a symbol of fearlessness, joy, and the unlimited quality of the spirit. The curved, wavy mane, the playful posture, the raised paws—all were characteristic features of this Tibetan representation.

But what was a Tibetan symbol doing in a hidden chamber of the Pyramid of Cheops, built 2,000 years before the spread of Buddhism? Her father had no connection to the religion, let alone Tibetan culture.

Mira leaned back and rubbed her tired eyes. The most logical explanation would be that someone in more recent times—perhaps in the last few centuries—had gained access to the chamber and added the symbol. Mainly looters and grave robbers, which, unfortunately, had been a frequent occurrence over the last 2,500 years. But Tibetan Buddhists? That was almost impossible.

So it must have been my father. The thought seemed absurd to her, but then so was a Buddhist snow lion in an undiscovered burial chamber of the Pyramid of Cheops.

The symbol stood in stark contrast to the uniform preservation and style of the wall paintings.

She opened a new browser tab and delved deeper into her research on Tibetan snow lions, even though her eyes already felt heavy and swollen. She read about their symbolic meaning in Tibetan Buddhism, their representation as guardians of sacred places, their connection to snow-capped peaks and pure heights. In Tibetan mythology, they often carried the thrones of Buddha, symbolizing unyielding joy and fearlessness on the spiritual path.

But it was another detail that particularly caught her attention. In some ancient Tibetan texts, snow lions were described as messengers between different worlds, as guides between this world and other planes of reality.

"Between worlds," she murmured as her thoughts wandered to the black pyramids on the murals, floating between earth and stars.

She glanced at her watch. Almost five in the morning. She had worked throughout the entire night without a moment's rest. Yet she felt no fatigue—only this burning sense of impatience, this urge to solve the puzzle her father had left her.

For she was now convinced that the Tibetan snow lion was no coincidence. It was a clue, a landmark, perhaps placed there by her father himself—or discovered by him and recognized as significant.

The morning sun was already beating down mercilessly from the sky when Mira left the air-conditioned hotel lobby and stepped out onto the streets of Cairo. She needed to get away from her thoughts, from the sterile environment of archaeological research—she needed the lively, chaotic hustle and bustle of the city to clear her mind.

Traffic was already in full swing, a frantic cacophony of horns, shouts, and humming engines. Dust and exhaust hung in the air, mingled with the smells of spices, grilled meat, and the ubiquitous aroma of black tea. People streamed through the streets, a kaleidoscope of traditional jellabiyas and modern jeans, busy faces under the already scorching Egyptian sun.

Mira drifted along, navigating the bustling alleys with the instinctive confidence she had developed during numerous research trips. She liked the chaos, the unfiltered vibrancy of Cairo—so far removed from the silent, timeless monuments she worked with, yet right next door. Here, there were no perfectly preserved murals, no enigmatic symbols from a distant past—just the pulsating present, which left no time for brooding. Dirty, loud, smoggy.

She found a small street café and ordered breakfast. This included a dish called ful medames, the most traditional Egyptian breakfast fare of all, made from stewed or mashed fava beans—a dish Hannibal Lecter might love—along with flatbread, tahini, and strong, sweet coffee. As she ate, she watched the hustle and bustle around her. Students with backpacks hurried past, merchants arranged their wares, taxi drivers loudly negotiated with potential passengers, and others argued loudly about politics, the weather, the economy, or whatever else.

She thought of her team, who were currently working on the discovery at base camp. They deserved to celebrate the find without being dampened by her gloomy mood. The discovery of the hidden chamber would electrify scientific circles, boost careers, and open up new perspectives on Egyptian iconography. It was a triumph—just not the one she had been looking for. They should celebrate and enjoy it, and she wasn't the right person to accompany them at that moment.

Her phone rang. Professor Markowitz's name lit up on the display.

"Mira! My star in the sky of archaeology!" His voice sounded euphoric, a rare state for the usually reserved academic. "I've looked at the pictures over and over again. Unbelievable! Absolutely groundbreaking!"

"Thanks, David." She tried to sound enthusiastic. "The team did an excellent job."

"The team! You made this discovery, Mira. Your intuition, your methodology. I've already spoken to the dean, to National Geographic, to the Metropolitan Museum. Everyone is absolutely thrilled!"

She smiled wearily. His enthusiasm delighted her, even over the phone. He had not only been her mentor, but also a fatherly friend during the difficult early years of her studies and the subsequent death of her mother.

"It opens all doors for us, my dear. All of them." His voice took on a solemn tone. "New research funds, expanded excavation rights, maybe even your own chair in the near future. You are the new superstar of archaeology—that's what you are."

"I'm happy," she said, hating herself for the lie. She should be happy. It should be the triumphant culmination of years of hard work. Instead, it felt like defeat, like another unsolved mystery, and that only made her guilt worse.

While Markowitz spoke enthusiastically about his plans for publishing and presenting the discovery, Mira's thoughts wandered to her mother. Fariha Najafi had never been able to accept that her husband had simply disappeared. For years she had waited for news, had pestered the authorities, had clung to every straw.

The uncertainty had finally consumed her, plunging her into a deep depression from which she never truly recovered. When cancer struck, she had ultimately lacked the strength to fight. Since then, Mira knew painfully well that a wordless disappearance without resolution was worse than the death of the family member in question.

"I'll be with you in 20 hours," announced Markowitz, pulling her out of her dark memories. "My flight leaves tonight. We have to celebrate this together, a fitting toast to one of the most significant discoveries of the last century!"

"I'm looking forward to it," replied Mira automatically, her gaze wandering over the busy street.

Something suddenly caught her attention. Two men—clearly not Egyptian, but European or American—were standing across the street. They wore light summer shirts and sunglasses, their posture carefully casual. But Mira didn't miss how their eyes kept wandering back to her, how they talked and nodded in her direction.

A nervous prickle ran down her spine. Was she being watched?

"Mira? Are you still there?" asked the voice of David Markowitz.

"Yes, sorry." She slowly got up and put some money on the table. "I have to go now. See you tomorrow."

She ended the call, put the phone away, and strolled seemingly aimlessly toward the busier market district. A discreet glance over her shoulder confirmed her suspicion: the two men had started moving, following her at a cautious distance.

A shiver of unease ran through her. Why would anyone be following her? Was it because of the discovery? Had the news already spread beyond scientific circles, whetting the appetite of treasure hunters or sensation seekers?

Or did it have something to do with the Tibetan symbol? With what her father might have found?

She plunged into the hustle and bustle of the Khan el-Khalili bazaar, navigating the labyrinth of narrow alleys and crowded stalls with practiced precision. Here, in the densest hustle and bustle of Cairo, it would be difficult to follow her without attracting attention.

She quickly turned onto a side street, then another, using her knowledge of the old quarter to her advantage. A quick glance back showed her that her pursuers were still behind her, even if they were clearly struggling to keep up.

With one last quick maneuver, she slipped into a fabric store, crossed it with an apologetic gesture to the surprised merchant, and stepped through the back exit onto a parallel alley. From there, she boarded the first minibus that would take her back toward her hotel.

As the crowded minibus fought its way through the heavy traffic, she tried to calm her racing heartbeat. Maybe she was imagining it all. Maybe the men were harmless tourists or businessmen. The combination of exhaustion and the emotional strain of the last few days could have distorted her perception. Who would be interested in an archaeology professor?

Her phone rang again, and she flinched so violently that the woman sitting next to her looked at her with a raised eyebrow. She expected it to be Markowitz, but it was an unknown international number. Hesitantly, she answered the call.

"Dr. Najafi?" A woman's voice, precise and with a slight French accent. "Ricarda Lefèvre from the European Space Agency. We met last year at the conference in Luxor."

Mira remembered. At the time, the ESA had helped map a temple complex using satellite data and had discovered hidden structures buried beneath the desert sand.

"Of course, Dr. Lefèvre. What can I do for you?"

"I have a few questions about the pyramids of Giza, specifically the Pyramid of Cheops." Lefèvre's voice sounded casual, almost too casual, especially given the timing, which was naturally conspicuous. "I'm particularly interested in the original edge lengths and how they've changed over time."

A strange request from a space agency.

"The original dimensions of the Pyramid of Cheops were approximately 230 meters at the base and 146 meters in height," replied Mira automatically. "Today's dimensions are smaller—approximately 207 meters at the base and 138 meters in height. To put that into perspective, each side of the base is about 2.5 city blocks, and if it were a skyscraper, it would be about 40 stories high."

"Thank you. What caused these measurements to change?"

"Primarily the loss of the outer limestone cladding, which was used as building material in the Middle Ages. In addition, erosion and slight seismic activity over the millennia have led to minimal deformations."

"Interesting." Lefèvre paused briefly. "And the pyramids of Chephren and Mycerinus? Similar changes?"

"Yes, proportional to their size. Why is the ESA interested in ancient structures, if I may ask?"

Another pause, longer this time.

"To be honest, I don't know exactly myself yet." Something in Lefèvre's voice had changed, an undertone that Mira couldn't quite place. "I heard you made an important discovery."

Mira blinked in surprise. The news had obviously spread quickly. "Markowitz didn't waste any time."

"Actually, I didn't hear about it from Professor Markowitz." Another strange pause. "Would you tell me about it?"

Something about this conversation felt wrong, but Mira couldn't quite put her finger on what it was. Still, the discovery would soon be made public anyway, if it wasn't already.

"We found a previously unknown chamber in the Pyramid of Cheops," she explained. "With exceptionally well-preserved wall paintings. Among them is an unusual depiction of the three pyramids of Giza—in black paint against a blue background, which apparently represents the night sky. What is particularly astonishing is that the image was copied on the adjacent wall."

There was a sharp intake of breath at the other end of the line. "Black pyramids? Are you sure?"

"Absolutely. The preservation is remarkable. The paintings also show priests in a meditative posture and a kind of . . . energy beam flowing from one of the priests to the pyramids."

A long silence followed, so long that Mira briefly thought the connection had been interrupted.

"Dr. Lefèvre?"

"Yes, I'm still here." The scientist's voice now sounded different, more controlled. "That's . . . highly interesting. I'll get back to you, Dr. Najafi. Soon."

The connection was interrupted, and Mira stared at her phone in confusion. What had that been? Why was the ESA's head of communications interested in ancient Egyptian structures? And why had the mention of the black pyramids triggered such a reaction?

The minibus reached her hotel, and she got out, carefully checking the surroundings for signs of her pursuers. Nothing. She had apparently shaken them off successfully.

Once in her room, she opened her laptop again and brought up the image of the Tibetan snow lion. In Buddhist tradition, these mystical creatures were not only symbols of fearlessness, but also signposts that could show the way to hidden treasures or wisdom.

Tibetan snow lions in an Egyptian pyramid. Black pyramids in the night sky. A priest who spoke to the gods. And a father who may have understood all this—and paid for it.

A sudden determination came over her. She opened a flight search engine and typed in "Cairo to Kathmandu." There was a flight tonight, with a layover in Dubai. She would miss Markowitz, raise questions, jeopardize her career.

But she had to do it. If the Tibetan snow lion was a clue—whether placed there by her father or discovered by him—then she had to follow the trail before someone else drew the same conclusions. Dr. Lefèvre's strange questions, the mysterious pursuers—something was going on here, and she had to find answers before it was too late.

With determined movements of her fingers, she booked the flight, then packed essentials into a small backpack. She would send Abdul a message, explaining that she had to attend to an urgent personal matter. He would inform the team and reassure Markowitz—hopefully.

As she pressed the Enter key, it felt as if she were erasing her career. Nevertheless, she didn't hesitate.

Her hand rested for a moment on her father's little leather book before she carefully placed it in her backpack. In addition to all the scientific notes and theories, it also contained a small note in the margin of one page that she only now truly understood.

"The mane shows the way through the gates of heaven."

9

The afternoon sun streamed through the tall windows of the CERN cafeteria, casting bright rectangles on the floor that frayed at the edges and seemed to flicker slightly. After hours of deliberations in closed conference rooms, the open dining area offered a welcome change. Lukas sat across from a visibly exhausted Carlos. The cups of cold espresso stood untouched between them, while around them they could hear the muffled conversations of other scientists who had also taken a break.

"Thirty-seven hours with only four hours of sleep," said Carlos, rubbing his reddened eyes. "Reminds me of when I was finishing up my doctoral thesis."

"I hear you," said Lukas. "We're too old for this." He rubbed his throbbing temples. For a while, the exhaustion had given him a strange clarity, as if the lack of sleep had blocked out unimportant thoughts, but now he was finding it increasingly difficult to keep his eyes open. He yawned loudly. "How many people in the world actually know about this now?"

Carlos thought for a moment. "The conference, the various observatories, selected government representatives . . . maybe five hundred? A thousand at most."

"That won't last long. The objects are getting closer every day. In a month, advanced amateur astronomers will be able to spot them."

There was a brief silence. What would happen when the news reached the public? Panic for sure? With the only way to soothe the masses being to point out that, despite giving off gravity waves that indicated they had more mass than the Sun, the objects hadn't destroyed Mars as they traveled by it. The trick would be not to mention that the objects appeared to be on a direct collision course with Earth.

Would prayer erupt around the planet? Would this discovery usher in a new era of scientific humility in the face of confirmation that humanity was not alone? A crisis of religion and faith? When something so impossible happened, it was impossible to predict humanity's reaction.

"Tell me about your communication ideas," said Carlos, pulling him out of his musings. "How do you talk to someone whose technological advantage is obviously enormous?"

Lukas looked up, his eyes like windows to a spirit who was seeking some kind of order in the vast uncertainty as the rain poured down.

"We've developed three parallel approaches," he began somewhat lamely, blinking against the fatigue. "The first is conventional and based on proven methods, directional high-power radio waves with various messages. We will send simple mathematical sequences, such as prime numbers, as the universal language of logic, binary-coded images similar to the Arecibo message of 1974, and physical constants as the common denominator of all existence in the cosmos."

He paused. "Well, constants that we *thought* were the common denominator. Until the objects made it clear to us that our understanding of physics is . . . lacking."

"Still makes sense," said Carlos. "If someone transmitted Newtonian physics to us, we'd know they must not have developed Einsteinian physics yet, but we'd still recognize it. So using the classic SETI approach, if I'm not mistaken, is a great idea."

Lukas sighed. "Our conclusion also. Why not? It's a bit like sending a message in a bottle into a starry ocean that makes our watery oceans seem minuscule. Nevertheless, we have to exhaust every possibility."

He took a sip of his now cold coffee and grimaced in disgust. "Our second approach is more experimental. We want to modify the Large Hadron Collider here at CERN to generate specific gravitational wave patterns."

"Yeah, that was mentioned during our presentation. Just how weak would these waves be?"

"Extremely. We'll be throwing a pebble in a pond and hoping our visitors have the means to see the ripples millions of miles away. Except we aren't positive we can even throw in a pebble. Theoretically, if we synchronize high-energy particle collisions with extreme precision, minimal gravitational waves should be generated. Dr. Mercer and Dr. Richter have already outlined the mathematical basis. The challenge lies in the implementation, but that's where the particle physicists come in."

"As much as I love your ripples-in-a-pond metaphor," said Carlos with a grin, "do you think you could give me the quantitative answer? This is science, not creative writing."

Lukas returned the smile. "Right. Everyone's a critic. According to our calculations, the waves we can create—*theoretically*—would be ten orders of magnitude below the detection limit of our own LIGO sensors."

"So *their* detectors just need to be ten billion times better than ours," said Carlos wryly. "How hard can a ten billion-fold improvement really be?" He paused. "I'm probably getting a little punch drunk, but imagine a cowboy sitting on a horse in 1850. You know, on a biological engine that operates at exactly . . . well, *one* horsepower. By definition. If someone told this cowboy about the power of heavy rockets we have today, he'd find it impossible to believe."

"That's just as bad as *my* metaphor," complained Lukas in amusement. "Besides, the mightiest rockets we have today only operate at twenty million horsepower, not ten billion. Although I understand it's quite tricky to get all twenty million horses into the engine." He laughed. "Not to mention cleaning up after them."

"Yeah. *Tricky* is one word for it."

"Here's the bottom line," said Lukas. "They'd need miracle tech to be able to detect our signal. But what the hell? What's another miracle among friends? These pyramids do seem to use gravitational waves for propulsion or communication, after all, so their sensors really could have the required sensitivity."

"How would you encode the message?"

"First, through frequency and amplitude—simple binary patterns, mathematical constants, perhaps even the geometric proportions of the pyramids themselves, as a sign of recognition—if that's even technically possible. I'm far from an expert in this area. Dr. Malik is working with a team of mathematicians and linguists on a syntax based on universal physical principles."

Carlos leaned forward, his face lit up with fascination.

"And the third approach?" he asked.

"LIGO."

"LIGO?" Carlos frowned and looked at him as if he had lost his mind.

"The idea is not to use LIGO itself as a transmitter," Lukas said more quietly. "That would be as technically nonsensical as it would be impossible. But we are investigating concepts in which the interferometers act as control units for a coupled mass resonator—superconducting oscillators that are set into extremely high-frequency asymmetric oscillations by modulated radiation pressure."

"I'm an astronomer, amigo."

"The theory is based on old work on mass-induced gravitational wave emission in the nano to micronewton range," Lukas continued, as if his friend had said nothing. "Previous models were considered too inefficient, but with new superconducting technology and quantum sensors, we could push into areas that were previously considered unthinkable." He smiled crookedly. "Basically, we would try to make space-time vibrate—but in a targeted, focused, and controlled way."

"Sounds like you're trying to do the impossible."

"And then some," agreed Lukas.

Carlos took a sip of his own coffee, his forehead creased in thought. "There is a fourth approach you might want to consider."

"I'm all ears."

"The objects are approaching Earth. What if they're already communicating, and we just haven't recognized it yet? Maybe the gravitational waves themselves are the message."

"Dr. Romano has suggested something similar." Lukas nodded slowly. "A team is already analyzing the fine structures of the wave patterns, looking for mathematical regularities that go beyond pure physics. But that's like deciphering a hieroglyph without the Rosetta

Stone. Remember, we've only known about the existence of gravitational waves since 2015."

There was a brief silence as both men pondered their thoughts, staring into their coffee cups with wrinkled noses. The cafeteria had gradually emptied, with only a few groups of colleagues and CERN employees still sitting at the tables, their voices muffled and tired like a lulling background noise.

"What about *your* group?" asked Lukas finally, trying to fend off sleep, the exhaustion in his eyes briefly replaced by scientific curiosity. "Have you made any progress with the visual data?"

"I almost forgot!" said Carlos, a spark of new energy in his demeanor. "In fact, we have made a significant breakthrough. We've combined all the observational data from the last few days—optical telescopes, infrared, spectral analyses, even some experimental quantum telescopes that are still in the testing phase."

"And?"

"We used a specially developed AI model that has been optimized for analyzing weakly reflective objects. It can reconstruct structures from fragmentary data, similar to how archaeologists can deduce the shape of an entire vessel from a few shards."

Lukas leaned forward, instinctively drawn in by the sudden intensity in Carlos' voice. "So? What did you find?"

"The objects are definitely pyramids, there's no doubt about that. But this is where it gets really strange." Carlos took a deep breath. "Lukas, these pyramids have almost exactly the same proportions and dimensions as the Great Pyramids of Giza."

A moment of absolute silence followed this revelation. Lukas stared at his friend, unsure if he had heard correctly.

"The Pyramids of Giza?" he repeated slowly. "You mean . . ."

"The Pyramid of Cheops, the Pyramid of Chephren, and the Pyramid of Mycerinus," Carlos confirmed with a nod. "The same arrangement, the same relative sizes—with some deviations, however—and the same proportions. The correspondence is accurate to less than five meters."

Lukas felt his heartbeat quicken. The idea seemed absurd, almost like a cosmic joke—three objects traveling from the depths of space toward Earth, taking on the shape of structures that humanity had built thousands of years ago. That in itself was highly improbable, but the fact that their sizes were almost identical seemed even more unlikely.

"It must be a spurious correlation," he muttered, as his mind tried to correctly classify these new implications, as it had so often done lately. "The probability of a random geometric match would be . . ."

"Astronomically low," Carlos finished his thought. "We're talking about a probability that is basically *zero*. There must be a connection. Even if the edge lengths don't match exactly, and the height also differs slightly, at least for two of the three objects."

Lukas rubbed his temples, behind which the throbbing had grown into full-blown pain.

"Maybe we really did misunderstand the communication. Maybe the shape itself is the message. A reference to something they know or have seen about us. As if they wanted to mirror something to us, as a sign that they recognize us."

"Or something they've *already* communicated to us," said Carlos quietly. "What if the pyramids of Giza themselves were not a human invention? This has been a conspiracy theory repeated so often it's basically mainstream. Because we still can't figure out how these things were built. And it's still an unanswered question why pyramids were built all over the world at different times and by different cultures."

The implication of these words hung between them like an invisible weight. To view the monumental structures, which for millennia had been regarded as evidence of human engineering, in a completely new light—as possible legacies or inspirations of extraterrestrial intelligence—was a thought that could shake not only their present-day society but the very foundations of human history.

"We shouldn't rush into pre-astronautics theories," Lukas finally warned, although the doubt in his voice was audible. "There could be other explanations. Maybe they've been observing our civilization for a long time and deliberately chose this shape as a distinguishing mark, just like you said."

"Or as a warning," Carlos added grimly.

A new voice suddenly joined their conversation: "Not *almost* the same dimensions—but *exactly* the same."

Both men looked up. Standing before them was a middle-aged woman with short, silver-gray hair and narrow, rimless glasses that gave her intelligent, sparkling eyes an analytical expression. Ricarda Lefèvre, the communications director of the European Space Agency (ESA). Lukas had already worked with her on several occasions when the LIGO project needed public support.

"Ricarda?" said Lukas in surprise. "How long have you been standing there?"

"Long enough."

"What do you mean, *exactly the same*?"

She sat down at her table without being asked, her movements precise and controlled like those of a robot. "I mean, the pyramids of Giza that we see today are not identical to those that were originally built. The outer limestone cladding that once covered the entire surface has weathered away over the millennia or been removed by local builders as building material. Erosion has worn away further centimeters. In total, the deviation between then and now is 7.8 meters for the Pyramid of Cheops, 7.1 meters for the Pyramid of Chephren, and 3.5 meters for the Pyramid of Mycerinus."

She leaned forward, her voice a mixture of professional sobriety and barely concealed excitement. "So what you see in the sky most likely corresponds to the original, exact dimensions of the pyramids as they were built 4,500 years ago."

"How do you know that?" asked Carlos in dismay.

"The archaeologist Mira Najafi is an old friend of mine." A subtle smile played around Lefèvre's lips. "One of the leading archaeologists specializing in Egyptian structures. We spoke on the phone an hour ago, and she confirmed it for me. The original dimensions of the Pyramid of Cheops correspond precisely to the measurements that your astronomical data should show for the largest of the three objects."

"You already know our data?" said Carlos, stunned.

"Agatha from your group—we were just having coffee."

The geometric echoes between humanity's oldest monumental structures and the mysterious objects approaching Earth could not be ignored. This had opened up a second implication that raised far more questions than it answered.

"If it's true," he began slowly, carefully sorting through his thoughts. "If these objects are indeed exact replicas of the original pyramids of Giza. We have to ask ourselves a critical question. Are these space pyramids mimicking one of our greatest historical monuments? Or is one of our greatest historical monuments mimicking *them*?"

He winced. "And by *them*, of course, I mean the ones on a collision course with Earth. The ones that could wipe us from existence on a whim."

10

The thin air of Kathmandu burned in Mira's lungs as she pushed her way through the crowded streets of the Thamel district. Tour buses unloaded tourists with colorful backpacks, motorcycles weaved through the crowds honking their horns, and street vendors touted their wares—from colorful prayer flags to "authentic" mountaineering equipment. The smell of incense mingled with exhaust fumes and pungent spices to create an olfactory fingerprint unique to this city.

In her hand, Mira held a laminated photo of her father—a snapshot from better days, showing him smiling in front of the pyramids of Giza, the scarab emblem clearly visible on his field hat. The corners of the picture were already worn from the countless times she had shown it to the locals since landing.

"Have you seen this man?" she asked for the hundredth time that morning, this time to the owner of a small guesthouse in the city center. "He was here maybe 15 years ago."

The man glanced at the photo and shook his head. "Fifteen years ago? I'm sorry, ma'am. Impossible to say. So many faces come and go."

Mira nodded wearily, thanked him, and continued on her way. The last 48 hours had been a whirlwind of airports, stuffy taxis, and endless questions. After her hasty departure from Cairo, she had landed in Kathmandu with nothing but her backpack, the photo of her father, and the vague hope that the Tibetan snow lion had led her here for a good reason.

The sun was already setting when she reached the end of her list of possible accommodations. One last hotel, off the main tourist trail, in a narrow side street of the neighborhood. The Lotus Haven, a 3-story building with peeling blue paint and a tattered prayer flag above the entrance.

The reception area was little more than a small room with a rickety desk behind which sat a young Nepalese man with a smartphone in his hand. He barely looked up when Mira entered.

"Excuse me," she began, handing him the photo across the counter. "I'm looking for this man. He's my father and may have been here about 15 years ago."

The young man glanced briefly at the picture, then shook his head.

"I'm sorry," he said with the typical friendliness of the Nepalese. "Fifteen years ago, I was still a child. I've only been working here for three years."

Mira felt exhaustion and frustration settle in her neck like a growing knot. This was the last address on her list. Another day without results. What had she been expecting? Talk about a long shot. Her intuition had seemed to push her here, and while it had often served her well, it was far from perfect. And it was asking an awful lot this time.

She noticed the older man sitting in a small alcove behind the reception desk, bent over a handwritten book. His hands were covered with age spots, his gray hair tied back in a careless knot.

"Could I perhaps speak with him?" she asked, pointing to the older man.

"That's my grandfather." The receptionist shook his head. "He hardly speaks English and no longer takes care of the business."

Something in Mira refused to give up. Not after everything she had gone through.

"Please!" she said emphatically. "It's important. He must have run the hotel back then, right? Maybe he remembers. You can translate."

The young man sighed, then turned around and said something in rapid Nepali. The old man looked up, his eyes magnified behind thick glasses. The grandson beckoned him over and handed him the photo.

The old man took it, held it close to his face, his eyes narrowed. Then something happened that took Mira's breath away: he nodded. A slow, deliberate nod, accompanied by a recognizable gleam in his eyes. A wave of hope washed over her.

"You know him?" she asked, and the receptionist hastily translated.

The old man replied in his language, and his grandson turned back to Mira.

"He says he has seen your father here, yes. But not recently."

Mira's heart began to race. A clue. After all these years, finally a concrete lead. "Are you sure?" she asked, almost afraid to believe it could be true.

Seconds later, the receptionist translated his grandfather's words. "As sure as an old man can be. He says he sometimes forgets things, but he never remembers things falsely."

"That's awesome!" she said excitedly. "Can you ask him what my father was doing here? Where he went?"

The receptionist translated, and the old man spoke at length, gesturing with his gnarled hands. His face showed a mixture of respect and the weariness of a long life.

"He says he doesn't know exactly what your father did. But my grandfather says he was a seeker."

"A seeker?"

"Someone who seeks answers, wisdom. He says there are many such people here. They usually go to the monasteries in the Himalayas. Especially to Samye or Jokhang."

The receptionist listened further. "Yes, he saw him last year. And he was definitely a seeker."

"Last year!" repeated Mira, feeling dizzy as the room spun around her. Could it really be? Was he still *alive*?

"Yes. Your father ended up at Samye. He had been in town for a rare visit, gathering supplies for a project of his. My grandfather tells me he didn't talk to your father personally, but saw him from a distance and remembered him by an unusual piece of jewelry that was hanging around his neck."

Mira's heart was now racing like a runaway train, crashing against her chest. Could she really have finally found her father? And alive?

"Can he describe this jewelry?" she asked excitedly.

The translator asked the question and relayed the short answer. "It was unusual. Not Tibetan or Nepalese. But it was quite striking. It looked like a fat golden key, with a ring on the top like a person's head, inlaid with topaz and emerald. It had strange markings carved into the body with tiny diamonds."

Mira's eyes widened into saucers. This was proof. Definitive proof in her mind. The man had described an old piece of jewelry her father had often worn—a beautiful ankh symbol on a leather cord. The ankh was perhaps the most recognizable symbol from ancient Egypt, often called the key of life, or the Egyptian cross, symbolizing eternal life. It had been a gift from her mother from the early days of their relationship.

So he *hadn't* left his wife. Why else would he have kept it with him?

I knew it!

"Please thank your grandfather for me," she said almost euphorically. "Profusely! This means more to me than I can ever explain."

Before she could say anything further, her phone rang. The French number she already knew and had saved after their last conversation: Ricarda Lefèvre.

She thanked the translator and his grandfather, making emphatic gestures of gratitude, and then answered the call on the fifth ring.

"Please excuse me," she said to the two men and took a few steps back. "Ms. Lefèvre?"

"Dr. Najafi." The ESA scientist's voice sounded clear, as if she were standing right next to her and not on another continent. "I just landed at Kathmandu airport. I think we should talk."

Mira froze. "You're here? In Nepal?"

"The café in the departure area of the international terminal in an hour. I'll be waiting for you." The connection was cut off before Mira could respond.

She stared at her phone, a queasy feeling spreading in her stomach. How did Lefèvre know she was here? And why had the woman followed her?

11

The airport café was almost empty, with most travelers rushing to their gates or standing in long lines at the check-in counters. Ricarda Lefèvre sat at a table by the window, a laptop in front of her, a cup of coffee in her hand. She looked fresh and rested, as if she had just returned from a short trip and not flown halfway around the world.

"Dr. Najafi," said Lefèvre with a brief smile, standing up to shake her hand. "Thank you for coming."

Mira took a seat, not letting go of her backpack. "How did you find me?"

"That's not important right now." Lefèvre closed her laptop. "I'm here to make you an offer."

"An offer?"

"The ESA needs your expertise. We're offering you a position as a consultant for a . . . special project."

Mira shrank back in confusion. "Uhh. . . thanks. I guess. But I'm not looking for a career change. As you know, I already have a job. At Yale University."

Lefèvre sighed. "Are you so sure about that?"

"What do you mean?"

"You ignored Professor Markowitz's calls. Intentionally, I assume."

Mira flinched. It was true. Since her hasty departure, her phone hadn't stopped ringing—calls from Markowitz, from Jason, from Abdul. She had ignored them all and finally put her phone on silent. The image of the Tibetan snow lion she had seen inside a hidden passage in the most famous of all Egyptian pyramids had burrowed into her brain, driving her to ignore everything except the search for her father.

"He can't have fired me," she said, more to herself than to Lefèvre.

The ESA scientist pulled out a tablet, unlocked it, and handed it to Mira. "Read for yourself."

The Egyptian Antiquities Journal website was open on the screen. The headline jumped out at her: "SENSATIONAL DISCOVERY IN THE PYRAMID OF CHEOPS: SECRET CHAMBER WITH ANCIENT IMAGES REVEALED."

Below it was a photo of Professor Markowitz and Dr. Abdelrahman, smiling in front of the entrance to the pyramid.

Mira skimmed the article. Her name was mentioned, yes—as a member of the research team, "unfortunately unable to give interviews due to personal commitments." The main discovery was attributed to Markowitz, who had noticed the anomaly "with his infallible scientific instinct." Dr. Abdelrahman was described as the "brilliant Egyptian partner" who had carried out the crucial analyses.

Her discovery. *Her* find. Her years of searching. Reduced to a footnote. She slumped in her chair as if her bones had melted into a viscous mass. It was easy to blame these men for stealing her thunder, but she had done it to herself. Who makes one of the greatest finds in history and then turns her back on it a moment later?

"There are more articles," said Lefèvre quietly. "In *National Geographic*, in *Scientific American*, in the *New York Times*. The same narrative everywhere. I think your mentor is angry."

Mira placed the tablet on the table, a dull feeling of numbness spreading through her. Markowitz had either seized the opportunity to take credit, or her actions had practically forced him to. The media rush must have been enormous—and insistent for a hero to interview. It hurt her more than she had expected, despite having brought this on herself.

"The monasteries will wait," continued Lefèvre. "Samye has been standing for over a thousand years. It will still be here in a few weeks."

Mira looked up sharply. "How could you know about that?" she said, stunned. "I just found out about it prior to your call." She looked ill. "Do you have me *bugged*?"

"No. But I did have you followed by the best. I had two men follow you in Cairo, but their professionalism left a lot to be desired. They stuck out like sore thumbs, and you obviously detected them.

The replacements I hired are so good they can blend into the scenery like an octopus."

"But why?" thundered Mira, outraged.

"We live in extraordinary times, Dr. Najafi." Lefèvre's tone remained even, almost gentle. "And the fate of the world hangs in the balance."

"The fate of the *world*?" she repeated in disgust. "Is this some kind of bad joke? You sound like a voiceover for a movie trailer. What's this really about?"

Lefèvre sighed once again. "I wish it were just a bad joke. I wish I were making it all up. You'll understand, I'm sure, when I reveal the big picture. But the bottom line is this: with stakes this high, the privacy rights of a single person unfortunately mean nothing. I needed to learn more about you before making my offer."

"What do you want from me?"

"Your expertise. Your perspective, to be precise." Lefèvre leaned forward. "We have a plane here at the airport, ready to take you to a place where we can give you the background you'll need to help us."

"Again, background on what? Help you how?"

"Help us understand pyramids." Lefèvre's gaze intensified. "And not just the ones on Earth."

A shiver ran down Mira's spine. "If you're trying to prove you're sane, you're doing a horrible job."

"There are things you don't know yet, Dr. Najafi. They could be related to your discovery in the new chamber." Lefèvre's voice dropped to a whisper. "Teams of the world's best scientists are currently working on a problem that you may be able to help solve. One that will affect us all."

Mira felt her heartbeat quicken. The murals. The black pyramids in the sky.

"I can't tell you more than that, not here." Lefèvre leaned back. "But I can assure you: what you will learn goes far beyond your discovery. It will change everything, forever."

If the woman were sane, Mira could surmise the gist of what this was about on her own. The woman was from a space agency, dropping a clue about pyramids in space. And Mira was the woman who had just discovered a depiction of pyramids in space in Egypt for the first time in recorded history.

Pyramids in space? It was absurd. Yet Lefèvre wasn't a homeless woman babbling to herself on the street. This was a woman from ESA, who had the resources to travel here after Mira at a moment's notice, and to discreetly place people so close to Mira that they were able to track her every movement, her every conversation.

So, as absurd as this was, she'd be a fool not to take it seriously.

"You're the leading expert on the Pyramids of Giza," continued Lefèvre, "with a fresh perspective. You understand Egyptian hieroglyphics perfectly and feel confident in ancient Egyptian culture. And you've already discovered connections that could be significant."

Lefèvre looked at her watch. "My offer is a one-time thing. If you decline, I'll call the second-best expert on my list."

The decision hung in the air between them like a tangible presence. Mira felt the weight, the significance of this moment. Something bigger was going on, something that went beyond archaeological discoveries and academic recognition.

And yet—the trail of her father was fresh. After 15 years of searching, she finally had a concrete lead. The monastery of Samye. A follower. A *seeker*.

And a sighting only a year earlier.

The excitement of a possible scientific revelation pulsed within her, mixed with a burning desire to finally learn the truth about her father's fate. Two paths diverged here, in this anonymous airport café.

Mira took a deep breath as a stanza from one of the most famous poems of all time drifted through her mind, unbidden. *Two roads diverged in a wood and I—I took the one less traveled by, And that has made all the difference.*

But in this case, which was the road less traveled? Pyramids in space? Or a Tibetan monetary? In this case, perhaps it was a toss-up.

No matter, this wasn't a choice that could be decided intellectually, or by a poem. She needed to follow her gut.

"I'm sorry, Dr. Lefèvre. I have to decline."

Lefèvre's eyebrows rose slightly. "Are you sure? You should know that this opportunity will not come again."

"My father was here." Mira's voice steadied. "Likely still is. After all these years, I finally have a concrete lead. I have to follow it before it goes cold."

"The pyramids will wait."

"So will the monastery."

Mira stood up and slung her backpack over her shoulder. "Whatever you've discovered, whatever you want to show me—it will have to happen without me. Or you'll have to give me more time."

"That's not going to happen." Lefèvre looked at her for a long moment, then nodded slowly and stood up. "But I understand. Family comes first."

"Thank you."

As she turned to leave, Lefèvre's voice stopped her once more. "Dr. Najafi—take care of yourself. The world may soon change in ways that are hard to predict, but it will be difficult."

Mira left the café with an uneasy feeling in her stomach. She was turning her back on monumental secrets and potentially groundbreaking discoveries. Ahead of her lay an unknown path into the mountains, following a father who had previously had nothing to do with Buddhism or even spirituality. The Islamic Revolution and the accompanying persecution of Sufis in Iran had robbed him of all faith.

But she believed the old man in the guesthouse. His accurate description of the ankh her father wore, combined with the out-of-place lion, was too much to ignore.

She had come all the way here, and she had struck pay dirt. She had run a marathon and was possibly a few feet away from the finish line. And her father was still alive!

She had to have answers. Finally. Why he had vanished. Why he had left clues so she could find the hidden chamber within Cheops, and then a further clue to bring her here. Why his discovery of a chamber in a pyramid in Egypt had led him to Buddhism of all things, and a monastery.

She had asked questions for 15 years and had thought she had imagined every possible scenario for what had motivated him to do what he had done.

But a monetary in Tibet had never been on her bingo card.

12

The United Nations conference hall in Geneva, normally a place of measured diplomatic discussions, was bathed in an atmosphere of tense urgency that morning. Security measures in and around the building had been raised to unprecedented levels. Even the usual press vehicles had been banned from the spacious parking lot, and the access roads were blocked off by Swiss security forces.

Lukas stood at the window of the preparation room and watched the arrival of the black limousines with tinted windows. Each one carried at least one head of state or government—a concentration of political power not seen in one place for a very long time.

"You look worried," remarked Carlos, who had stepped up beside him.

Lukas tugged at his tie, which felt as if it were choking him.

"The most powerful people in the world expect me to tell them in just 30 minutes how we intend to make contact with extraterrestrial objects that, according to current forecasts, will collide with us at full speed and wipe us out. So *worried* isn't quite the right word."

"Just remember, they're just as scared as you are. Probably more."

Lukas snorted. "Really? That's what you're going with to calm my nerves? Why not go with the old standard, 'imagine everyone in the audience in their underwear."

"I'd never suggest that. Have you *seen* them? Many of these people are in their seventies. Imagining them in their underwear is something you really don't want to do."

Lukas laughed. It turned out Carlos had helped calm him down, after all.

His presentation was ready on the table, carefully compiled from the results of the last three weeks of intensive work by his communications group. Twenty of the best minds in physics, linguistics, mathematics, and exobiology had worked day and night on communication concepts that were now to be implemented on his recommendation. If he messed up and they didn't get the green light, all that work would be for nothing.

Dr. Elena Volkova, a brilliant Russian physicist, and Dr. Mei Zhang from the Chinese Institute of High Energy Physics joined them. Both would later assist in describing the CERN experiment.

"Are the technical details really correct?" asked Lukas, pointing to the relevant slides. "I don't want to raise false hopes or embarrass myself."

Dr. Zhang nodded. "The calculations have been checked several times. Theoretically, it's possible. If these objects use gravitational waves to communicate, then this is our best chance of being understood."

A member of the organizing team appeared in the doorway. "Dr. Heuer? Five minutes."

Lukas nodded, picked up his documents, and followed the man through the long corridors of the UN building. Carlos and his colleagues walked behind him, a small procession of science on its way to meet the world's most powerful.

The conference room itself was smaller than Lukas had expected. The main hall hadn't been chosen, but rather a more discreet room, apparently for particularly sensitive consultations. Instead of the usual rows of delegation desks, there was a large circular table with about 30 seats. Most of them were already occupied.

Lukas recognized President Morales from the US, President Chen from China, German Chancellor Schneider, French President Dubois, and other leading politicians whose faces he knew only from news broadcasts. Some were talking quietly, others were studying documents or typing on tablets. Everyone looked up as the scientists entered the room.

Dr. Lawrence Kellerman of the International Science Council, who was chairing the meeting, rose.

"Ladies and gentlemen, may I introduce Dr. Lukas Heuer and his team. Dr. Heuer is the one who discovered the three objects and is the head of the international communications group. Today he will be presenting the strategies we've developed so far."

Lukas stepped up to the lectern while Carlos and the other colleagues took their seats at a side table. He put down his notes, took a deep breath, and activated the presentation on the large screen behind him. "Ladies and gentlemen, heads of state and government," he began, his voice firmer than he felt inside. "Three weeks ago, humanity made an unprecedented discovery.

"Three artificial objects, pyramid-shaped and clearly not of terrestrial origin, are moving on a direct course toward Earth." He showed images of the three black pyramids. They had improved after several of the world's most powerful telescopes had been pointed at the objects and had taken measurements over long periods of time.

"These structures generate gravitational waves of astonishing strength and coherence, suggesting a highly advanced technology beyond our current understanding. They appear to be of intelligent origin and may be attempting to make contact."

He saw some of those present becoming restless. US President Morales raised his hand.

"Dr. Heuer, could you explain once again in simple terms what gravitational waves are? Not all of us have a background in theoretical physics."

Lukas nodded. "Of course, Mr. President. Gravitational waves are like ripples in the fabric of space and time itself. When you throw a stone into a pond, waves form on the surface of the water. Similarly, massive objects or events in the universe—such as collapsing stars or merging black holes—create waves in space-time. These waves travel at the speed of light and can be detected with very sensitive instruments."

"And these . . . pyramids deliberately generate such waves?" asked German Chancellor Schneider.

"That appears to be the case, Chancellor. The gravitational waves emanating from them show regular patterns that indicate deliberate modulation—similar to how we modulate radio waves to transmit information."

"But that may also *not* be the case."

"That's also true," he admitted. "Since this is technology that is completely superior to ours and, well . . . violates what we know about physics, the gravitational wave emissions could have a variety of causes. But since our known physics suggests such waves could only be made by objects so massive they should have already caused our extinction, despite their distance, I, for one, am okay with that."

The members of the audience frowned, shrank back, cringed, and made other expressions indicating that his point hadn't been lost on them.

Lukas continued with his presentation, showing diagrams of the recorded wave patterns and explaining how they differed from natural gravitational wave sources. Then he got to the heart of his presentation.

"Our communications group has developed three parallel approaches to contacting these objects. We recommend pursuing all three simultaneously, as we don't know which one is most likely to succeed."

He moved on to the next slide, which illustrated the first approach.

"Approach one is conventional: directional electromagnetic signals. We will use the world's most powerful radio telescopes—including FAST in China and Arecibo II in Puerto Rico—to send focused signals to the objects. These signals will contain mathematical sequences, prime numbers, physical constants, and binary-coded images—similar to the historic Arecibo message of 1974, but much more complex and information-rich."

Chinese President Chen nodded appreciatively. "The FAST telescope is ready. Our scientists have already begun calibrating the transmission parameters."

"Excellent, Mr. President. International cooperation is truly crucial here."

Lukas moved on to the next slide. "Approach two uses optical and infrared lasers. We'll send out synchronized laser pulses from multiple locations around the world, forming complex patterns. This method offers higher bandwidth and enables the transmission of more detailed information."

He explained the technical aspects of laser communication when some questions arose as to whether laser bombardment could be considered an attack, before moving on to the third and most controversial approach.

"Approach three is experimental and without historical precedent." He took a deep breath. "We propose modifying the Large Hadron Collider at CERN to generate controlled gravitational waves."

A murmur rippled through the room. French President Dubois leaned forward, his brow furrowed.

"*Generate* gravitational waves? With a particle accelerator? Is that even possible?"

"Theoretically yes, Mr. President." Lukas signaled to Dr. Zhang, who stepped up to the podium.

"The Large Hadron Collider is the most powerful particle accelerator in the world," explained the Chinese physicist. "In its 27-kilometer-long underground ring, we accelerate protons to 99.9999991% of the speed of light. To put that in perspective, at that speed, one could make 14 round-trips between Washington and Beijing per *second. Round-trips.*

"Also at that speed, precisely as Einstein predicted, the mass of a proton is 7,245 times greater than if the proton were at rest, and time slows for it by the exact same factor. One second to the proton is 2 hours to us."

She switched to a technical diagram of the LHC. "Our idea is to modify the accelerator so that we can generate synchronized collisions at specific points in the ring. Each collision produces a tiny gravitational wave—far too weak for us to detect. But through precise synchronization, we can superimpose, amplify, and modulate these waves so that the extraterrestrials might be able to measure them."

"We borrowed the idea from lasers," added Lukas. "What makes laser light so much more powerful than normal light? The fact that the light is produced so it's *coherent*, meaning all the light waves have the same wavelength, are perfectly in phase with each other, and travel in exactly the same direction."

"Exactly." Dr. Zhang nodded. "We would turn the entire accelerator into a gravitational wave transmitter that generates coherent, modulated waves, however marginal they may be. Still not nearly strong enough for us to measure, but with luck strong enough for these . . . objects to measure."

British Prime Minister Blackwood frowned. "If we can't measure the output, how do we know we're succeeding?"

Lukas sighed. They had wondered the same. "It's a valid question," he said. "We have to take it on faith. But not entirely. If you roll a boulder off a cliff, you don't have to see it fall to know it did. The technical challenge was immense, but we've been able to get extreme precision when it comes to the synchronization—trillionths of a second. The LHC's control systems have been significantly improved in recent years, with quantum computers controlling the collision sequences."

"And what message would we send?" asked President Morales.

"The same as we described when we reviewed the communication plan using electromagnetic signals," replied Lukas. "Not that this is really necessary. Coherent gravitational waves by themselves imply an intelligence trying to reach out."

Indian Prime Minister Sharma, who had remained silent until then, raised his voice. "What are the risks?"

Lukas hesitated, then decided to be completely honest. "There are several risk factors. First, we've never attempted to use the LHC in this way before. The modifications could have unforeseen consequences. Second, we don't know how the objects will respond to our signal. They could interpret it as a threat or react differently than we expect."

"Could it damage the accelerator?" asked President Chen.

Dr. Zhang replied, "It's possible. The high-energy physics community would normally need years to plan such an experiment, with extensive safety tests and simulations."

"What's the worst that could happen in the event of a critical error?" Schneider wanted to know.

"The LHC could be irretrievably destroyed."

"Would there be a danger to the civilian population?"

"None at all," said Lukas, shaking his head.

"As I see it," said President Morales, "it's a no-brainer. Yes, there's a small chance the ring is destroyed. But if we can't attract the attention of these flying pyramids, there's an *immense* chance that the *Earth* is destroyed."

A tense silence followed this statement.

After the presentation there was a short break during which those present had drinks and discussions in small groups. Lukas took the opportunity to moisten his dry throat with water and mentally prepare for the question-and-answer session that would inevitably follow.

When the meeting resumed, President Morales opened the discussion: "Dr. Heuer, you brought up the possible risk of the objects, or the *beings* riding along, if there are any, interpreting our attempted communication as a threat. I assume you've spent many hours discussing this possibility with the finest scientific minds on the planet. What conclusions have you drawn?"

"The threat of inaction is just as great as the threat of action," said Lukas. "The objects are already showing signs of attempting to communicate through their gravitational wave patterns. They appear to be sending messages, which we aren't understanding. Not responding could be just as risky as responding. Imagine someone knocking repeatedly on your door and you don't answer. Are you being rude? Unfriendly? Are you hiding just behind the door with a shotgun in your hand?

"Being intelligent means being curious. These objects—or any beings along for the ride, as you mentioned—will notice that we're here, with or without a response. Through communication, we at least have the chance to avoid misunderstandings."

Japanese Prime Minister Tanaka, who had been listening quietly until then, spoke up with a strong accent and measured tone: "In human history, first contact between civilizations with markedly different levels of technology almost always ends badly for the less developed culture."

"An important historical objection, Mr. Prime Minister. However, there is one crucial difference: Earthly conquerors were typically motivated by resource needs, territorial expansionism, or ideological convictions. An interstellar civilization that has developed the technology for interstellar travel and gravitational wave manipulation is unlikely to have material shortages that would justify conquest. There would simply be nothing for them to gain here."

"I would tend to agree," said President Chen. "Except that our logic and motivation may be entirely different from theirs."

"Unfortunately, that is also true. Ultimately, we have to work with uncertainty and accept that any consideration is subject to anthropomorphism."

The British Prime Minister interjected again: "What if this . . . gravitational wave communication fails or is misunderstood? Do we have a contingency plan?"

Lukas exchanged a glance with Carlos.

"To be honest, Madame Prime Minister—no. We have no effective defense plan against objects of this nature. We'd have better luck stopping a jet fighter with a *Nerf Ball*."

An oppressive silence spread through the room.

"Then it looks like we don't have a choice," said the American president. "We have to try it. And it has to work."

After another two hours of intense discussion, a vote was taken. The heads of state unanimously decided to pursue all three communication approaches.

"One last question," said President Chen. "Who will lead the CERN experiment?"

Dr. Kellerman cleared his throat. "The International Science Council proposes that Dr. Heuer serve as deputy director, while the main leadership will be entrusted to Professor Wei Lin."

Lukas felt his stomach tighten. Professor Wei Lin was undoubtedly a brilliant physicist and Nobel Prize winner—but he hadn't been involved in the development of this specific concept.

"Professor Lin is an excellent choice," continued Kellerman. "His work on quantum chromodynamics is groundbreaking, and as a sign of our global cooperation, his leadership will send an important signal."

Politics. Of course. China had to play a significant role to demonstrate international unity. Lukas understood the necessity, but the disappointment still gnawed at him.

"Dr. Heuer?" asked Kellerman. "Do you agree with this arrangement?"

Lukas felt all eyes in the room on him. This was about more than personal ambition or scientific recognition. It was about the future of humanity, about first contact with an extraterrestrial intelligence.

"Of course," he said, forcing a polite smile. "Professor Li is an excellent choice. I look forward to working with him."

"Wonderful."

When the meeting ended and the leaders left the room, Carlos approached him and put a hand on his shoulder.

"Everything okay, amigo?"

Lukas watched as President Chen engaged in lively conversation with President Morales—two world powers, temporarily united in the face of a possible cosmic threat.

"It has to be okay," he replied quietly. "We don't have time for personal animosities. We're down to three weeks."

Lukas swallowed hard. Not that it mattered. If these approaching objects truly represented a cosmic Grim Reaper, then having 3 weeks, or 3,000 *years*, would make no difference."

13

The path to Samye Monastery wound through a landscape of overwhelming grandeur, surrounded by the mighty peaks of the Himalayas. It smelled of damp leaves and mysticism. Mira followed the narrow, well-trodden path that led steeply up the mountainside, panting. In the thin air at over 10,000 feet, every breath burned in her lungs.

"Slow down, Doctor," said Dorje, her Sherpa guide, with a smile. "The mountain will wait. Has waited a thousand years."

She nodded, too breathless to reply, and stopped to take a sip of water. The preparations for this expedition had been rushed—a local tour operator in Kathmandu, hastily assembled equipment, hardly any time to acclimatize to the altitude. Her fitness was not what it should have been—too many years in air-conditioned laboratories and dusty archives, too little time in the open air.

Dorje waited patiently, his weather-beaten face calm and friendly. He was a man of perhaps 50, with a lean, sinewy body that seemed to handle the incline with ease, despite the heavy weight. His clothing was a practical mix of traditional Tibetan elements and modern outdoor gear.

"Why Samye Monastery?" he asked as Mira stowed her water bottle away. "Most tourists want to see Potala or Jokhang. Samye is . . . different."

"I'm . . . looking for . . . someone," she replied, panting. "My father. He came here . . . a long time ago."

Dorje nodded thoughtfully. "Many seekers come to Samye. Oldest monastery in Tibet. Founded in the eighth century. Has many answers. But not very popular with tourists."

They continued their ascent. The path became steeper, winding through rocky outcrops and sometimes over narrow wooden bridges spanning gorges. The vegetation became sparser, the air clearer. The majestic peaks of the Himalayan range towered above them, eternal guardians in their white coats.

After another hour of arduous climbing, Dorje suddenly stopped and pointed ahead. "There. Samye."

Mira looked up and felt her breath catch—this time not from exertion.

The monastery lay before them like a vision from another time. Built on a plateau that seemed to have been carved out of the mountainside, the whitewashed walls gleamed in the clear sunlight. Golden roofs shimmered, red and blue accents adding lively splashes of color. She had read on the internet that the entire complex was laid out like a mandala—a cosmic diagram representing the universe. At the center stood the main temple, Utse, surrounded by smaller buildings and Buddhist stupas, which looked like white stone bells.

"It's beautiful," whispered Mira.

"A sacred place," replied her guide. "The universe in miniature. The central temple is Mount Meru—the cosmic mountain at the center of the universe. Surrounded by four continents and eight islands."

The last section of the path led gently uphill, and soon they reached the massive wooden gate that marked the entrance to the monastery. It was decorated with colorful paintings—scenes from the life of Buddha, mythological figures, protective deities with grim faces.

Dorje spoke briefly with a monk who was "guarding" the gate, explaining their request in rapid Tibetan. The monk looked at Mira with calm curiosity, then nodded and motioned for them to enter.

Inside the monastery, there was an atmosphere of deep tranquility that stood in sharp contrast to the overwhelming nature that surrounded it. The courtyard was paved with smooth stones, worn down by centuries of meditative footsteps. Monks in dark red robes moved at a measured pace through the complex, some carrying water jugs or bundles of firewood, others sweeping the floor with simple rush brooms.

"Wait here," said Dorje. "I will talk to the abbot."

Mira wearily sat down on a low stone bench and let her gaze wander over the complex. The architecture was a fascinating mixture of Tibetan, Chinese, and Indian elements—a reflection of the cultural crossroads that Tibet had always been.

After about 20 minutes, Dorje returned, accompanied by an elderly monk with a kind, wrinkled face. His eyes were dark and clear, his posture upright despite his obviously advanced age.

"This is Lama Tenzin," said Dorje. "He speaks English and can help you."

The monk placed his palms together in front of his chest and bowed slightly. "Welcome to Samye, daughter of the West. Dorje says you're looking for someone."

Mira stood up hastily and returned the gesture somewhat awkwardly.

"Yes, my father. He came here 15 years ago." She took the laminated photo out of her bag and handed it to the monk. "Dr. Dariush Najafi. He's an archaeologist. He disappeared while conducting research in Egypt, but I have reason to believe he came here. And that he was still here a year ago."

Lama Tenzin looked at the photo with an inscrutable expression. Then—an imperceptible nod, a barely perceptible flash of recognition in his eyes that meant the world to her at that moment.

"I know this man," he said calmly. "Please follow me."

Mira felt her heart skip a beat. After all these years, all the searching—a simple confirmation, delivered with the matter-of-factness of a weather report.

Her Sherpa guide gestured for her to go ahead while he awaited her return. The monk led her through a side entrance into the main building. The floor beneath their feet consisted of polished wooden planks that creaked softly under their weight, as if sharing secrets from times past.

They reached a larger room whose wide-open windows revealed a view of the snow-capped peaks in the distance. About 20 monks sat here in the lotus position on low cushions arranged in neat rows. Their eyes were closed, their hands resting in front of them in various ritual poses—mudras. Not a single muscle moved in their faces; only the barely perceptible rising and falling of their chests indicated that they were alive at all.

Lama Tenzin led Mira quietly through the room, taking care not to disturb the meditators. She followed on tiptoes, impressed by the palpable atmosphere of deep contemplation that filled the room.

They went through another door into a smaller, more private room. A single window let in the clear light of the high altitude, which fell on a simple seating area with cushions and low tables. Calligraphy with Tibetan characters hung on the walls.

The monk pointed to a cushion. "Please sit down."

Mira complied, suppressing her nagging impatience as Lama Tenzin poured tea into two small bowls with painfully slow, flowing movements. The aroma of butter tea filled the room—a Tibetan specialty she had encountered during her brief preparation in Kathmandu but hadn't yet learned to love.

"Your father is no longer here," the monk said abruptly as he handed her a bowl.

Mira, who was just about to accept the warm bowl, froze. "No longer here? But you said you knew him."

"I do." Lama Tenzin sat down with a graceful movement. "He was here. For many years. But he is no longer here."

A painful ache spread through Mira's chest. So close—and yet another dead end.

"Do you know where he went?" she asked with undisguised disappointment.

The monk sipped his tea before answering. "Before we talk about that, I would like to hear your story. What brings the daughter of Dariush Najafi to us after all these years?"

A strange calm emanated from him, a presence that seemed both ancient and completely present. His dark eyes seemed to look directly into Mira's soul, not searching or judging, but with a deep, comprehensive curiosity that was not demanding, but unexcited and sincere.

"It's a long story," she said hesitantly.

"Time is a strange concept," replied the monk with a subtle smile. "Sometimes it stretches endlessly, sometimes it disappears completely. Here in Samye, we have learned to observe its flow without being carried away by it."

Mira took a sip of the salty, buttery tea to gain time. Then she began to tell her story—about her father, his disappearance, her mother's death, her years of searching. She told him about the pyramids, the hidden chamber, the Tibetan snow lion on the murals. She spoke of her difficult time in college, which she had only survived thanks to Markowitz, her suicide attempt, and the strength she had found in the hope that everything had meaning and that her father might still be alive.

Lama Tenzin listened silently, his face calm and attentive. When she had finished, there was silence in the room for a moment, interrupted only by the distant sound of a bell.

"The stories we tell ourselves shape our reality," he said finally. "They are like clouds in the sky—sometimes dark and threatening, sometimes bright and beautiful. But the sky itself remains unaffected by them."

"With all due respect," replied Mira, a hint of irritation in her voice, "what I just recounted wasn't a story. These were the facts of my life."

"Of course." The monk smiled gently. "But even facts we organize into stories, give them meaning, weight, and thereby shift their essence. Your father disappeared back then—that's a fact. That he abandoned you—that's a story you have formed from it."

Mira wanted to disagree, but something in his words touched a sore spot. "How could I have seen it any other way? He never came back."

"Sometimes we travel paths we didn't foresee," said Lama Tenzin. "The river finds its way to the sea, even when it encounters obstacles. It doesn't fight against the rock; it flows around it."

"Are you saying that my father . . . that he didn't leave voluntarily?"

"I'm saying that terms like 'voluntarily' or 'involuntarily' are sometimes too simple for the supposed complexities of life." The monk poured more tea. "Your father came to us with a deep wound in his soul and great concern for the future. Not physically—his body was strong. But his mind was burdened by a realization he couldn't bear."

Mira leaned forward. "What realization?"

"He never said clearly, and I spoke little English at the time. I've only learned it in recent years. I think he was afraid of the future, of an event he believed he could foresee."

Lama Tenzin made a sweeping gesture. "He spoke of black pyramids in the sky, of a cycle that closes after 4,500 years, but is not a cycle at all. And of a great danger."

Mira's eyes widened. This was just like the hieroglyphs in the secret chamber. Just like the cryptic notes in her father's book. And the cryptic words of Lefèvre. Could it all be connected? Mira's heartbeat quickened.

"What happened to him?" she asked, her voice thick with emotion. "Please tell me. I feel as if I was so close to reuniting with him at last."

"He studied our texts, learned our meditation techniques. He sought a way to bridge the gap between science and wisdom, between seeing and knowing." The monk leaned forward slightly. "Did you know that your ancient Egyptians and our Tibetan masters have more in common than most people realize? Both recognized that death is not the end, but a transition. They called it gods; we call it the oneness of all things."

Mira thought of the Egyptian books of the dead, of the elaborate burial rituals that were supposed to prepare the deceased for their journey to the afterlife. "That's true."

"Your father understood this connection better than most." A brief shadow flitted across Lama Tenzin's face. "He believed he had seen something that he had to unravel to save the future. A memory of ancient knowledge. It was a message, I think."

"A message about what?"

"About the true nature of reality. About the fabric that connects everything." The monk folded his hands in his lap. "You know, in the Buddhist tradition, we speak of 'Indra's net'—a cosmic net with jewels hanging at its junctions. Each jewel reflects all the others. Infinitely. Nothing exists on its own."

Mira rubbed her temples. The high altitude, the exhaustion of the journey, the monk's cryptic words—it all just confused her. "Please,

Lama Tenzin. I've been looking for my father for 15 years. Where is he now?"

The old man looked at her with deep compassion. "I'm sorry that you've carried what wasn't your burden for so long. Your father made his decision out of love—not only for you and your mother, but for all life. I'm convinced of this after almost 15 years of accompanying him on his spiritual quest."

Something in the way he spoke gave Mira a cold premonition.

"You speak of him in the past tense."

"Time is a strange concept," the monk repeated. "Do you know what *tukdam* is?"

Mira shook her head.

"I will show you," Lama Tenzin said gently. "When you are ready."

A wave of emotions washed over Mira—hope, fear, confusion, sadness. She had searched for so long, had dedicated her life to this quest. And now, at the apparent end, an answer awaited her that she couldn't understand.

"I *am* ready," she said, her voice little more than a whisper, not knowing what this monk was actually talking about.

He rose with the flowing ease of decades of practice. "Please follow me."

They returned to the larger room with the meditating monks. The atmosphere was unchanged—timeless, silent, filled with an almost tangible concentration. Lama Tenzin slowly led her through the rows of seated figures.

"Your father is sitting at the very back on the left," he said quietly.

"He . . . he's here?" She almost choked as she spoke. Her heart began to pound, and her palms became sweaty.

"Yes."

They reached the last row of meditators. The monk stopped and pointed to a figure at the end of the row.

At first glance, the man was no different from the other monks. He wore the same dark red robe, sat in the same upright posture, his hands folded in a mudra, his head shaved bald. But as Mira stepped closer, she recognized her father's unmistakable features despite his wrinkled face.

She froze as if struck by lightning. Tears ran down her cheeks.

"Father?" she whispered incredulously and walked toward him, torn between the urge to rush to him and the desire to respect the sacred silence of this place.

He didn't respond. His eyes remained closed, his face calm and unmoving.

"He cannot hear you," Lama Tenzin said gently. "He is in tukdam."

She didn't listen to him.

"His mind has already left his body, but his consciousness still lingers."

Mira knelt before her father, desperately searching for a sign of life.

"Father," she whispered more urgently. "It's me, Mira. Your daughter."

No response. Not the slightest twitch of a muscle.

With trembling fingers, she touched his hand. It was cool, but not cold—strangely firm, as if it were made of wax instead of flesh and blood. She searched for his pulse, first at his wrist, then at his neck.

Nothing.

"He's not breathing," she said, panic in her voice. "He has no pulse!"

"No," Lama Tenzin replied calmly. "Physical life has almost ceased. What you see is the tukdam state—the lingering of consciousness in the body after death to prepare for the transition. It's a sign of the greatest progress in meditation. He's already been in this state for 7 days."

Mira stared at her father, unable to comprehend what she had heard. After 15 years of searching, she had found him—only to learn that he had died 5 days ago. And yet here he sat, upright, showing no signs of decay, as if simply meditating on a particularly profound problem.

"Why?" she finally managed to say, tears streaming down her face. "Why didn't he come back? Why did he leave us?"

Lama Tenzin knelt beside her. "He carried a realization that was too heavy to bear alone. But he freed himself from it and found unity."

"What realization?"

"I don't know. But he was very peaceful." The monk lowered his voice even further.

Mira stared at her father's peaceful face. The features she had known so well as a child had aged and matured, but were still recognizable. Fifteen years—lost, irretrievably.

"He loved you and your mother," continued Lama Tenzin. "He often spoke of you. But he believed he was protecting you by staying away, and he knew that he could only find what he was looking for if he devoted the rest of his life to this cause."

The tears now flowed freely, wetting Mira's cheeks, dripping onto the polished wooden floor. All the years of searching, of hope, of disappointment—they came crashing down on her like a tidal wave breaking through all the dams.

"What . . . what happens to him now?" she asked in a choked voice.

"His consciousness is preparing for the next journey. In a few days to a few weeks, the tukdam state will end, and his body will begin the natural process of decay. We will then bury him according to our traditions."

"How . . . how long?"

"Sometimes it takes up to three weeks. No one can predict it. It is a blessing."

Mira gently placed her hand on her father's cool cheek. Five days too late for a final conversation. Five days too late for explanations, reconciliation, farewells.

"He left something for you," said Lama Tenzin quietly. "Come. I'll show you when you're ready."

Mira couldn't take her eyes off her father, this empty vessel that had once housed the man who had taught her to read, who had told her stories, who had loved her.

"I need . . . a moment," she whispered. *He looks so alive!*

The monk nodded understandingly and withdrew, leaving her alone with what remained of her father—an empty body, seemingly deep in meditation, maintaining the illusion of life one last time before succumbing to the inevitable.

In the silence of the monastery, surrounded by the meditating monks, Mira felt a strange calmness rise within her—not peace, not yet, but the first faint hint of it. The certainty that her search had at least come to an end. That she now knew what had happened to her father.

The answers to her other questions would have to wait. For now, she was simply a daughter who had finally found her long-lost father—albeit too late for a reunion in this world.

14

The CERN control center buzzed with activity. Three weeks had passed since the meeting with the heads of state—three weeks of restless work, during which a team of over 200 scientists and technicians had worked to transform the world's most powerful particle accelerator into something it had never been designed for: a gravitational wave transmitter.

Lukas stood in front of the main monitor wall and looked at the diagram of the 27-kilometer-long underground ring that stretched beneath the French-Swiss border. Colored lines indicated the status of the various systems, the digital heartbeat of the gigantic machine.

Their biggest technical challenge had been retrofitting the superconducting magnets. They had to be able to change their field strength faster than ever intended. The risk of a quench—a sudden loss of superconductivity—was not insignificant. The magnets operated at temperatures close to absolute zero—about –460 °F—cooled by liquid helium. If an area became too warm and lost superconductivity, enormous electrical resistance would be created. The stored energy would be released as heat, which could lead to a chain reaction. Worst case, this would lead to a catastrophic failure of the cooling systems, overheating, and possible damage to the magnets and beam pipes. In previous quench events, parts of the accelerator were out of service for months.

They had taken as many precautions as possible in the short time they'd had available. They had added additional helium reserves, improved emergency drainage systems for electrical energy, and strict monitoring protocols. But the risk they were taking was considerable.

The tension in the control room was so palpable you could cut it with a knife. Forty-eight hours. That was all the time the politicians had given them before the repurposed Large Hadron Collider had to speak to the pyramids in the only language anyone thought they might understand.

Lukas stood in CERN's main control room, eyes fixed on a minor temperature spike in Sector 23—0.12 Kelvin above nominal. Within tolerance—barely—but it gnawed at him.

"Dr. Wu," he called to the lead engineer for the magnet systems. "Take a look at this." He gestured to the monitor he had just read.

"Not ideal," she said. "But the fluctuation is still within tolerance limits. It could also be a sensor error."

"Or a sign of an incipient problem in the cooling system," noted Lukas. "We should postpone the test sequence until we're sure."

Professor Li, who had returned from a final meeting with government officials, joined them. "Is there a problem?" she asked.

Lukas explained the situation. "We're scheduled to conduct the test in two days. But if we postpone it another 24 hours, that should give us time to thoroughly check the cooling system."

"The temperature deviation is within acceptable parameters." Li shook his head. "The schedule was set by the coordination committee and agreed upon by all participating governments. A delay would cause diplomatic complications."

"With all due respect, Professor, technical problems don't adhere to diplomatic schedules. If a quench occurs, we'll be dead in the water."

"Noted," said Li, his tone remaining polite but firm. "But the decision has been made. The pyramids are approaching, and we've been given no leeway." Li put a hand on Lukas's shoulder. "I understand your concerns, I really do. But orders are orders. The test will proceed as planned."

"Can we at least set up additional monitoring systems and put an emergency team on standby?"

"Of course. A sensible precaution."

The next 48 hours passed in feverish activity. On the day of the test, the atmosphere in the control center was one of subdued tension. Scientists and technicians took their positions, checked systems, exchanged quiet words. Monitors hung on the walls, displaying live feeds from various parts of the accelerator.

Lukas sat at the main console, Professor Li next to him. In front of them was a tablet with the communication protocol, the mathematical sequence they wanted to send as their first message.

"Final system check," announced the lead technician.

The voices of the various department heads echoed through the room.

"Magnetic system ready."

"Beam control ready."

"Cooling system ready. Sector 23 under observation."

"Target mechanisms ready."

"Emergency systems on standby."

Li turned to the team. "Begin the test sequence."

The tension in the room rose noticeably as the various systems were booted up. The particle beam was first accelerated to normal operating parameters, then brought into the special configuration for the gravitational wave experiment.

"Beam stable at 99.9999991 percent light speed," reported one technician.

"Phase shift modules activated," followed another.

"Ready for the first pulse."

Li looked at his watch. "Begin the sequence in T minus ten seconds."

The countdown was running. Lukas felt his heartbeat quicken. They had tested, simulated, and calculated intensively—but this was the moment of truth, the attempt to communicate with alien objects that made use of technology humanity could only dream of.

"Three . . . two . . . one . . . initiate sequence."

The first group of protons was deflected from its trajectory and hit the first target. Data streams lit up on the screens as the sensors analyzed the effects.

"First pulse successful," reported Dr. Wu. "Beam parameters normal, target intact."

Lukas allowed himself to breathe a sigh of relief.

Further pulses followed, rhythmic, according to the precise pattern they had calculated. Each impact emitted a tiny gravitational pulse, too weak to be measured individually, but in their entirety—according to theory—they would superimpose to form a coherent wave.

"Sequence running normally," reported a technician. "Pulse 17 of 250."

Lukas watched the data with rapt attention. So far, everything was going according to plan. The beam control was working with picosecond precision, the targets were withstanding the impacts, the magnets were working . . .

A shrill alarm interrupted his thoughts.

"Temperature rise in sector 23!" shouted Dr. Wu. "The third magnet segment is heating up rapidly!"

"Quench!" Lukas jumped up. "Implement emergency shutdown!"

"Emergency shutdown not responding!" replied Wu seconds later, panic in her voice. "The temperature is continuing to rise."

Red warning symbols flashed on the screens. The sound signals from the various alarms overlapped into a cacophonous symphony of urgency.

"Beam parameters are destabilizing," reported another technician. "We're losing control of the focus."

Lukas's mind raced. The defective magnet continued to heat up and would soon reach a critical point. If the heat caused the surrounding liquid helium to evaporate, the sudden increase in pressure would have catastrophic consequences.

"Is anyone still in Sector 23?" he asked sharply.

A glance at the personnel tracker confirmed his fears: a maintenance team was in the adjacent tunnel to carry out inspections during the test.

"Three technicians in the access tunnel to Sector 23-24," confirmed the security officer. "Evacuation team is on its way."

But Lukas knew it might be too late. At the rate the temperature was rising, there were minutes at most before a catastrophic pressure increase would occur in the cooling system.

"I'm going down," he said resolutely and turned toward the door.

"That's crazy!" shouted Li. "The safety protocols . . ."

"You don't have time for a full evacuation." Lukas was already moving. "Keep trying to stabilize the system. I'll get the technicians out. The rest is lost."

He ran through the corridors of the CERN complex and took the elevator to the basement, which led to the accelerator's tunnel system. A map of the system ran through his head—he had to find the shortest route to access point 23-B.

When he reached the tunnel, he was greeted by the clinical silence of the underground facility, interrupted only by the distant hum of the machines. He reached for an emergency communicator on the wall.

"Dr. Heuer here. Where exactly is the maintenance team?"

"About 300 meters from access point 23-B, towards sector 24," came the distorted reply from the control room. "Dr. Heuer, the situation is deteriorating. The pressure in the cooling system is rising rapidly, you . . ."

Lukas dropped the receiver and started running, his footsteps echoing through the vaulted tunnel. The emergency lighting cast ghostly shadows, and an unpleasant vibration could be felt in the floor—a sign that the accelerator was no longer functioning properly.

After 200 meters, he saw them—three figures in the blue overalls of CERN technicians, talking quietly—there was no alarm down here and apparently no communication link with their sector.

"Get out of here!" he shouted. "We have a critical quench in Sector 23!"

The technicians looked up, confusion and then concern on their faces.

"*Run!*" screamed Lukas at the top of his lungs just as pressure blew an exit hatch open, breaking the leg of one of the technicians instantly and slicing a deep gouge in his thigh. The injured man issued a bloodcurdling scream of agony.

Lukas rushed over to him and slipped under his shoulder to support him. "Come on!" he shouted again. "The cooling system will fail at any moment!"

They began their retreat as quickly as the injured technician would allow. The vibrations in the floor grew stronger, and an eerie creaking and groaning filled the tunnel—the sound of metal under extreme stress.

"Dr. Heuer," a distorted voice came from a speaker that was apparently still working. It was Li. "The pressure has reached critical levels. You have 60 seconds at most until—"

A loud crash interrupted the transmission, followed by a hiss that quickly intensified into a roar. The lights flickered.

"The coolant is leaking!" one of the technicians shouted. "If the liquid helium evaporates—"

"Faster!" urged Lukas, now almost carrying the injured man.

They still had about 50 yards to go to reach the safety bulkhead separating the access area from the main tunnel. Behind them, they could now clearly hear the hiss of escaping gas and a metallic groan as the jet pipes and magnets deformed under the sudden rise in temperature.

A tremor ran through the floor, so strong that they almost lost their balance. The lighting failed completely, only the red emergency lights remained active, bathing the tunnel in an eerie red glow.

"Almost there!" gasped Lukas, who was now carrying the full weight of the injured technician.

The safety bulkhead was in sight, about 15 yards away. Behind it was the access shaft with the elevator to the surface.

Suddenly, there was a sound that made Lukas's blood run cold—a sharp crash, followed by a rumble of thunder, as if a huge wave was moving through the tunnel. The shock wave of the escaping coolant.

With his last ounce of strength, he pushed the three technicians through the bulkhead, followed them, and slammed the emergency lock shut. The massive steel bulkhead closed with a dull thud—just as the shock wave reached it and struck it like a giant hammer.

They were thrown to the ground as dust trickled down from the ceiling and small debris fell around them. The roar on the other side of the bulkhead was deafening, but gradually weakened as the energy of the explosion dispersed throughout the tunnel system.

Finally, an eerie silence prevailed, interrupted only by the gasping of their breaths, the occasional crackling of cooling metal parts, and the whimpering of the injured technician.

Lukas pressed down hard on the man's wound, and soon was handed clothing to use as a bandage to help staunch the flow of blood. He finally rose, staring at his bloody hands.

The injured man groaned and whispered to himself in shock.

They made their way to the emergency elevator that would take them to the surface.

When they finally stepped out of the elevator shaft, they were met by a rescue team. Medical personnel immediately attended to the injured man while security guards cordoned off the area.

Professor Li rushed toward Lukas. "Are you okay?"

"It's not my blood," responded Lukas rapidly. "How bad is it?"

"A quench in sectors 23 and 24. The pressure relief valves failed, causing an explosion in the cooling system. We have significant damage to at least two kilometers of the ring."

"And the experiment?"

Li shook his head. "Failed. We couldn't even transfer ten percent of the planned sequence." He looked directly at Lukas. "You were right. We should have listened to your warnings."

Lukas wiped dust and sweat from his face.

"That doesn't matter now," continued Li. "The important thing is that we're standing here talking." He glanced toward the main building, where journalists and camera crews were already gathering. "But we're done here. The LHC will be out of operation for months, if not longer."

Lukas suddenly felt very tired.

"You should get some rest, Dr. Heuer. You saved lives today."

Lukas winced. There was an old adage he believed in, *he who saves one life saves the world*. And he was proud that he'd been able to save lives. Three of them. But his goal was to save *billions*.

And in that, he had failed completely.

Lukas looked up at the ceiling. Somewhere out there, the three black pyramids were approaching Earth—unstoppable, enigmatic. And now humanity had no possible means to communicate with them.

"We need a new plan," he said quietly. But he knew there wouldn't be one. Not now.

15

The laptop cast its bluish light on Mira's face, while beyond the small monastery room the Tibetan sky revealed the first stars. She had been given simple accommodation in the guest wing of Samye Monastery—a modest room with a narrow bed, a wooden table, and a low window that offered a view of the snow-capped peaks.

The browser displayed scientific articles about the phenomenon Lama Tenzin had called *tukdam*. She read with the methodical thoroughness she had internalized during her academic training, taking notes and comparing sources. Immersing herself in her research helped her to suppress the pain of her father's condition—albeit only temporarily. She felt endlessly alone. And now she didn't even have a job anymore.

Tukdam, she learned, was a state that some advanced Tibetan meditators could enter after clinical death. While the body was dead by medical standards—no pulse, no breathing, no brain activity—it remained unusually fresh for an abnormally long time, without the usual signs of decay such as odor, discoloration, or stiffening. Their bodies didn't even get cold.

A 2021 paper in *Frontiers in Psychology* described a study in which Tibetan monks in the tukdam state were examined using modern medical methods. A research team from the University of Wisconsin-Madison, led by Dr. Richard Davidson, had performed EEG measurements, MRI scans, and biochemical analyses on the bodies of deceased individuals who, according to Tibetan tradition, were in tukdam.

The results were astonishing. More than astonishing. Impossible! At least according to everything humanity thought it knew about death and decomposition. Based on millennia of human experience with countless human bodies, within five days after clinical death, the skin of a human would turn greenish-black, and massive bloating would occur from the release of internal gases. A human face would swell, tongue protruding and eyes bulging. Dark branching patterns would appear under the skin as blood vessels broke down, and reddish-black liquid would leak from the nose, mouth, and anus.

After seven days, the duration her father had been in room temperature conditions without any pulse, his face should have been almost entirely unrecognizable. And anyone who entered the room he was in would be gagging from a profound, pungent stench that had often been described as a combination of rotting meat, sewage, and overripe cheese.

Her father's condition flew in the face of the entirety of human experience. Yet the Wisconsin researchers and other groups had confirmed it. Those in tukdam did indeed show a significantly lower rate of decomposition than normal, their body temperature magically remaining far warmer than it had any right to be, and in some cases, their skin elastic and alive for up to three weeks after clinical death. Nevertheless, the researchers couldn't detect any measurable brain activity or other signs of life that would explain this phenomenon.

A Tibetan doctor, Dr. Tenzin Wangyal, who was trained in both traditional Tibetan medicine and Western medicine, had proposed a fascinating theory. That the tukdam state could be related to subtle energies that modern science wasn't yet able to measure. He had pointed to studies showing that certain enzymes and proteins in the cells of tukdam practitioners remained active for an unusually long time—as if part of the body hadn't yet "learned" that it had died.

From a Buddhist perspective, several sources explained, tukdam represented an intermediate state in which subtle consciousness still lingered in the body, even though the grosser life functions had already ceased. During this time, consciousness prepared for its transition to the bardo state—the intermediate phase between death and rebirth.

Mira leaned back and rubbed her tired eyes. The scientific explanations were insufficient, the spiritual interpretations beyond her rational understanding. The only certainty was that her father was dead—and that even his death was as mysterious as his disappearance 15 years ago.

But she was also heartened. The impossible seemed to be happening all the time.

How could tukdam not be a household word? This was a fantastic, supernatural reality that everyone should know about, not just scattered handfuls of researchers and monks. Proof that there was so much more to reality, to life and to death, than emerging human minds could possibly fathom. That humanity, arrogantly believing it had begun to understand science, nature, and reality, had barely scratched the surface.

So maybe her father *wasn't* really dead. Maybe there was an afterlife. Maybe it was all a simulation. The bottom line was that nothing could be ruled out, and anything seemed to be possible.

She closed her laptop and stepped over to the window. The mountain air was bitterly cold and crystal clear, the starry sky of an intensity she had never experienced before. So many stars, so many worlds. And somewhere out there, in that immeasurable vastness, her father had seen a connection—a connection to the black pyramids that had ultimately cost him his life.

A wave of grief and anger suddenly washed over her. Even if there were an afterlife, she'd been denied the chance at a reunion with her father. She had searched for 15 years, had subordinated her career, her personal relationships, her entire life to this search—only to arrive too late. To find her father as an empty shell, trapped in an incomprehensible state between life and death.

She pressed her forehead against the cool windowpane and let the tears flow freely.

* * *

The next few days passed in a fog of grief and confusion. Mira moved between her room and the meditation room, where her father still sat in the same position. She watched him for hours, looking for a sign, a movement, an indication that something of him was still present.

Nothing.

The monks treated her with quiet kindness, bringing her food and tea, but otherwise leaving her alone. Only Lama Tenzin visited her occasionally, talking to her about her father, telling her about the years he had spent in the monastery. But these stories felt like tales about a stranger—not about the man she had known.

On the seventh day, her depression reached a low point. She had hardly slept, hardly eaten, lost in dark thoughts. What was she to do? Where was she to go? The search that had given her direction and purpose for so many years was over. All that remained was emptiness and all the scorched earth she had left behind.

She walked slowly to the main temple, where she knew Lama Tenzin was meditating at this time of day. She found him in a quiet corner, his eyes closed, his hands resting in his lap.

She waited quietly until he opened his eyes and gave her a gentle smile.

"I am lost," she said bluntly, her voice breaking.

The old monk looked at her with infinite compassion. "The feeling of being lost is often the beginning of realization."

"I don't know what to do now. Where to go. What the meaning of . . . everything is."

Lama Tenzin pointed to the floor next to him. "Sit down."

Mira sat down, awkwardly trying to get her legs into a comfortable position.

"The search for your father has led you here," said the monk. "Perhaps it was his wish that you come here—not only to find him, but to discover something else."

"What could that be?"

"What he himself found here." Lama Tenzin folded his hands. "Let me introduce you to meditation while you are here. It will calm your mind and help you find your way. We call it the pathless path. Perhaps there you will find answers that I cannot give you."

Thus began Mira's introduction to the practice of meditation. Every day she met with Lama Tenzin, learning the basics of mindfulness, concentration, and inner observation. At first it was a struggle—her restless mind jumped from thought to thought, from memory to memory, from worry to worry.

"Like a monkey jumping from branch to branch," Lama Tenzin once said with a smile. "That's how the untrained mind is. You are the branch." He chuckled almost childishly. "Be patient with yourself."

After a week of daily practice, she began to experience brief moments of stillness—moments when the constant stream of thoughts was interrupted and an unexpected clarity shone through like sunlight through gaps in the clouds. She began to understand the metaphor that she was the sky and thoughts were nothing but passing clouds.

"This is only the beginning," the lama encouraged her. "The mind is like a glass of cloudy water. If you let it stand still, the suspended particles gradually sink to the bottom and the water becomes clear."

In the second week, he introduced her to more advanced techniques. She learned visualization meditations, in which she created and dissolved inner images; sound meditations, in which the deep tones of Tibetan singing bowls led her mind into deeper states; movement meditations, slow, conscious gestures that connected body and mind.

The depression did not completely disappear, but it changed. The sharp edges of the pain softened, the darkness became less impenetrable. Sometimes, when she meditated in the morning light, she even felt moments of pure joy—unconditional, without reason, like a flower blooming from the ashes.

"The Buddha taught that everything is impermanent," explained Lama Tenzin. "Not only life, but also pain. When we stop fighting it, it loses its power over us. As with the Borg, resistance is futile."

Mira blinked. "You've seen *Star Trek*?"

"We're monks, not barbarians." Tenzin chuckled cheerfully with his typical childlike joy.

In the third week, he began to introduce her to the deeper aspects of the Tibetan meditation tradition. They learned about Dzogchen, the "Great Perfection," a practice aimed at recognizing the inherent purity and completeness of the mind; about Mahamudra, the "Great Seal," which explored the nature of reality beyond conceptual thoughts.

These were difficult, often confusing teachings, full of paradoxical statements and unfamiliar perspectives. But to Mira's own surprise, she began to see meaning in them—not on an intellectual level, but as a direct experience in her meditation.

Some days she visited her father in the meditation room, sat quietly beside him, and practiced her exercises. His body still showed no signs of decay, but something had changed—a subtle quality she couldn't name. It was as if a barely perceptible presence was gradually receding.

On the twenty-first day of her practice, Lama Tenzin came to her, his face more serious than usual.

"Your father will soon leave the body completely," he said bluntly. "The tukdam is coming to an end."

Mira felt her heart contract. Although her father was already clinically dead, the preservation of his body in the tukdam state had represented a last, thin thread of connection. His final departure would sever that thread for good.

"How do you know?" she asked.

"The signs are visible to those who know how to read them. Subtle changes in skin color, in the energy surrounding the body." The lama placed a hand on her shoulder. "You've made remarkable progress in your meditation over the past few weeks. I believe you're ready."

"Ready for what?"

"In the Tibetan tradition, we believe that consciousness is particularly receptive to contact at the moment of final transition. You could meditate next to your father as he leaves his body, and perhaps . . . experience a connection."

Mira looked at him incredulously. "Is that possible?"

"In the usual sense? No. You will not have conversations or exchange thoughts as you do in life." Lama Tenzin smiled gently. "But there are sometimes deeper levels of communication—beyond words, beyond thoughts. A recognition from mind to mind."

She thought of the black pyramids, of all the puzzles her father had left behind. Would she find answers? Or was this just another step into a labyrinth with no exit?

"I'm ready," she said finally.

The following morning, Lama Tenzin prepared a special place in the meditation room. He placed a cushion for Mira next to her father, lit butter lamps whose golden light danced gently on the walls, and burned juniper as a cleansing ritual.

The other monks had left the room to give them privacy. Only Mira, her father, and Lama Tenzin were present.

"I will guide you through the initial phase," explained the lama. "Then I'll leave you alone. Just follow your breath, without expectations, without a goal. Let whatever happens happen."

Mira sat down next to her father. His body still looked unchanged—his posture perfect, his face peaceful, no signs of decay despite the weeks that had passed since his clinical death. And yet she now sensed what Lama Tenzin had meant—a kind of withdrawal, a diminishing presence, as if an invisible light were slowly fading.

She closed her eyes, felt the cool breeze on her skin, smelled the sweet scent of burning juniper, heard the soft crackling of the butter lamps.

Lama Tenzin's voice guided her into meditation, calm and rhythmic.

"Let your breath flow naturally . . . Observe how it comes and goes . . . Feel how your body rises and falls with each breath . . . When thoughts arise, recognize them, let them pass like clouds in the sky . . ."

His voice grew quieter, more distant, until it finally fell silent. Mira sank deeper into her meditation, following her breath like an anchor in stormy seas. Again and again her thoughts drifted away—to her father, to the pyramids, to her uncertain future—and again and again she gently brought her attention back to her breath.

Gradually, something changed. The usual sounds of the monastery—distant bells, occasional footsteps, the creaking of old wood—seemed to fade away. Instead, a feeling of spaciousness arose, as if the walls of the room had dissolved and her consciousness expanded into a larger space.

Her perception of her body also changed. The familiar boundaries of skin and bone became blurred, permeable. Warmth spread from her chest, flowing through her arms, her legs, her head—not uncomfortably, but like a gentle glow from within.

With this change came an unexpected clarity. Thoughts still came, but they had a transparent quality, as if she could see through them into a deeper, quieter space behind them. They were impersonal. And in that space there was a presence. Not separate from her, not outside her, but somehow interwoven with her, like water mixing with water.

An image formed in her mind—not like an ordinary visual thought, but clearer, more stable, with a quality of immediacy. She saw the underground chamber she had discovered in the Pyramid of Cheops. The murals with the black pyramids in the night sky, the priests in meditative posture, the beam of light connecting them.

But something was different. The stone table in the middle of the room seemed to be upside down, or perhaps it was her perspective that was reversed, as if she were looking down from the ceiling.

She focused her attention on the table, trying to understand this strange image. Was it a memory? A hallucination? A message?

The more intensely she concentrated, the clearer the image became. The upside-down table now seemed to be the key, a symbol whose meaning hovered at the edge of her understanding like a word on the tip of her tongue.

A wave of realization washed over her—not in words or thoughts, but as a direct experience. The table wasn't upside down. Her perspective was. To understand, she had to see things from a different angle—literally and metaphorically.

The image became more intense, more vivid, as if an invisible presence wanted to draw her attention to it. She kept seeing the upside-down table.

Suddenly, the image disappeared. The chamber, the table, the murals—everything dissolved like mist in the morning sun. Instead, she felt a movement, a flow, as if something was passing by her, gently brushing against her and then moving on—like a breeze blowing through an open window and then disappearing. It was a sacred moment that warmed her with a strange familiarity.

Mira opened her eyes, blinking in the dim light of the meditation room. Lama Tenzin knelt before her, his face calm and compassionate.

"He is gone," the monk said softly. "In this moment."

"I know," she replied, looking at her father.

Outwardly, he looked the same as before—same posture, same peaceful face. And yet something was fundamentally different. The subtle presence she had felt just a moment ago was gone. All that remained was the shell, the empty vessel.

"I saw something," she whispered. "The chamber in the pyramid. The table—it was turned over. Or maybe it was my perspective. I think there's something under the table. Something hidden."

Lama Tenzin nodded as if he had expected nothing less. "Your father often spoke of this table. He said the key was not on it, but under it. But he also said that he would only be the pathfinder for those who would walk the path."

"Maybe he meant me." The realization struck her with sudden clarity. "He knew I would come. He was waiting for me."

"Perhaps. Or perhaps your Dharma was waiting for you." The old monk rose slowly. "We will prepare the funeral rites for your father. Various traditions must be performed for a tukdam when he dies."

"I have to go back," said Mira, suddenly filled with an urgency that surprised even her. "To Egypt. To the Pyramid of Cheops. I have to look under that table."

Lama Tenzin smiled, a smile full of warmth and understanding. "I thought you would say that. Your father left something for you—for this moment. Come."

As she took one last look at her father, Mira no longer felt sadness—or at least not only sadness. It was a more complex feeling, a mixture of farewell and new beginning, of loss and discovery. The circle had closed, and at the same time a new one had opened.

Whatever was hidden under the table—hopefully, it would give her insights into the secrets her father had taken with him to the grave.

And maybe, just maybe, it would also help her understand why he had left back then—and why he had led her here, to this remote place, to this threshold between worlds.

When she went into Lama Tenzin's room with him, he held out a leather booklet, very similar to her father's old notebook. She opened it and found a single note inside. It contained coordinates, including three black pyramids drawn underneath, just like the markings. She immediately recognized that it was the Pyramid of Cheops. She wouldn't be surprised if it was, more precisely, the chamber she had discovered.

"That's the chamber with the table," she murmured. "Why didn't you give this to me right away?"

"I believe that he would have wanted you to find what *he* found here," replied Tenzin. "Something led him here, and you had to see it before continuing on your path," he added with a peaceful smile. "Don't lose yourself in the world of things, Mira Najafi. All forms are unstable and transient, but your consciousness is not."

16

The cold slowly crept through Lukas's jacket as he sat on the hood of the silver Hyundai they had rented that morning in Geneva. The car was still warm from the engine, but the Alpine air on this September evening was bitterly cold, especially here at an altitude of almost 7,000 feet. Carlos handed him a beer from the small cooler they had brought with them. Tea might have been the more rational choice, but the occasion offered no reason for rationality.

"Here's to better times, amigo," said the Chilean, clinking his bottle against Lukas's.

Lukas took a sip, letting the bitter drink linger on his tongue as his gaze wandered over the majestic landscape that stretched out before them. The evening sun gilded the snowfields on the surrounding peaks. Deep below them, a narrow road wound its way through a valley, tiny cars crawling along like toys.

After the disaster at CERN, they had both felt the need to get some distance—from the hectic emergency meetings, the excited media reports, and the concerned looks of their colleagues. So they had taken a day off and driven to the mountains to find clarity, or at least a moment of peace, however fleeting it might be.

"You know," said Carlos after a while, "when I saw the movie *Close Encounters of the Third Kind* as a kid, I always thought that if aliens ever came to Earth, they would want to talk to us with colorful lights and music. Simple sounds, simple signals. Universally understandable."

Lukas nodded. "And now we have three black pyramids approaching Earth and not responding to any of our attempts at communication. Maybe we should paint hieroglyphics in the clouds," he added in frustration.

"No response to radio waves, no response to lasers, no response to optical signals. It's as if they're completely ignoring us."

Lukas took another sip and let his gaze wander to the horizon, where the first stars were appearing in the darkening sky. Somewhere out there, invisible to the naked eye, the alien objects were approaching. In eight months, they would reach Earth—without humanity having the slightest idea what would happen then.

Carlos continued with a rolling Spanish accent. "I mean, they have to be ignoring us, right? Any species that advanced should be able to easily contact a backward civilization like ours."

Lukas's gaze wandered to the stars, which now appeared more and more numerous in the night-blue sky like tiny buttonholes. The Alpine air was so clear that the Milky Way was visible as a pale band as the darkness thickened around them. "Maybe we're no more noteworthy to them than a harmless strain of bacteria is to us," he said quietly. "We may find certain aspects of bacteria fascinating, but we don't try to communicate with them. Their understanding is too limited, or in this case, non-existent. What would be the point?"

"A rather discouraging perspective." Carlos reached for a second beer bottle. "Although we can stretch that metaphor in far worse ways. We may not communicate with common bacteria, but sometimes we bring soap." He cringed. "Or *bleach*."

An uncomfortable silence followed this remark. The threat that might emanate from the pyramids was a constantly present specter that none of them could completely dismiss.

"What's your best guess as to what they are?" asked Lukas.

Carlos took a long sip before answering. "I have many theories. None of them particularly reassuring." He waved his fingers in the air as if trying to paint complex pictures. "Theory number one: they're probes, pure machines, sent by a distant civilization to collect data. No communication necessary because they're only supposed to observe. Maybe some kind of galactic surveillance system."

"Possibly," said Lukas. "So they aren't programmed to respond, only to observe and collect data. A kind of Prime Directive."

"But Starfleet's Prime Directive aims to avoid revealing oneself to less developed civilizations so as not to influence their development. They've already revealed themselves."

"True. What's your next theory?"

"They're remnants of a long-lost civilization. Autonomous units that still follow preprogrammed patterns but have no one to return to. Ghost ships wandering through the galaxy."

Lukas winced. "Right, like a galactic Flying Dutchman."

"Theory number three," said Carlos. "They're here to colonize or conquer. Or, you know, *decontaminate*."

"Well, our only hope is that they aren't aware they're doing us any damage. At least that way, we have some chance of stopping them. Vanishingly small, but a chance. If they really are intent on wiping us out, we're at their mercy."

"The Japanese prime minister reminded us of human history in this regard," muttered Carlos. "He spoke generally, but it isn't hard to find specific examples. The Aztecs against the Spanish. The Aborigines against the British colonizers. Human history is full of such asymmetrical encounters. They never end well for the technologically inferior side."

Night had now completely descended on the mountains. The temperature had dropped further, and their breath formed little clouds in the air. But neither of them made any move to get into the car or start the journey back. The silence of the mountains, the clarity of the night sky, the absence of human noise—all this offered a welcome contrast to the hectic pace and fear of the past few weeks. Here they were just two friends with beer and gloomy thoughts.

"Theory number four," said Carlos after a while. "They're here to help. Maybe they're not responding to our primitive attempts at communication because they know we wouldn't understand them. Maybe they're waiting for us to be ready—intellectually, spiritually, socially."

Lukas smiled weakly. "That sounds like a science-fiction movie from the seventies. 'The Day the Earth Stood Still' or something."

"Sometimes reality imitates art." Carlos shrugged. "At least it's a more comforting idea than the alternatives."

Lukas laughed. "*Anything* is a more comforting idea than the alternatives."

A sudden flash made them both look up. A shooting star shot across the sky in a short, bright streak.

"We should make a wish," said Carlos in a whisper.

Lukas closed his eyes briefly, an ironic smile on his lips. What should he wish for? That the pyramids had peaceful intentions? That they would simply pass by Earth without causing any damage? Or something more personal—professional recognition, a second chance with Lisa, an easier life?

He sighed. None of these personal items would matter if the Earth were crushed like a hummingbird egg.

"How is Professor Li?" he asked instead, pushing his thoughts aside.

Carlos's face darkened. "Not good. He was dismissed and will probably never get a senior position again. The Chinese government has recalled him. They're making him the scapegoat for the accident."

"That's unfair. He was just implementing the decisions that came from above. The politicians wanted results, fast and without regard for the usual safety protocols. I think he was under extreme pressure."

"Like all of us. Fairness is rarely a factor in politics. They needed someone to blame, and he was the official head." Carlos took a sip of his beer. "By the way, the repair costs for the LHC are estimated to be at least three billion euros. The reconstruction will take years."

Lukas nodded grimly. The accident had not only destroyed their communication project, but also severely damaged one of humanity's most important scientific instruments. High-energy physics had suffered a severe setback, just when it was perhaps most urgently needed.

"So what will become of you now?" asked Carlos after a while.

"Me?" Lukas looked thoughtfully at his beer bottle. "I'm working as a consultant for various government agencies dealing with the pyramid situation. But to be honest, I feel useless. We tried everything we could think of, and nothing worked. Now all we can do is wait and hope. What about you? What are your plans?"

"Back to Chile, to the VLT. We'll continue to observe the pyramids, collect data, look for patterns." Carlos shrugged. "Science goes on, even if we don't get any answers, we can't just close our eyes."

They were silent for a while, each lost in their own thoughts. The stars twinkled above them, cold and indifferent. In the distance, an animal howled—perhaps a fox or coyote.

"Do you know what concerns me most?" said Lukas finally. "Not the question of whether they are peaceful or not. But the question of why. Why now? Why are they coming to Earth right now?"

"Maybe it's pure coincidence," said Carlos. "The galaxy is big, the time spans are immense. Maybe our paths just happen to be crossing at this particular moment."

"But what if it's not a coincidence? What if there's a reason—a reason we don't understand because we're asking the wrong questions?"

Carlos looked at him thoughtfully. "What kind of reason do you imagine?"

Lukas searched for words. "I don't know exactly. But sometimes I feel like we're overlooking something fundamental. It's like we're trying to solve a 3-dimensional puzzle with 2-dimensional thinking." He sighed. "Which, as anyone who has ever read *Flatland* by Edwin Abbott will tell you, is impossible to do."

"Flatland?" repeated Carlos, raising his eyebrows.

"Really? I thought everyone had read *Flatland*. By the time they were ten."

"Yeah, not so much. Tell me about it."

"An incredible book. Even more incredible, written all the way back in 1884. It was brilliant. Abbott found a way to give readers an intuitive grasp of how the fourth dimension would appear to 3D beings like us, something our minds aren't capable of truly understanding. He did this by analogy. By presenting a scenario we *are* capable of understanding: describing how our 3D universe would appear to *2D beings*."

"Interesting."

"Very. He basically imagines a universe that exists on a flat piece of paper stretching on to infinity, and all inhabitants and objects are simply drawings on this paper. Everything in existence is smashed flat and can't lift itself from the paper."

"Right," said Carlos. "Because there is no third dimension of height."

"Exactly. The idea is that the 2D beings would think our abilities were so extraordinary that they would appear magical. A square 2D vault filled with 2D money would be impenetrable to them. But we could just reach down from above and take the money from the middle of the vault with ease. Hell, we could reach inside their 2D bodies and remove their organs if we wanted. To them, their organs would just seem to vanish."

"That's a pretty grisly example. But I see what you mean. By analogy, a 4D being could reach in and snatch *our* organs."

"Right. Coming in through a dimension we can't even comprehend exists. And they could do it without breaking our skin or touching any other part of our bodies. An entrance inside of us that we can't conceive is there, just like Flatlanders, unable to lift themselves from the page, can't see the route we're taking from above."

He paused to let this sink in. "And we could appear to do all kinds of other miraculous things. We could materialize or vanish instantly, or even teleport—just by stepping off the paper and back on somewhere else. We could appear to grow and shrink instantly as we pass through their plane. Think of forcing a pointy ice-cream cone through a piece of paper. To beings on the paper, the cone would first appear as a dot, then a small circle, and then a rapidly expanding circle as the cone passed through."

He waited a few seconds and then sighed. "I could go on forever, but I'll stop here. I've digressed enough. But it really is fascinating to think about."

"Definitely," said Carlos. "And Abbott had great insight as to how to best try to understand what isn't understandable. By focusing on what is."

"Okay, so what can we understand?"

Carlos slid off the hood and stretched. "Well, we understand that the pyramids out there in space are nearly identical in size to the ones in Giza. That has to be a key."

"I agree. But I've thought about possible explanations for this until my brain began to hurt, and I got nowhere."

Carlos frowned. "Yeah. Same here. But that doesn't mean we shouldn't keep trying."

"The worst part of all this is that we'll probably die without getting any answers. If I could just satisfy my curiosity, just know how it's all really connected, I swear I could die happy."

Carlos nodded and raised his bottle of beer, clinking it against his friend's. "Whatever happens," he said, "I'm glad we're in this together. Experiencing the end of the world is less scary with a friend by your side."

Lukas felt a lump in his throat. The melancholy of the evening, the devastating reality of their situation, the uncertainty of the future—all of this mingled with the warmth of their long friendship. "Very true," he replied earnestly.

They remained silent for over a minute. Finally, Lukas sighed. "We should head back. It's getting colder, and tomorrow morning is the next crisis meeting."

Carlos nodded, collected the empty bottles, and stowed them in the cooler. "Who's driving?"

"Me. I drank less."

They got into the car, and Lukas started the engine. The heater kicked in, blowing first cold air, then gradually warmer air into the interior. Before driving off, Lukas took one last look at the starry sky. So clear, so infinite, so alien—and yet for millennia the reference point for human navigation, for scientific discoveries, for philosophical contemplation.

Somewhere out there were the pyramids, approaching Earth, driven by unknown motives and unimaginable technology. Before the next summer, if nothing changed, the pyramids would arrive and collide with the Earth, crushing the world like an elephant stomping on a grape.

17

The morning sun gilded the snow-covered peaks as Mira crossed the courtyard of Samye Monastery with her backpack. Her Sherpa, Dorje, was already waiting, his weather-beaten face calm and patient. When he saw her, he smiled broadly and waved.

The descent would be easier than the ascent three weeks ago, but it would still present its challenges. Lama Tenzin stood at the gate to see them off. The last few days had been filled with funeral rituals for her father.

In accordance with Tibetan tradition, Mira had opted for cremation—her father had dedicated his life to exploring the hidden, and now his remains were to return to their elemental components, free and unbound.

"Thank you for everything," said Mira to Lama Tenzin, placing her palms together in a respectful gesture. "I cannot put into words what this time here has meant to me."

The old monk simply smiled. "Words are often inadequate for the most important experiences. How do you feel now?" he said with his typical, somewhat awkward politeness, which she found so endearing.

Mira thought for a moment and took her time. No rush, no hasty thoughts.

"The grief is still there. But it's as if space has opened up around it. I can't express it any better than that."

"A very apt description." Lama Tenzin's eyes lit up. "In Buddhism, we speak of the Four Noble Truths. The first is the truth of suffering—dukkha. All life contains suffering, dissatisfaction, pain. The second truth teaches us that this suffering has a cause—our attachment, our desire, our clinging to impermanent things, basically everything the eye sees, the ear hears, and the hand touches."

He made a sweeping gesture that encompassed the monastery, the mountains, the sky. "The third truth is that there is an end to suffering. Not through the disappearance of pain, loss, or separation—these remain part of life. But through changing our relationship to them. The 'space' you describe is exactly that—recognizing that grief is allowed to be there without you identifying with it. Again, like clouds in the sky—sometimes they're dark and heavy, but the sky itself remains untouched."

"And the fourth truth?" asked Mira.

"There's a path that leads to the end of suffering—the Eightfold Path of right view, right intention, right speech, and so on. The practices you have learned here are part of that path. Take them with you, continue to practice them, even when you're back in your world." He tilted his head briefly. "Especially then."

Mira nodded gratefully. "I'll try."

"You'd better." He chuckled. "Oh, before I forget." Lama Tenzin reached into his robe and pulled out a folded piece of paper. "Your father wasn't the only Westerner to seek refuge here in recent years. An American scientist, Dr. Alexios Pappas from MIT, spent several months here. A brilliant mind—quantum physicist and neuroscientist. He and your father had long conversations."

Again, she had the feeling that he had known exactly when he wanted to give her the note. "At the right time," he would have said if she had asked him. Mira took the paper with the contact information written on it.

"Do you think he might know something?"

"Possibly. In any case, it might be worthwhile to talk to him." The monk folded his hands and smiled warmly. "Go with mindfulness, Mira Najafi. You will always have a place here if you desire it."

18

The pyramid complex at Giza lay bathed in golden morning light as Mira's taxi reached the parking lot. After two exhausting days of travel—from Tibet to Kathmandu, from there to Delhi, and finally to Cairo—she felt exhausted but determined. The vision she had during her meditation of the overturned stone table, along with Lama Tenzin's words, had given her new direction and clarity. That experience was now helping her avoid falling into despair as she stood before the ruins of her career.

She had kept her cell phone off during her entire stay at the monastery, and when she finally turned it back on at the airport in Kathmandu, she was hit with a flood of messages that was nothing short of biblical. Many hundreds from colleagues, friends, and journalists, and more than 20 from Markowitz alone, the subject lines increasingly urgent in tone. Dozens of missed calls from Jason, Abdul, and other team members. Even several messages from Ricarda Lefèvre with the cryptic request to call back "on an urgent matter."

Mira had decided not to respond to any of them—not now. Her priority was clear: she had to get back to the hidden chamber, had to look under the stone table, had to find out what her father had left there.

With purposeful steps, she walked to the entrance of the archaeological site where her research team had set up camp. The massive structure of the Pyramid of Cheops rose before her, illuminated by spotlights that made its millennia-old presence even more impressive.

She showed her ID at the security gate. The security guard frowned as he looked at it, turned it over in his hands several times, and then inserted it into a reader, which emitted an unpleasant beeping sound.

"This ID card is no longer valid, Doctor," he said finally in his heavily accented English.

"There must be some mistake. I lead the Yale University research team that discovered the new chamber. I am the discoverer."

"I'm sorry." The man shook his head regretfully. "Your name is no longer on the access list. The ID card is marked as expired. I can't let you through without a valid ID card."

"Call Professor Markowitz. Or Dr. Abdelrahman. They'll confirm who I am."

"I have my instructions, Professor, and I don't know these people." His voice remained polite but firm. "I'm just scanning the papers. If you would like to apply for a new access card, please contact the Supreme Council of Antiquities administration during office hours."

Mira felt frustration rising within her. Without her recent meditation training, it would have done more than rise. It would have shrieked from her vocal cords like a little girl auditioning for a role in a horror movie. "Listen, I was only away for a short time. There must be some misunderstanding."

"That's possible." The security guard shrugged. "But I still can't help you."

You are the sky, these are just clouds, she reminded herself, taking a deep breath and forcing herself to remain calm. Anger wouldn't help here.

"All right. Could you please notify someone from my team? Tell them that Dr. Najafi is here."

The man nodded reluctantly, picked up the phone, and spoke briefly in Arabic. After hanging up, he pointed to a nearby bench. "Please wait there."

Mira sat down, her backpack heavy on her lap. The sun rose higher above the horizon, and a warm breeze began to blow. Around her, the first tourists of the day flocked to the entrances, chattering loudly, wearing sun hats, and with skin glistening with sunscreen.

Almost an hour passed as the shadows grew shorter and the grounds gradually filled up. Finally, Mira noticed two figures approaching the security gate—Jason and Dr. Abdelrahman. Her heart leapt with hope. Surely they would clear up this misunderstanding.

She stood up and walked toward them, a smile on her lips. "Jason! Abdul! I'm so glad to see you. Apparently there's a problem with my access pass."

But their faces remained impassive. Jason avoided looking at her directly, and Abdul wore an expression of cool professionalism.

"Dr. Najafi," said the Egyptian archaeologist with a curt nod and a distance in his voice that shook her. "Your sudden return surprises us."

"I had to attend to a personal matter. I'm sorry I couldn't let you know sooner." She looked back and forth between the two of them. "Can one of you clear up this misunderstanding? I have to get back to the chamber."

Jason glanced uneasily at Abdelrahman, then back at the floor. The older archaeologist slowly shook his head.

"There's no misunderstanding, Dr. Najafi. Your access has been officially revoked."

Mira stared at him in disbelief. The fact that he was addressing her formally stung her. "Revoked? On what grounds?"

"Breach of contract. Unexcused absence. Failure to respond to official communications." Abdul listed the points with clinical precision. "Professor Markowitz made this decision in consultation with the university administration and the Supreme Council."

"That's ridiculous! I discovered the chamber! It was my research that—"

"And then you just disappeared." Dr. Abdelrahman's voice became sharper. "Without explanation, without handover, in the middle of a critical project. In fact, many of us were worried you had *died*. Do you know how many uncomfortable questions we had to answer about your disappearance?"

Before Mira could answer, both men looked over her shoulder. She turned and saw Professor David Markowitz walking toward them with measured steps. His gray hair was more disheveled than she remembered, his posture tense.

"David," she said, relief in her voice. Despite the emails, despite the obvious complications, he had been her mentor, her supporter for years. He would understand.

"Mira." His tone was cool, formal. He motioned for Jason and Dr. Abdelrahman to leave. "Go ahead. I'll be right there."

The two nodded and left without another glance at Mira. She remained alone with Markowitz in front of the security gate, the guards discreetly out of earshot.

"What the hell got into you?" asked Markowitz, his voice low but intense. "I'm relieved you're still alive, I am. But in a way, that makes me even *angrier*. Gone for almost a month without a *word*? No phone call, no email. Nothing! Do you know what was going on here?"

"David, I can explain. It was a personal emergency, I had to—"

"A personal emergency doesn't justify ignoring every attempt to contact you. We were worried, Mira! I reported you missing to the police!"

Shame flooded through her. In her focus on finding her father, on her own journey, she hadn't considered the impact her sudden disappearance would have on others.

"I'm so sorry," she said quietly. "I can only say that I found my father, long thought dead, in the most remote regions of Tibet."

"Tibet! Really?"

"Yes. I found him there. After a 15-year search. I know that isn't excuse enough, but it's all I can offer. I know I let you down. I let everyone down. But I have an urgent need to get back to the chamber. Now. There's something I need to check. Something important."

"So you're in Tibet for God knows how long and suddenly you realize you have this urgent need to see a chamber that the rest of us have been begging you to return to since you vanished?"

She winced. "Yeah, I'm afraid that sums it up a lot better than I'd like."

"Tell me what you're after?"

She hesitated, and his face hardened.

"I thought so." The disappointment in his voice hit her like a slap in the face. "The chamber is currently being thoroughly documented and analyzed, under the direction of Dr. Abdelrahman and myself. Your involvement in this project is over."

"David, please. You've known me for 14 years. Have I ever done anything to abuse your trust?"

"Not until now, no. But that's irrelevant. You're like a madman who slaughters a family and then points out you've never had so much as a parking ticket before. What you've done is inexcusable. It's no way to treat colleagues, Mira. *Friends*. People who've invested their time and money in you. And their careers."

His voice now sounded more sad than angry. "I risked my reputation for you, Mira. Entrusted you with a team, research funds, a career opportunity. And you just disappear, drop everything, don't respond to any messages. We thought you were dead? Who can't type a one-sentence text message or make a five-minute call? This is the 2030s. Even Tibet has cell coverage now. How am I supposed to understand that?"

"You're not. Now that I've come back to reality, even I don't. I can only say again that I found my father."

Mira opened her mouth, then closed it again. How could she explain what had happened? The search for her father, the monastery in Tibet, the tukdam state, the meditation, the vision? It would sound crazy, irrational, unprofessional.

And even if he understood every word, he was right. How to explain not even taking a few minutes over such a long stretch of time to reach out to them?

"As I told you, I found my father. But what I didn't tell you was that he was in a remote monastery in Tibet, with no reception, and no internet. And that he died before I could talk to him. Before he even knew I was there. I was devastated. I see now that my psyche couldn't handle it. I withdrew into myself. The monks took me in and taught me meditation. I must have fled the real world while I recovered from my loss. It was like I was curled into a fetal position, with a monastery taking the place of a womb."

Markowitz's expression softened slightly. "I'm sorry to hear that, Mira. Really. But before any of that occurred, you had to make the decision to travel to Tibet and abandon the most important archaeological project in at least a decade, and your colleagues who were facing a storm of inquiries."

"I let you down," said Mira. "I know that. But trust me now, David. What I'm looking for in the chamber could be even more significant than the chamber itself. It has to do with the black pyramids, with the hieroglyphics, with something my father discovered."

"Then tell me, and I'll look into it. That's all I can offer you."

"I don't know exactly."

"You don't know exactly? What does that mean?"

"It's hard to say."

"Mira, I trusted you." He shook his head. "I defended you when others questioned your theories. But I'm sorry. You're no longer part of this project. Your position at the university expires at the end of the month and won't be renewed. If you wish to submit a formal request to visit the excavation site, you can do so through the usual channels."

"David—"

"Goodbye, Mira." He turned away. "I'm sorry for your loss. And I truly hope you find what you're looking for."

She watched him walk through the security gate, respectfully allowed passage by the guards, and return to the excavation site. The Pyramid of Cheops rose behind him, massive and impenetrable, its secrets locked tight within its stone heart. Her former workplace now seemed as distant and inaccessible to her as Fort Knox.

Mira was left alone, her backpack heavy on her shoulders, the Tibetan wind now just a distant memory in her hair. The stone table in the hidden chamber, the possible secret it held, now seemed unattainable—behind closed doors and broken relationships.

But there was something within her that had been born at Samye Monastery. A calmness, a clarity that transcended momentary obstacles. She would find a way back into the chamber if it was the last thing she did.

She could see no other choice.

19

The conference room in the basement of the CERN main building had never been open to the public. Originally designed for top-secret discussions about nuclear research during the Cold War, it was equipped with state-of-the-art eavesdropping protection, had no windows, and only one well-controlled access point. Today, it served as headquarters for "Project Black Delta"—the international crisis team dealing with the approaching arrival of the black pyramids.

Lukas immediately noticed the change in the composition of those present when he entered the room with Carlos. Where scientists had previously been in the majority, uniforms of various colors now dominated the scene. High-ranking military officers from various nations, with all kinds of insignia on their chests, sat together in small groups, talking quietly and exchanging notes. At the front of the room, a massive video wall had been installed, currently displaying the flags of various nations—ready for the heads of state and government to join the meeting.

"This doesn't look good," muttered Carlos as they looked for their seats.

Lukas nodded grimly. The increasing militarization of the project was an unmistakable sign of the direction in which the discussion was heading. Science had provided no answers, established no communication. Now those whose job it was to respond to threats with force would take over.

They took their seats next to Dr. Elena Volkova, the Russian physicist who had been involved in the failed LHC experiment. Her expression was tense, her eyes tired.

"Have you heard the news?" she asked quietly. "The pyramids haven't slowed down, as was assumed yesterday. A measurement error, it seems."

"That would have been too good to be true," he replied.

The fact that the three objects had not changed reinforced a feeling that had been plaguing Lukas for weeks—the feeling that they were overlooking a crucial piece of the puzzle, a context that would explain everything. But nothing occurred to him or caught his attention.

His gaze fell on a man he hadn't seen at the meetings before—a dark-skinned man with short gray hair and distinctive glasses, who was engrossed in conversation with Ricarda Lefèvre from the ESA.

"Who is that?" he asked Elena.

"Professor Nkosi Mbeki, an Egyptologist from South Africa. ESA brought him in to investigate the connection between the space pyramids and the Egyptian pyramids when it came out that they had the same edge lengths."

"An Egyptologist?" Carlos raised his eyebrows. "Interesting twist."

Before they could continue their conversation, a gong sounded and Dr. Lawrence Kellerman from the International Science Council stood up.

"Ladies and gentlemen, please take your seats. The heads of state and government will be joining us shortly."

A bustle of activity filled the room as everyone took their seats. The video wall flickered, and one after another, the faces of the world's most powerful politicians appeared—President Morales of the United States, President Chen of China, German Chancellor Schneider, French President Dubois, and a dozen other leaders.

"I hereby open the eighteenth meeting of Project Black Delta," began Kellerman. "I remind you once again that this meeting and everything related to Black Delta is strictly confidential." He paused briefly and looked around the room. "Unfortunately, the situation hasn't changed since our last meeting. Dr. Volkova?"

Elena stood up and stepped up to the lectern. In a calm voice, she presented the latest data—the unchanged trajectory of the pyramids, the continued constant emission of gravitational waves.

"Based on our models, the forecasts remain unchanged," she summarized. "If they continue on the same course, the objects will collide with Earth in just under eight months. However, the gravitational effects will cause massive damage weeks before that. Again, we *think*.

Based on the pyramids' effect on Mars, not based on what we calculate their mass to be. Based on their *mass*, Mars should be nothing but dust right now, and we should be staring up at tidal waves as tall as skyscrapers. Well, we would be if we still had a planet, which we wouldn't. When you fully accept that you don't really understand gravity, or physics, anymore, anything is possible."

"Thanks," said the US president with a wry smile. "That's a complete lack of precision only a politician could admire. But, bottom line, based on its effects on Mars, you still expect it to have about the same gravitational effect on other objects as our Moon."

"Exactly."

"Thank you," said Kellerman. He gestured to the South African. "Since the objects bear a striking resemblance to the Egyptian pyramids, we've asked Professor Mbeki, under the leadership of the ESA, to share his perspective on this aspect. Professor?"

The South African Egyptologist stepped forward, his posture calm and dignified. Lukas noticed some of the military and scientists in the room rolling their eyes or exchanging skeptical glances. The divide between scientific disciplines was often deep, and the humanities were not always taken seriously by the "harder" sciences—not to mention the military.

"Thank you, Dr. Kellerman." Mbeki's voice was deep and melodic, with a slight South African accent. "The connection between the Egyptian pyramids and the cosmos is deeper and more complex than most people realize. The ancient Egyptians had a highly developed understanding of astronomy that went far beyond simply observing the stars."

He activated a presentation showing hieroglyphics and astronomical diagrams.

"Egyptian cosmology didn't view the sky as a separate entity, but as an integral part of a holistic universe. The goddess Nut embodied the sky itself—her body, studded with stars, arched over the earth. The sun god Ra traveled daily in his solar barge across the sky to the west. At night, he traveled through the underworld to get back to the East so as to be reborn the next morning."

He showed a picture of the sun god in his barge, pointing out that its Egyptian name had been translated to *The Boat of a Million Years*.

"Particularly relevant to our situation is the alignment of the pyramids. The three great pyramids of Giza are aligned exactly with the stars of Orion's Belt—a constellation that the Egyptians associated with Osiris, the god of the underworld and rebirth. This alignment is so precise that it reflects the relative brightness of the stars—the Pyramid of Cheops, the largest, corresponds to Alnitak, the brightest of the three belt stars."

Mbeki switched to an overlay of Orion's Belt with the pyramids of Giza, which showed the astonishing correspondence.

"Furthermore, the Great Pyramid contains precise astronomical information. The descent and ascent angles of the inner passages correspond exactly to the angles at which certain key stars could be seen in the sky from Giza—in particular, Sirius, which was associated with the goddess Isis, and Alpha Draconis, the North Star at that time."

He paused briefly, as if to give those present some time to process this information.

"The modern pre-astronautics theory, often criticized but never completely refuted, postulates that this precise astronomical knowledge may not have been of purely terrestrial origin. The perfect north-south alignment of the pyramids with a deviation of less than a tenth of a degree, the use of pi and the golden ratio in their proportions, the incredible precision of the stone setting—all of these point to a knowledge that seemingly exceeded the technological capabilities of the time. By *a lot*."

Lukas guessed that many of the scientists would be rolling their eyes at this point, as pre-astronautics was often considered pseudoscience in serious academic circles. The fact that unknown flying objects were approaching Earth, whose dimensions corresponded exactly to those of the pyramids of Giza, helped them to take it very seriously.

"There are also numerous depictions in Egyptian temples that show unusual scenes," continued Mbeki. "Figures traveling in 'sky barges', columns of light shining down from the sky, gods who appear to be operating advanced devices."

He showed a picture from the temple of Dendera that was often interpreted as a 'light bulb'—an elongated structure with a snake-like shape inside, reminiscent of a primitive electric lamp.

"The hieroglyphs in the Serabit el-Khadim mine complex on the Sinai contain inscriptions that speak of 'those who came from the sky'. The Papyrus of Tulli, whose authenticity is disputed, describes 'fireballs' that came down from the sky during the reign of Thutmose III."

German Chancellor Schneider cleared her throat on her screen. "Professor Mbeki, this is undoubtedly fascinating. But is there any indication in Egyptian mythology as to what these visitors wanted at that time? Or how one might communicate with them? In short, is there a solution in these ancient texts that is relevant to us today?"

Mbeki smiled slightly. "A direct solution? No, Chancellor, at least not yet. But these traditions suggest that there may have been contact in the past—and that the pyramids themselves may have been a kind of communication or orientation point for these contacts."

Mbeki finished up and Kellerman gave the floor to General Isaac Williams, Chairman of the US Joint Chiefs of Staff.

A tall man in the brown military uniform of the Marines stepped forward. His face was angular, his short gray hair cut with military precision. He radiated the kind of natural authority that only decades of command experience could confer.

"Ladies and gentlemen," he began without preamble, "I've been given the thankless task of trying to prepare the world's military for the worst-case scenario. And I've heard all the metaphors. An ant against a sledgehammer. A crystal chandelier against a nuclear bomb. Even Wile E. Coyote against the Road Runner."

He shook his head. "But even if there's the slightest chance we can do something, we have to *try*. With human extinction on the table, it seems we can spare some time and effort on this, even knowing it's likely futile."

Lukas was impressed. He appreciated the man's clear-eyed view of what they would likely be up against, and that he wasn't trying to sugarcoat the reality of it.

The general activated a presentation on the main display showing various weapon systems.

"Together with our NATO allies, our Chinese partners, space agencies such as NASA, ESA, and JAXA, and private space companies like SpaceX and Blue Origin, we've evaluated the following options. First, kinetic impactors—projectiles with significant mass that can be directed at targets at high speed. The most advanced systems currently available are the US Navy's railgun platforms, as used on the Zumwalt class."

The hologram showed a satellite-like structure with a long, cylindrical protrusion.

"These electromagnetic guns can accelerate tungsten projectiles at speeds of up to 35,000 miles per hour, or 10 miles per second. Since the rounds weigh up to 40 pounds and are traveling 30 times faster than a fired bullet, you can imagine there is basically no structure on Earth they can't penetrate. We currently have 6 such platforms in service."

He switched to another image.

"Second: high-energy laser weapons. The latest generation of laser cannons are 500-kilowatt solid-state lasers, which can direct concentrated beams of energy at a target. However, I've been told that their effectiveness against objects that absorb virtually all electromagnetic radiation is questionable."

Another image appeared.

"Third: and here we enter a sensitive area, the nuclear option. The most powerful of these weapons currently in existence are the American B83-1 with an explosive power of 1.2 megatons. We still have 90 of them, which in theory can also be used in missiles optimized for use in space."

Lukas exchanged a concerned glance with Carlos. The situation was developing exactly as they'd feared.

General Williams deactivated the hologram and looked around the room with a serious expression.

"I'm afraid these are our best options. If the objects decide to behave as if they have the two solar masses the gravity waves say they do, obviously these weapons will be turned to paste before they get close. On the other hand, they'd turn *us* to paste at the same time. If the objects decide to continue to behave like our Moon, the weapons can reach them. What kind of damage they can do, if any, remains to be seen." He shook his head. "But one doesn't need to be a scientist to recognize the kind of damage a high-speed collision with these objects can do to *us*. Getting hit by an asteroid may have caused the extinction of the dinosaurs. But getting hit by the equivalent of our Moon . . . Well, suffice it to say, that wouldn't be fun."

He paused. "Questions? Comments? Thoughts? I'll open the floor."

Lukas quickly stood, and the general nodded in his direction. "Go ahead."

"With all due respect, General Williams," he began, his voice steady, "we should discuss the risk-reward proposition here. What are the chances an attack succeeds versus the chances an attack, well . . . pisses them off."

Williams smiled. "Well phrased. And we have given this considerable thought. There is no way to know. Under your scenario, they're just playing billiards with the Earth, perhaps somehow unaware that we can't survive this game. Or maybe they *are* aware, but are playing a game of chicken. Terrifying us out of our skin for the sheer joy of it. But at the last second they'll say, just kidding, and veer off. Or tone down the gravity thing."

He paused. "But then, we fire our puny little bows and arrows at a reinforced tank—another metaphor I've been hearing—and they get *enraged*. Imagine the nerve of these barbarians we won't talk to, they say to each other. They're trying to scratch our tank. With little provocation. Well, other than the fact that we'll soon be driving them into extinction. Now we're *really* mad. Now we're going to drive them into *double* extinction."

The general paused for a long moment for this to sink in. "So, yes, it's possible we will piss them off. But highly unlikely. Just as unlikely as it will be for our weapons to prevail. It's a toss-up. But if we're going down, it had better be through action rather than cowering in a corner so as not to offend the thing trying to kill us. For better or worse, it just seems more . . . human."

Lukas blew out a long breath. "I didn't expect you to dismantle my argument so thoroughly, General, or for me to agree with you when you were done. But I do. Well-reasoned. But before we try this option of last resort, I say we need to keep searching for other options. The similarity to the pyramids of Giza isn't a coincidence. There must be a connection, a context that we don't yet fully understand. If there has been contact in the past, as Professor Mbeki suggests, then there must be a way to renew that contact without using nuclear weapons."

Chinese General Zhao rose. Unlike Williams, he wore a simple uniform without excessive adornment, but his presence was no less authoritative. "Dr. Heuer, we're all in full agreement here. We are not—how do you say it?—dumb military men who have hammers in their hands and see nails everywhere." His English was precise, albeit with a distinct accent. "We couldn't support the continued search for alternatives any more emphatically. It's simply a matter of contributing our expertise so we're prepared for the worst-case scenario, if all other options fail."

There were approving nods from everyone in the room.

Professor Mbeki stepped forward again. "If I may make a suggestion: the striking similarity to the pyramids of Giza points to the possible significance of this place. Perhaps we should position a team directly there to conduct further investigations."

"A careful mix of scientists and security forces on the ground could be a good idea," agreed the US general. "We should look for the connection, for sure. At the same time, we'll be getting our weapons systems ready for a last-ditch effort, praying like hell it doesn't come to that."

Over the next 20 minutes, a detailed discussion developed about the practical implementation of this two-pronged approach. Lukas felt his initial tension ease somewhat. The militarization of the project was progressing, but the military wasn't acting as pigheaded as those in the movies would have one believe.

"In summary," said President Morales finally, "we're tasking the military and space agencies to jointly develop a defense strategy that will only be activated in an extreme emergency. At the same time, the scientific teams will intensify their communication attempts, with a particular focus on the possible historical connection to the pyramids of Giza. A joint team of experts will be sent to Giza to examine the pyramids more closely on site."

He looked around the room, both at those physically present and at his colleagues on the screens.

"Are there any objections to this proposal?"

No one spoke up.

"Then this proposal is unanimously accepted. The details will be worked out in the respective working groups. We will meet again in three days to evaluate the progress."

When the connection to the heads of state was disconnected and those present began to leave the room, Carlos stepped next to Lukas. "Well, that went a lot better than I thought it would," he said.

Professor Mbeki approached them, a thoughtful expression on his face. "Dr. Heuer, Dr. Mendoza. I'd like to hear your thoughts on some aspects of Egyptian astronomy, if you have a moment."

"Sure." Lukas looked at the Egyptologist curiously.

"I didn't mention everything I know in my presentation," said Mbeki quietly. "There are texts—very old, somewhat controversial texts—that speak of a 'great cycle,' a return of the 'sky gods.' The exact time of their return isn't mentioned because the Egyptian calendar was based on years, but also on cycles and certain religious units. If we could establish a temporal connection, we would at least know more."

"Could it be that the Egyptians foresaw the arrival of the objects?" said Lukas. "Is that what you're saying?"

"Not their arrival," said Mbeki. "Their *return*."

"That would be astonishing," said Carlos, his eyes widening. "But even if that were the case, it would be of little use to us if we can't pull a rabbit out of a hat. Or, better yet, a papyrus scroll with a clear solution inscribed on it."

"If I can't pull off that magic trick, it won't be for lack of trying," said the Egyptologist. "There is one more thing. The ESA contacted me because they're working with David Markowitz, whose team recently discovered a chamber in Cheops, now called the *Star Chamber*."

"A new chamber in the pyramids was discovered?" said Lukas in surprise.

"Yes, by an archaeologist named Mira Najafi. Do you know her?"

Lukas shook his head. "Never heard of her. What exactly did she discover?"

"That's the interesting thing. No one seems to know exactly. She disappeared shortly after her discovery. But Dr. Lefèvre from ESA believes it could have something to do with black pyramids in the sky—depicted on a millennia-old mural—*twice*. Side by side. That's very unusual and could actually point to a kind of cycle. Possibly suggesting the Egyptians had dealt with these objects and knew that they'd return."

"That would be fantastic news," said Lukas. "I'd love to know the pyramids were here before without wiping us out. That wouldn't be a guarantee, but it would sure make me feel a whole lot more optimistic."

A shiver of renewed hope ran down Lukas's spine. The missing piece of the puzzle they were so desperately searching for—could it be hidden in the depths of an ancient pyramid?

"I think we should be part of the team that goes to Giza with Mr. Mbeki," he said to Carlos. "Maybe we'll find answers there."

"Or questions we didn't even know to ask," added Mbeki with an enigmatic smile. "I'd be honored if you'd accompany me."

20

The ringing of her phone jolted Mira out of the restless half-sleep she had been experiencing for the past few nights. She reached for the device, expecting another call from Markowitz or perhaps a call from Ricarda Lefèvre, who had decided to stop ignoring her. However, the number on the display was Egyptian—she had apparently even saved it.

"Hassan?" she asked sleepily, remembering that she had tried to call him the night before.

"Dr. Najafi." The smoky voice on the other end sounded surprised. "It's been a long time."

Hassan el-Farouq was a contact at Cairo University who had served as her guide on her first research trip almost eight years ago. He moved effortlessly between the academic world and the darker corners of Cairo, knew people in places that weren't in any guidebook, and had always brought her to her workplace before the first tourists arrived.

"I need your help, Hassan." Mira looked out the window of her modest hotel room, which had been chosen with a view of the Nile and her tight financial situation in mind. "Can we meet?"

"Sure." A short pause followed. "Café Riche in an hour?"

"See you soon."

***

Café Riche in downtown Cairo was a historic place where revolutionaries and intellectuals once gathered. Today, it was a popular meeting place for tourists and locals alike, a link between the old and the new, just like Hassan himself.

He was already sitting at a table in the back corner, a thin man in his fifties with sharp eyes and a well-groomed mustache. In front of him stood a cup of Turkish coffee, as black as the expensive suit he wore—a sign of his rise to associate dean of the history department.

"Mira." He rose halfway as she approached. "It's good to see you. I heard about your discovery. Impressive, really impressive!"

She sat down across from him, noticing the sparkle in his eyes—a mixture of professional curiosity and personal interest.

"Thanks for making time on such short notice, Hassan."

"Are you kidding? You're a celebrity! Or at least you should be. A great rise, an even greater fall—who would I be if I didn't take advantage of the interview you apparently denied to the world's media?" He smiled broadly, revealing a gold tooth.

A waiter brought a second cup of coffee without being asked, and she murmured a quick "Shokran."

"So," he began, leaning forward, "a hidden chamber in the Pyramid of Cheops. After all these centuries of research. The scientific community is electrified."

Mira suppressed a sigh. She didn't have time for technical discussions, but she knew that Hassan considered information to be currency. She had to pay before she could ask for favors.

"A tunnel, probably used during construction and then sealed. The chamber itself seems to have a ritual character." She sipped her coffee, strong and sweet. "The most interesting thing is the wall paintings—they show the three pyramids of Giza, but strangely depicted in black against a blue night sky."

Hassan's eyes narrowed slightly. "Black pyramids? That's unusual. The traditional depiction would be in natural sand colors."

"Exactly. And there are also priests who seem to be communicating with these black pyramids." She paused, wondering how much she should reveal. "But I'm not here to talk about my discovery."

"Of course not." Hassan leaned back, a knowing smile on his lips. He didn't even sound disappointed. "You're here because you need something."

Mira lowered her voice and leaned forward conspiratorially before speaking. "Remember when I wanted to go to Sinai? You advised me to take a firearm. You said you knew the right people."

The academic froze for a moment, his face becoming expressionless. "That was years ago, Mira. And it was dangerous advice that would get me into trouble today."

"I want to go back to the Sinai." A lie, but a necessary one. The truth would frighten even Hassan.

"The Sinai hasn't actually become any safer." He looked around, lowering his voice even further. "But why are you asking me? There are official channels for organizing expeditions, with security forces and everything."

"You know how bureaucracy is." She held his gaze. "I don't have time for endless applications and permits."

Hassan studied her face as if trying to decipher a complex panel of hieroglyphics.

"What's so urgent, Mira? What are you really up to?"

"I can't tell you." She thought of her father, of the vision she had had during meditation, of what might be hidden on or under the stone table. "Not now, at least. But it's important, Hassan. More important than you can imagine."

Long seconds passed, during which only the soft clinking of cups and muffled conversations could be heard.

"No weapon," he said finally. "The contacts aren't available for that anymore. But . . ."

He took out a pen and scribbled an address on a napkin. "These people can help. Whatever you're planning. They can accompany you or something. But I warn you: be careful."

Mira took the napkin and put it in her pocket. "Thanks, Hassan."

He grabbed her hand and held it tight. "Listen, Mira. Cairo has changed. It was never safe for a woman alone, but now? Just be careful. Very careful."

* * *

The address took Mira to a neighborhood of Cairo that, for good reason, didn't appear in any tourist guide. Imbaba, once a notorious center of Islamist activity, had been pacified, but it was still a place where it was better not to be out after dark—especially alone and as a Western woman.

The taxi had refused to take her there directly, dropping her off at the edge of the neighborhood instead.

"Farther not good, lady," the driver had said, the fear in his eyes more understandable than his broken English.

Now Mira continued on foot, her head covered with a scarf, her posture deliberately inconspicuous. The narrow streets were a labyrinth of people, smells, and sounds. Children played among piles of garbage, old men smoked hookahs in shabby cafes, and everywhere she felt the piercing stares following her—the stranger, the intruder, the outsider, even though she was veiled.

With every step deeper into the neighborhood, her unease grew. What was she doing here? Was it worth it? She could be robbed, kidnapped, or worse at any moment. And for what? A vague vision, a last desperate hope of finding answers?

No, I know what I saw and felt.

The address turned out to be a dilapidated building with crumbling plaster, surrounded by street vendors hawking everything from fake designer watches to dubious electronic goods. A rusty iron balcony hung precariously over the entrance.

Mira took a deep breath and stepped inside. The narrow corridor smelled of damp and something unidentifiable. A bare bulb provided barely enough light to see the steps leading up.

On the first floor, she followed the hallway to a door with peeling green paint. A quiet conversation drifted through the thin wood. She knocked, twice short, once long, and then scolded herself for acting like an idiot.

The conversation on the other side fell silent. Footsteps approached the door.

"Meen henaak?" A rough male voice speaking hard Arabic.

"Ana sadiqat Hassan." *I am a friend of Hassan's.* Her Arabic was rudimentary, but she hoped it would suffice.

The door opened a crack. A dark eye scrutinized her, then the door opened wider.

The room behind it was surprisingly spacious, albeit sparsely furnished. Three men sat around a low table, one with a scar running across his face, one young with nervous eyes, and one older, with the demeanor of someone who routinely gave orders.

"American." The older man spoke English with a strong accent. "What do you want?"

Mira swallowed. "I'm looking for someone who can take me to the Pyramid of Cheops at night," she replied finally without preamble.

A brief, surprised silence followed, then an amused snort from the man with the scar. The older man said something in Arabic, too fast for her to understand, whereupon the chuckling man fell silent.

"Why?" he then asked in English.

"That's my business."

She opened her bag and pulled out an envelope. With deliberately calm movements, she placed it on the table, opened it, and let the men see its contents. Five thousand US dollars in used hundred-dollar bills. A large part of her savings. "Five thousand now. Another five thousand when I'm out."

The men exchanged glances, unreadable to her.

"Dangerous," said the older one. "Many guards. Dogs."

"I know. That's why I need help. Consider this a test run. If you do this job well, I'll have many more jobs for you later."

The man with the scar grabbed the envelope and counted the bills with practiced movements. Mira felt her heart racing. This was the moment when everything could go wrong. She was alone in a dilapidated building with three strangers who were obviously operating on the wrong side of the law, and she had just presented them with a considerable sum of cash.

The older man nodded to the younger one, who got up and left the room. Mira felt panic rising within her. Had they decided to simply rob her? Or worse?

She had tried to prevent them from just taking the five grand, or worse, by holding out a carrot. Steal the money, and that's all they would ever get from her. But do the job, and they'd get the second half of the payment, followed by further jobs, which didn't really exist, but held the promise of riches to come if they played fair with her now.

"When?" asked the older man as the man with the scar pocketed the money.

The simple question brought her back to reality. They were still negotiating. "Tonight."

A short, barking laugh that made her flinch. "Quick, American. Very quick."

"I don't have much time."

The door opened again, and the younger man returned, accompanied by a fourth—also a young man, perhaps in his early twenties, with alert dark eyes and a mischievous smile that seemed strangely out of place in this environment.

"This is Faisal," said the older man. "He will guide you. He has been there many times."

In the past, Mira would have been furious at the thought—a grave robber, a looter of cultural treasures. Now he was her last hope.

"Salam." Faisal nodded to her, his gaze open and direct, without the threatening aura of the other men. "We'll meet at sunset on the western edge of the necropolis. Bring dark clothes—and money."

***

Twilight had settled over the Giza Plateau. The last tourists were leaving the area as the security guards began their night shift. The mighty pyramids cast long shadows across the desert like silent guardians of a bygone era.

Mira waited at the agreed-upon meeting point, dressed in black jeans and a dark sweater, a backpack with the essentials on her back—flashlight, water, gloves, a small tool kit. Her heart was pounding in her throat and she paced nervously back and forth. What she was planning to do was not only illegal, but potentially dangerous. The corridors of the pyramid were a labyrinth, and if she were discovered . . .

"Ready?" Faisal appeared out of nowhere beside her, dressed in dark jeans and a jacket, his face now partially covered by a black cloth, giving him the appearance of a Bedouin from times past.

Mira nodded. "The security guards patrol with dogs."

"I know, but not everywhere. And we have arrangements." His smile flashed briefly. "Come on, we have to wait until it's completely dark."

They retreated into the shadows of an old wall, watching night fall over the desert landscape. Faisal whispered his plan to her. On the western edge, there was a spot where the fence had been damaged and only provisionally repaired.

"Security here is like everywhere else in Egypt," he whispered. "Strict on paper, full of holes in reality. It's all a question of baksheesh," he added, the Persian word for gift, but typically used to mean *bribe*.

When darkness was deep and the stars were twinkling above them, Faisal gave her a sign. In the distance, they could see a group of young men approaching the guard post at the southern gate, shouting and waving loudly. The guards responded—not with alarm, but with welcoming gestures.

"Now." Faisal led her to the fence, where a section had been patched with simple wire. With practiced movements, he cut through the wire, creating an opening just large enough to crawl through, sand and dust flying everywhere.

Dogs barked in the distance, but the guards seemed to deliberately ignore them, too busy with whatever was being passed to them through the fence.

Crouching low, they hurried across the open terrain, using every mound and shadow for cover. The massive silhouette of the Pyramid of Cheops rose before them in the night sky, ancient and intimidating.

"Where is the entrance?" asked Faisal quietly as they reached the foot of the pyramid.

"The north side. The main tourist entrance." Mira led him around the base of the pyramid, always careful to stay in the shadows. "From there, we have to go to my former team's base camp, and then through a newly discovered tunnel to the chamber."

Faisal gave her a strange look. "You're brave, American. Or desperate."

"Both," she replied dryly.

They reached the entrance, a modern steel structure that protected the original entrance. The door was unlocked and easy to open.

The passageway in front of them led steeply down into the darkness. Mira turned on her flashlight, directing the beam at the floor to minimize the risk of being seen from outside.

"The base camp is in the Great Gallery area," she whispered.

Faisal nodded. "I'll go first. If anyone's there, I can distract them."

"There's no one there at this time of night."

They moved cautiously through the ascending passageway that led to the Great Gallery. The air became more stifling, the dust of millennia swirling with every step. As they approached the end of the passageway, they heard voices—and Mira recognized one of them immediately.

Markowitz.

"Shhh." She pulled Faisal back into the shadows. "My former boss is here," she whispered. "And probably others from my old team. We need a distraction."

"I thought no one was here at this time of night?" he hissed accusingly.

"Not usually. Apparently that's changed. You have to distract them."

Faisal frowned. "Distract them how?"

"Anything that will lure them away. A noise, an intruder, I don't know! You're the criminal."

"You want me to play the intruder?" His voice was low but sharp.

"Just for a few minutes. Lead them away, then disappear. I'll pay you well for it."

A brief, tense moment followed as Faisal looked her over appraisingly. Then he nodded reluctantly.

"Five minutes. No more. And if I don't see the money . . ."

"You will!" she whispered impatiently, shooing him away.

He retreated, disappearing into the darkness of a side corridor. Mira waited, her heart pounding against her ribs.

After what felt like an eternity, there was a loud rumbling, followed by a shout in Arabic. Voices grew loud, hasty footsteps receded.

Mira counted to twenty, then ventured forward toward the makeshift base camp.

To her horror, it was not completely deserted. Markowitz and Abdul were sitting together, bent over a tablet, engrossed in quiet conversation. Mira crouched behind one of the massive boxes of equipment, her breath shallow, her pulse racing.

" . . . unusual energy signatures," she heard Markowitz say. "The ESA wants to install more measuring devices."

"The hieroglyphs mention a 'key to heaven,'" replied Abdul Abdelrahman. "But we haven't found anything."

Mira froze.

A sudden clang in the distance made both men look up. Faisal was obviously doing his job well.

"What the hell was that?" muttered Markowitz.

"I'll go check," offered Abdelrahman, getting up. "Maybe the others are having trouble."

Markowitz nodded, grabbed his flashlight, and followed him. The moment their footsteps faded, Mira scurried out of her hiding place, her gaze fixed on the narrow passageway leading to the newly discovered tunnel system.

The former construction workers' tunnel was now exposed, supported by modern metal struts, the walls marked with measurements and scales. Mira crawled through, ignoring her aching elbows and knees. Her experiences in Tibet drove her forward, fueled by the vision of her father and the knowledge that she had overlooked something important.

After about 50 yards, the tunnel opened into the chamber she had discovered—the "Star Chamber," as it was now officially called. The room was brightly lit by makeshift lamps, the walls covered with the fascinating images she knew so well: the black pyramids in the night sky, the meditating priests, the beam of light connecting them.

But the chamber wasn't empty. There were measuring devices everywhere—sensors, computers, cameras. And in the middle, next to the stone table, stood Jason, her former assistant.

He looked up, his eyes widening in disbelief. "Dr. Najafi?"

Mira put a finger to her lips, silently pleading for silence. Jason's hand was already moving toward his radio.

With two quick steps, she was at him, pressing her hand over his mouth.

"No," she whispered urgently. "Please, Jason. I can explain everything."

His eyes were wide with surprise, but he didn't resist her grip.

"I need to check something," she continued, her voice an urgent whisper that sounded so desperate it surprised even her. "Something about the stone table. I must have overlooked something. After that, you can arrest me or whatever you want. But please, let me check."

Slowly, she took her hand away from his mouth, ready to put it back immediately if he tried to shout.

Jason stared at her, his face a mixture of rejection and pity. Mira didn't know which hurt her more.

"Dr. Najafi, what are you doing here? How did you get in?"

"It doesn't matter. Please, Jason. It's important."

A long moment of hesitation followed, during which only their breathing and the soft hum of the measuring instruments could be heard. Then he nodded slowly. "All right. But quickly. I don't want to lose my job because I helped you do something illegal. Don't touch anything, that's the deal!"

21

Charles de Gaulle Airport in Paris awoke at dawn to its usual hustle and bustle, but Lukas hardly noticed the crowds around him. He stood with Carlos and Professor Mbeki at the gate for private planes, waiting for the ESA aircraft that would take them to Cairo. His thoughts were still revolving around yesterday's conference at CERN.

"This is completely normal," he said with a wry smile, taking a sip from his coffee mug. "Every physicist knows that one day he might have to try to stop an extinction-level threat by studying a 4,500-year-old pyramid."

"Is that what they teach you guys in Physics 101?" said Carlos with a smile.

"Yeah. That Force equals Mass times Acceleration. And that you can find answers to cosmic mysteries by studying Giza. And also, you know, that when you're dealing with outer space pyramids, force might *not* equal mass times acceleration, after all. Hell, *mass* might not even equal mass."

"Sí, amigo. The irony is remarkable," agreed Carlos, grimacing. "But no more so than learning those wacky new-age pyramid-power fanatics might have been on to something."

Professor Mbeki, who was searching through his leather bag, looked up. "Maybe it's not as ironic as it seems. The ancient Egyptians understood things about the cosmos that we're only rediscovering today. Their knowledge of precession, stellar cycles, mathematical relationships—it wasn't primitive, it was highly advanced."

Lukas was about to reply when his phone began to vibrate. At the same time, he heard the characteristic tones of Carlos's and Mbeki's devices. All three instinctively reached for their phones.

A text message from Dylan Mercer appeared on Lukas's display: "Watch Pulse Global News immediately. Everything is out. Link: PGN.com/breaking-alien-pyramids"

A cold shiver ran down his spine. With trembling fingers, he opened the link, while Carlos and Mbeki did the same beside him.

The PGN logo filled the screen, followed by the red "BREAKING NEWS" headline: "ALIEN OBJECTS APPROACHING EARTH—GOVERNMENTS CONFIRM EXISTENCE!"

A serious-looking blonde news anchor stared into the camera: "Good morning, I'm Alice Shannon with an unprecedented story that could shake the world. We're receiving confirmed reports that three massive, pyramid-shaped objects of extraterrestrial origin are currently on a direct course toward Earth. These objects, which according to our informants have exactly the same proportions as the pyramids of Giza, were discovered weeks ago by international gravitational wave detectors, but the information has been kept secret until today."

The image changed to a computer-generated representation of the three black pyramids in space.

"According to leaked documents from the international 'Project Black Delta,' the objects will reach Earth in about eight months. However, certain physical effects could have catastrophic consequences weeks before their arrival."

"My God," whispered Carlos. "Who the hell leaked this?"

Lukas scrolled through more news apps. It was the same everywhere: BBC, Sky News, Al Jazeera, Deutsche Welle—all the major news outlets were reporting on the pyramids. His hands trembled slightly as he switched from one article to the next.

"This is going to be chaos," muttered Mbeki, shaking his head.

A livestream from the White House appeared on his screen, where an emergency press conference was taking place. President Morales stepped up to the lectern, flanked by representatives from NASA, the Pentagon, and various scientific institutions.

"My fellow Americans and citizens of the world," the president began in a serious voice, "I am here to speak to you today about a situation of unprecedented magnitude. It is true that three unknown objects are approaching our planet. These objects exhibit characteristics that indicate they are not of natural origin."

He paused, his hands clasped around the lectern.

"I want to emphasize that these objects do not currently pose an immediate threat. An international team of the world's best scientists is working around the clock to understand their nature and establish communication. We have no reason to panic."

Lukas snorted softly. "No reason to panic?" he said in disbelief. "Let's see if the world believes him."

As if his words had been prophetic, social media began to explode. Lukas scrolled through X, Instagram, and Facebook while the president continued to speak.

"#Alieninvasion" was already trending worldwide. Videos of people flocking to supermarkets flooded the feeds—and not even 15 minutes had passed. A clip from New York showed crowds forming in front of banks to withdraw cash.

A tweet from a user named @SurvivalPrepperXX read: "I TOLD YOU SO!!! The pyramids were always landing pads! Buy weapons and canned food, NOW!!!"

Another, from @CosmicPeace3000: "This is the moment humanity has been waiting for. First contact = evolution of consciousness. We will ascend to the stars! #WelcomeHome"

Religious reactions were not long in coming either. The Vatican announced an extraordinary address by the Pope. Evangelical preachers in the US declared the pyramids to be either messengers of God or harbingers of the apocalypse.

A video from Cairo showed thousands of people pouring into the streets. Some knelt down and prayed, others held up signs reading "Welcome Back, Ancient Ones" and "The Pharaohs Return."

"Look at this," said Carlos, holding up his cell phone. The screen showed a live stream from Tokyo, where people were flocking to subway stations as if an air raid were imminent.

Meanwhile, financial news reported a dramatic slump in global markets. The Dow Jones had fallen by over 20 percent, the Nikkei by 25. Trading was suspended. Cryptocurrencies skyrocketed, while gold and other precious metals also exploded.

A Sky reporter from London looked grim: "Spontaneous crowds have gathered here at Piccadilly Circus. Reactions range from panic to a kind of messianic euphoria. The British government has canceled all non-essential flights and declared a state of emergency."

"Dr. Heuer?" A woman in uniform approached them. "I'm Captain Mueller. Our flight is ready, but . . ." She hesitated and glanced at her own cell phone. "We've just received instructions to postpone all non-essential flights. The airspace over several major European cities is closed."

Lukas exchanged a concerned glance with his companions. "How long will this last?"

"No one can say for sure. But I have special permits for scientific missions. We can fly, but we have to take a detour over the Atlantic. That will add about two hours to the flight time."

"Then we'd better take off right away," said Lukas without hesitation.

As they walked to the plane, Carlos's cell phone rang. He answered and spoke excitedly in Spanish. After a few minutes, he ended the call.

"That was my sister from Santiago," he explained. "The Chilean government has placed the observatory under military protection. No one can get in or out without special permission. They're afraid of sabotage or protesters."

On the plane—a modern ESA Gulfstream G650—Lukas tried to relax, but his cell phone wouldn't leave him alone. The messages were coming in by the minute.

Reports of mass meditations were coming in from India. Hundreds of thousands of people were gathering at sacred sites to pray for peaceful contact. A Hindu guru declared in a viral video: "The vimanas are returning! The ancient scriptures predicted it!"

In Russia, President Petrov allegedly put the strategic nuclear forces on high alert. Similar reports came from China and the US, but no one could tell what was written out of sensationalism and what was really true. Lukas doubted these stories were, simply because the governments of the world had been desperately working shoulder to shoulder now for some time behind the scenes.

Particularly disturbing were the reports from the Middle East. Various extremist groups interpreted the arrival of the pyramids as a sign of the beginning of a Holy War. In Syria and Iraq, spontaneous fighting broke out between different factions that had previously lived in a fragile peace.

"This is a nightmare," muttered Lukas as he scrolled through the news. "Humanity will tear itself apart long before the pyramids even get here."

"It's chaos now," said Professor Mbeki, "but I suspect it's much worse because of the initial shock. Once that wears off, I'm hopeful that things will settle down, at least a little. I find the reaction in Africa quite interesting. Look here." He showed his tablet. "In Mali, the Dogon tribes are gathering. They claim their ancestors told them about the return of the 'Nommo'—amphibious beings from Sirius who brought knowledge to humanity."

"You mean different ancient cultures have similar traditions?"

"Not just similar—astonishingly specific. The Maya spoke of Kukulkan, who came from the sky. The Sumerians spoke of the Anunnaki. The Aborigines in Australia have the Wandjina—sky beings who brought them laws and knowledge."

"Every culture had its gods," noted Carlos, looking out of the window at the Mediterranean far below. "And they always came from the sky. The ancient Greeks and Romans were no different. You do have to wonder about what motivated these so-called gods. Are they Jane Goodall, studying apes? Are they teaching apes sign language just to see if they can? Are they molding us for greatness? Or are they just entertaining themselves?"

These same questions were being asked around the world by hundreds of millions of people. In the following hours, theories piled up on their cell phones—everything from invasion, to rescue, to cosmic tests for humanity.

An online article in the *Wall Street Journal* quoted several scientists: "The fact that these objects have the shape of the pyramids of Giza can't be a coincidence. It points to a deeper connection between human civilization and extraterrestrial intelligence than we previously assumed."

Another article from *Nature* speculated: "If these objects have been here before, as ancient texts suggest, and human civilization has survived, their return could be a periodic event—a kind of cosmic inspection or contact."

Lukas found this theory reassuring until he read on: "However, circumstances may have changed since the last visit. Human technology has developed exponentially. We may be judged differently this time."

A shiver ran down his spine. What if humanity failed the test?

His cell phone buzzed again as they were already over North Africa, the light brown plains stretching out below them. A Pulse Global News alert: "MASS PANIC IN SEVERAL MAJOR CITIES—LOOTING AND VIOLENCE ON THE RISE."

The accompanying video showed burning cars in Los Angeles, broken shop windows in London, and crowds of people streaming through the streets of Mumbai.

"Civilization is collapsing before our eyes," he muttered. "How are we supposed to find a solution?"

"Perhaps," said Mbeki thoughtfully, "that is precisely the test. Not our technology or our weapons, but how our species responds to the unknown."

An hour later, as they flew over the Nile Delta, Lukas's cell phone rang again. This time it was an unknown American number with an area code that probably indicated rerouting via the Internet.

"Dr. Heuer? This is Director Patterson from NASA. I'm calling you on the direct orders of President Morales."

Lukas felt his stomach tighten. "What can I do for you, Director?"

"The situation has changed dramatically since the information became public. The global public is demanding answers and action. The heads of state and government have agreed on a new plan."

"What plan?" Lukas's uneasy feeling intensified.

"A manned mission. We're sending a spacecraft to the objects to establish direct contact before they reach Earth. This should reassure the public and give us back the initiative."

"A manned mission? That's extremely risky. And very short notice, isn't it?"

"Less risky than waiting and watching civilization collapse in panic," replied Patterson dryly. "The mission will launch within the next six weeks and give them new hope and something to focus on."

Lukas sighed. Psychological manipulation. Something governments had been using more and more frequently to control populations. A placebo effect. Pretend to be proactive. Pretend to be confident and have solutions and hope like hell that would placate the masses.

"Will the mission be armed?" asked Lukas.

A short pause. "Of course. Better to have arms and not need them, than to need arms and not have them."

Lukas closed his eyes. "I see."

"You're being ordered to Houston to head the scientific advisory board. And we need your friend Carlos here also. Your flight has already been booked. You'll fly back from Cairo tomorrow morning."

"But I'm on my way to Giza to examine the newly discovered chamber. It could contain crucial information."

"Dr. Heuer, with all due respect, the time for archaeological expeditions is over. We need you for a mission that could determine the fate of humanity. The president says this is non-negotiable. You and Carlos are the faces of this discovery. The poster boys, so everyone can see that the discoverers of these objects support the project."

The line went dead.

Lukas stared at his cell phone, overcome by a feeling of powerlessness. Through the small airplane window, he saw the first outlines of Cairo emerging in the twilight. Somewhere down there, in a millennia-old pyramid, answers could be hidden that could change everything.

Instead, he'd be inside the arrow they were shooting at the tank. Not an ideal place to be.

Carlos had overheard the entire exchange. "When they were preparing you to study pyramids in Physics 101," he said to his friend, "did they have a section on useless space missions?"

Lukas sighed. "I assume you know the old adage: there are only two things one can be certain of—death and taxes."

Carlos nodded.

"Well, adding a third is long overdue. There are three things one can be certain of: death, taxes, and governmental posturing."

He looked out the window once more at the lights of Cairo. Somewhere down there, the pyramids of Giza waited—silent witnesses to a past that had suddenly become the future.

But would humanity squander its chances to solve this puzzle by focusing on show rather than substance? If so, it wouldn't be the first time.

But in this case, it would certainly be the last.

22

A pitying expression flitted across Jason's face as Mira moved around the stone table. Her fingers gently stroked the cold surface, as if she could sense the secrets of millennia through mere touch. The Tibetan snow lion, carved into the limestone, seemed to watch her with its timeless eyes—silent, judging, waiting.

"Dr. Najafi," said Jason softly, his tone like a gentle cloth carefully spread over the mind of a madwoman. "Perhaps you should . . . You know, fatigue and stress can lead to misinterpretations."

Mira didn't look up. "I'm not overworked, Jason. And I'm not hallucinating."

Inwardly, she repeated the meditation Lama Tenzin had taught her. Thoughts are just clouds passing through the sky of your consciousness. They come and go. They are not personal. The doubts, the fear, the uncertainty—all just passing clouds that had no power over her unless she allowed them to.

The stone table remained silent. Its surface was smooth, except for the snow lion, no carvings, no hieroglyphs, no hidden mechanism. Mira circled it for the third time, bent down low, examined the edges from every conceivable angle.

"Dr. Najafi, please." Jason stepped closer, his voice now more urgent. "You've already lost your job because of this . . . this fixation. Professor Markowitz was furious."

"Markowitz doesn't understand anything," she muttered as she knelt down to inspect the table legs. "He only sees what he expects to see, and he judges too quickly."

Jason sighed, a sound like the distant rumbling of a collapsing sand dune. "You were a brilliant scientist. One of the sharpest minds in our field. Why are you clinging to . . . to what, anyway? A vision? A dream?"

Mira paused, her hands resting on the cool limestone floor. She had to consider the possibility that he was right. Was all this just a daughter's desperate search for her father's legacy? A self-delusion fueled by grief and loss?

"What did the sensors show?" she asked abruptly.

Jason blinked in surprise. "What?"

"The sensors." She pointed to the measuring devices that filled the room. "Markowitz and Abdul mentioned unusual energy signatures."

"Oh." He seemed uncertain for a moment. "I'm not sure I'm allowed to talk about that."

"Jason, please." Her voice sounded pleading, even to her own ears. "What did you find?"

He hesitated, glancing nervously toward the tunnel entrance. "Weak magnetic anomalies."

"When did these measurements begin?"

"About two weeks ago." He seemed relieved to be talking about something concrete. "Professor Markowitz has brought in specialists. The ESA is involved."

"That could mean there are metallic alloys in the walls." Mira slowly got up, brushing dust off her knees.

"Dr. Najafi, I'm sorry, but I have to ask you to leave now." Jason gently took her arm. "Be reasonable. Whatever you hope to find, it's not here."

His touch was like an anchor pulling her back to reality. The despair in his eyes mirrored her own—the only difference was what they were despairing about. He feared for her sanity; she feared that she might fail, that she might not make the connection between this place and her father before it was too late.

"One last try, Jason." She pulled her arm away from him. "Just one last look."

He hesitated, then nodded resignedly. "Two minutes, no more. Then I'll call the others."

Jason turned away, reaching for his radio. At that moment, a thought shot through Mira's mind, bright and clear as the morning star on the eastern horizon.

"Grave robbers!" she suddenly exclaimed.

"What?" Jason turned around, confused.

"Grave robbers." Mira now spoke more quickly, excitement vibrating in her voice. "They used cheap materials—clay, lime plaster—to cover their tracks. I explained it to my students a few weeks ago. You were there."

"Yes, but . . ."

"My father knew that too, of course." Her eyes shone with new determination. Before Jason could react, she reached for his tool belt and pulled out a small archaeological chisel.

"What are you doing?!" He lunged forward, but it was too late.

Mira had already placed the chisel on the underside of the stone table and struck. The material crumbled surprisingly easily—not the hard limestone of the original table, but an elaborate replica made of lime plaster and clay.

"Stop!" Jason tried to wrest the chisel from her, but Mira worked with feverish precision.

"Look!" She pointed to the crumbling pieces under the table. "This isn't original. It was added! Replicated!"

Jason froze as the false bottom gave way and a small compartment appeared—a cavity carefully carved into the stone table and sealed with clay. Inside lay a notebook, its leather cover bearing the characteristic signs of wear that Mira recognized immediately.

"I'm so stupid," she whispered as she carefully pulled out the book. "My father must have thought I would discover this right away."

Jason stared at her find in bewilderment, seeming to have suddenly forgotten the radio in his hand.

With trembling hands, she opened the notebook. Her father's familiar, precise handwriting filled the pages—a final message, a legacy that had been waiting for her. Jason stood motionless, his face a mixture of shock and reluctant fascination.

"He hopes that someone wise will find the notes, hence the disguise," Mira read aloud, her voice little more than a whisper. "Preferably his daughter, if she were to follow in his footsteps, but that's just his hope. I would certainly make a good archaeologist."

Jason remained silent while Mira continued reading, her eyes flying over the densely written pages, and she actually managed not to cry. It was as if her father were speaking to her. Like a time capsule.

"He writes about an ancient papyrus—the Book of Thoth-Hermes, only fragments of which have survived and which experts dismiss as a mythological construct."

Her voice grew stronger as she read. "It tells of the 'star barges of the gods' that return to Earth every 4,500 years. The priests called them the 'black fires in the sky' because they swallowed all light like flames swallow wood."

Jason stepped closer, his scientific interest clearly piqued.

"Four thousand five hundred years?"

Mira nodded, her fingers gliding reverently over the pages. "He writes that the last documented visit took place during the reign of Pharaoh Djedefre—around 2,500 BC."

"So if they return every 4,500 years," said Jason. "They'd be due back . . . " Jason did the simple math in an instant, and his eyes widened.

"*Now*," confirmed Mira. "They'd be due back now. At least approximately."

She thought back to Lefèvre's cryptic words and her questions about the pyramids. "Oh my God! They know!"

"Who knows?" asked Jason. "And what exactly?"

But she barely heard him. She continued leafing through the pages, her fingertips dancing over her father's words as if they were relics from another time.

"The high priests possessed a technique," she read aloud, "in which they communicated mentally with the gods who came from outer space in pyramids. It required them to remain in a realm between life and death. They have to be talking about tukdam."

"Tuk what?"

"Tuk *dam*. Practiced by Tibetan monks to this day. They're able to remain between life and death for weeks."

Jason frowned. "Between life and death? What the hell does that even mean?"

"Some monks can remain in a meditative state for days or even weeks after clinical death. The body shows no signs of decay, and consciousness lingers in an intermediate sphere. I've seen it myself, and tukdam has also been scientifically studied and proven."

"Impossible. If that were true, it would be one of the biggest global news stories ever."

"You'd think so, wouldn't you? But apparently not."

She continued leafing through the pages, her eyes widening at the next few lines.

"If I'm right and the cycle soon reaches its next point," she read, *"humanity must be prepared to relearn what it has forgotten about the spiritual world since the ancient, advanced civilizations existed. Fortunately, there are neuroscientists who are seriously exploring the potential of the human mind. But I think the Far East is generations ahead of them in this regard . . ."*

Jason shook his head in disbelief. "It's a lot to digest. Archaeologists are always going off about wild theories, Mira, you know that."

"Not this time," she said. "Look at the black pyramids on the wall, Jason. Which just happen to be repeated twice. Consider the magnetic traces in this chamber. Consider the three pyramids from space racing toward Earth at this very moment. Given all that, you'd be a fool not to believe it."

She closed the notebook and held it out to Jason. "Here, read it for yourself. My father was a brilliant archaeologist, you know that as well as I do. He wasn't crazy."

Jason hesitantly took the book as Mira walked to the back of the chamber, where the murals shimmered in the pale light of the work lamps. The seven priests—six of them lying lifeless in a row, one standing, connected by a beam to the black pyramids in the sky, speaking to the pharaoh at the same time.

A golden diagram of the universe above it all, concentric circles inscribed with hieroglyphics. The Sun at the center, the planets in their orbits, beyond them the stars. And at the very edge—three triangular symbols, so black that they stood out even against the already dark background.

"Tukdam," Mira whispered reverently. "The ancient Egyptians must have known about it?"

She pointed to the six priests lying in the mural. "This depiction—I always thought they were dead. But what if they *weren't*? What if they were in that intermediate state I just described? In such deep meditation that their consciousness lingered even after physical death."

Mira stepped closer to the wall. "Look at the seventh priest—he's standing, but the beam connects him to the pyramids and the pharaoh at the same time. What if he served as a kind of mediator? A translator between worlds?"

Jason was now standing next to her, his initial skepticism giving way to a reluctant fascination.

"And you believe your father discovered this connection? Between Tibetan meditation practices and ancient Egyptian rituals?"

"Not only that." Mira turned to him, her eyes shining in the dim light. "He believed that we had to communicate with them again. The black pyramids are returning, Jason. Just as it was predicted, after more than four millennia. My father deciphered the cycles and timelines. That must be it."

She looked back at the mural, at the three dark triangles in the cosmic firmament. "The Egyptians didn't just have contact with the pyramids in space—they left instructions for future generations on how to do so again. When the time came."

"Instructions?" Jason's voice wavered between skepticism and astonishment.

"Yes. Contact with what they interpreted to be gods." Mira pointed to the complex painting, her hand hovering over the symbols like a conductor over a cosmic orchestra. "These are instructions. That's why it's an identical copy. It has to happen again, just like it did back then. Of course, the pharaohs must have believed that they would last forever, just like their empire."

Jason hesitated, then leafed through the notebook. His eyes widened when he came across a certain passage. "He writes here about meditation as a form of communication. About consciousness transformation as the key to understanding."

"How else could the Egyptians of that time make contact?" said Mira. "They didn't have satellites or radio towers. These symbols here—they mean 'Gate of Heaven' and 'Voice Without Sound'. The ancient Egyptians believed that communication with the gods could not be achieved through language, but by other means. That must be it."

She paused. "In Tibet, while meditating alongside my father, I had a vision. This room, this table, turned upside down. It was no coincidence. It was a message. I was supposed to look under the table."

"Dr. Najafi . . ." Jason now sounded uncertain, his scientific mindset in conflict with the writings of a famous scientist. His inner conflict was easy to sense. "Assuming all this is true, what does it mean for us? Should we share this with the world? Have everyone take a crash course on meditation?"

She considered for several long seconds. "No. They depicted priests. A limited number. Not even the pharaoh was included. So maybe this isn't meant to be a mass communion. At least not yet. But we should definitely share this with the European Space Agency. I have a contact there. A woman named Ricarda Lefèvre."

"Yes." Mira reached for the notebook, her determination solidifying like concrete under the hot Egyptian sun. "The ESA. That's what I'll do. Even if I have to fly to Brussels and wait outside the entrance until she shows up."

A sudden noise from the tunnel made them both jump. Voices were approaching—Abdul and the rest of the team were returning.

"Quick." Jason grabbed Mira's arm. "There's a second exit, a maintenance tunnel."

"At the junction?" she whispered. "That dead ends."

"No. The geologists unblocked it." He led her to the exit of the chamber. "It leads outside, to the western slope."

"The geologists uncovered it." He led her to the exit of the chamber. "It leads outside, to the western slope. Take the notebook with you."

Mira hesitated. "Why are you helping me?"

A brief, resigned smile flitted across his face. "Because I've been working in this room for two weeks, and . . . I really liked you."

He shook his head as if he couldn't believe what he was saying. "You were a good professor. But I'm going to have to report what happened here. The scratched underside of the table and the compartment will raise questions."

The voices were getting closer. Mira clutched the notebook.

"Thank you, Jason."

"Go to the ESA." He gently pushed her toward the tunnel. "Find Lefèvre. And . . . good luck."

Mira disappeared into the darkness of the tunnel, her father's legacy clutched tightly in her hands. Behind her, she heard the voices of Markowitz and Abdul entering the room after she had crawled around the bend. She also heard Jason, but couldn't make out what he was saying.

Her father had indeed had a plan and had seen something he believed in so strongly that he had sacrificed the rest of his life for it. He had shown her the way, and she would not let his sacrifice be in vain. She would carry the flame forward and use his insights—no matter what.

The cool night air greeted her as she crawled out of the hidden exit. Above her stretched the desert sky, a velvety black embroidered with countless stars—and somewhere out there, still invisible to the naked eye and unbeknownst to Mira, three pyramid-shaped objects were approaching Earth.

With her father's notebook pressed to her chest, she set off into the night, driven by a vision older than the pyramids themselves—and yet never more relevant than in this cosmic moment.

23

The sirens of the police escort cut through the hot Cairo air like blades of lava as their convoy made its way through the congested streets to the Giza Necropolis. Lukas sat in the back seat of the armored vehicle between Carlos and Professor Mbeki, his gaze shifting between the chaos outside and his cell phone, which was constantly receiving new messages about the global reaction to the pyramid revelation. It was more of the same, with the difference that China was completely suppressing the news, and it was virtually non-existent there, while in the West, a large part of the population apparently didn't want to know about it and dismissed it as "government propaganda" designed to distract from economic problems. The more creative minds even considered it all to be AI fake news.

"Tell me again that this was a good idea," muttered Carlos, wiping the sweat from his forehead. "You don't usually turn down the President of the United States, Lukas. Especially not when he needs you for a mission that could decide the fate of humanity."

Lukas looked up from his phone, which was showing a livestream from New York—burning cars, looting, people marching through the streets with signs protesting the government, liars, and alien conspirators.

"We're not turning him down," he replied. "We're taking a detour. If there are answers hidden in the pyramid that could help us prevent this catastrophe, then a few hours' delay is worth the risk."

"Well, we're committed now," said Carlos fatalistically. "So I guess we're about to find out."

Professor Mbeki, who had hardly said a word since they landed, looked out at the street through the small bulletproof window.

"The question is not whether it's worth it," he said thoughtfully. "The question is whether we still have a choice."

As they approached the Giza Plateau, the magnitude of the situation became clear. What Lukas had seen on the news on his cell phone was nothing compared to what was happening here. The normally wide Pyramid Street was clogged with a sea of people—tens of thousands, all streaming in the same direction, their arms raised to the sky, chanting slogans, waving banners.

"My God," whispered Carlos.

The Egyptian military had assembled massive forces. Tanks blocked the main access roads to the plateau, soldiers in full gear formed human chains, and military helicopters circled overhead with their rotors roaring. Announcements in Arabic echoed from loudspeakers, mingling with the roar of the crowd to form an apocalyptic crescendo.

"What are they saying?" Lukas asked their driver.

"They're telling people to disperse and go home. That the area is closed for security reasons." The policeman shook his head. "But these people won't leave. For them, the pyramids aren't just tourist attractions—they're a connection to their ancestors. They probably believe as much as you do that the answers to their questions can be found here."

Lukas couldn't blame them.

Their convoy turned into a side street that was being kept clear by soldiers. Lukas could see the faces of the people through the window—a mixture of awe, despair, and wild hope. Many held up homemade signs with inscriptions in Arabic that he couldn't decipher.

A young man in torn clothes hammered on the window of their vehicle and shouted something in Arabic. His eyes were wide open, his face covered in sweat.

"He says he wants to see the chamber," the driver translated. "The secrets of the ancestors are there for everyone."

Lukas felt a strange sense of connection to this unknown man. Weren't they all looking for the same answers? For an understanding of what was happening to their world?

Their small convoy of emergency vehicles finally reached the outer security perimeter of the Giza Plateau. Here, the military presence was even more intense—checkpoints, barbed wire, heavily armed soldiers. At least a dozen helicopters circled in the sky.

"It looks like a war zone," muttered Lukas as they were guided through the security checks on foot.

"In a way, it is," replied a familiar voice.

Ricarda Lefèvre from ESA was waiting for them at the main checkpoint, accompanied by an elegant middle-aged man in an expensive suit.

"Dr. Heuer, Dr. Mendoza, Professor Mbeki," she greeted them, while the cries of the crowd continued to echo in the background. "May I introduce Deputy Prime Minister Rashid, the representative of the Egyptian government."

The Egyptian official bowed slightly and shook their hands one after the other.

"Welcome to Giza, gentlemen. I wish the circumstances were a little simpler." His English was perfect, but Lukas could hear the tension in his voice. "We are pleased by your spontaneous visit."

"Thank you very much." Lukas looked up at the mighty ancient structures, which glistened in the sun as if in an oven. Their sheer presence was overwhelming.

"The situation is extraordinary," continued Rashid as they were guided to the Pyramid of Cheops. "Since the news about the objects you discovered was released, we've counted over 200,000 people trying to reach the plateau. Not just from Egypt—from all over the world. We have flights from New York, Tokyo, Mumbai. They all want to go to the pyramid; they all believe that the answers can be found here."

Lukas nodded. The power of the collective human psyche when confronted with the unknown was frightening and reminded him of lemmings.

They approached the entrance to the Great Pyramid, which was supported by steel beams. A ring of soldiers surrounded it, their rifles at the ready, eyeing them sternly, but they stood to attention when they recognized Rashid. The roar of the crowd at the outer fence could be heard here as a continuous background noise, interspersed with the rhythmic drone of helicopters.

As they passed the last checkpoint, Lukas noticed a disturbance. About 20 yards away, two soldiers were struggling with a wriggling figure—a small, dark-skinned woman who was fighting violently against her arrest.

"Lefèvre!" she shouted over the noise. "Ricarda Lefèvre! I have the answers! Listen to me!" The woman kicked and writhed as the soldiers dragged her away. Her voice was hoarse with despair: "The chamber! Under the table! I found the answers!"

"Who's that?" asked Mbeki, pointing to the scene.

Lefèvre didn't look in that direction and shrugged. "Just one of countless lunatics. In the last few hours, dozens of . . . well . . . lunatics, have been arrested for illegally entering the premises at night. Everyone thinks they have the solution, everyone wants to see the chamber and then thinks they know everything."

Lukas watched as the woman was led away, her protests fading into the distance. Something about her desperation, the way she had called out to Lefèvre, made him doubt. How many of these lunatics knew the name Ricarda Lefèvre and could recognize her from a distance?

But it was too late to follow up—they had already arrived at the entrance to the pyramid.

The contrast was dramatic. Outside: chaos, noise, an angry crowd. Inside: the millennia-old silence of the stone tomb, interrupted only by the muffled hum of the temporary lighting.

They followed a narrow descending passageway that led to the heart of the pyramid. The walls around them were built of perfectly cut limestone blocks, each weighing several tons and fitted together with a precision that would impress even modern engineers.

"The Star Chamber is about 30 meters below the King's Chamber," explained Lefèvre as she turned on a flashlight. "It was only recently discovered by a team led by Professor Markowitz and archaeologist Mira Najafi."

"How?" asked Carlos. "This pyramid has been explored for centuries."

"The entrance was hidden. Since 2023, there have been new discoveries thanks to new technological approaches, but Professor Mbeki can certainly explain that much better."

"Where is Najafi now?" asked Mbeki, instead of offering an explanation.

Lefèvre hesitated. "Gone. She turned her back on her discovery and went to Tibet."

Mbeki raised his eyebrows in surprise but said nothing.

They reached a small opening in the wall, barely wide enough for one person. Modern LED lights had been installed to illuminate the tunnel behind it. The ESA communications chief crawled on all fours, and Lukas, who was uncomfortable in confined spaces, soon began to sweat. The air smelled slightly of dust but was dry.

"Here it is," said Lefèvre at some point as they finally squeezed through another gap and entered an open area. "The Star Chamber."

Lukas straightened up, his joints cracking. The room was rectangular, perhaps 8 meters long and 5 wide, but the ceiling was unusually high, almost 3 meters, which immediately caught his attention. That alone would have been enough to make him pause for a moment. But it was the walls that completely threw him off balance.

Every surface, every niche, every single centimeter was covered with hieroglyphs and colorful depictions. Not just faint or weathered—no, they were preserved in a way he, as a layman, had never seen before. The colors looked fresh. No comparison to the King's Chamber or other famous tombs he had seen in documentaries. Something about this environment—the temperature, the humidity, perhaps even the isolated location deep inside the pyramid—had preserved this room perfectly.

Lukas slowly turned in a circle, trying not to stumble as his gaze slid along the walls. His eyes lingered on the north wall. Against a blue background—he assumed it was meant to represent early dawn—three pyramids were depicted. Their arrangement was unmistakable: the classic formation of Giza, with the third slightly offset. But their color confused him. They were not yellowish or ochre as usual, but deep black, just like the ones they had discovered at the South Observatory and visualized for the first time. Not a shiny black—more like a void that swallowed light.

Next to the pyramids was a crescent Moon, silvery and clear. Lukas frowned. A Moon motif? To his knowledge, Egyptian iconography was always dominated by the sun and its rays.

Below them sat seven figures in a meditative pose. Priests, he guessed. The typical side view, hands raised, eyes closed. Six of them were painted in pale, almost transparent colors—he vaguely remembered that this stood for the deceased. But the seventh was different. Strong colors, almost glowing. And a ray of light emanated from his chest, pointing directly upward—toward the black pyramids.

"Unbelievable," he whispered.

Carlos and Mbeki followed him into the chamber. Carlos seemed just as impressed as he was, but for Mbeki, this was clearly not his first visit.

"That's not all," said Lefèvre. "Look at the east wall."

Lukas turned around. The east wall showed exactly the same image—the same night sky, the same stars, the same three black pyramids, identical in every detail, as far as he could tell.

"Why twice?" he asked, his gaze shifting back and forth between the two walls. "Why did they paint the same image twice?"

Professor Mbeki stepped closer to the walls, his glasses glinting in the LED light. "It's a mystery," he explained. "In all of Egyptian art, I have never seen a picture duplicated in the same chamber—or anywhere else. The Egyptians were masters of symbolism—every element in their wall paintings had a specific meaning, a specific purpose."

"Could it represent the past and the future?" asked Carlos. "A coming and going?"

"Possibly," replied Mbeki, but he didn't sound convinced. "Or . . ." He fell silent, his eyes widening slightly.

"Or what?" pressed Lukas.

"Or it shows a cycle. A return. The first image could represent the first visit, the second the second—the current one, as I already wanted to explain at the crisis meeting."

A shiver ran down Lukas's spine. "If the ancient Egyptians had known that the pyramids would return. And had predicted the timing of their return. Then they must have also known what happened during the first encounter."

"And perhaps what will happen during the second," said Carlos.

"Perhaps," said the professor. "Unfortunately, it will be difficult to find out."

Lukas moved closer to the walls and searched for further details. Tiny hieroglyphs were carved between the stars, so small that they were barely visible to the naked eye.

"Those are numbers," explained Mbeki. "Time references. They differ between the first image and the second. But so far, we haven't been able to make sense of them. Egyptian timekeeping was very complex. They knew about years and seasons and the movement of the Earth around the Sun, but their cosmological knowledge was mixed with their mythology and beliefs in their timekeeping. That's what makes it so difficult to translate into our calendar."

The silence in the chamber was absolute. Lukas could hear only his own heartbeat and the muffled roar of the crowd far above them.

"They knew," whispered Carlos. "The ancient Egyptians knew when the pyramids would return. I didn't want to believe it, but they must have known. This can't be a coincidence."

"At least it seems as if the objects have been here before," said Mbeki, somewhat more cautiously.

"But why?" asked Carlos. "What is the *purpose*? What happened the first time, and what will happen this time?"

"Whatever happened the first time, they lived to tell the tale," said Lukas. "Well, sort of. This art isn't exactly a detailed video file. But the world survived. The Earth was still spinning on its axis after they left. In my view, that's the most encouraging thought I've had in a very long time."

"Amen to that," said Carlos.

Lukas paused. "I need to make a call," he said. "I'll just step outside for a moment to get reception. Carlos, can you take some photos?"

"Don't worry," said Lefèvre. "I have enough high-resolution photos to drown you in."

"Great," he said, and then began to make his way back outside. When he reached the entrance, the shrill ringing of his phone pierced the silence. The sound was almost obscene in the mystical atmosphere of the pyramid.

"Excuse me," he muttered to the soldiers and reached for his phone. The display showed an American number from Washington, D.C.

"Dr. Heuer, this is Director Patterson. Where the hell are you?"

Lukas cleared his throat. "We're, uh, stuck in traffic, sir. The situation here in Cairo is chaotic. We're on our way to the airport."

"Stuck in traffic?" Patterson's voice became sharper. "Dr. Heuer, the Air Force plane has been waiting for you for *three hours*. The authorities are breathing down my neck, and soon the president will be too! We have a mission to plan that could decide the fate of humanity, and I won't accept any more lame excuses. You're stalling."

"Sir, I understand the urgency, but—"

"No 'buts,' Doc! You have exactly one hour to be on that plane, or I will personally make sure you never see the inside of a government-funded lab again. Is that clear?"

"Yeah, threats aren't all that effective when the end of the world is around the corner," said Lukas. "But I'll be there."

The line went dead.

Lukas stared at his cell phone while Carlos and Mbeki, who had caught up with him, looked at him expectantly.

"We have to go," he said finally. "Right now."

It was good to have seen the chamber with his own eyes, but time was up.

Outside, chaos awaited—the screaming crowd, the circling helicopters, the armed soldiers. A little way off stood the Deputy Prime Minister with a staff of officers. Lukas headed toward him.

"Deputy Prime Minister?" he called over the noise, pointing upward. "Could we borrow one of your helicopters?"

24

The rough grip around Mira's upper arms was relentless, as if she were being held by clamps. Two Egyptian soldiers led her down the steep steps of the pyramid, their heavy boots echoing like hammer blows on the millennia-old stone. She had hidden her father's notebook deep inside her jacket, where it now pressed against her ribs like a second, throbbing heart—the only proof of the truth she had discovered.

She had hidden in the dark corridors of the pyramid for hours. She had crawled through narrow tunnels, pressed herself into the darkness at the right moments, becoming another nothingness among the shadows of millennia. But in the end, they had found her—with search dogs that had tracked her through the labyrinth of stone.

When they stepped into the glaring daylight, the sight hit her like a slap in the face of pure madness. Now she knew why so many soldiers had searched the pyramid.

The sun was already high on the eastern horizon, a merciless fireball bathing the chaos on the Giza Plateau in a surreal, blinding light. Tens of thousands of people as far as the eye could see—a crowd pressing against the barriers like a raging storm surge against a crumbling dike.

The crowd was a seething sea of colors and voices: men in white robes chanting Arabic prayers, women in headscarves clutching their children and singing rolling melodies, European tourists or journalists with cameras desperately trying to document the incomprehensible events unfolding before them.

Thousands of soldiers formed a living, armored fence between the crowd and the pyramids. They looked like beetles trying to hold back an army of ants. Here and there, the metal of armored vehicles flashed between the uniforms.

Dozens of helicopters thundered through the air like mechanical vultures—military helicopters, news helicopters, police helicopters. Their rotor blades whipped up swirls of sand that swept across the plateau, filling the air with a fine, suffocating dust. The roar mingled with the general noise to create a soundscape that was difficult to bear.

To the west, a police escort approached with sirens wailing and blue lights flashing. The vehicles—black limousines with tinted windows, armored transporters, motorcycle officers—held a perfect military formation. Mira recognized the small flags on the antennas: diplomatic missions, government officials, maybe even foreign military personnel.

She fought against the soldiers who relentlessly dragged her down the steps. Her feet kept slipping on the stone, smoothed by millions of visitors, but the two men simply dragged her on.

"I need to speak to the government!" she shouted in English, her voice almost breaking.

Then she tried her rudimentary Arabic: "Ana mehtagah atakallam ma'a al-hukumah!"

The soldiers didn't respond. Their faces were as expressionless as stone masks, their eyes hidden behind dark sunglasses that reflected the chaos around them in miniature. Either they didn't understand her, or they were completely indifferent.

"Important information!" she shouted desperately, her voice almost breaking. "Malumat muhimmah! Ana a'rif!"

One of the soldiers said something in Arabic to his colleague, a short, sharp word that sounded like a curse. The other laughed—a cold, contemptuous sound. They dragged her farther down the steps, their boots scraping on the stone like fingernails on a slate.

In the distance, near the parked government vehicles, Mira recognized a familiar figure. Ricarda Lefèvre stood in the middle of a group of four men in dark suits—two Europeans, a tall African, and an Egyptian official in a pinstriped suit.

"Lefèvre!" she shouted over the deafening noise, her voice breaking with the effort. "Ricarda Lefèvre!"

The ESA employee was only about 20 yards away, but she might as well have been on another planet. Lefèvre was engrossed in a serious conversation, her posture tense, her gestures hasty and urgent. The men around her glanced alternately at the pyramids and the sky, as if expecting an answer from the cosmos at any moment.

"I have the answers!" Mira shouted with a force born of pure desperation. "Listen to me!"

Mira kicked and writhed in the soldiers' iron grip, her feet searching in vain for purchase on the smooth stones. Every muscle in her body tensed against her bonds, but it was futile. The grip did not loosen. Despair spread through her like poison, cold and paralyzing, as the ESA employee didn't even turn to her. She was so close! But then—one of Lefèvre's companions looked in Mira's direction!

"The chamber!" she shouted with her last ounce of strength, her voice now nothing more than a hoarse croak. "Under the table! I found the answers! I know how to communicate!"

Her words were drowned out by the roar of a helicopter flying low overhead, enveloping her in a hurricane of sand and dust.

When she could see again, Lefèvre and her group were gone.

Tears of frustration burned in her eyes as the soldiers dragged her to one of the waiting police cars. It was a white limousine with blue stripes and Arabic characters on the sides, the windows barred like a mobile cage.

As they approached the vehicle, Mira cast one last desperate glance back at the pyramids. The three monumental structures towered into the sky like stone guardians of eternity, unchanged for millennia—and yet no one understood what they were trying to tell them.

The back seats of the police car smelled of cheap disinfectant, old sweat, and the fear of a hundred detainees before her. The metal of the handcuffs cut into her wrists as the car finally started moving and fought its way through the narrow, cleared path through the crowd.

As they later drove through the streets of Cairo, Mira pressed her face against the barred window. The city had become a cauldron of human emotion. Traffic chaos reigned in the streets, as if everyone had set out at the same time to get somewhere—to their families, to the mosques, to the churches, to the government buildings, away from everything or into the middle of the unknown. Even for Cairo, the chaos was enormous.

Crowds gathered in front of the city's large mosques, their voices joining in a polyphonic prayer that drifted through the open windows of the police car. In front of Coptic churches, people knelt on the sidewalks, their hands raised to the sky. Street vendors hastily sold cobbled-together talismans and amulets, while others barricaded their shops.

Everywhere, electronic display boards flickered with breaking news in Arabic and English: "SPACE OBJECTS APPROACH EARTH," and "SCIENTISTS BAFFLED BY PYRAMID SIGNALS," and "MILITARY ON HIGH ALERT," and "WORLD LEADERS CONVENE FOR EMERGENCY SESSION."

The world reacted as humanity had always reacted to the unknown—with a mixture of awe, terror, and a desperate search for answers.

Her father had reacted differently. But he was dead, and Mira had failed to get his knowledge to the right people—a devastating realization.

Her father's notebook pressed against her ribs, its weight reminding her of her failure as if it were a brick. The answers were so close—and yet separated from the world by bars, uniforms, and human ignorance.

The police station in central Cairo was a brutalist concrete block from the 1970s, its gray facade marked by decades of decay and neglect. Rusty stains ran down the walls like tear tracks, and the few windows were fitted with bars that were more reminiscent of a prison complex than a police station.

Inside, the chaos was the same as outside on the streets—only concentrated and amplified by the low ceilings and poor ventilation. Overwhelmed officers rushed back and forth between desks, phones rang incessantly, and people talked over each other in harsh Arabic. The noise was a wall of voices, shouts, and metallic clanging.

A fat officer with a sweat-drenched face yelled orders, while another desperately tried to get a fax machine to work. A woman in handcuffs cried loudly in front of a desk, while a man in a torn suit argued with a younger police officer.

Mira was led down a long corridor that smelled of Lysol and cold sweat. The walls were painted with peeling green paint, and bare light bulbs provided a yellowish, flickering light.

The cell she was locked in was a small room with bare concrete walls covered in countless scribbles—names, dates, curses in Arabic script and occasionally in Latin letters. A narrow cot with a thin, stained mattress stood against one wall, next to a rusty bucket that served as a toilet. The only window was no bigger than a shoebox, barred and looking out onto a bare concrete wall, as if it were a depressingly monotonous picture.

She sat down on the mattress, which creaked and gave way under her weight. Her father's notebook was still safely hidden under her jacket, but what use was it here? What good was all the knowledge in the world when it was trapped behind bars?

Despair crept through her veins like ice. Outside, the world was preparing for an encounter for which it was ill-equipped. Somewhere, generals and politicians were sitting around conference tables, planning military responses to a threat they didn't understand.

She closed her eyes and tried to apply the breathing techniques Lama Tenzin had taught her. Thoughts are just clouds drifting across the sky of consciousness. But today the clouds seemed to be made of lead, heavy, dark and stormy.

After what seemed like an eternity, the cell door opened with a rusty squeak. A policeman in a worn uniform, his badge hanging crookedly on his chest, nodded to her.

"Phone call," he said in broken English, his voice hoarse from cheap cigarettes. "One call. Twenty minutes."

He led her down the corridor back to the main area of the station, back to the chaos.

On a narrow desk in a corner stood an old black telephone, its receiver so worn that the original black had faded to a dirty gray. The spiral cord was patched in several places with tape, and the whole thing looked like it came from the 1980s, which was probably the case.

Next to the phone, a middle-aged man in a wrinkled brown suit was waiting. He was thin and had the tired eyes of someone who had seen too many hopeless cases. Obviously a lawyer—probably the kind routinely assigned to foreigners in trouble because they could speak English.

"Miss Najafi," he said with the practiced tone of a man who had already had hundreds of such encounters. "I am Mahmoud Al-Rashid, your legal counsel. You have a phone call, 20 minutes."

"Only 20 minutes?"

"That's the rule." He opened a worn leather briefcase and pulled out a form. "I strongly advise you to contact your embassy. The American embassy can help you get out in a few days. That's the usual procedure for trespassing and vandalism in particularly serious cases."

"Trespassing and vandalism?" Mira shook her head, a movement that expressed all her despair. "I don't have a few days."

Al-Rashid frowned and looked at her over the rim of his glasses. "Miss, you have been arrested on serious charges. Trespassing in a World Heritage Site. Vandalism of artifacts of inestimable cultural value. These are serious offenses, but with diplomatic assistance, we can—"

"You don't understand." Mira reached for the phone receiver, her hand trembling with impatience. "I know how to solve the problem with the objects in space."

The lawyer blinked as if she had just declared that she could fly with the snap of her fingers. He turned to the two police officers standing nearby watching them and spoke quickly to them in Arabic. Mira understood only fragments, but she heard the words "maschuna" and "maghnuna"— crazy, insane.

The police officers laughed, a short, harsh sound that contained no trace of humor. It was the laughter of men who had heard it all before—every crazy claim, every wild story, every desperate lie.

Al-Rashid sighed and shook his head.

"Miss Najafi, I understand that the current circumstances are extraordinary. The news about these objects in space has unsettled us all." He made a complicated gesture with his fingers. "But you need to keep a cool head now."

"Give me the phone."

The lawyer looked at her for a long moment, his face a mixture of professional sympathy and resigned acceptance of the idiosyncrasies of his desperate clients. Finally, he shrugged and nodded to the police officers, who moved back a little—far enough to give her some privacy, but close enough to prevent any attempt to escape.

She dialed the only number that still made sense to her, the one she knew by heart because she had stared at it obsessively over the last few days.

25

The Johnson Space Center in Houston lay beneath the Texas sun like a temple to human ambition—a cathedral of steel and glass where the dreams of a species that now fought against the inevitability of a cosmic phenomenon took shape.

Lukas sat in the air-conditioned terminal of the private spaceport, staring at his cell phone, its display flooded with an endless stream of messages. He'd received 384 interview requests in the last 24 hours. Spiegel, BBC, Al Jazeera, Reuters, AP—the entire world press suddenly seemed eager to hear his voice.

"Dr. Lukas Heuer, the man who discovered the end of the world," as the *New York Times* had called him. He had truly imagined his fame differently.

In the past, he would have dreamed of being printed on the front pages. As a young postdoctoral fellow, he had imagined what it would be like to be in the spotlight, to be the scientist whose name would be associated with an epoch-making discovery. He had never imagined that discovery might mean the final apocalypse.

"Everything okay, amigo?" asked Carlos, who was sitting next to him and looking at him with concern.

"Hundreds of journalists want to know if we're all going to die. To be precise, they want to know how we're all going to die." Lukas shook his head and pushed his cell phone away. "As if I had an answer to that."

"The TV experts have done their own calculations and have painted any number of vivid, and often conflicting pictures of what's in store for us."

A black SUV pulled up in front of the terminal. Two men in dark suits got out—without knowing them, Lukas knew immediately that they were from the Secret Service.

"Dr. Heuer? Dr. Mendoza? We'll take you to the main building."

The drive through the large complex revealed a facility in a state of emergency. Military convoys moved through the streets, checkpoints controlled every intersection and every entrance and exit, and helicopters circled overhead. It was clear that a project was being worked on here that was a make-or-break endeavor. The Johnson Space Center had become a fortress.

They passed through three security checks before being allowed to enter the main building, which normally served as mission control for manned space flights.

"Welcome to Project Osiris," said a familiar voice as they were guided through a narrow corridor to a conference room.

Director Patterson was already waiting for them there. The room, whose walls were covered with huge displays, was surprisingly small.

The screens showed blueprints, orbits, technical specifications, and, repeatedly, the three black pyramids inexorably approaching Earth. The room itself exuded an energy of desperate determination—history was being made here under the pressure of time. How it would turn out was literally written in the stars.

"Osiris was a god in the ancient Egyptian religion," said Patterson. "A divine being associated with fertility, the afterlife, resurrection, and the cycle of nature. Hopefully, the entirety of humanity won't soon be in need of resurrection or the afterlife. But why not hedge our bets? And we can use the help of an ancient deity about now, however we can invoke it."

The NASA director sighed deeply before continuing. "What we discuss here remains strictly confidential, even though the existence of the project is public knowledge."

He pointed to an oval table around which a dozen people had already gathered—a multinational team of engineers, scientists, and military personnel. Every face told of sleepless nights and the burden of impossible decisions. Some were obviously Chinese, as Lukas immediately noticed.

"Dr. Li Lin from the Chinese National Space Administration," said Patterson, pointing to an elegant middle-aged woman whose eyes reflected the sharpness of years of space experience. "Jean-Luc

Dubois from ESA. Colonel James Harrison, our mission commander. And Dr. Elizabeth Reeves from SpaceX, our technical director."

"We have five weeks," began Patterson without preamble as the holographic displays came to life. "Five weeks to plan, implement, and launch a mission that would normally require years of preparation. This is only possible thanks to the unprecedented cooperation between NASA, ESA, SpaceX, and the Chinese Space Agency. Along with the unimaginable sums of money the international community is raising to save Earth. We're currently rewriting the book on international cooperation—under the most extreme conditions humanity has ever experienced."

Dr. Reeves of SpaceX activated a holographic representation of a spacecraft floating in the air like a silver tower. Every line, every component spoke of the fusion of human engineering with the urgency of survival.

"Our Starship Block Three forms our backbone," she explained with a precise pronunciation that uncomfortably reminded Lukas of one of his particularly strict elementary school teachers. "Its payload capacity for low Earth orbit is 150 tons, and it has an interior volume of 1,300 cubic meters. The Raptor-3 engines generate 280 tons of thrust per unit—39 for launch, 13 for orbital maneuvers and vacuum optimization."

The holographic display broke down into components, each one a masterpiece of engineering. "The heat shields are made of TUFROC—Ultra-High Temperature Ceramic Matrix Composite—developed for temperatures up to 2,500 degrees Celsius. This is crucial because we'll be flying at speeds that would pulverize conventional materials, especially during re-entry."

She's counting on a return, thought Lukas. *Very optimistic.*

Jean-Luc Dubois took over seamlessly with a soft French accent. "But a standard starship is far from sufficient for what we have in mind. Airbus Defense and SpaceX are jointly modifying the entire crew section with the Columbus II life support system—an advancement of what we perfected for the International Space Station."

A new holographic display materialized—the interior of the spacecraft, a complex network of pipes, computers, and life support systems.

"The Environmental Control and Life Support System—ECLSS—recycles 99.7 percent of the water and 97 percent of the oxygen," Dubois continued. "The carbon dioxide scrubbers are based on the latest generation of metal-organic frameworks—MOFs—which achieve an efficiency that would have been unthinkable until 2030. We're talking about a closed biosphere for 6 people over 8 months."

"Thank you." Dr. Lin leaned forward, her voice carrying the confidence of a nation that had risen from developing country to space power in just a few decades. "The Chinese CNSA is contributing our latest QDT-40 ion engines," she said. "Four of them, each with 40 kilonewtons of thrust at a specific impulse of 4,750 seconds. That's three times the efficiency of chemical engines. They will be launched into orbit by a Long March 10 and automatically attached to the spacecraft with a kind of clamp."

Lukas stared at the technical data dancing around the holographic spacecraft. "Eight-month mission? How far exactly are we flying?"

Colonel Harrison, whose face looked strangely pinched, as if his breakfast had gone down the wrong way, replied with the sober clarity of a soldier: "Eight months round trip. The objects are currently about 120 million miles away, moving on a trajectory that will bring them to Earth in seven and a half months. With conventional chemical engines—Hohmann transfer orbits—the round trip would extend beyond our life support capabilities. We thought it was important to be able to make it back to Earth alive."

Lukas cringed. "Yeah, good thinking," he said grimly.

A new display showed orbits, trajectories that wound through the solar system like cosmic dance steps.

"The ion engines enable continuous low thrust over months," said Dr. Lin. "Spiral acceleration to a speed of 72 kilometers per second relative to the Sun—which is about 45 *miles* per second," he added for the benefit of the Americans. "That reduces the flight time to 2 months and 23 days if we launch in 5 weeks."

"The power supply," Dr. Reeves continued, "is provided by an experimental nuclear reactor—KILOPOWER Mark IV with 20 kilowatts of continuous power. Highly enriched uranium-235 in micro-heat pipes, coupled with Stirling generators. The system is designed to function reliably at minus 260 degrees Celsius in space. Only 13 degrees above absolute zero. For those without technical backgrounds, absolute zero is the lowest possible temperature in our universe, at which even the motion of atoms stops dead in its tracks."

Carlos, who had been listening silently until now, spoke up: "The radiation exposure during an eight-month flight will be enormous. How will you protect the crew?"

"Hydrogen shielding," replied Dubois immediately. "Twenty centimeters of polyethylene around the crew capsule, enriched with boron-10 for neutron capture. In addition, there will be active electromagnetic shields—superconducting magnetic coils that generate a bipolar magnetic field of 0.5 tesla. This deflects most of the cosmic radiation. Together with the water tanks arranged around the living module, this provides formidable shielding."

Lukas admired the technical brilliance, but one question still burned in his mind. He hesitated. "It all sounds like a scientific miracle. But something is obviously missing."

"The weapon systems," said Patterson, finishing the unspoken sentence.

The atmosphere in the room changed noticeably. Dr. Lin opened another image on the display at the head of the table—cylindrical objects that rested like sleeping dragons in the cargo holds of the spaceship.

"Nine modified thermonuclear warheads," she said in a voice that suppressed any hint of emotion. "Originally B83-1 warheads with 1.2 megatons of explosive power each, the delivery systems have been completely redesigned for space use by a joint venture between Lockheed Martin, Arianespace, and the Beijing Institute of Space Technology."

Harrison took over: "The challenge in space is the lack of atmosphere. No shock wave, no thermal transfer like on Earth. The energy must be transferred through X-rays and gamma rays, as well as through direct neutron flows."

"So 10.8 megatons total," said Carlos incredulously. "If I'm doing the math right, that's over 700 times Hiroshima."

"Your math is correct," said Harrison. "Each warhead is equipped with an autonomous guidance system—ring laser-assisted navigation coupled with star sensors for absolute positioning. Ignition is provided by implosion lenses made of octogen-based explosives, optimized for space temperatures."

"The launch vehicles are modified Falcon 9 first stages with Merlin 1D engines," added Dr. Reeves from SpaceX. "Each one can direct its payload to within 10 meters of a target, even at speeds of several miles per second."

Lukas felt his stomach tighten. The technical perfection of the destruction was both impressive and terrifying. "Colonel, with all due respect, these objects manipulate space-time itself. They generate gravitational waves with an intensity that exceeds our models. What makes you think that even the most powerful nuclear weapons will have any effect? Or even get anywhere near the objects?"

The questions hung like shadows over the room. Harrison stared at the warheads displayed before he replied, "Because we have no alternative, Dr. Heuer."

"Even if they reach the target and detonate," said Dr. Lin. "They're likely to have little to no effect. The density of these pyramidal objects is extraordinary. But this is the best we can do. I see it, not an attempt to *destroy* the objects, which I believe won't happen, but as a gentle, polite knock on the door. Letting them know someone wants to say hello."

Lukas's immediate reaction was pure contempt. Ridiculous. But the longer he thought about it, the more he had to admit: it wasn't any more preposterous than the other theories on the table. A huge stretch, yes—but still more plausible than the idea of the nukes actually destroying the pyramids.

He swallowed hard. Or, the other alternative, that this puny attempt at aggression would annoy them enough to take a reflexive swat at the nest that spawned such a pesky gnat.

"I'll remind this gathering again," said Patterson, "that deploying the nukes is a measure of last resort. We'll still be trying everything we can to communicate with them—without a nuclear love tap at their door."

Dr. Reeves activated a new display. "To further this thought," he said, "we've come up with another way to hopefully communicate using gravitational waves—through the use of rapidly rotating neutronium masses."

"Neutronium?" asked Carlos. "That's impossible to handle."

"*Almost* impossible," corrected Dr. Lin. "The Beijing National Laboratory has stabilized microgram quantities in magnetic containment fields. Enough to generate weak gravitational waves. *Theoretically*. Even if our detectors were a trillion-fold more sensitive, *we* couldn't detect them. The waves should be orders of magnitude weaker even than those we were trying to produce in CERN. But at least it's *something*."

Dubois added, "In parallel, we have quantum communication systems—entangled photon pairs with a coherence time of several hours. If the objects are using quantum mechanical communication protocols, we might be able to reach them with that."

"We'll also cover the full electromagnetic spectrum," added Dr. Reeves. "From radio waves to gamma radiation."

"Ten-meter radio telescope, infrared spectrometer, X-ray and gamma detectors. All coupled with AI systems that can test millions of communication protocols simultaneously."

"I assume all of this has to be assembled in orbit," said Lukas.

"Yes," replied Patterson. "It will be complex, but we have experience with that thanks to the shuttle era."

"How many crew members?"

"Six," said Patterson. "The perfect balance between redundancy and resource consumption. Two American astronauts—Colonel Harrison and Dr. Michael Torres, both veterans of space missions.

Two Chinese taikonauts—Major Wei Lin and Dr. Liu Xiaoming, both with experience in long-term missions on the Chinese space station."

Dr. Lin nodded. "Major Wei spent 518 days continuously in space. Dr. Liu is a quantum physicist and xenobiology specialist."

"As for the other two seats, Dr. Heuer, you already know that these are reserved for you and Dr. Mendoza, as the discoverer of the objects, and as the face to the public. You two are roughly more famous than God about now."

Dr. Reeves activated a final presentation—a massive floating platform in the middle of the ocean. "The launch will take place from the planned Floating Launch Platform Alpha, 800 kilometers southeast of Cape Canaveral. The platform is 200 meters long, 100 wide, with a payload capacity of 20,000 tons."

"Why the ocean?" asked Carlos.

"We've done some things with the nuclear devices we've never done before," said Reeves. "The risk that they'll go off upon launch is nearly infinitesimal, but why not make sure humanity is as safe as possible?"

"Right," said Lukas. "We'd hate to destroy ourselves before the objects get the chance."

"I promise you though," said Patterson. "You have nothing to worry about. The launch will happen without incident. You'll have four months in space to continue attempts at communication, which we've just described. While you're traveling, the brightest minds in the world are working on ideas. We need to be able to implement appropriate solutions onboard. That will be your job."

Lukas nodded, reminded of a short story he had read as a kid, in which four astronauts set off to reach the nearest star, placed in suspended animation for 500 years. The twist was that human progress didn't slow during their journey. Upon arrival at Alpha Centauri centuries later, they discover habitable planets already colonized by advanced human societies. Faster-than-light travel was invented on Earth not long after their departure, allowing later ships to overtake and surpass them.

Four months wasn't 500 years, but perhaps the collective minds of humanity would come up with a solution, after all.

Lukas's cell phone began to vibrate, the modern buzz breaking the meaningful silence of the moment like a wrong note in a symphony.

"Excuse me," he muttered, silencing the device.

Patterson nodded. "Training begins tomorrow at zero five hundred. Years of intensive preparation, compressed into five weeks. Centrifuge tests, vacuum chamber simulations, zero gravity training, complete medical and psychological evaluation. You'll be pushed to your physical and mental limits, I can tell you that much."

The meeting dissolved like stars at dawn. Lukas walked out of the building into the open air, where the Texas heat enveloped him like a firm embrace. But he needed that. The warmth on his skin, the tingling of his pores opening up to form beads of sweat. It was all real, not a dream. His cell phone vibrated incessantly—a digital cacophony of questions he couldn't answer, from people seeking answers he didn't have.

Finally, he gave up and answered the next call, ready to berate the inevitable journalist for getting his private number.

"Dr. Heuer?" The voice sounded different than expected—older, with a slight Greek accent, and imbued with an urgency that went beyond the mere curiosity of a journalist. "This is Dr. Alexius Pappas from MIT. I need to speak with you. Urgently! I think I have an idea of how to make contact with the aliens."

26

Mira had now spent three days and three nights in the cell, whose concrete walls enclosed her thoughts like a modern sarcophagus. Time seemed to take on a different quality in this room without clocks, without natural light, and without distractions, where only the faint reflection of the neon lighting from the corridor seeped through the barred windows.

Her lawyer, Mahmoud Al-Rashid, visited her twice on the first day and once on the second. His words were a maze of legal terms that slid over her ears like water over stone. Trespassing, vandalism, bail negotiations—all concepts that seemed to exist in another reality, far removed from the cosmic truths that were being squandered within her.

Food came three times a day: a small ration of water in a plastic cup that tasted of disinfectant, two slices of dry bread, and a dollop of hummus served on a paper plate. Mira ate mechanically, without tasting anything, her thoughts wandering to the black pyramids that were inexorably approaching Earth—that much she had gleaned from the television broadcasts at the station.

It should have shocked her, but she saw the announcement only as final proof that her father had indeed given his life for something greater than himself, and that his notes were not fantasies. She read them over and over again, especially since they were the only thing that provided her with distraction. Apparently, the two leather booklets had been left with her in a small display of mercy.

On the first day, despair crept through her bones like a cold liquid. She lay on the thin mattress and stared at the ceiling, where water stains formed strange patterns that looked like hieroglyphics of an unknown language.

The sounds of the police station penetrated the walls: the ringing of telephones, the voices of the officers, the metallic banging of doors. Every sound was a thorn, reminding her that the world was turning while she was trapped in this cage of concrete and bureaucracy.

But on the second day, when the darkness of despair was at its deepest, she remembered the words of Lama Tenzin: "When you are trapped in the cave of suffering, become the cave itself. Accept the darkness, and it will become your kind teacher."

She sat cross-legged on the narrow cot, closed her eyes, and began to meditate. At first, her mind was like a stormy sea, full of waves of fear, frustration, and impatience. But gradually, with each conscious breath, the surface began to smooth out.

Thoughts are just clouds passing across the sky of consciousness. The old monk's words became a mantra pulsing through her veins. Despair was a cloud. Fear was a cloud. Even the urgency of her mission was a cloud—important, but only relatively so, not absolutely, not the essence of her consciousness.

In the silence of meditation, she found a space that was larger than the cell, wider than the walls, deeper than her circumstances. It was the same space she had felt in the monastery of Samye when she sat at her father's side and received the vision of the overturned table. A space beyond time and space, where consciousness itself was the landscape.

On the third day, she meditated almost around the clock, sinking deep into herself. She ate her meals without leaving her meditative posture, chewing slowly and consciously, considering each bite a gift. Water became the nectar of mindfulness, bread the substance of the universe.

In those quiet hours, she understood something fundamental about the nature of her imprisonment: The bars were real, the concrete walls solid, but what was truly imprisoned was only her body. Her mind, her consciousness, could travel. It could expand, connect with the cosmic fabric that permeated all things, and return to its origin. She was just a wave in the ocean of the cosmos, a part of it, but never separate. A momentary elevation, fleeting yet precious, a single step in a complex dance.

This realization was not depressing, but liberating.

Could there even be mistakes if every form was merely an expression of consciousness? If nothing could exist without an observing consciousness?

The ancient Egyptians knew it, she thought in a moment of clarity. They understood that communication could not be achieved through words or signals alone, but through consciousness itself. Through the mind. While they were less technologically advanced than modern humans, perhaps they were much more advanced spiritually. How much of their research went into exploring consciousness rather than technology?

On the fourth morning, Mira awoke not from sleep, but from a deep meditation that had lasted all night. She felt refreshed, as if she had drunk from a source beyond the physical world. A gentle joy permeated her.

The sound of heavy footsteps in the corridor made her open her eyes. It wasn't time for food, and the footsteps sounded different—more shuffling, less routine.

The cell door opened with the familiar squeak and scrape of rusty hinges. Her lawyer, Al-Rashid, stood there, but his usual weary resignation had given way to a different energy—a mixture of surprise and professional excitement.

"Miss Najafi," he said, his voice sounding brighter than usual. "You're free. Someone paid your bail, and the American Embassy intervened."

Mira rose slowly from the cot, her movements fluid after the long hours of meditation.

"Do you know who?"

"I'm not sure, but I think whoever you called—it worked." Al-Rashid stepped aside, and a figure appeared in the doorway that Mira recognized immediately.

Ricarda Lefèvre was dressed in a wrinkled, steel-gray pantsuit that bore the marks of long days of travel. Her blonde hair was tied back in a tight bun, and her blue eyes scrutinized Mira like those of a hawk.

"Dr. Najafi," said the ESA communications chief with her precise, slightly French-tinged pronunciation. "I didn't expect to find you here of all places in the world. You really have fallen far."

Lefèvre's voice conveyed more pity than reproach.

Mira stepped out of the cell, her father's notebooks clasped tightly in her fingers. A few days ago, those words would have hurt her, but now, after the transformative experience of the last few days, they bounced off her like raindrops on glass.

Because she hadn't fallen at all. Her journey had allowed her mind and soul to *expand*.

"I found important answers," said Mira. "You wouldn't be here if you didn't believe that too."

Lefèvre sighed, and for a moment, the professional mask fell from her face. The fatigue beneath it was unmistakable. "That was you on the plateau, calling to me. Wasn't it?"

Mira nodded. "It was."

"I'm sorry. I didn't recognize you, and didn't have time. I've been working 20-hour shifts since . . ." She made a vague gesture toward the ceiling. "Well, since the end of the world was announced, I guess."

It was the first time Mira had seen Lefèvre as a human being and not just as an official. The woman in front of her was obviously exhausted to the bone, driven by a responsibility that fate had placed in her hands.

Lefèvre looked at her for a long moment. "You obviously have powerful allies, Dr. Najafi, that much is certain. Very powerful. I'll explain everything on the way."

* * *

The taxi fought its way through the chaotic traffic of Cairo to the airport. The city was still a cauldron of human emotions—crowds in front of religious sites, military vehicles on the streets, electronic display boards announcing breaking news about the cosmic visitors in various languages. But apparently, the security forces had managed to establish an acceptable level of order in the meantime.

At the airport, they didn't drive to the commercial terminal, but to a remote area for private flights. A sleek Gulfstream G-5 in US Air

Force colors was standing on the runway, its turbines already warming up.

"US Air Force?" shouted Mira over the noise as they got out of the taxi.

"Your allies have influence," replied Lefèvre simply.

The flight was long and turbulent, as if they were already within the gravitational influence of the cosmic visitors. First westward over North Africa and the Canary Islands, then a stop in Madeira, where they stayed just long enough to refuel, and then farther westward across the Atlantic.

In the luxurious cabin of the Gulfstream, they sat across from each other, separated by a small table covered with coffee cups and documents. The gentle hum of the engines provided a soothing backdrop for their conversation.

"Tell me everything," said Lefèvre after they had flown in silence for a while.

Mira opened her father's notebook, the leather-bound pages rustling softly. Her father's handwriting seemed to live and breathe in the subdued cabin lighting.

"My father was no ordinary archaeologist," she began. "He searched for connections between the great cultures of humanity. He believed that certain strands of knowledge were passed down through history, from civilization to civilization."

She conveyed how her father's notes had led her to discover the Star Chamber. Then she went on to recount her journey after deciding to leave Cairo for Tibet, including her father's death in the tukdam state. Lefèvre listened attentively, her eyes betraying nothing of her thoughts.

"The Book of Thoth-Hermes," continued Mira, "describes a cycle of 4,500 years. The 'star barges of the gods' returning to Earth. And the way the ancient priests communicated with them."

"And that would be?" asked Lefèvre.

"Up here." Mira tapped her temple. "Not through technology or language, but through consciousness itself, the realm they attached as much importance to as we attach to science and technology. The ancient Egyptians were a thoroughly spiritual society that attached more importance to the mind than anything else. I believe the murals show six priests in the tukdam state—the intermediate state between life and death—and a seventh who acts as a mediator, a kind of medium."

"Medium?" asked the European woman, raising her eyebrows. "You mean like those women who hold séances around a circular table and pretend to talk to ghosts?"

"No. Of course not. I mean someone capable of such a deep state of meditation that they can open themselves up to communication. A different kind of communication. With the dead or with something else entirely. But unlike the mediums you mentioned, they don't come out of their trance to accept a big check from a gullible client. Instead, I doubt any of them actually wake up at all. Somewhere in the deepest contemplation, the line between life and death is extremely thin. My father traveled along it and didn't return. He died in tukdam."

"Right," repeated Lefèvre thoughtfully. "Which you've already described. And which I'm still trying to wrap my head around."

"The fact that there is now evidence of its reality is a huge step forward for our civilization," said Mira. "Western neuroscientists have finally begun to recognize and try to understand this seemingly impossible state of consciousness."

Mira looked out of the small cabin window. Below them stretched the Atlantic Ocean, an endless blue that revealed the curvature of the Earth.

Lefèvre had revealed nothing of her own thoughts throughout the conversation. Her face was the perfect mask of a diplomat, impenetrable and professional. "Dr. Najafi," she said finally, "what you describe is extraordinary. But you surely understand that extraordinary claims require extraordinary evidence."

"The evidence is everywhere. The Star Chamber clearly shows the very phenomenon we are facing today. The gravitational waves measured by Dr. Heuer. The neurological patterns of meditators in the tukdam state and their similarity to the priests in the mural. We just have to recognize the connections left to us by the ancient Egyptians."

When the coast of North America finally appeared on the horizon, a thin strip of land between the sky and the sea, Mira felt something change inside her. The days in captivity had transformed her. She knew exactly what had to be done.

***

At dusk, Dulles International Airport glittered like a shining jewel. The Gulfstream taxied to a remote hangar, where two men were already waiting for it.

The first was tall and slim, with dark blond hair and the thoughtful eyes of a scientist. His posture betrayed both intelligence and a certain emotional reserve. This had to be Dr. Lukas Heuer, the German physicist Mira now knew from the numerous news outlets she had consulted during the flight.

The second man was slightly older, with graying temples and a stately belly. He wore horn-rimmed glasses on his broad nose, and his eyes were small but sparkled with intelligence and warmth.

"Dr. Najafi," said Heuer as they stepped off the plane. His voice was polite but cool. "I'm Lukas Heuer."

"Dr. Heuer." Mira shook his hand. "It's hard not to recognize you."

A shadow flitted across his face and he smiled wryly. "Unfortunately, that's true."

"Mira! It's so good to finally meet you in person." The other man stepped forward, a warm smile spreading across his face. They shook hands.

"Dr. Pappas." The relief in her voice was unmistakable. "Thank you! I know it couldn't have been easy after we spoke for you to find a way to convince the powers that be to come rescue me."

"You have nothing to thank me for. I've long admired you and your work. So when you say you have ideas that might save humanity, I'd be a fool not to take you as seriously as you deserve."

He stared at her with what seemed like affection. "And I spent several months at Samye studying with your father and Lama Tenzin," he said softly.

"Yes," she replied with a look of joy on her face. "I look forward to hearing all about that."

"And I'll regale you with that experience as soon as we have some downtime. But to give you a quick summary, both your father and the Lama are great men. And your father never stopped loving you and your mother. Not for an instant."

Mira's eyes teared up at this, but she fought to regain control of her emotions. "Thank you," she whispered, barely able to keep tears from flowing from watery eyes.

"Come," said Lukas, gesturing to a waiting vehicle. "We have much to discuss, and time is running out."

"Does that mean you believe me? Believe Dr. Pappas?"

"Dr. Pappas's theories are very . . . interesting," replied the German evasively. "And since we currently have no alternatives, I'm grateful for any creative approach, no matter how unconventional. And I'm willing to go to Herculean lengths to see this through."

Mira raised her eyebrows. "Herculean lengths? I see. Does that mean you'll be performing twelve labors? You know, like killing a multi-headed monster?"

Lukas laughed. "No. But I did manage to set up a meeting with a single-headed *man*. Perhaps not at the level of Hercules, but he is the most powerful man in the world, so it was a bit of a challenge. I'm pretty sure he's not a *monster*, but let's find out."

"We're going to the White House," explained Lefèvre, and Mira blinked in surprise.

"I have a good relationship with the president," added Lukas. "Enough to get you and Dr. Pappas an audience. But you'll only get one chance to convince him of your idea. So we're counting on you to be extraordinarily persuasive."

27

The White House welcomed them like a temple of earthly power amid the cosmic crisis looming over humanity. The colonnades glowed in the gathering night of Washington as if nothing had happened, as if three pyramid-shaped objects were not inexorably approaching Earth, as if the fate of human civilization were not at stake. Presumably, that had been the builders' intention: to convey permanence.

Lukas sat in the back seat of the armored limousine and looked at the iconic building through the tinted windows. Next to him sat Carlos, nervously tugging at his jacket collar, while across from him, Dr. Pappas waited with the stoic calm of a man who had dedicated his life to the scientific exploration of the deepest mysteries of human consciousness. Mira Najafi gazed out the window with the focused attention of an archaeologist trained to notice the tiniest details. Ricarda Lefèvre, meanwhile, studied her notes as if this were just another workday like any other.

Four days had passed since Lukas had left Houston without permission. Four days during which astronaut training had continued while he and Carlos, together with the MIT researcher, had searched for an alternative solution. One that didn't involve a nuclear knock on the door.

The motorcade—three identical black limousines, escorted by motorcycle police and followed by SUVs full of Secret Service agents—rolled through the security checkpoint at the south gate. Here began the ritual of power that had remained unchanged for centuries: the careful examination of every person who wanted to enter the inner sanctum of American democracy.

Secret Service men and women greeted them with polite but unyielding professionalism and searched them from head to toe.

"ID, please," said the first agent, a middle-aged woman with short gray hair and eyes that registered every detail.

Lukas handed over his passport and green card, watching as the agent entered his details into a tablet that immediately communicated with the security databases of half the world. His name, his face, his fingerprints—everything was checked against lists of millions of people, sorted by threat level and security clearance, in a matter of seconds.

"Dr. Lukas Heuer," she said finally. "Gravitational wave researcher, currently working for NASA on Project Osiris. Approved."

"Right," he muttered.

Carlos was next. "Dr. Carlos Mendoza, Chilean citizen, astronomer at the European Southern Observatory. Project Osiris employee. Approved."

Next was Pappas.

"Dr. Alexios Pappas, American citizen, professor of neuroscience at MIT. Special clearance from the Office of Science and Technology Policy. Approved."

Mira hesitated for a moment before handing over her passport. Lukas noticed the tense line of her shoulders, the memory of the Egyptian police cell still fresh in her mind.

"Dr. Mira Najafi, American citizen, archaeologist." The agent paused, glancing at her display. "Recently released from custody in Egypt. Diplomatic intervention. Approved under supervision."

Lefèvre was last. "Ricarda Lefèvre, French and Luxembourgish citizen, communications director of the European Space Agency. Diplomat. Approved."

The next checkpoint took them through metal detectors. Every wire, every electronic component, every metallic object was registered and analyzed. His wristwatch was examined for minutes, as if it might contain explosives that physics hadn't yet discovered.

Then came the screening: full-body scanners that sent X-rays through their bodies and produced 3-dimensional images of their skeletons, organs, and hidden objects. Lukas thought about the irony—here they were, five people who possibly held the fate of the species in their hands, being screened like suspects at an airport.

"Cell phones, tablets, and all electronic devices in the lockers," an agent instructed them. "You'll get them back when you leave the building."

Lukas put his smartphone in the gray metal locker and felt a strange sense of relief. For four days the device had been a constant source of stress—the endless messages, calls, interview requests. Now, at least for a short time, he was free of it.

The third checkpoint was psychological in nature: a short interview with a Secret Service agent who asked questions designed to expose lies or hidden intentions.

"Purpose of your visit?"

"To advise the president on matters of national security concerning objects in space," replied Lukas.

"Have you ever had contact with foreign intelligence services?"

"Not knowingly, no."

"Are you currently under the influence of alcohol or drugs?"

"No."

The questions continued, a litany of paranoia that seemed absurd to Lukas. Who had time for such things nowadays?

Finally, after 15 minutes, an agent led them through the actual security gates into the White House itself.

The entrance hall was a work of art made of marble and history, every stone steeped in the decisions of dozens of presidents. Portraits of past heads of state looked down from the walls with more or less stern expressions—Washington with his stoic idealism. Lincoln with the melancholy of the Civil War. Roosevelt with the determination of World War II.

Lukas felt the weight of history in these rooms. This was where the decision had been made to drop atomic bombs on Japan. This was where Kennedy had mastered the Cuban Missile Crisis. This was where people had decided on war and peace, life and death, for millions. And now they were here to deliberate on the fate of the entire human species in the face of extraterrestrial visitors.

A marine in an immaculate uniform—every button polished, every crease precisely ironed—led them through a corridor whose walls were adorned with paintings of American landscapes.

"The president is expecting you in the Oval Office," said the Marine calmly, gesturing to a door flanked by Secret Service agents.

The Oval Office—the heart of American power, the room where the most important decisions in the free world had been made for generations. Lukas felt his palms getting sweaty as they approached the famous door.

The room that opened up before them was smaller than Lukas had expected, but filled with an aura of power that was almost physically palpable.

The famous "Resolute Desk" dominated the side in front of the windows, made from the wood of a British ship that had been trapped in the Arctic—a symbol of perseverance in the face of impossible circumstances. Behind it hung the American flag and the flag with the presidential seal, their colors glowing in the subdued light of the table lamps.

President Morales rose from his chair behind the desk. He was a man in his late sixties, whose gray hair and deep furrows around his eyes betrayed the burden of office. His movements were those of a man who had slept too little, drunk too much coffee, and had to make too many impossible decisions. Lukas could relate.

"Dr. Heuer," said the president, his voice carrying the rough texture of exhaustion as he pointed to the two sofas. "As you can imagine, in this situation, I have no time for social niceties. You'll need to get right to the point."

Lukas nodded respectfully. "Understood. I'm grateful for your time, Mr. President."

"I sincerely hope you have a good explanation for why you disappeared from Houston for four days despite ongoing astronaut training." The tone was sharp but not hostile—the voice of a man accustomed to getting direct answers to direct questions. "There's a list of thousands of scientists who would kill to be on board the *Hope*."

"I know. But I felt this was too important to take any other action."

"So what is this about? And who are these people you've brought with you?"

"You already know Dr. Carlos Mendoza. This is Dr. Ricarda Lefèvre, Director of Communications at ESA. Dr. Alexios Pappas, neuroscientist at MIT. And Dr. Mira Najafi, archaeologist and Egyptologist from Yale."

Morales scrutinized the visitors with the keen attention of a man accustomed to assessing people quickly. Only when he sat down on one of the sofas did they settle down as well.

"Mr. President," began Lukas, spreading his hands, "Dr. Pappas and Dr. Najafi have come up with a . . . promising . . . approach to communicating with the objects. One not based on technology."

Morales leaned back, skepticism clearly visible on his face.

"A non-technological approach to communication? With extraterrestrial intelligences? What does that even mean?"

"May I, Mr. President?" asked Pappas politely.

Morales nodded.

The MIT scientist cleared his throat and began to speak in the melodious voice of a university professor: "Mr. President, let me begin with the current state of neuroscience in relation to human consciousness. Despite decades of intensive research, we still only have a superficial understanding of consciousness—the most fundamental characteristic of human existence."

He paused, apparently gathering his thoughts.

"We know that the human brain contains approximately a hundred billion neurons, each of which is connected to thousands of others. It is the most complex structure in the known universe. These networks generate electrical patterns—brain waves—that we can measure with EEGs. During wakefulness, beta waves between 13 and 30 hertz dominate. In deep meditation or REM sleep, we see theta waves between 4 and 8 hertz."

Morales listened attentively, his hands folded on his crossed legs.

"But here's where it gets interesting," continued Pappas. "Over the past 20 years, we have observed states of consciousness in experienced meditators that lie outside these normal parameters. Gamma waves above 40 hertz, sometimes up to 100 hertz—frequencies that correlate with extraordinary mental clarity and a sense of unity with the universe."

"And that means?" asked Morales.

"It means that human consciousness is capable of states that we thought impossible until recently. Tibetan monks who have been meditating for 50 years can consciously change their body temperature by several degrees, slow their heartbeat until it's barely measurable, reduce intestinal activity and their entire metabolism to a minimum, and reach states of consciousness that they describe as *oneness*."

Lukas watched the president's face. The initial skepticism gave way to cautious attention.

"Modern neuroscience has confirmed some of what Far Eastern traditions have been teaching for millennia," continued Pappas. "Consciousness isn't just a byproduct of neural activity. It's a fundamental aspect of reality, possibly as fundamental as matter and energy."

"You're talking about the 'hard problem of consciousness,'" said Morales, clearly taking Pappas by surprise. "It isn't widely known, but I had a near-death experience when I was in my twenties. Ever since, I've been an interested layman in the subjects of life and death, consciousness, and so on. But please go on and say what you were about to say."

Pappas wasted no time. "As you know, then, what's called the *hard problem of consciousness* asks why we have subjective experiences at all? Why aren't we just biological computers that process information without 'experiencing' anything? How can a bunch of simple, individually unconscious cells collectively produce our conscious experience as humans? Materialistic neuroscience has no definitive answer to that."

Lukas wasn't sure he had a clear grasp of what Pappas meant, but decided to remain silent.

The president, however, read his body language like a book. "Dr. Pappas," he said, "can you elaborate on this just a little for my friend Lukas here. And Carlos. This isn't really their field."

"Of course, Mr. President. I can definitely get it across better. We, as scientists, now know a lot about the brain in purely physical terms—how neurons fire, how information moves around, how the brain controls behavior, solves problems, and so on. These are considered the "easy" questions, which doesn't mean they aren't impossibly hard to actually figure out, but that's what they're called."

He arched an eyebrow. "So what's the *Hard Problem*? It's a problem we can't reduce or explain away with just physics: why does any of that brain activity feel like something from the *inside*? Where do subjective experiences come from? For example, what is it like to feel pain? Taste chocolate? Be happy?

"No matter how detailed the description of brain chemistry, wiring, and electricity gets, we can never fully explain why there's an inner experience attached to it. Imagine explaining to someone born blind what the color red 'looks like.' You could describe wavelengths of light, cone cells in the eye, brain areas lighting up, and so on, but you'd never convey the actual experience of *redness*."

Lukas and Carlos exchanged glances. "Thank you," said Lukas for them both. "That was quite helpful. I think we've got it."

"Great," said Pappas. "It turns out that Far Eastern philosophies have been exploring this hard question for millennia. Buddhism, Hinduism, Taoism—they all describe consciousness as the fundamental fabric of reality from which all phenomena arise.

"Since the 1920s, we've known that observing a quantum system changes its state. The observer's consciousness seems to play a fundamental role in the structure of reality. Famous physicists such as Henry Stapp and Stuart Hameroff argue that consciousness and quantum mechanics are inextricably linked.

"More recent theories have suggested that we may be living in something like a computer simulation in which our surroundings are procedurally generated only through our conscious observation. In other words, phenomena such as quantum entanglement and the measurement process suggest that reality is not completely determined until it's observed. This is comparable to 'lazy rendering' in computer games—the world is only 'loaded' when the player looks at it."

"Now *that's* something I *am* familiar with," said Lukas enthusiastically. "Further support for the simulation theory comes from the smallest unit of the universe, the Planck length. It seems to be a limit for spatial resolution. Below that, 'distance' no longer makes sense.

Which is reminiscent of the pixel structure of digital simulations—space may not be continuous, but quantized like a grid."

He paused. "The Bekenstein-Hawking limit and the holographic principle state that the amount of information in a space is proportional to its area. *Not* its volume. And while this contradicts all intuition about 3D space, it sounds exactly like a 2D data structure simulating 3D. There's a great deal of evidence that our reality is far more complex than it appears, and that our consciousness plays a central role in it."

Morales turned to Mira. "You look like you have something to add, Dr. Najafi. We may be short on time, but now isn't the time to be shy."

Mira leaned forward slightly, her voice calm but firm. "Yes. I'd like to tell you about a specific phenomenon that could confirm these theories in practice, or rather, highlight the central importance of consciousness. It's called tukdam—a Tibetan term for a state of meditation that occurs *after* clinical death. Have you heard of it?"

Morales shook his head. "No. Which is surprising, since this is the kind of topic I've been interested in for a long time. If it's true, it's well hidden."

"What aspects of consciousness and near-death have you studied?" asked Pappas.

"The near-death experiences of others. Extensively. There are now highly credible documentaries and books on the subject. Accounts from numerous people who've been on the brink of death or clinically dead before resuscitation. They share astonishing commonalities. Individuals report being able to observe their own bodies and events from above. Traveling toward a bright, welcoming light, and experiencing overwhelming feelings of peace, joy, and love. And so on. Many also report heightened awareness, altered perception of time, and a sense of entering another realm."

"Is that what *you* felt?" asked Pappas.

The president nodded. "It is."

"Can I assume you're familiar with the case of Pam Reynolds?" asked the MIT scientist.

"I am," said Morales. "But why don't you provide a quick summary for those here who aren't."

"Of course. In 1991, Pam Reynolds, a 35-year-old American, underwent a rare 'standstill' brain surgery for a giant basilar artery aneurysm," he began, clearly drawing from a lecture he'd given at MIT countless times. "To access the aneurysm safely, surgeons induced hypothermic cardiac arrest. Her body temperature was lowered from 98 to 60. Her heartbeat and breathing were stopped. Her EEG showed no brain activity, and blood was drained from her head, rendering her clinically dead by every medical standard. Her eyes were taped shut, and her ears were plugged with speakers emitting loud clicks to monitor brainstem function."

He paused. "After recovery, Reynolds reported a profound near-death experience, including an out-of-body perspective where she floated above the operating table, accurately describing the unusual bone saw and overhearing specific conversation among the surgical team. These details were later verified as correct by the medical staff, including the neurosurgeon."

Lukas's mouth almost dropped open. Tukdam and now this. How were so many people unaware of these seemingly supernatural cases that science seemed to now have confirmed?

"Thank you," said Morales. "A far more concise description of the case than I could have managed. But, please," he added, motioning to Mira. "We never let you finish. You were about to describe something you called tukdam."

"Right," said Mira, quickly gathering her thoughts. "Some Tibetan monks can remain in a state that Western medicine can't explain for days or even weeks after cardiac arrest and brain death. Their bodies show no signs of decay, their posture remains upright, their facial features are relaxed, and there is no rigor mortis."

Morales considered. "You said *Western* medicine. Can I assume that means that our science has verified some of these claims?"

"*All* of these claims. Scientists at the University of Wisconsin and the Max Planck Institute systematically investigated these cases. The findings are clear: these people are in a state of consciousness beyond our current understanding."

The president remained silent for several long seconds, appearing to be deep in thought. "Okay, given my background and what I'm already convinced is true, I'd be the last to argue that the human mind doesn't contain any number of surprise capabilities. So where is this leading?"

Mira took a deep breath. "Mr. President, I believe that forty-five hundred years ago, the ancient Egyptians were also confronted with the arrival of the same pyramid-shaped objects we're seeing. But because their culture focused on the mind rather than our science and tech, they found a solution that we haven't."

"You're basing this on findings from the Star Chamber in Giza?" said Morales.

"Yes, partially. But the bottom line is that I'm absolutely convinced we can't communicate with them using any of our science and tech. We've tried everything the world can think of, and we've failed. Why? Because these objects will only respond to communication through consciousness itself. The murals in the Star Chamber show six priests in the tukdam state and a seventh who acted as a mediator between them and the sky gods."

Dr. Pappas nodded his agreement. "Quantum physics teaches us that information may be transmitted at levels we can't yet measure. Quantum entanglement has repeatedly demonstrated that particles can be linked with each other, such that an action on one instantaneously affects the action of the other—even across distances as vast as the entire known universe. If consciousness is indeed a quantum phenomenon, then there could be forms of communication that our current instruments can't detect."

"The Egyptian priests appear to have realized that human consciousness could serve as a kind of interface to higher-dimensional intelligences," added Mira. "We desperately need to try that same solution today."

Morales leaned back, his face impenetrable as stone. Finally, he issued a loud sigh. "Even if you're right, we don't have any ancient Egyptian priests at our disposal, do we? Although, perhaps we could convince these Tibetan monks of yours to help."

Dr. Pappas smiled faintly. "We have another alternative, actually. Which is why I'm here."

"Don't keep me in suspense."

Pappas opened his briefcase and took out a small vial filled with a clear liquid. "We have this. A psychoactive compound I've discovered."

He placed the injection module with a steady hand on the small table between two sofas. "What you see here is what I've named Nirolex. It's the result of 12 years of translational neuroscience. It isn't a sedative or a hallucinogen, but a targeted consciousness modulator. Our goal is to use it to induce defined neural states that have previously only been observed in the most advanced meditation practitioners—or, in some cases, through substances such as psilocybin, which is found in many mushroom species."

He pointed to a tablet computer resting on the table. "Can I borrow that for a moment?"

Pappas's fingers flew over the device, and less than a minute later, turned the display for all to see. It now showed a complex spectral diagram of the human brain.

"What you see here is what is known as frontoparietal gamma coherence—a pattern documented by Professor Richard Davidson at the University of Wisconsin in these Tibetan monks we've been speaking so much about. Monks with over 10,000 hours of meditation practice. These synchronized high-frequency patterns occur spontaneously during deep awareness—during presence without a stream of consciousness. Until now, they were considered non-pharmacologically reproducible."

He tapped gently on the injection module. "That changes with Nirolex. The active ingredient takes effect after about five minutes. Nirolex works through three synergistically coordinated mechanisms. First, through the selective modulation of GABA-A receptors in the thalamus. Neurologically speaking, the thalamus is our filter to the world—it decides what we consciously perceive. Second, by hitting the same serotonin receptor activated by psilocybin, it helps a subject achieve expanded awareness of inner processes, a kind of shortcut to deep meditation. Third, it stabilizes certain frequency patterns via the modulation of T-type calcium channels. These channels are crucial for the rhythmization of neural networks."

"Which all means *what*?" asked Morales.

"Within minutes, our test subjects under Nirolex show the same neural activity patterns as experts who have honed meditation for decades."

"Why haven't I heard of this drug before now?" asked the president.

"It isn't approved. We've only begun studying it in human patients. But it's become absolutely clear that it opens a door—not to an escape from reality, but to a deeper, unfiltered perception of it. Bottom line, it's the first scientifically controlled access to an expanded state of consciousness."

"Sounds too good to be true," said the president.

Pappas winced. "It does have one problem that's been holding it back." He took a deep breath. "It only works once. It's still unclear why, but the brain develops some kind of immunity to it after one use."

"All we'll need is one use," said Morales. "We should try it immediately."

"I already did," admitted Pappas. "I had several of my test subjects try to contact the pyramids right after I spoke with Mira about the idea. All reported the same thing. They felt as if they were connecting with something amazing, a unique otherness that they describe as totally alien to human experience. But the connection was too tenuous. Whenever they were at the height of their expansion of consciousness, they felt as if they experienced too much noise. Like the consciousness of billions of beings was drowning out the unique signal they were trying to channel. It was like trying to see the contours of a bright object through thick clouds. They could see the glow, but couldn't hone in on the shape."

Morales shook his head in contempt. "So you tried and failed," he said angrily. "You should have led with that! Why have you wasted my time?"

Pappas winced again. "Because I don't think we failed at all. I think our success was just drowned out. And just barely based on the interviews I conducted with the test subjects. Bear with me. If Mira is right, the ancient Egyptians were able to connect with the objects from Earth. But the world population back then was only about thirty million. Thirty million—far less even than the population of California today. So they were able to connect to the alien despite the noise from thirty million conscious minds. But now the world population exceeds *eight billion*. More than 250 times the ancient population. I think *that's* what's holding us back."

The president's eyes narrowed. "I see," he responded. "And I get where you're going with this. We're sending a ship to meet them in space."

"Exactly!" said Pappas. "Exactly. I propose this be attempted again on your Project Osiris mission. It isn't that we need to get closer to the objects to succeed. It's that we need to get as far away from the *noise* as we possibly can before we give it a try. To get the clearest signal. Especially since, given the nature of the drug, we'll only have one shot at it."

Morales remained silent, still fuming.

"I know it isn't a perfect situation," pleaded Pappas. "But I can't urge you enough to give this a green light. I'm absolutely convinced it will work. I can send you videos of what the subjects told me. It's pretty compelling, even though we ultimately failed."

There was a lengthy silence in the room. It seemed as if no one even dared to breathe.

"I'll consider it," said the president finally, still looking infuriated by Pappas's bait and switch. "I thought this was too good to be true," he added. "And I was clearly right. I wish like hell I hadn't been, for once."

28

The Willard InterContinental Hotel towered over Pennsylvania Avenue like a marble witness to American history, its neoclassical columns reflecting the golden light of the setting sun into their room. Lukas and Carlos were to spend two nights here, in luxury financed by taxpayers, while the world's powerful debated the fate of humanity.

Lukas and Carlos could have had separate rooms but decided to share one. Their friendship was the glue that seemed to hold them together in these times when the laws of physics and the limits of what was possible seemed to be renegotiated daily.

The room was a temple of American elegance and decadence: high ceilings with stucco work, heavy curtains in royal blue, antique furniture that told stories of generations of diplomats and state guests. Two queen-size beds, a desk, a refrigerator, and a TV that they refused to turn on. The last thing they needed was to watch more reports of disaster and impending doom.

Lukas sat by the window and looked down at the streets of Washington, where life seemed to flow on. People walked along the sidewalks, cars jammed in rush hour traffic, tourists photographed the White House—a spectacle of normality that seemed almost surreal in the face of the cosmic crisis.

"How crazy has everything become?" muttered Carlos, who was lying on his bed staring at the ceiling. "How did we get to this point? Did we really just visit the White House to discuss using mind-expanding drugs to prevent an extinction-level event?"

Lukas laughed, a sound that contained more despair than mirth. "My father once told me that science is like a maze—you think you know the way until you turn the next corner and realize that the maze is bigger than you ever imagined."

"Then your father was a wise man." Carlos sat up, his dark eyes thoughtful. "But maybe that's what good science is all about—being open to expanding the treasure trove of human knowledge, even if it comes from the most unlikely sources."

"You mean we should consider this another experiment?" Lukas turned away from the window.

"That's exactly what I mean, sí." Carlos stood up and began pacing the room—an old habit he had when thinking about complex problems. It used to drive Lukas crazy, but now he saw it as a charmingly quirky idiosyncrasy. "And what an experiment. We're talking about the nature of consciousness itself. About the possibility that mind and matter are fundamentally connected. About a form of communication that would go beyond our current understanding of information and causality."

An electronic ringing interrupted him. Lukas's cell phone vibrated on the nightstand, followed a few seconds later by Carlos's device. Both stared at the displays: Director Patterson, NASA Johnson Space Center.

Lukas sighed. "For the twelfth time today."

"The *thirteenth*," corrected Carlos with a grin. "I've been counting. Which means I've learned something new about you. Great at tensor calculus. Not so great at *addition*."

Lukas laughed as the phone finally stopped ringing. Neither of them felt like listening to Patterson's inevitable tirade about irresponsibility and insubordination. They knew what he would say: that astronaut training was losing critical time, that every day counted, that they were neglecting their duty to the mission.

But here, in this luxurious hotel room above the streets of the capital, another mission seemed to be taking shape—one not based on nuclear warheads and millions of miles of travel.

A loud knock at the door made them both look up. When Lukas opened it, Mira Najafi rushed into the room. Her dark eyes were wide, her posture tense. "Have you heard the news?" she asked.

Lukas and Carlos exchanged confused glances. "What news in particular?"

Without asking permission, Mira went to the TV and turned it on.

The large screen came to life, showing the familiar NewsNation studio with its red "BREAKING NEWS" banner. "Four more pyramid-shaped objects have appeared in the solar system," said the news anchor with the controlled drama of someone who was professionally accustomed to announcing disasters.

"Initial reports from NASA confirm that one of the objects is located near Jupiter and is already causing measurable disturbances in the gas giant's storm bands. Two more objects have been detected beyond Neptune's orbit, while a fourth has appeared in dangerous proximity to the Sun."

The image changed to a computer-generated representation of the solar system, in which seven black pyramids floated like gravestones in the cosmic landscape. The characteristic three images of the pyramids of Giza were a familiar sight between Earth and Mars.

"According to initial calculations, none of the new objects appear to be heading for Earth," continued the spokesperson. "But scientists confirm that they are clearly related to the three pyramids originally discovered. The most disturbing thing, however, is that they have literally appeared out of nowhere, which is puzzling astronomers worldwide."

Lukas stared at the screen, feeling his stomach tighten. His cell phone started ringing—Patterson again. Now he understood why the director had been so desperate to reach them.

"This doesn't change the mission," said Carlos finally, but his voice sounded less confident than usual. "It just makes the whole phenomenon even more mysterious. How can something appear out of nowhere?"

"Maybe they haven't," replied Mira thoughtfully. "Maybe they've always been there, they just haven't shown themselves."

Before any of them could respond, Ricarda Lefèvre entered the room through the still-open door. She looked even more tired than usual, almost skeletal.

"The president and his closest advisors, together with the Chinese and Europeans, have made a decision," she said without further ado. "The project Dr. Pappas just pitched the president will be officially integrated into Project Osiris, under the leadership of Dr. Pappas and Dr. Najafi."

"Thank God," said Lukas with a sigh of relief.

"I'll second that," said Carlos, smiling for the first time in days.

Mira simply plopped herself down into one of the armchairs, as if an unbearable weight had been lifted from her shoulders.

"The initiative has been designated as *Project Mindmeld*."

Lukas snorted. Was there anything in science that *Star Trek* hadn't influenced? He glanced at Lefèvre, and something about her expression troubled him. Her eyes showed no joy or triumph—only deep, professional exhaustion.

"What's the catch?" he asked.

Lefèvre sighed. "It's been agreed that an expert on the drug, Nirolex, and meditation techniques is needed on board the *Hope* for the project to work at all. Someone who understands the neurochemical processes and can intervene in an emergency."

Lukas felt his heart sink. "Meaning there's no room at the inn for me." He hadn't thought that far ahead, but it should have been obvious that if Pappas's project was approved, a change of crew would be required.

"No," said Lefèvre quickly. "Your presence on the *Hope* is non-negotiable. It's still possible that ideas will be generated from other scientific disciplines that an accomplished gravitational wave physicist like you will need to implement. *You're* definitely going, Dr. Heuer. But I'm afraid that Dr. Mendoza no longer will be."

Lukas looked at Carlos and saw the disappointment in his friend's eyes, which he was bravely trying to hide.

"Dr. Pappas would like to give Dr. Najafi priority," Lefèvre continued. "She's more experienced in meditation. She can also easily learn how to administer the drug and maintain the necessary equipment in the remaining four and a half weeks."

"Then I'm not going either," said Lukas firmly. "If my friend is being left out, I'd rather stay here. There are plenty of gravitational wave researchers who are at least as good as me, if not better."

Carlos put a hand on his arm, his smile sad but genuine. "I appreciate that, amigo. Really. But you have a responsibility now—not just to the whole world, but also to me. You aren't just a gravitational wave researcher, you're one of the faces of hope for the whole world. Don't forget that. I'll support you from Mission Control."

29

Over the next four and a half weeks, the Johnson Space Center turned into a buzzing hive. Mira woke up every morning at five o'clock in her Spartan accommodation on the NASA site, feeling the weight of what lay ahead with her first breath.

The days flowed into one another like waves in the ocean, a constant ebb and flow, demanding and intense, leaving her every muscle aching and her head buzzing each evening. Ten to twelve hours of joint training with Lukas and the two pilots—Colonel James Harrison from the USA and Major Wei Lin from China, two people whose calm competence gave her hope that they might actually survive. Then another five to six hours of specialized training, separately, each in their own field of activity, tailored to their tasks for the mission.

"The human brain," explained Dr. Pappas one Tuesday afternoon in the sterile environment of the neuroscience lab, "is an instrument of unimaginable precision. But like any instrument, it must be understood before it can be mastered." His fingers glided over the surface of a holographic brain model on a touch display.

Mira absorbed every word, her notebooks filling with diagrams of neural networks, dosing protocols, and emergency procedures. The Nirolex system was a work of art in microelectronics and pharmaceutical precision—eight individual injection modules, each calibrated to the specific neurological profiles of the crew members, except for the two pilots. Four for the planned mission and four as redundant replacements.

"It's administered subcutaneously via these microneedles," explained Dr. Elizabeth Kozlov, a physician with the patience of a teacher and the precision of a surgeon. "Five milligrams per kilogram of body weight, dissolved in 20 milliliters of sterile saline solution.

Absorption takes three to five minutes, and the full effect is achieved after about eight minutes. The half-life is eight hours."

Mira practiced on dolls, on simulators, on volunteer test subjects, until her movements took on the fluid elegance of years of experience. She learned to handle the modules like a musician handles their instrument—with respect, precision, and an intuition that eventually transcended conscious thought. Later, she repeated all of this for two days on a total of 100 parabolic flights in microgravity.

The physical training was hard and pushed her to her limits. Every day. In the centrifuge, a mechanical monster made of steel in a cramped round chamber with ugly bathroom tiles, they learned to endure the G-forces of launch—that brutal embrace of acceleration that could make the human body many times heavier, placing great strain on the vascular system and bones.

"Breathe in a controlled manner according to the pattern we discussed," shouted Colonel Harrison through her headset as the centrifuge pressed them into their seats with five times the force of gravity. "Tense your abdominal muscles. Fight against fainting."

Mira felt the blood drain from her head, a gray veil narrowing her field of vision and black veils closing in from the sides. But she fought, focusing her thoughts to a point of clarity, to that calm center she had found in her meditation.

In zero-gravity training, in addition to their hundred flights for medical training in 0g—the "vomit comet," as NASA veterans affectionately called the modified aircraft—they learned to optimize their movements in zero gravity. Thirty seconds of free fall, during which the human body shed its earthly shackles and, for a brief time, became what it would be in space: weightless, without up or down, high or low.

Lukas moved with surprising grace in zero gravity. His normally tense shoulders relaxed, his face took on an expression of peaceful concentration. In these moments, Mira recognized the man he might have been before the discovery of the pyramids—the scientist who explored the mysteries of the universe with the curiosity of a child. At that moment, she somehow felt sorry for him and sensed something of the burden that must rest on his shoulders as the face of the discovery of the supposed end of the world.

"You have a natural talent for this," remarked Major Wei after a particularly elegant maneuver in which Lukas had pushed himself from one wall to another, turning around the transverse axis. "Most people become frantic from the unfamiliar impulses triggered by every touch and every movement. You dance with it, you glide. That's exactly the right way to do it."

Lukas issued a rare smile.

In the technical training sessions, the starship revealed itself to be an astonishingly simple marvel of technology that was quite straightforward. Each system was clearly labeled and, from her point of view, intuitively structured: the life support system with its complicated oxygen and carbon dioxide cycles, the navigation systems with their wide touch displays, the communication systems, the radiator controls, and much more. Overall, she was impressed by what the SpaceX engineers had achieved.

Lukas spent hours every day studying the scientific instruments. The quantum communication system consisted of crystals and precision lasers that sent entangled photons through a vacuum tube. The magnetometer array registered even the faintest magnetic disturbances.

"Each instrument shows us something that our senses can't perceive," he explained to Mira during a break. "When we encounter the pyramids out there, these are our only means of understanding their true nature."

He didn't say "if at all," but it was clear from his expression. In recent weeks, no new ideas had emerged from the international commission of experts or the public, which apparently significantly reduced his hope that someone would come up with a groundbreaking idea.

Mira just nodded and watched how Lukas had changed in recent weeks. The pain of Carlos's absence was still there, but the intense work was obviously helping him get over it. He was becoming calmer and more focused with each passing day.

Her own training was different, but just as intense. While Lukas explored the secrets of the scientific onboard systems, she learned about the mysteries of human consciousness from a medical and neurological perspective and tried to learn as much as possible about how the drug worked.

All six crew members trained together and apart, depending on their responsibilities. She and Lukas were the only two without any experience in space. Colonel James Harrison and Dr. Michael Torres from NASA had flown a number of missions, as had Major Wei Lin and Dr. Liu Xiaoming from the Chinese Space Agency.

The simulator was a decommissioned Block 3 starship that served as an exact replica of the *Hope*, with fully functional systems. This allowed them to simulate everything they would encounter out there. Here, they not only learned about the technical systems, but above all, how to work together in a confined space without small problems turning into major conflicts.

"In space, a dispute over minor issues can jeopardize the entire mission," warned Dr. Patricia Williams, the mission psychologist. "You must learn to address your problems quickly and directly without taking it personally."

Mira realized that this was mainly directed at her and Lukas, as the four experienced astronauts were already carefully selected and experienced personality types who were perfect for such missions.

They practiced various scenarios: system failures, medical emergencies, disagreements about priorities. Mira noticed that everyone reacted differently to stress. Lukas became calmer and more thoughtful. Colonel Harrison spoke more directly and concisely. Dr. Torres made more jokes. Major Wei remained polite but firm. Dr. Liu became very quiet and focused.

"You complement each other well," observed Dr. Williams after one of the last long exercises. "That will be the most important thing when you're out there."

Parallel to these joint training sessions, Mira spent five to six hours a day with Dr. Pappas and his medical team. She learned everything about the Nirolex system—from its chemical composition to the smallest details of its application.

With Dr. Pappas, Mira delved deeper into the mysteries of human consciousness than she had ever thought possible. The Nirolex system was more than just a drug—it was a key to doors that humanity had been trying to open for millennia.

"The critical phase is between 8 and 12 minutes after the injection," Dr. Pappas explained as she practiced the application on a volunteer. "During this time window, consciousness opens up to states that are normally only achievable in the deepest meditation. The patient is fully conscious, but the normal filters of perception are loosened. This is precisely when it's most important that you gently guide the others to lead them even deeper. Nirolex is only a door opener; you have to walk through it yourself."

She practiced the application again and again until every movement became automatic. Opening the sterile module, preparing the injection, monitoring vital signs during the critical phase. Her notebooks filled with EEG patterns, heart rate variations, the subtle signs of a consciousness in transformation.

"What do you see?" she asked one of the test subjects, a young NASA engineer whose EEG curves showed the characteristic gamma waves.

"It's like a fog lifting," he replied in a voice imbued with quiet humility. "I breathe. I am. Something is dissolving. Ah."

In moments like these, Mira felt a deep resonance with the meditation experiences of her time in Tibet. She was familiar with what the engineer was describing—those moments of clarity in which the boundaries between here and there, between self and non-self, blurred, where duality became non-duality.

The penultimate evening came like the sunset at the end of a long journey—inevitable, yet strangely surprising. The weeks had felt like a single fever dream, like a small eternity, and yet had passed at breakneck speed.

They had already been in quarantine for two days, shielded from the outside world in a sterile bubble of filtered air and under constant medical supervision by doctors in chemical protection suits. No risk of infection was allowed to jeopardize their mission; replacement candidates were standing by in case even one of them fell ill. But of course, after all this, no one wanted to have to back out.

Mira sat in her Spartan quarantine room at night and looked out through the small window at Houston. The city sparkled like a field of stars, each light the home of a person counting on them to succeed.

Her hands rested calmly on the open notebook in her lap—pages full of diagrams, protocols, notes containing the condensed knowledge of five weeks of intensive preparation. She thought of her father, of his notes under the stone table, of the millennia-old wisdom she now hoped to carry into space.

A soft knock on her door made her look up. Through the small window, she saw Lukas with a faint smile on his face.

"Can't sleep either?" he asked through the intercom.

"Who could?" she replied.

They sat down on the floor, their backs against the wall of the living room with the pool table. The entire accommodation supposedly dated back to the Apollo era and had a certain shared apartment character, where one could almost forget that they were on the cutting edge of human technology and were attempting something that had never been dared before.

"Are you afraid?" asked Lukas after a while.

Mira thought for a moment. "Not of dying," she said finally. "But of failing. Of holding the key in our hands and still not being able to turn it when it matters."

"You won't fail, Dr. Najafi," said Lukas with a certainty that surprised her. "I've seen you work over the last few weeks. Your dedication, your thoroughness. You're ready."

"*We're* ready," she corrected him gently. "And shouldn't we start using first names?"

"Right. I'm Lukas." He held out his hand to her.

"Mira."

He smiled, and she recognized in that smile the man who had turned the pain of Carlos's absence into a new kind of determination. The weeks of training had not only turned them into budding astronauts, but also into something rare and precious: a team ready to attempt the impossible.

Outside, the Earth continued to turn, people went to sleep and would wake up, go to their jobs, love their families, argue, debate, play sports, meditate, ponder the meaning of life, and look up at the stars. And it was their job to make sure that continued.

"Aliens," she said into the darkness at some point. "I've studied pyramids for a long time," she added in amusement. "But I always thought the aliens would arrive in flying saucers. Who knew?"

He laughed.

"Are you leaving anyone behind?" asked Mira.

"No. I'm newly divorced."

"Oh. I'm sorry."

"How about you? Who are you leaving behind?"

She shook her head. "Not a soul. My father was my last relative, and he died in Tibet, as you know."

"Yes. I'm sorry."

"Don't be," she said gently. "It all led me here. He gave his life for what I believe will end up being the greatest purpose there is. And we should look on the bright side," she added sarcastically. "If we fail, you won't have to deal with divorce lawyers, and I won't have to hassle with inheritance tax."

"Yes, taxes," agreed Lukas. "The true scourge of humanity."

Both neophyte astronauts laughed.

"At least no one will call and ask why we haven't been in touch for so long," she added with a chuckle.

"I have a confession to make," said Lukas, and it was clear they had suddenly become punch drunk as laughter had released the unbearable pressure that had been building for some time. "This was my childhood dream. When anyone asked me what I wanted to do when I grew up, I always gave the same answer: my dream is to fly to a trio of super-massive space pyramids in a spaceship crammed with nukes."

They chuckled, a wonderfully bizarre moment.

"Dare to dream," said Mira.

30

The Texas air carried an unusual warmth for a late autumn evening, as if even the seasons had been thrown off balance by what humanity would attempt the next morning. Lukas sat on one of the wooden chairs on the porch of the quarantine house and gazed at the *Hope*, which stood in the distance on its launch pad like a 40-story monolith—ironically the same height as the Cheops pyramid. The mighty rocket was illuminated by spotlights, its silver steel shell standing out sharply against the darkening sky.

The six crew members had gathered here spontaneously after the official briefing had ended. Colonel James Harrison and Dr. Michael Torres sat relaxed at the wooden table, their legs dangling in the air like children. Major Wei Lin had fetched a chair and sat with the calm demeanor of someone who had made patience an art form. Dr. Liu Xiaoming, on the other hand, leaned against the railing and gazed thoughtfully into the distance.

Lukas sat next to Mira, her hands resting in her lap, but he could see the tension in her strained, slightly raised shoulders. They had become closer in the days leading up to the mission than either had expected.

"Five billion people will be watching," noted Dr. Torres, shaking his head. "That's more viewers on livestreams and TV than all the Olympic Games combined."

Lukas felt his shoulders tense up. "Great," he said sarcastically. "That doesn't put any added pressure on us at *all*."

Mira laughed.

Colonel Harrison opened a bottle of beer with a loud hiss. He then opened five more and passed them around until everyone had one in their hand.

After they had all clinked bottles and taken a long, reverent sip, Harrison looked at Mira. "There's something I'd like to understand," he said. "This *Mindmeld* project. The idea is to meditate and expand consciousness and thereby talk to aliens. How is that supposed to work without it just being hallucinogenic fantasy, like a drug trip?"

"Really?" said Mira. "In all this time, no one walked you through the Mindmeld part of the operation?"

"Just the basics."

"I suspect you just see the human brain as a sort of biological computer, don't you?"

He affirmed that he did, and she spent several minutes walking him through the hard problem of consciousness, including the example of trying to explain the color red to a blind man. "So our minds are a lot more than a biological computer," she concluded. "Rational thinking is just one aspect of human consciousness."

"But rational thinking has given us science, technology, and medicine," said the colonel.

"Yes and no. For incremental progress, rational thinking can do wonders. But the big leaps forward, those often come from somewhere else. Epic scientific breakthroughs most often spring from eureka moments, when the analytical mind becomes still and a deeper kind of knowledge emerges. Einstein called it intuition. Kepler spoke of divine inspiration."

Lukas realized that he was nodding. "She's right. The theory of relativity, quantum mechanics—the most important discoveries in physics often came as sudden flashes of inspiration."

"But these eureka moments can still be explained rationally," insisted Harrison. "The subconscious processes information behind the scenes and makes connections. It works on a thorny puzzle day and night without us knowing it while we attend to friends, meetings, movies, and other duties that require our conscious attention. When our subconscious finally solves the puzzle, it presents it to us—seemingly from out of nowhere."

"Maybe," said Mira. "But maybe it's something else. Maybe consciousness isn't just a product of the brain, but a fundamental aspect of reality itself."

"What do you mean?"

"Think of quantum physics. Observation changes the observed system. The observer's consciousness plays a fundamental role in the structure of reality. Some physicists even argue that consciousness doesn't arise from matter—matter arises from *consciousness*."

She paused. "Look up at the stars, Colonel. Every photon that reaches your eyes has traveled for years or centuries or millennia. But it only exists in the moment it interacts with your consciousness. Without an observer, they are just probability waves in a quantum mechanical field."

"That's one interpretation of quantum mechanics, not the only one."

"True. But it oddly reflects philosophies that have been taught for millennia by the great spiritual traditions. Which claim that the universe is not only made up of matter and energy, but of consciousness. That we are not separate observers, but part of a larger, self-aware cosmos, and that everything is one great consciousness."

"Is there any evidence of that?"

"Yes. I'll share something I find particularly intriguing." She went on to describe near-death experiences and the case of Pam Reynolds, in particular.

"NDEs involve profound, expanded states of consciousness," continued Mira when she had finished. "Like feelings of complete unity with everything, which many report when their brain activity is severely reduced, flat-lined, or entirely *absent,* as was the case with Pam. If consciousness was just a function of the mind, imprisoned in the brain, you'd expect it to vanish when the brain shuts down. But it does the opposite of that. In fact, it seems as if our brains are *preventing* us from experiencing this universal consciousness. So, when brain function drops sharply, the filter weakens—allowing more of that vast, connected awareness to come through. Which is why consciousness seems to feel so incredibly expanded precisely when the brain is *least* active."

Harrison looked on thoughtfully. "I have to admit, that is pretty intriguing. Anything else you find equally intriguing while we're at it?"

"As a matter of fact, yes," said Mira. "I've been doing reading in molecular biology. The more we learn about the astonishing, *ridiculous* complexity of a single cell, the more impossible the idea that it could arise by random chance becomes. Not in the lifetimes of a trillion times a trillion universes. So is there a Creator? If so, who made the Creator? If not, who made the universe? At the end of the day, we understand nothing."

Lukas was mesmerized by this woman, in more ways than one.

"One last thought on consciousness before we change the subject," she said. "When you sit quietly, or especially when you meditate, you start noticing something odd: thoughts just come and go on their own. Feelings come and go. Even the sense of "I" or "me" is just another thought that shows up sometimes. There's no fixed little boss inside who controls everything.

"It's all just happening in one big field of awareness—like clouds moving across the sky. The sky doesn't own the clouds. The sky is the space where clouds appear and disappear. So you don't really have a life, like you have a phone or a dog. You *are* a life. You're the living, aware energy that's already happening—right now—and all thoughts, including those about 'my life' are just waves on that ocean."

"Wow," said Lukas. "I can actually feel my brain melting as I try to make sense of what you just said."

Mira laughed. "Yeah, if only we had the time, there's a great monastery in Tibet that can help you with that problem."

Harrison was now absently rolling the now-empty beer bottle back and forth between his large hands. "What does that mean for our mission?"

"It means that communication can take place not only via electromagnetic waves or gravitational signals. Consciousness could communicate directly with consciousness, on a level deeper than language or symbols. I'm convinced of that, which is why I'm so sold on this Mindmeld idea."

Harrison sighed. "Why not?" he said. "If the Vulcans can do it, even a half-breed like Spock, why can't we?"

"That's the spirit."

Dr. Torres had been silent until now, but he interjected. "I was skeptical when I first heard about this Nirolex. But then I spoke with some of the test subjects. They all described the same thing—a feeling of connection with everything, a knowledge without words."

"That's exactly what I believe the ancient Egyptian priests experienced," added Mira. "They understood that consciousness is the key to communicating with the gods—their words for extraterrestrials, I suppose."

Harrison was silent for a long time. The stars grew brighter as the last remnants of daylight faded. Finally, he sighed. "I, for one, look forward to finding out. One thing is indisputable: the universe is far stranger than we can possibly comprehend. The good news is that, no matter what, once our mission starts tomorrow, we won't be bored."

He raised his eyebrows. "Dead, maybe. But surely not bored."

31

The cockpit of the *Hope* enveloped Mira like a cocoon of carbon fiber and titanium, a microcosm of human engineering on the edge of cosmic infinity. She lay in her seat, the straps pressing against her shoulders and hips, while her heartbeat hammered against her ribs with such intensity that it almost hurt. Nervousness was too weak a word for what she was feeling—it was a symphony of awe, fear, and electrifying anticipation.

Above her arched the cockpit's panoramic window, through which she could see the azure sky of Florida, still innocent and peaceful before it would transform into the velvety black of space. The other five lay in similar seats arranged around her, each encased in the white pressure suit designed to protect them in the event of an accident.

The hours leading up to this moment merged in her memory into a kaleidoscope of rehearsed procedures and mounting nervousness. The wake-up call at four in the morning, the traditional astronaut breakfast—scrambled eggs, steak, toast, all easily digestible and high in protein to fortify the body for the rigors of launch. The medical examination, during which every pulse, every breath, every blood pressure reading was documented. Putting on the space suits, a complex process involving attached tubes, cables, and life support systems that transformed them from biological beings into technological hybrids. All of this surrounded by NASA and SpaceX technicians who cared for them like bees care for their queen.

The last phone calls with their families, the short, intense conversations, while she herself had talked quietly with Lukas and had become painfully aware that no one would miss her if something were to happen today. Finally, the walk-out, the ceremonial march to the launch pad, while cameras from all over the world followed their steps. They waved in different directions and smiled broadly, precisely timed according to the briefings, even though Mira, at least, had been nauseous.

"*Hope*, this is Launch Control. What is your status?" Commander Patricia Wells's voice crackled through the communication system.

"Launch Control, this is *Hope*," replied Colonel Harrison with the calm professionalism earned over 17 space flights. "All systems nominal. Crew ready for final launch preparations."

Mira listened as Harrison and Major Wei worked through the checklist, their voices a soothing song in her ears.

"Main engines?"

"All Raptors green. Fuel pressure nominal."

"Life support?"

"Oxygen 100 percent, CO2 scrubber active, temperature control nominal."

"Navigation?"

"GPS lock confirmed, inertial system calibrated, flight computer ready."

The checklist was a litany of safety precautions, a prayer to the gods of physics and engineering. Each item was steeped in the blood and sweat of countless engineers who had invested years of their lives to ensure that these six people would leave Earth alive, and generations of astronauts who had paid for the first steps of their profession with their lives.

"*Hope*, external fueling complete. Fuel tanks 100 percent full. Countdown to ten minutes. Starting now."

Mira felt the subtle vibration of the rocket as the fuel hoses were retracted. Beneath her lay 300 tons of liquid oxygen and methane, a controlled explosion waiting to be unleashed. At that moment, the *Hope* was the most complex object humanity had ever created—a fusion of science, technology, and the collective hopes of an entire civilization.

"T-minus ten minutes and counting," announced Launch Control.

Mira turned her head toward one of the small cameras mounted in the cockpit. Somewhere out there, five billion people sat in front of their screens, holding their breath, praying to their various gods, hoping and fearing. Children in school classrooms, families in their living rooms, scientists in research facilities, politicians in crisis centers—all united in this one moment of human audacity, unable to do anything but wait.

Everything had been staked on this one card. Not only the technological resources of multiple nations, but the hopes of an entire species, which for the first time in its history was consciously encountering intelligence from the stars.

"T-minus five minutes. All stations, prepare for launch sequence."

The last few minutes stretched out like centuries. Mira checked her straps and the HUD systems on her helmet one last time, then closed her eyes and took a deep breath, searching within herself for that quiet place she had found in meditation.

"T-minus one minute. Engines in launch mode."

The deep rumble of the Raptor engines penetrated her bones, a mechanical heartbeat announcing the life of the rocket. The *Hope* trembled like a living being, or perhaps it was just her galloping pulse.

"T-minus thirty seconds."

"Twenty."

"Ten."

"Nine."

She held her breath.

"Eight. Seven. Six."

"Engine ignition!"

The world exploded in light and thunder. Seventy-five meganewtons of thrust pressed Mira into her seat as if a giant hand were trying to crush her. The rumble of the engines merged with the pounding of her heart.

"Liftoff! *Hope* has left the launchpad," she heard the sober voice of Launch Control over the radio.

Through the window, Mira saw the few clouds above them rapidly growing larger. The launch pad, which minutes earlier had been her world, became a tiny dot in an expanding landscape on her screen. Florida spread out below them like a detailed map, crisscrossed by the silver veins of rivers and the geometric patterns of human cities and towns.

"*Hope*, this is Launch Control. Everything good from down here. Speed 400 meters per second and climbing."

The first phase of the ascent was a battle against Earth's gravity, a tug-of-war between the ancient force that pulled everything down and the human will to break free from it. The 33 Raptor engines converted chemical energy into kinetic motion with an efficiency that bordered on magic.

"Mach 1 achieved," reported the Major calmly. "All systems nominal."

They broke the sound barrier. Everything vibrated and shook.

"Maximum dynamic pressure," said Harrison. "Max Q. Engines reduced to 80 percent."

This was the most critical moment of the ascent, when the combination of speed and air density exerted the greatest stress on the rocket's structure. The *Hope* was shaken by invisible forces like a dog that had sunk its teeth into unruly prey.

"Max Q overcome. Engines back to full power."

At an altitude of 40 miles, the sky began to change. The blue gave way to a deeper indigo, then a purple reminiscent of the edge of space. Mira felt gravity losing its hold on her, degree by degree, mile by mile.

"Eight hundred meters per second. One hundred kilometers altitude reached."

They were now officially in space, but not yet in orbit. That was the difference that most people didn't understand—space was just altitude, but orbit was speed. They not only had to climb high enough to escape the atmosphere, but also had to get fast enough to continuously fall around the Earth without ever touching it.

"MECO—Main Engine Cut Off," announced Harrison. "First stage jettisoned."

The engines fell silent, and suddenly there was an eerie quiet. Mira felt her body press against the straps—they were now falling freely, carried only by their speed and the curvature of space-time around the Earth.

"Second stage ignition in 30 seconds," reported Launch Control.

The six slightly smaller vacuum-optimized Raptor engines roared to life. This phase of the ascent was more elegant, a precise orbital maneuver that would carry them into perfect orbit.

"Orbital insertion burn begins . . . now."

For the next four minutes, the engine burned with mathematical precision, changing their velocity by exactly 600 meters per second. It was a ballet of physics, choreographed by Newton and Kepler, executed by computers and human calculations.

"Engine cut off. Orbital insertion complete. Congratulations, *Hope*. You're in orbit," announced Starbase Mission Control with a hint of celebration. While they had trained at the NASA facility in Houston, the mission was being controlled from SpaceX's launch facility in Starbase, Texas.

Mira allowed herself a long exhale. Only now did she realize that she had been squeezing Lukas's right hand with her left the whole time.

When she glanced at him from the side, he just smiled.

Through the window, she saw Earth in all its breathtaking glory. The curvature of the horizon, the thin blue line of the atmosphere, the continents and oceans, all in a clarity that no photo could ever capture. Mira felt tears welling up in her eyes—not just because of the beauty, but because of the sheer improbability of this moment.

"*Hope*, this is Mission Control. We have you on the scopes. Perfect orbit, 280 kilometers altitude. Prepare for rendezvous with the equipment package."

The next phase of their mission was another precisely calculated maneuver: thirty kilometers ahead of them waited an unmanned vehicle loaded with equipment that had been too heavy to carry during launch. The thermonuclear warheads, each a huge rocket in its own right, were waiting later in the same orbit.

"Rendezvous burn in five minutes," reported Major Wei. "Target distance 34 kilometers."

The *Hope*'s control rockets fired in precise pulses, changing its orbit by a few meters per minute. It was a lesson in patience and precision—in space, there was no rush, only the mathematical certainty of orbital mechanics and trust in the computers' calculations and their input from the sensors.

"Visual contact with target," called Dr. Torres. "Twelve o'clock, two kilometers away."

The equipment package floated in front of them like a metal asteroid, its solar panels glistening in the sunlight. Robotic arms came to life as AI systems took over the complex choreography of docking.

"Docking initiated," confirmed the synthetic voice of the onboard computer after several minutes. "Monitoring structural integrity during transfer."

Mira watched with fascination as robotic arms moved with a precision that human hands could never achieve, connecting cables, sensors, cooling systems, and data links with silent equanimity.

"Installation of the scientific package 80 percent complete," reported Mission Control.

Then they reached the nuclear weapons.

"Weapons system now being integrated."

The thermonuclear warheads were handled with even greater care, each secured individually in specially designed mounts after the *Hope*'s hull hatches had opened. It was a strange irony—the same species that had created these instruments of destruction was now sending them into space to potentially enable peaceful communication with an alien intelligence. Mira felt as if she were marching out with a white flag of truce while simultaneously concealing a sharpened knife behind her back.

"All systems integrated and tested," the onboard computer announced after an hour. "*Hope* is ready for her interplanetary mission."

"*Hope*, this is Mission Control Starbase. Everything looks excellent."

Seconds later, they heard the voice of Commander Wells. "We have an update on the secondary objects. The four newly discovered pyramids are not approaching Earth but are moving through the solar system at the same speed as the original three objects. Their purpose remains unclear, but they appear to be forming a coordinated formation, that much is certain."

Their mission remained the same—to make contact with an intelligence likely beyond human comprehension. Now it had just become stranger and more complex.

"Roger that, Starbase," replied Harrison. "We're heading for the original three objects."

"Affirmative. Burn time for primary injection: 14 minutes, 20 seconds. You have the green light for departure burn."

After being gently pressed into their seats for 14 minutes and ejected from Earth's orbit, Major Wei activated the ion engines, a whisper of electrified xenon that gently sent them on their journey.

"Ion engines nominal. Acceleration one-tenth G. Velocity change commencing . . . now."

Mira felt the gentle pressure against her back, barely stronger than the weight of a feather. But this delicate force would accelerate them over the next few months to speeds that would carry them to the pyramids, where the fate of humanity would be decided.

She had made a career out of studying pyramids, but she had to admit, leaving the Earth to do so had never seemed like an option.

Through the window, the Earth began to slowly shrink, from a world to a blue jewel floating in cosmic darkness. They were now travelers between worlds, pilgrims on a journey that would either lead them to first contact—or result in the extinction of humanity.

32

The *Hope* moved steadily through the darkness between planets, carried by the gentle, tireless power of its ion engines. Fourteen days had passed since its launch from Earth, fourteen days of continuous acceleration that carried them deeper into the vastness of the solar system. Lukas floated in his work area and gazed at the stars, which now looked different than they did from Earth—sharper, clearer, no longer refracted by the atmosphere, but in their original cosmic purity.

With the ion engines continuously accelerating the ship, they would reach the objects in 110 days—including the reversal maneuver and braking phase. But that was only half the physics that awaited them.

"From day 80 onwards, we'll feel the first gravitational effects," Dr. Torres had explained during one of the morning briefings, his voice calm and clear, as if he were talking about a simple banality. "Well . . . *maybe*. Maybe not. The truth is, we've been dealing with physics well beyond our understanding, so our predictive power is . . . unclear. The gravitational waves we detected from Earth mimic those of small neutron stars, but that doesn't mean the actual mass or tidal field behaves classically. Space-time itself *may* begin to deform in ways we can't predict. But I emphasize *may*."

Lukas nodded, his fingers gliding over the display of his tablet, which showed the calculations. He had worked it out himself with his colleague, poring over the formulas Einstein had developed more than a century ago during endless nights. The gravitational wave signature suggested enormous effective mass—perhaps two times that of the Sun—but the real gravitational influence was clearly *much* weaker, or focused in a directed pattern human scientists didn't understand.

"The tidal forces could destabilize our instruments," warned Wei Lin, his calm voice tinged with technical concern. "From day 90 onwards, we must expect systematic drift errors in the sensors. If the objects are directing their gravitational gradient toward us—like a beam—the stars will appear to change their positions, as if the universe itself were distorting."

"And from day 100," added Lukas, "we'll physically feel what it means to approach objects that can manipulate the fundamental forces of the cosmos. Our bodies may experience tidal forces that no human has ever felt before—again, assuming the influence sharpens as we close in."

Mira sighed. "So, to summarize, we basically have no fricking idea what will happen."

Lukas smiled. "Well, we have an *idea*. Based on how these objects have acted so far. We just can't count on them to behave. They seem able to disregard any law of physics they want to on a whim. So while we don't expect them to turn into an immense top hat filled with enormous bunny rabbits, if they wanted that to happen, I wouldn't bet against them."

"Right," said Major Wei. "But based on what we *think* we've learned, we should be able to get quite close."

"What do you mean by that?" asked Mira.

"He means that each object's bark is worse than its bite," said Lukas. "If the objects were as massive as their gravitational distortions suggest they are, Earth would have already been torn to pieces. And don't get me started on why they haven't crashed into each other. It's like putting two electromagnets within an atom of each other and watching as every steel object in sight slams into them, yet they, themselves, remain separated."

Mira grinned. "So I understand about as much of what's going on as you do," she said in amusement, "and I didn't even have to study physics."

Lukas winced. "Sure, Mira, rub it in. Thanks."

She laughed, but Harrison turned serious once more. "All I know is that when we reach the limit of what's possible in terms of tidal forces," he said, "we're supposed to accelerate back toward Earth.

I'm still hopeful that Xiaoming, Michael, and Lukas will determine that point early on."

"We'll certainly give it our best," said Lukas. "It was a lot easier when you could count on universal constants not changing on you. As I just said, the gravitational waves they emit don't provide any direct conclusions about their actual mass or local field."

He paused. "We need to be ready for anything. We'll have to stay alert for the first signs of gravitational effects, regardless of what our calculations tell us."

Mira smiled. "I don't know about you guys," she said wryly, "but I'm hoping like hell to see a giant top hat filled with bunnies. If the pyramids can hear me now and would like to show off, that's something I'd truly love for them to conjure up."

* * *

The *Hope*'s habitat module had been specially designed for its unprecedented challenges, a technological masterpiece based on decades of research for future Mars missions. Sixteen yards high and eight yards in diameter, it provided six people on four carefully planned decks with everything they needed to survive in the cosmic void.

The lowest deck housed the critical systems—water treatment, life support, and power distribution. Above that were the laboratories and computer stations, where hopefully the scientific work would take place once they were close enough.

The third deck was their social hub, with the galley, the common area, and the communication systems that connected them to an ever-distant Earth. Above, closer to the stars, were six tiny private cabins, each no larger than a phone booth, but with a porthole that offered a direct view of the shared interior.

Microgravity was a constant, invisible companion that determined every aspect of their lives. Objects floated with sluggish elegance when released, liquids formed perfect spheres that drifted through the air, and the human body slowly adapted to an existence in which the concepts of "up" and "down" had lost their meaning. In the early days, Lukas had learned to move with small, controlled jerks, shuffling along the ubiquitous handrails like an acrobat in a 3-dimensional circus without a net, just like on parabolic flights.

His days followed a precise, almost ritualistic rhythm that brought structure to the monotony and confinement. After waking up at six o'clock ship time—an arbitrary but necessary construct in a world without sunrise—he spent two hours doing intense physical training. The training device was a complex construction of rubber bands, resistance systems, and rotating elements that gave the body the illusion of weight and combated the creeping degradation of muscles and bones. Without this daily ritual, his muscles would atrophy within weeks, his bones would lose density, and his cardiovascular system would adapt to the lack of stress—a biological surrender to weightlessness.

"It's almost like moving meditation," Mira had remarked one morning as she watched him train, having finished her own exercises. And she was right—the repetitive movements, the conscious struggle against mechanical resistance, the rhythmic breathing created a state of concentration that made them forget the endless space around them for precious minutes. On some days, Mira even guided him, Xiaoming, and Michael, introducing them to simple mindfulness and breathing exercises, which at least Lukas continued to practice before falling asleep and after waking up because they helped him to be calmer and sleep better.

Most of his waking hours, however, were spent on the scientific tasks that formed the heart of their mission. The sensor systems' software was his personal responsibility and obsession. Hour after hour, he sat in front of the displays, checking millions of lines of code, simulating scenarios that could have come from science-fiction novels.

What would they measure when they got close to the objects? What unusual signals might occur? How should the computers respond to phenomena beyond all human experience? He programmed routines for gravitational anomalies, for distortions of space-time, for energy signatures that weren't in any textbook.

The communal meals had been James Harrison and Wei Lin's idea, a conscious act of social life—three times a day, all six of them gathered in the common area to share not only food, but also human connection, conversation, and the warmth of community in the cold of space. The food itself was a carefully planned mix of freeze-dried rations and hydroponically grown plants from the small but productive greenhouse. Tomatoes that glowed like ruby-red jewels, lettuce with leaves of unreal freshness, herbs that released their essential oils into the recycled air of the ship—tiny, precious reminders of life on Earth that shone with particular intensity in the sterile environment of the spacecraft.

"Who would have thought that a tomato tastes more intense in space than on Earth?" joked Michael one afternoon as he carefully maneuvered a slice into his floating mouth, a movement that was equal parts ballet and science.

Eating in microgravity was actually an art in itself, a daily lesson in physics and mindfulness. Crumbs could get stuck in air filters and block critical systems, liquids formed perfect spheres that drifted through the cabin and had to be caught before they entered electronic systems. Every bite was a conscious act, every meal an exercise in patience and precision that required mindfulness. James even joked regularly that they were all master meditators now and didn't need drugs.

The daily interviews were their most important connection to distant Earth, an electronic window through which five billion people followed their journey. Every day at 2 p.m. ship time, they tuned in to news channels or streaming platforms, answered questions from journalists around the world despite the already noticeable signal latency, and shared their experiences with their fellow humans who were eagerly awaiting news from space.

These interviews were more than just public relations or media spectacle. They were a psychological outlet, a vital connection to home that reminded them that they were drifting alone in the cosmic vastness, but for a very good reason. In the infinity of space, where the silence was so complete that it seemed to ring in their ears, the human psyche could become fragile, could lose itself in the realization of its own insignificance.

Sleeping in microgravity had initially been one of the greatest challenges for Lukas, a nocturnal struggle with the absence of weight and orientation. In his tiny cabin, he was wrapped in a specially designed sleeping bag that was attached to the wall like a chrysalis. There was no bed in the traditional sense, no pillow to rest his head on, no mattress to support his body. Instead, he floated in a shell of technical fabric, while the walls of the cabin enclosed him and safety straps prevented him from bumping into them. The darkness was absolute—deeper and more complete than any night on Earth, untouched by moonlight or the distant glow of cities. In this total blackness, he often dreamed of Earth, of gravity and wind and the feel of grass beneath his bare feet.

Daily washing, on the other hand, was a complex experiment in fluid dynamics and surface tension. Water formed shimmering balls that had to be captured and wiped away with special absorbent cloths before they could get into the electronics. Soap couldn't simply be rinsed off—it had to be removed mechanically, a time-consuming procedure that required patience and skill. Every day began and ended with these small, intimate rituals of personal hygiene. Sometimes he wished he were a robot.

What helped with all this were the many jokes that James, Michael, and Mira often cracked. They seemed to find something funny in everything and unerringly lightened up any tedious work.

He experienced a new intimacy with Mira, which permeated their life together. It was a bit maddening, but being inside cramped quarters on the *Hope,* on a mission to save humanity, wasn't exactly conducive to fostering *physical* intimacy. Still, he was grateful for the non-physical kind.

Mira was simply Mira, her daily meditation no longer a foreign, exotic practice, but a natural part of their shared rhythm. Wei spoke openly about his family back home, his wife Mei and his daughter Zhishao, showing photos and videos that had been transmitted through millions of miles of vacuum. Xiaoming proudly showed pictures of his orchids, explaining the years of patience it took for a bud to open.

Torres told vivid stories of his motorcycle rides through the mountains of Colorado, of the freedom of the open road and the roar of the engine. They became a family, born of necessity and nourished by the shared experience of traveling through the vacuum as a tiny island of life with an indescribable burden on their shoulders.

They often spent their evenings together in the common area, floating in front of the large panoramic windows and gazing out at the stars, which shone with a clarity that was impossible on Earth. Earth itself had long since shrunk to a bluish dot, barely distinguishable from the countless other stars. Mars shimmered as a reddish dot in the distance, but it too was many millions of miles away. They existed in an in-between space, between worlds, between the known and the completely unknown.

"If it weren't for this eerie threat we're hurtling toward," said Lukas one evening as he sipped a cup of synthetic coffee, whose taste was a faint reminder of Earth beans, "I might even enjoy this very special shared living situation with you guys."

"It's beautiful, isn't it?" agreed Mira. "This simplicity. No distractions, no unimportant worries—just one big one instead of many small ones." She smiled mischievously. "Just us, the stars, and the impending apocalypse."

As if on cue, a loud alarm began to wail.

33

The alarm cut through the silence of the *Hope* like an axe blow. Red pulsing warning lights bathed the spaceship in eerie shadows.

"Navigation error! System conflict!" reported the voice of the on-board computer with mechanical urgency.

Lukas floated away from Mira to his console. The numbers on the displays danced wildly, so that at first he didn't even understand the nature of the problem. But as he nervously licked his lips, he recognized a pattern: coordinates that had been stable minutes ago were now jumping back and forth between different values. The visual representation of the starry sky on the secondary monitor flickered. Constellations became distorted. The ship could no longer orient itself.

"James, what the hell is going on here?" shouted Torres, who had now arrived in the cockpit. His voice echoed tinny through the connecting corridor to the lab. "The inertial data doesn't match the optical navigation."

Harrison stared at his instruments. "The star sensors are reporting conflicting positions. Vega is simultaneously at zero-twenty-five and zero-twenty-seven degrees."

"That's physically impossible," muttered Wei Lin as his fingers flew over the navigation controls. "I'll check the calibration of the optical array right away. Maybe a lens has come loose, but . . ."

A jolt went through the ship. Very slight, but noticeable. Lukas reflexively reached for a handrail, even though it was hardly necessary in zero gravity. "That wasn't engine thrust, was it?"

No one answered him.

"Telescope data coming in," reported Xiaoming. He had activated the autonomous deep-space sensor on board, which regularly mapped the starry sky. "Something's wrong. See for yourselves."

Lukas switched over. Several bright stars appeared on the display—but some were distorted, duplicated, visible in elongated arcs. Others had disappeared completely.

"What the hell . . ." whispered Torres.

"Some kind of warping effect," said Lukas. "The pyramids. Their influence is bending space around us. The light from the stars is being deflected. We don't see where the stars are. We see where their light comes from after passing through the distortion. The two are no longer the same."

Liu Xiaoming frowned skeptically. "But we're still eighty million miles away."

"That's right. But the effect is strong enough—and focused enough—to cause local compression of space-time," explained Lukas. "Three sources, perfectly aligned, and the warping amplifies in the region we're entering."

"And that would result in what we're experiencing?" asked Harrison.

"Yes. And more. It could distort our entire perception of space, even here on board, if it gets worse. We'll see a curved reality."

"I'll take a look at the inertial platform," said Wei Lin. "If the inertial sensors are also spinning, then it's more than a measurement error."

"Inertial navigation in space?" asked Mira. "I thought that was used more in airplanes?"

Lukas nodded. "True, but modern spacecraft use it too. Inertial sensors, MEMS gyroscopes, fiber optic systems—they measure acceleration and rotational motion independently of external references. They're our last redundancy."

"The gyroscopes are showing phantom movements," said Wei again. "The ship thinks it's rotating slightly. But according to visual comparison, we're not rotating."

"When space itself is being rhythmically distorted, it creates a shifted inertial frame," said Lukas. "This isn't a technical failure. This is a physical environment we've never entered before. The sensors can't possibly work normally."

A shrill tone interrupted the discussion. "Course correction initiated," reported the onboard AI. "Deviation from target trajectory detected."

"Stop!" yelled Harrison so loudly that Lukas flinched as if he had been struck. "Shut down the engines! Now!"

Torres audibly hammered on the manual override in the cockpit.

"Ion engines deactivated. But they've already accelerated. We have minimal vector impulse," the quantum physicist shouted down the corridor.

"How big was the maneuver?" asked Lukas, his mouth dry.

"Zero point three meters per second to starboard. Then a counter-correction of 0.28 to port."

"So they almost canceled out," muttered Lukas. "The autopilot system saw a deviation that wasn't real—and then actively created one while tilting at phantom windmills."

"A classic control loop error," said Wei. "Feedback loop from faulty sensors and automatic correction. If we don't stop this, we'll start to stagger."

"Then we'll shut it down," decided Harrison. "But we need immediate redundancy. We're flying by sight—and our sight is deceiving us."

Lukas pondered, the shrill alarm not exactly helping him concentrate.

"Radio navigation," he said finally. "Time difference measurement with the Deep Space Network."

Wei Lin lifted his head from his console and nodded slowly. "Goldstone, Madrid, Canberra?"

"Three stations, evenly distributed across the globe. They transmit time signals continuously. If we analyze the signal propagation times, we can triangulate our exact position—regardless of optical distortion."

"But doesn't that take a long time?" said Harrison. "At our distance—what is it, eight light minutes?"

"Eight and a half," confirmed Wei. "But we don't need to measure absolute times, just the differences in propagation time. And those are in the microsecond range. That means we can determine our relative position with high precision."

"I'll write a new script," said Lukas. "We can analyze the phase of the carrier signals. Phase comparison methods provide the best resolutions."

Harrison nodded briefly. "Do it! Michael, establish radio contact with Goldstone. Wei, prepare a secondary inertial monitoring system. I want to know if the ship itself is starting to generate movement patterns."

"Connection to Goldstone established," called out Michael Torres a few seconds later. "The signal is strong."

"Madrid is online," reported Wei. "Canberra is next."

Lukas was completely immersed in his code. He had isolated the pulse transmission of the carrier signals, recorded their frequency modulations, uploaded the Earth's triangulation grid, and simulated the interference patterns.

"Data stream stable," said Wei. "All three stations are now transmitting synchronously."

"Then let's go," said Harrison. "Start the measurement, Lukas."

Lukas's fingers danced across the interface. The algorithm went online—four parallel evaluation routines that converted all runtime differences into positions with split-second accuracy. A map of interplanetary space appeared on his display—and the *Hope* was a red dot on it.

"We're exactly on course. Deviation less than two kilometers. That is within our navigation limits. The course was correct from the start."

"That means . . ." Harrison turned to Torres. "The auto-corrections could have destabilized us for days."

"If we hadn't noticed," said Wei Lin, "we would have shot ourselves off course at some point. And never known why."

"I'm deactivating the optical navigation," announced Harrison. "From now on, only radio and inertial sensors."

The red warning lights went out. The display calmed down.

Lukas sat in front of the central navigation display and stared at the updated star charts. He frowned.

"That can't be," he muttered.

"What can't?" asked Wei, who was sitting at a nearby terminal, alarmed.

"The distortion effect—it's gone. The constellations are back exactly where they should be. No more warping."

The major floated over to him and looked at the screen. "Maybe it was just a temporary overlap? Could have been some kind of interference pattern."

"Possible," said Lukas thoughtfully. Then he turned to the rest of the crew in the lab. "Harrison, I have a theory."

"I'm all ears," said Harrison, coming closer and catching himself on a handrail.

"What if the space-time warping we observed wasn't permanent? Maybe the pyramids generate their influence in a kind of pulse pattern—intermittently. Like a rotating lighthouse. We're only affected when we're in the focus of this 'beam'."

"As good a theory as any, I suppose," said Wei. "But if correct, this means we could experience the same effect again at any time."

"Yes, but there's something else." Lukas activated a recording of the sensor logs. "The distortion didn't just drop to zero. It decreased in an exact logarithmic curve—as if it were being dampened. Not simply switched off, but like a mechanical vibration compensator."

"Like a system that's stabilized from the outside," murmured Liu.

"Or," added Torres, who had come from the cockpit, "like a system that realizes it's causing interference—and regulates itself."

For a moment, no one said anything.

"You mean the pyramids . . . reacted?" said Wei skeptically.

"I'm not saying they're intelligent or conscious in themselves," said Lukas. "But they may be following a protocol. When they sense that their environment is being destabilized, they reduce their influence."

"If so, this gives us even more reason to wonder why they don't respond to any attempts at communication," said Harrison thoughtfully.

"We should continue to monitor the patterns," said Wei. "If they do conform to your lighthouse metaphor, we may be able to identify a periodicity."

"And our course?"

"Stable for now," said Lukas. "Everything is calm for the first time in hours. But I recommend manually checking the position every five minutes—just to be on the safe side."

Harrison nodded and patted him on the shoulder. "Good work. We'll remain vigilant. And continue collecting data. Maybe the pyramids will tell us more than we thought."

34

The alarm tore through Lukas's dreams of Earth like daggers through silk. Red lights pulsed through his tiny cabin, transforming the peaceful sleeping quarters into a cave of warning and urgency. His body was instantly wide awake, floating out of his sleeping bag into the cold, recycled air of the ship without any conscious decision on his part.

"Everyone to the control center!" Torres's voice echoed through the *Hope*'s onboard speakers. He sounded raw with tension. "Emergency! Now!"

Lukas pushed himself off the wall and glided through the dark corridor, his eyes still gritty. The *Hope*'s artificial night had been brutally interrupted at four in the morning ship time. The other crew members were already floating out of their cabins, shadows in the darkness, hastily dressing.

"What do we have?" called out Harrison as he struggled into his jumpsuit and floated down the corridor.

"The inertial system is going haywire!" replied Torres from the lab, his voice strained with adrenaline.

They reached the control center. Torres floated in front of the consoles like a conductor in front of a mad orchestra, his face wet with sweat despite the cool temperature. His fingers danced frantically across the displays, desperately trying to make sense of the chaos of data.

"For 20 minutes," he gasped, wiping the sweat from his eyes. "The IMU is continuously registering phantom accelerations. The ship thinks it's rotating around three different axes at the same time."

Lukas floated over to the sensor data, his scientific training automatically taking control of his panic. The numbers on the screen made no physical sense. "Zero point zero three degrees per second yaw rate? At zero point zero two degrees pitch? That's completely impossible with our current flight configuration."

"The autopilot wants to constantly countersteer," said Torres, pointing to another console. "I manually deactivated it before it tore us to pieces."

Wei Lin hastily activated the navigation consoles, his fingers moving frantically but precisely across the keyboard. "Radio navigation shows no deviation at all. We're absolutely stable on course according to navigation."

"But the gyroscopes are saying something completely different," muttered Xiaoming, floating over to the technical displays.

"The inner platform reports continuous rotation around the Z-axis, plus periodic fluctuations around X and Y."

Harrison floated between the consoles like an admiral on the bridge of a sinking ship. "Torres, when did this begin? Precisely."

"Three forty-four, thirty-seven seconds," replied Torres without hesitation. "It started slowly with minimal deviations. Then the values became exponentially more extreme."

Lukas studied the data streams with the intensity of an archaeologist deciphering an ancient inscription. "Show me the exact timestamps and the complete progression curve."

Torres transferred the data to Lukas's screen. A complex curve slowly built up, showing the apparent rotation of the ship over the past 20 minutes.

"This is definitely not a random sensor error," said Lukas slowly. "Look at the pattern. It's far too structured."

The curve swung up and down rhythmically, not chaotically, but in precise, mathematically predictable waves.

"Periodic," Wei realized after a moment of intense observation.

"A maximum about every 40 seconds, then a minimum, then a maximum again."

"Forty seconds," repeated Lukas, and somewhere in the depths of his scientific memory, something began to ring a bell. "Wait. That sounds familiar."

Lukas stared at the continuous logs of the inertial measurement unit and hull stress sensors. The approaching pyramids had been sending subtle distortions through the ship for weeks—effects too faint for Earth-based detectors to catch, but now growing strong enough that the *Hope* itself was acting as an unwilling witness.

"What are you doing?" asked Torres, floating closer, his voice still strained with stress.

"Testing a hypothesis," replied Lukas as his fingers pecked at the keyboard like the beak of a bird of prey. "If my guess is correct . . ."

He pulled up the last four hours of IMU logs, autopilot correction timestamps, and hull micro-stress readings. A clear, repeating pattern emerged when he overlaid them: a faint but unmistakable sinusoidal oscillation in the phantom accelerations.

"There," he said, pointing at the screen with a trembling finger. "The distortions are perfectly constant and periodic. It's just like our last problem a week ago."

Liu hovered closer until his nose was almost touching the display and studied the overlaid graphs. "What's the exact period?"

Lukas ran quick calculations, syncing the timing of the glitches against the autopilot burns and the subtle stretching they all felt in their bodies. "It's 0.025 hertz. That corresponds exactly to a period of 40 seconds."

"Holy shit," whispered Torres. "Exactly the same period as our phantom rotation."

"Resonance," said Lukas, and the realization hit him like a physical blow to the pit of his stomach. "Whatever is coming from the pyramids is causing our entire inertial system to resonate."

Harrison floated over to them, his face a mask of professional control. "Explain that in a way that an old pilot who has no idea about physics can understand."

"The pyramids are emitting some kind of rhythmic distortion," explained Lukas, trying to use simple language. "Weak, but perfectly consistent. Our gyroscopes and acceleration sensors are reacting to it like a tuning fork being made to vibrate by another tuning fork."

"But we're not actually moving off course?" asked Wei, confused.

"Absolutely not. But the ultra-sensitive inertial sensors think we are. The distortion minimally warps the space-time around us. The instruments interpret these tiny warps as real movement of the ship.

The optical distortion we saw earlier wasn't there either, but a hallucination of the on-board AI. It's designed to perform real-time, reality-constant interpretation calculations. It adjusted the telescope data to match what the inertial systems were telling it."

Harrison grimaced. "This could be an even bigger problem than we thought. If the autopilot continuously tries to correct, it will systematically waste our fuel or make the ship completely unstable."

As if on cue, a new, even shriller alarm sounded. The ion engines ignited automatically with a low hum.

"Automatic course correction initiated," the computer reported in its emotionless voice. "Unintended rotation around Z-axis detected. Correction maneuver being performed."

"Stop! Stop immediately!" yelled Harrison, floating to his command console. "Deactivate all automatic correction systems! Now!"

The engines fell silent after exactly two seconds, but the damage had already been done.

"Too late," said Wei, studying his navigation data. "We've already lost 0.4 meters per second of delta-v in the wrong direction."

Torres shook his head, his despair palpable. "At this rate, we'll use up our entire fuel reserves in less than a week."

"We need a solution," said Harrison with the authority of a man accustomed to making decisions in crises. "And we need it fast."

Lukas intensely studied the overlaid logs—IMU phantom movements matched against the timing of corrections, hull stresses, and even the subtle tidal-like tugging they felt in their own bodies. The correlation was mathematically perfect, not even a millisecond of deviation. "Digital signal processing," he muttered, feeling a solution forming in his mind. "We need to filter out this exact frequency from the IMU data."

"Can you really do that?" asked Torres hopefully.

"With the precise timing and waveform we've extracted from the sensor logs, definitely," replied Lukas, his spirits slowly returning. "I'll program an adaptive filter that works in real time."

"How long will that take?" asked Harrison.

"Twenty minutes for the complete spectral analysis of the pattern. Another 20 to 30 minutes for programming and integration."

"Then get started," ordered Harrison without hesitation. "Torres, you help him with whatever he needs. Wei, you monitor the navigation continuously and report any further anomalies. Xiaoming, you check all other systems for similar resonance effects."

The next few minutes passed in feverish, concentrated work. Lukas analyzed the timing and amplitude patterns with the meticulousness of a Swiss watchmaker. Whatever was coming from the pyramids was not a single frequency, but a highly complex, multi-layered rhythm. He wondered if this was a new pattern, or one they hadn't recognized from farther away.

"Interesting," he muttered, delving further. "Three superimposed primary rhythms with different phases."

Torres hovered over his shoulder and watched the analysis. "Main period 40 seconds, we already have that. But there are also harmonic overtones."

"Exactly. At 20 seconds and about 13.3 seconds. Each pyramid seems to have its own characteristic signature. The same primary rhythm, but with distinct deviations."

Lukas programmed a complex adaptive filter that could remove all three fundamental periods plus their harmonics from the inertial system data in real time. The code was mathematically sophisticated and had to work millisecond by millisecond. In the end, he had the onboard AI check and improve his code.

"Programming completed in three minutes," he announced as his eyes scanned the results.

"The phantom rotation is getting dramatically stronger," warned Liu from his console. "Now -0.08 degrees per second around the Z-axis."

"The system thinks we're spinning out of control," noted Wei, not for the first time.

"Almost done," Lukas assured him. His last lines of code implemented the real-time correction with multiple redundancy. "Filter is fully programmed and ready for integration into the main system."

Torres took on the critical task and transferred the code to the IMU system. "Okay, that should do it."

The inertial sensor readings jumped wildly, as if possessed by an invisible demon, then suddenly stabilized at normal, steady values.

"Rotation zero degrees per second," reported Liu with undisguised surprise. "Acceleration zero. All parameters back in the nominal range."

"The filter is working perfectly," confirmed Torres in relief. "IMU now showing perfectly stable values."

Harrison cautiously activated the autopilot, ready to intervene immediately if necessary. "Automatic system back online. No error messages, no correction commands."

The red alarm lights went out one by one. A peaceful silence returned to the control center. Lukas slumped down and sighed deeply.

"Damn good work, everyone, especially you, Lukas," said Harrison, his voice carrying sincere admiration. "But what does this mean for our mission in the long term?"

Lukas looked thoughtfully at the continuous logs of the sensor patterns. "The distortions become measurably stronger the closer we get to them. The resonance effects will increase exponentially."

"Is that because of us?"

"I don't think so. It's because of our observation horizon. Imagine you're standing in front of a lighthouse. From a distance, you only perceive the distant glow, but with your face directly in front of it, you feel like you're being scorched by the sun. But that's not because the distortion itself is more intense, it's because we're now in range of multiple overlapping rhythms."

"Wow," said Mira with a wry smile. "Two lighthouse metaphors in a row. Who'd have thought it?"

"Can we still continue the mission safely?" asked Wei, ignoring Mira's attempt to lighten the mood.

"With the adaptive filter, yes, definitely. But I have to monitor and adjust it continuously. The patterns are changing slowly but steadily, and that will only increase."

Harrison activated long-range communication with distant Earth. "Mission Control Starbase, this is *Hope*. We've successfully resolved a second technical issue caused by the effects of the target objects.

Our inertial system was in destructive resonance with the incoming distortion."

The inevitable eight-minute delay seemed to last an eternity this time.

"Hope, this is Starbase," came the reply at last. "Understood and acknowledged. Please send us all technical details for analysis. What is the current status of your system stability?"

"Completely stable after successful filter implementation," replied Harrison. "Mission will continue without delay. But we must warn you: the effects are increasing exponentially, and sooner than expected."

Lukas floated back to his workstation and watched the hypnotic patterns of the sensor distortions on his screens. The pyramids were communicating with the universe in an ancient language of distorted reality.

"Lukas?" said Torres quietly, floating next to him.

"What's going on?"

"The fundamental resonance period. It doesn't match the calculated mass of the objects. It's systematically too low and at the same time too high at the peak."

"But that doesn't make sense." Lukas opened the ship's clock and compared the data from the three atomic clocks on board. Then he had Starbase send him a comparative timestamp. Torres was absolutely right—it made no sense. "Time dilation," he whispered, his voice carrying reverential fear.

"Time dilation?" said Mira, raising her eyebrows. "What's that, exactly?"

"It falls out of Einstein's equations. Objects at a higher speed or in higher gravity environments experience time more slowly than those at lower speed or in lower gravity environments. But the slowing of time is negligible until you get to a healthy fraction of the speed of light.

"At light speed, time stops *entirely*. But even at 10% of light speed—which is a scorching 670 million miles per hour—your 24-hour day would feel only 7 minutes slower. GPS satellite timestamps have to be adjusted 37-millionths of a second each day to account for this effect."

Lukas paused, looking vexed. "But here's the thing. Based on the apparent gravity and velocity of these objects, the effect we're seeing is *wrong*." He raised his eyebrows. "Unless," he added slowly, feeling a frightening realization forming, "they exist differently than in the space-time described by Einstein."

"What are you talking about?" asked Harrison, coming over to them. "Do we have a new problem?"

Lukas looked at the strange data, messages from a reality beyond all human experience. "The pyramids emit some kind of directed, rhythmic distortion. A focused warping of space. Normally it would spread evenly, but here it appears modulated, as if it carries coded information. Or is waiting for a resonance in return."

The *Hope* continued to fly through the endless night between the stars, its critical instruments now protected from the resonance of space itself. But just how long could they survive if they continued to encounter cosmic forces that apparently regarded time and space as malleable tools?

35

Mira sat cross-legged in her small cabin, her eyes closed, her breathing steady. Ten days had passed since the inertial system crisis. The *Hope* flew steadily through the darkness between worlds.

I breathe in and am aware of my inhalation, she thought—no, she felt. *I breathe out and am aware of my exhalation.*

This was one of the first techniques Lama Tenzin had taught her to calm her mind. Simply follow her breath consciously. Calm her mind. Open herself to what lay beyond her thoughts.

Click.

Mira opened her eyes. The sound came from the wall. A metallic click like a faulty relay.

Click-click-click.

She waited. Listened. The *Hope* was full of noises—fans, pumps, computers. But this was different.

Click-click-click.

Rhythmic. Almost like a heartbeat, but slower. She stood up, floated to the wall, and pressed her ear against the cold metal surface.

Click-click . . . click-click . . . click-click.

The sound was everywhere. In the walls, in the floor, on the ceiling. As if the whole ship had a strange pulse.

She activated the communication system. "Lukas? Can you hear me?"

No answer.

"Lukas, this is Mira. Is everything normal with you?"

Silence.

Mira floated out into the corridor. The red lighting was dimmed for the night phase. Shadows danced on the walls, taking on strange shapes as if they were being projected onto the polymer structures.

Click-click-click.

The sound followed her. She moved toward the control center. Her steps—no, her floating movements—seemed to be in time with the clicking. For a moment, she thought she was walking, just like she had done what felt like an eternity ago on Earth.

Torres was sitting in front of the screens in the control center. His eyes were staring into space.

"Michael?" She touched his shoulder.

He turned slowly. His pupils were dilated. "Do you see them too?" he whispered.

"See what?"

"The pixels. The ship is disintegrating. Billions of tiny squares are drifting into space."

Mira looked around. Everything looked normal. Metallic, solid.

The consoles glowed, the servers hummed.

Torres pointed to the window. "Look. Really look."

She followed his gaze. For a moment—just a tiny fraction of a second—she saw it too. The walls dissolved into countless glowing dots that drifted into the vacuum like cosmic dust.

Then everything was normal again.

"Michael, when did this start?" she asked, concerned.

"An hour ago. At first, I thought I was tired. But it's getting worse."

Click-click . . . click-click.

The sound grew louder. Mira felt her heartbeat adjust to it. Slowing down. Deepening.

She activated the communication system. "All crew members to the control center. Immediately."

After five minutes, the others floated in. Harrison looked tired. Wei Lin was holding his head. Liu moved strangely, slowly, as if seized by some sort of rigor.

"What's going on?" asked Harrison.

Mira's expression was grim. "Do you hear that clicking?"

Harrison listened. "What clicking?"

"There. Everywhere. It's rhythmic."

Wei Lin nodded slowly. "Yes. For 20 minutes now. I thought it was coming from the computers."

Xiaoming said nothing. He stared at the ceiling as if he were watching something fascinating.

"Xiaoming?" Harrison floated over to him. "Everything okay?"

"The pyramids," whispered Liu. "They're here. Right in front of us."

Mira looked out the window. Only stars and darkness.

But then—for a heartbeat—she saw them too: three giant black triangles hovering in front of the *Hope*. So close that they filled her entire field of vision. Menacing gods from another reality. They dominated the entire universe, miles high, blacker than nothingness.

She blinked. The pyramids were gone again.

"They're hallucinations," she said aloud. More to herself than to the others.

Harrison floated over to his command console. "All systems normal. No alarm. But . . ."

He fell silent. Stared at the screens.

"James?" Mira floated over to him.

"The numbers," he muttered. "They change in time with . . . with that clicking." He stared at Mira as if suppressing panic. "You didn't secretly inject us with Nirolex, did you?"

"No, of course not!" Mira looked at the displays. The navigation data jumped up and down slightly. In sync with the click-click-click.

Dr. Pappas's voice echoed in her memory: The brain is an electrical network, and frequencies can influence it. Delta waves, theta waves—they occur naturally, but they can also be induced.

"Frequencies," she said quietly.

"What?" said Torres.

"Pappas explained it to me—the brain works with electrical waves. Delta at 0.5 to 4 hertz. Theta at 4 to 8 hertz."

Click . . . click . . . click.

She counted along. About two seconds between clicks. Zero point five hertz.

"Delta waves," she whispered. "Those are delta waves!"

Wei Lin shook his head as if waking from a dream. "What are you talking about?"

Mira floated over to Lukas's workstation. The German was hanging onto a handrail, staring into space. She called up the composite structural integrity and inertial anomaly log—the same multi-sensor fusion display Lukas had used to discover the 40-second resonance pattern.

There it was. A new, dominant low-frequency oscillation had appeared in the hull micro-strain gauges, atomic clock desynchronization residuals, and even the faint periodic tugging they all felt in their own bodies. The main period: exactly two seconds—0.5 hertz.

"The distortion pattern," explained Mira. "The tidal/resonance effect coming from the pyramids now has a dominant component at 0.5 hertz. That's delta-wave territory—the exact frequency range the brain produces during deep, dreamless sleep."

"And that means what?" asked Harrison.

"This frequency corresponds to the delta waves of the brain," replied Mira. "It directly influences our consciousness."

Torres laughed. A strange, hollow sound, almost hysterical. "The ship is trying to get into our heads."

Click-click . . . click-click.

The hallucinations came in waves. Mira saw the walls pulsing like living organs. She saw shadows moving where there should be none. She watched Xiaoming slowly begin to disappear, becoming transparent.

She concentrated on her breathing. *In . . . out . . . in . . . out.*

Thoughts are just clouds. Consciousness is the sky.

The visions subsided. Not completely, but enough to think clearly.

She had read five books on neurology during the flight because she had felt superfluous while Lukas serviced his instruments and the others had their technical tasks. So she had studied.

Dr. Buzsáki's book on brain rhythms. Dr. Steriade on states of consciousness. Dr. Llinás on the intrinsic oscillations of neurons.

"We need to apply acoustic masking," she said suddenly.

"What?" asked Harrison again.

"White noise. In antiphase to the fundamental frequency. That can neutralize the effect."

Torres shook his head. "I don't think that helps."

Mira floated over to the *Hope*'s audio system. Her fingers danced across the controls. "If we generate a counter-signal—exactly the same frequency, but phase-shifted by 180 degrees—we can cancel out the waves."

Click-click-click.

The hallucinations grew stronger. Wei Lin suddenly spoke in a strange rhythm: "Time . . . is . . . a . . . circle . . . that . . . turns . . ."

Xiaoming floated to the wall and began to stroke it as if it were alive.

Mira worked feverishly. She programmed the *Hope*'s audio generator. Zero point five hertz, phase-shifted, across all speakers. If she wasn't fast enough, the others would go crazy, and who knew what damage they could cause?

The 0.5 hertz resonance was the key. It *had* to be. This frequency lay exactly in the delta band of human brain waves, that slow, deep rhythm between 0.5 and 4 hertz that Dr. Buzsáki had described as the basis of consciousness. She recalled the neurological texts she had studied during the endless hours of the flight.

The brain was an electrical network of eighty billion neurons oscillating at precise frequencies. Dr. Steriades's research had shown that delta waves were produced when the thalamus—possibly the central hub of consciousness—sent its rhythmic discharges through the cortex. These slowest of all brain waves normally only opened their gates during deep sleep.

But the infragravitational waves of the pyramids had presumably superimposed themselves on these natural rhythms, causing the network of neurons to resonate like tuning forks, causing each other to vibrate—just as Lukas had metaphorically described previously. The resulting states of consciousness—the hallucinations, the altered perception—hadn't been chaotic disturbances, but the brain's natural response to external delta stimulation.

Her solution was based on a fundamental principle of wave mechanics: destructive interference. Two waves of the same frequency, but phase-shifted by 180 degrees, canceled each other out like light and shadow blending into gray. She had programmed the *Hope*'s audio system to generate a counter-signal at exactly 0.5 hertz—inaudible to the conscious ear, but perceptible to the neurological system, which registered these frequencies as electromagnetic vibrations.

The white noise acted as an acoustic shield, neutralizing the foreign delta waves before they could reach the thalamocortical loops of their brains. The mathematics of the AI program she used was elegant: signal plus inverse signal equals zero. Their perception of reality returned to normal, freed from the cosmic rhythms that had led their neural networks into unknown territories of consciousness.

A deep hum filled the ship. Barely audible, but noticeable in the bones.

Click . . . click . . . cli . . .

The rhythmic clicking fell silent.

Harrison blinked as if awakening from a dream. "What happened?"

Torres shook his head. "Where did the pixels go?"

Wei Lin stopped speaking in rhythms. Xiaoming turned away from the wall, and Lukas seemed to awaken from his stupor.

"The distortion pattern," explained Mira. "It oscillates in the delta frequency range. That directly affects our brain waves."

"And the counter-signal?" asked Harrison.

"It cancels out the effect. Like noise-canceling headphones, if you will." She rubbed her face. "It really worked!"

Xiaoming floated over to them. He looked pale as a ghost. "I saw . . . strange things."

"We all did," confirmed Torres. "Damn scary."

"Maybe that's their way of making contact," she thought aloud. "It can't be a coincidence that they're sending out a signal that affects our brains in this way."

Harrison activated communication with Earth. "Mission Control, this is *Hope*. New problem with target objects. We believe they can generate infragravitational waves that cause neurological disturbances."

The nearly nine-minute delay seemed to last forever.

"*Hope*, this is Starbase. Roger that. What is the status of the crew?"

"Stable after implementing acoustic masking, thanks to Dr. Najafi," replied Harrison. "Mission will continue."

Mira floated to her workstation. Waveforms danced across the screens. Three different frequencies now. Zero point zero two five hertz for resonance. Zero point five hertz for consciousness. And a new one at 8 hertz—theta waves.

"It won't stop," she said to the others. "The closer we get, the more frequencies they'll send."

Lukas came to her. "Can we mask them all?"

"Theoretically, yes. But . . ." She hesitated. "Maybe we shouldn't."

"Why not?"

Mira thought of her meditation, of the moments between waking and dreaming, when the boundaries of reality blurred. "If they're trying to communicate, aren't we blocking their message?"

"You want to deliberately expose yourself to their influence?" asked Harrison incredulously.

"Yes!" she replied emphatically. "What do we have to lose?"

"She's right," said Lukas. "Of course she is. We came out here to try to communicate—*not* to pretend our nukes will act as a friendly tap on their door. The odds our mission succeeds, in my view, are astronomically low. We're destined to die along with all of humanity if we can't get a handle on this. So what's the worst that can happen? We give ourselves over to these potential signals, we go crazy, and eventually die.

"But what's the *best* that can happen? We communicate with them. Tell them we're bacteria they may not have noticed and that we'd appreciate it if they didn't use any bleach on us."

"Exactly," said Mira. "We should lean into this chance. Now is the time to use Nirolex. Let's not be meek. If we're going to go for it, we should *go for it*. This could well be the moment we've been waiting for. The objects are so close now that we'll soon be able to see them with our own eyes."

"But on Nirolex, the four of you will be out of the picture," said Harrison. "It'll just be me and Wei left. Given the problems we've seen over the past three weeks, which the four of you have mostly solved, we likely won't be able to handle any more surprises."

Mira grinned, surprising everyone. "We've already stipulated we're betting our lives on this. So yeah, emergencies could arise. You place your bet and you take your chances. The Hertz are ideal for deep meditation. This is our window! Maybe they really are coming back, and our presence reminds them of their contact with the Egyptians 4,500 years ago. And now they're pushing open the door."

"They're preparing us," said Lukas. "They're tuning our consciousness. Like an instrument."

Harrison sighed. "Yeah. Maybe. Still annoying that such highly developed beings/objects couldn't just send a light signal, a radio message, or whatever, to communicate with us."

"That frustration has eaten away at us all from the very beginning," said Lukas. "I get that. But you know in your heart Mira is right. And the plan has always been to try communicating using Nirolex. We've been waiting to get as far as we possibly can from the noise of eight billion human minds, but now is the time. If the ship is destroyed tomorrow, being a little farther from Earth at the time won't help us."

He paused. "I'm a scientist by training," he continued. "But it's time to throw out meticulous logic and insistence on certainty. In short, as you Americans like to say, it's time to take a leap of faith."

36

The *Hope's* laboratory had become more cramped. Four medical beds were arranged in a circle like the points of a compass. Mira moved carefully between the medical instruments she had meticulously prepared over the last two hours. The gravitational pull of the three pyramids was now strong enough to tug at the ship's structure and accelerate it—yet only in unpredictable bursts, as if the objects were deciding, moment by moment, how much of their true mass to allow into our reality. The walls of the *Hope* creaked under the tidal forces, groaning as though the ship itself were protesting the selective, capricious nature of the gravity pressing against it.

"The gravitational surges are increasing," reported Harrison over the communication system from the cockpit. "Whatever Mindmeld is supposed to do, you'd better do it now, Mira. I can't wait much longer with Plan B!"

Mira nodded without replying as she calibrated the complex Nirolex injection system. Each of the four cannulas was programmed with an individual dosage protocol. Dr. Pappas had taught her that the dosage of Nirolex was absolutely critical—too little, and the neural stratum would not open sufficiently. Too much, and they could lose themselves in the depths of their own brains.

"The cannulas are sterile and ready," she announced, more to herself than to anyone else. "The injection system is programmed for one-button activation. As soon as I press the trigger, we'll all receive our specific dosage at the same time."

Lukas was already lying on his couch, his normally tense face showing unusual calm. The weeks in space had changed him—the scientist's harshness had given way to a deeper serenity.

"Are you sure this will work?" he asked quietly. "The connection between consciousness and . . . whatever is waiting for us out there?"

He shook his head and rolled his eyes. "Strike that. How can you possibly be sure? As we've pointed out countless times, when physics, mass, time dilation, and gravity work any way they want to, there's nothing we *can* be sure of."

"Like you said, when our science fails us, all we have is our gut and our intuition. And our faith." She smiled serenely. "But all this being said, yes, Lukas, I'm sure it will work. Feel better now?"

His smile joined hers just as he felt the small prick of the needle.

Torres lay on the second couch, his usual lightheartedness replaced by concentrated silence. "I've been in a lot of dicey situations," he muttered as Mira pushed the cannula into his vein, "but this is different. Risking my life is one thing. But risking my sanity? That's an even harder pill to swallow."

"I understand," said Mira. "But there's no turning back now. All you can do is embrace it. Think of it as an experiment under extreme conditions."

"Yeah, not really helpful. But to be fair, given all the surreal things that have happened since Lukas spotted these objects, I could already be mad. You know, lying in a mental hospital somewhere, thinking I'm on a ship called *Hope,* travelling to space pyramids. At least if I am already crazy, I'm proud of my imagination. These aren't your ordinary fever dreams."

Liu Xiaoming, the third participant in their experiment, lay there with his eyes closed, his breathing already in the rhythmic pattern he had learned in his own Chinese meditation practice.

"In traditional Chinese philosophy," he said quietly, "there is a concept called Wu Wei—acting without acting, knowing without thinking. Maybe that's what we'll try today."

"That's very close to what Tibetan monks call *rigpa,*" replied Mira. "The original awareness beyond all conceptual constructs."

She attached the cannula, her movements fluid and confident. The practice with Dr. Nicholas had ultimately made her an expert—even in zero gravity, which was now, of course, no longer perfect. The slight pull of the extraterrestrial objects was already noticeable, drawing her toward the back wall, which forced her to hook her feet under the couch.

Finally, she floated to her own bed, the fourth in the circle. With practiced movements, she inserted the cannula into her left hand. The slight pain of the puncture was familiar, almost soothing. She held the activation button in her right hand, an inconspicuous black device that had the power to transport four human brains to realms that experienced meditators took decades to reach.

"Harrison, Wei," she spoke into the communication system. "We're starting now. Monitor our vital signs. If there are any complications, follow the emergency protocols…"

"Understood," replied Harrison. His voice was professional, as always, but with an underlying concern he couldn't quite hide. "We have you on all monitors. Whatever happens, I wish you Godspeed."

Mira closed her eyes and felt the familiar weight of responsibility on her shoulders. Four lives were in her hands—and with them very likely the future of the human species. If her theory was correct, they were on the verge of establishing a conscious communication between humanity and an extraterrestrial intelligence. If they failed . . . well, they were all out of options.

"Relax, close your eyes," she began in the calm, hypnotic voice she had learned from Lama Tenzin. "Let all the tension flow out of your bodies. Together, we will embark on a journey deeper than any human experience before. Your breath will be your guide. Don't cling to anything—no thoughts, no expectations, no fears. Be open to whatever may come. Don't even cling to your breath, for it flows all by itself, without your intervention. You will breathe."

The ensuing calm flowed through her veins like liquid moonlight, cool and luminous. Her thoughts slowed down, like a film on a screen playing at half speed, and she felt that she was the screen and not the film running on it.

"Be aware of all things that are perceived, that come and go, effortlessly," continued Mira, although her own voice already seemed to be fading into an echo, as if coming from a great distance. "If you do get distracted, it's okay. Just bring your attention back to your breath. Not on breathing as an action, but on the breath itself—the subtle in and out that connects life and consciousness. Effortlessly and freely."

Their bodies on the stretchers began to relax; she could feel it. The GABA receptors in the thalamus modulated themselves, the usual filters of consciousness dissolved like morning mist before the sun—aided immensely by the drug. But even that was just a thought and therefore relative.

"Feel your body becoming heavier . . . and lighter at the same time. As if you were sinking into warm, deep water, but also as if you were detaching yourself from it and rising. Both sensations are true and both are illusions."

Mira's own consciousness began to expand. The boundaries between her individual mind and her surroundings slowly blurred. She could sense the presence of the others—not as separate personalities, but as facets of a larger, collective consciousness.

"Focus your attention on the space between breaths. In the pause between exhaling and inhaling lies a silence deeper than any silence. There, in that space, our true journey begins."

Mira let the final words linger for a moment, then, with a subtle movement of her finger, she activated the small audio device she had prepared earlier. Her own recorded voice—calm, steady, and identical in tone—continued the guidance seamlessly, leading them deeper while she allowed her awareness to fully dissolve into the silence behind the words. The recording would carry them forward now, her presence still felt in every syllable, even as she, herself, journeyed beyond speech.

Lukas felt his scientifically trained rationality dissolve like salt in water. His thoughts, normally precise and linear, began to move in spiral patterns. The equations of relativity danced before his inner eye, transforming into living geometries of light and meaning.

Torres experienced his memories of motorcycle rides through Colorado condensing into a single, timeless experience of movement and freedom. The road, the wind, the feeling of speed—everything merged into a pure state of being, beyond any narrative structure.

Xiaoming felt the Chinese characters he had known since childhood become 3-dimensional mandalas, carrying complex philosophical truths in their curves and angles. His grandfather's calligraphy became a living river of meaning and beauty.

"Now," said Mira's pre-recorded voice after an appropriate interval, "open your awareness to what lies beyond the personal. You are no longer separate individuals. You are facets of a consciousness greater than the sum of its parts."

That was the moment when the transformation truly began. She began to dissolve. An indescribable fear opened up before her like a black hole promising death. Her terror was so essential, so elemental, that it blew everything apart.

She let herself fall.

The boundaries of her personality dissolved, not into the vacuum of space, but into something much more fundamental—into nothingness.

But then something new opened up. She—no, *it*—saw how the 3-dimensional world she had considered the only reality all her life was only a thin shadow of what it was experiencing.

Time ceased to flow linearly. Past, present, and future existed simultaneously, not as a sequence of moments, but as coordinates in a multidimensional space that was not space in the sense of height, width, or length. She could see her birth and her death, not as separate events, but as two aspects of the same eternal moment. Her life was not a story that spanned years, but a complete pattern that existed in a single, timeless present.

Lukas witnessed the gravitational distortions become visible structures—not just abstract data, but as if space-time itself were alive, a living, breathing fabric that formed the bodies of the universe, a structureless superstructure. He understood now why the effects had been so erratic: the pyramids weren't exerting gravity in the rigid, predictable way of ordinary matter. They chose when and how deeply to intersect with our 4-dimensional slice of reality. The pyramids were there, but not as three separate objects traveling through space, but as three points of contact of a single, multidimensional being that existed in realms that human language couldn't describe and whose imprints on the map of time were nothing but shadows of what it really was.

Torres no longer saw his motorcycle rides as linear movement through space and time, but as patterns in a complex network of possibilities. Every decision he had ever made—to turn left or right, to stop or continue—existed simultaneously, creating branching realities that were all equally real and equally illusory.

Liu no longer experienced Chinese philosophy as an abstract concept, but as a living truth. Tao was not just an idea, but the underlying structure of reality—the flow of being that connected all things and transcended them all at the same time.

And then, in a moment of collective clarity, they recognized the entity in its entirety.

It was not what they had expected. Not an extraterrestrial intelligence in the conventional sense, not a consciousness that existed in time and space like themselves. It was something much more fundamental—an aspect of reality itself, a realm of existence that encompassed all possible realities simultaneously.

The being existed in six dimensions—three of space, one of time, and two more that human language couldn't describe because human consciousness never had access to them. From its perspective, the entire history of the universe was a single, complex pattern, a mandala of energy and information in which every moment, every place, every possible future was present simultaneously.

The pyramids of yesteryear, which had been recreated in Giza, and the three objects now approaching Earth were not separate events separated by millennia. They were a single phenomenon, a nexus where a 6-dimensional being interacted with the 4-dimensional reality of humans. A single moment.

The "arrival" of the pyramids wasn't a movement through space, but a kind of bow wave of the entity's movements in higher-dimensional space.

Mira felt her consciousness dissolving further into something greater, even though its contours had long since blurred. She was no longer Mira Najafi, archaeologist and seeker of truth. She was a point of attention in a cosmic consciousness that encompassed all possibilities simultaneously, without thoughts and without "I," the most common thought.

She experienced not only her own life, but the lives of all humans who had ever existed or would ever exist, not as stories, but as presence. Humanity was not a collection of separate individuals, but an oscillating pattern in a complex wave field, a single chord in a symphony of unimaginable beauty and complexity. But even that was only relative.

The being didn't communicate through words or symbols that required thought, but through direct transmission of the experience of consciousness, interaction with its essence. It showed them how reality was truly structured—not as solid matter moving through empty space, but as a flow of information and consciousness that manifested all possibilities simultaneously. Every decision they had ever made existed in parallel possibilities. Every thought they had ever thought was a point in a multidimensional space of observation.

Lukas realized that his scientific discoveries were not his personal achievements, but moments of clarity and presence. The theory of relativity, quantum mechanics, the discovery of gravitational waves—all were part of a larger pattern, a slow evolution of human consciousness toward an understanding of its true nature.

Torres saw that his love of movement, speed, and the freedom of the open road had been a longing for this greater reality—a state of being in which all boundaries were removed, in which consciousness could move freely, unshackled by thought.

Xiaoming understood that millennia-old Chinese wisdom had always pointed to this truth. The Tao, the Qi, the teachings of Buddha, Jesus, Zarathustra, Tolle, Meister Eckhart, the concepts of Yin and Yang—all were attempts to describe the multidimensional nature of reality as consciousness in a language understandable to 3-dimensional beings living in the world of form.

And then, in a moment of complete clarity, they got the message.

In the depths of meditation, Lukas's individual consciousness dissolved into something greater, the echo of his decades of scientific training awakened in him—as a mere, impersonal memory at that moment, as the universal language of physics that suddenly took on a whole new meaning.

The being they had just encountered existed in a reality that he was only beginning to understand through the most advanced theories of modern physics. It was an inhabitant of what M-theory postulated as 11-dimensional space—those hidden dimensions beyond our familiar four that had been considered mathematical necessities since Kaluza and Klein, but empirically unattainable. Here, in this state of expanded consciousness, abstract mathematics became a living experience.

While Einstein had described gravity as a curvature of 4-dimensional space-time, Lukas now realized that this curvature itself was only the shadow of higher-dimensional movements. The being moved through 6 expansive dimensions of space-time, for which time was not the relentless flow experienced by humans, but a navigable coordinate—comparable to the way humans could move freely through 3-dimensional space.

What humans experienced as causality—that causes produce effects, that the past shapes the present—was, for the being, an illusion of limited perspective. The entity saw Einstein's entire block universe as a single, simultaneous object. Past, present, and future were not temporally separate states, but geometric coordinates in that higher-dimensional space through which it could move with the same ease that a bird glided through the air.

The pyramids—both those that appeared in ancient times and the cosmic visitors now—had never been separate phenomena. They were projections, cross-sections of a single 6-dimensional body projected into different areas of 4-dimensional space-time. Like Lukas's fingers pressed onto a 2D plane and appearing as 5 separate circles, the being manifested itself simultaneously in different eras of human history—a timeless event that fragmented humans' linear perception into seemingly separate encounters.

The pyramids represented a nexus—an intersection where higher-dimensional reality briefly kissed the linear world of humans, leaving echoes in stone and in consciousness.

Through his expanded perception as a conscious substrate of the universe, Lukas realized that the being not only had access to alternative timelines, but had to perceive all possible branches of reality as a single, complex structure. What quantum mechanics described as superpositions—all possible states existing simultaneously until a measurement caused them to collapse—was the natural landscape of existence for the being. It saw not only the reality that had come to pass, but the entire spectrum of all realities that could have come to pass, would come to pass, or had come to pass in parallel dimensions.

It was no *wonder* that the entity hadn't responded to their attempts at communication.

Dark matter and dark energy, those mysterious components that made up 95 percent of the universe but remained invisible to human instruments, were simply normal matter and energy existing in the additional dimensions to the entity. What astronomers measured as cosmic anomalies were the shadows of higher-dimensional structures projected into 4-dimensional space-time—like the 2D shadow of a 3D hand appearing as a barking dog on a child's wall.

Gravity itself, the most fundamental of all forces, was not only the curvature of space-time, as Einstein had understood it, but also a shift in 6-dimensional meta-space. Black holes, those extreme curvatures of space-time that trapped even light, were merely nodes where higher-dimensional geometry folded into lower dimensions—vortices in a cosmic river flowing in realms that human senses could never reach.

As these insights flowed through Lukas, he understood that the Calabi-Yau spaces of string theory—those compact, rolled-up dimensions that should exist at every point in normal space-time—were simultaneously open to the being. It moved through these extra dimensions with the same awareness with which a human being crossed a room from north to south or from east to west.

The deepest revelation was that the being didn't see a star ignite or explode, but perceived the entire life cycle of the star—from the protostar phase through the main sequence to the supernova and neutron star—as a single, simultaneous structure. All gravitational influences, all interactions with other stars, all possible observers who would measure this star from different perspectives existed as a single, complex 6-dimensional object in its consciousness.

For the being, what humans experienced as a person's life—birth, growth, aging, death—was a single, timeless state, a 4-dimensional worm wriggling through the apple of space-time. It didn't see Lukas as a man who was born, became a physicist, and would one day die, but as a complete, simultaneous pattern—all his moments, all his decisions, all his possible life paths existed simultaneously in its reality.

This realization was both humbling and liberating. The human experience of time, of transience, of the fear of death—all of these were illusions of limited dimensionality. In the higher-dimensional reality, everything existed simultaneously, *eternally*, in a state of timeless perfection—and there, too, a part of his consciousness always existed, inseparably connected to everything, because it *was* everything.

The experience began to stabilize. They found a new kind of unity that preserved their individual identities as soon as they returned and felt their bodies again, but at the same time enabled a deeper connection. They were still Mira, Lukas, Torres, and Liu, but they were also parts of something greater that they had now seen. They were part of the structure of the universe, and how could it ever be otherwise, when everything was interdependent?

Slowly, the impressions began to fade. The multidimensional geometries dissolved, the timeless perspectives on the past and future shrunk back into a linear flow. But something had fundamentally changed. A window had been opened in their consciousness that would never be completely closed again.

They opened their eyes—all four at once, as if connected by invisible threads. The *Hope* laboratory materialized around them, but it looked different than before. More solid and at the same time more transparent.

Mira began to laugh, and the others joined in. It was not the laughter of madmen, but the laughter of pot-bellied Buddhas.

"Did you feel that too?" asked Lukas at some point, his voice full of awe.

"Yes, and I think it will always be with me," replied Torres, and indeed, they could perceive the thoughts and feelings of the others like a faint radio station in the background of their consciousness.

"The pyramids," said Liu quietly. "They're not what we thought. They are . . ."

"Consciousness packaged in a different physical form," said Mira, finishing the sentence for him. "A catalyst for what we might become."

They sat in reverent silence, but the silence wasn't uncomfortable or empty. It was fulfilling and healing.

37

Hours after their Nirolex journey, the silence in the cockpit of the *Hope* still had the quality of a cathedral after the last prayer. Lukas hovered in front of the sensor consoles, his mind still empty and yet full at the same time, in a deep peace that was beyond description, when Harrison jumped up like a man who had seen ghosts.

"They're shrinking!" Even his excited voice couldn't break the silence. It was always there, behind all things, as Lukas realized. "The pyramids—they're getting smaller!"

Wei Lin stared at the navigation displays, his fingers darting across the controls. "The gravitational anomalies are weakening. Space-time . . . it's smoothing out again, I think."

Lukas moved toward the sensors, his movements now fluid in zero gravity. The numbers on the screens told a story that his scientifically trained rationality could hardly comprehend. The resonance and gravity effects they had been experiencing were fading like morning mist before the rising sun.

"The object size is decreasing exponentially," he murmured as his eyes combed through the data. "Mass at 70 percent . . . 50 percent . . . 20 percent of the original values."

"And now?" Harrison floated next to him, his eyes widening in incredulous fascination.

"Zero," whispered Lukas.

"They're gone," said Mira serenely. "*It's* gone. As if it never existed."

"It?" said Harrison. "Was it a being? Did you talk to it? I thought you were just having crazy, drug-related hallucinations?"

Mira smiled. "It might have seemed that way at first, but our hallucinations, as you call them, became the same one. We became a sort of human nexus—four minds merging into one shared field of awareness—in direct communion with the nexus of objects. All seeing the same visions."

She paused in delight. "Only it wasn't really a nexus of objects at all. The three pyramids here, and the four others many millions of miles away, were all part of the same being. Not really a being as we understand it, more of a conscious natural phenomenon, an entity, but without the pillars of a personality, without an individual self."

Harrison shook his head. "I think you're still hallucinating," he said. "What you just said is the most tangled mess of metaphysical nonsense I've ever heard. Sounds cool and mystical, but what the hell are you talking about? How can these objects separated by millions of miles be a single entity? It's absurd."

Lukas grinned. "You've never read *Flatland* by Edwin Abbott, have you? I guess Carlos isn't the only one. I'll tell you all about its absurd implications later, but for now I'll just answer your question. The entity exists in a universe with two higher dimensions than ours. Our brains can't possibly comprehend what it would be like to live there, but we can draw analogies, as Abbott did, by considering how we, as 3D entities, might appear to 2D beings."

He held up his hand, spreading her fingers wide. "Imagine a 2D being living on a flat piece of paper. They can't see up or down because that's a dimension—a direction—they're incapable of moving in, or even perceiving. If I press my five fingers down onto that plane, they see five separate circles. To them, those circles are distinct things—maybe even a perfect triangle pattern if I arrange my hand that way. They have no concept of a 3D hand, no way to see the palm connecting the fingers. To them, the circles are separate entities. But we know it's just *one* hand. *One* living thing, briefly touching their reality."

Harrison considered. "I'll be damned. I really didn't think you could ever get that to make sense. I stand corrected."

Mira nodded. "Perfectly explained, Lukas." She turned to Harrison and Wei to continue. "So the pyramids were the same. A single multidimensional being—or consciousness, or phenomenon—intersecting our 4-dimensional space-time in three places here, and four places a long way from here. What we saw as seven separate objects was just the cross-section of something far greater. One entity. One presence. No individual self, no personality as we understand it—just a conscious natural force expressing itself through our limited slice of reality."

An amused smile came over Harrison's face. "Right. Expressing itself by giving us the finger, so to speak."

Mira laughed. "Well, not just the middle one, but seven of them."

Mira's laughter suddenly turned to tears, which now leaked from the corner of her eyes and began rolling down her cheeks. "And this isn't the first time it touched us," she continued softly. "Because in the same way this single entity can appear to us to be in two separate places at once, it can appear to be in two different *times*. Forty-five hundred years ago, the pyramids of Giza were built after the same fingers pressed down in a different moment, and Egyptian priests communed with the entity. To the entity, both contacts are happening right now. Ancient Egypt and today are just two fingers of the same timeless hand."

She wiped tears away with the back of her hand. "It's hard to describe the emotions I feel right now. I've devoted much of my life to the study of the pyramids of Giza, and now I have an understanding of them well beyond what I even thought was *possible*. My life's work is more complete than I imagined it could ever be."

Lukas couldn't help but take her in his arms and hold her, not to comfort her, but to share the joy she was feeling at this unexpected revelation, one that gave her an entirely new perspective on . . . everything.

"I'm really happy for you, Mira," said Harrison. "But at the risk of returning to the more mundane, I just want to be crystal clear about what happened. So you made contact with this being. So what then? You just politely asked it to leave? And then it *did*?"

"Not really," said Mira as Lukas separated from her once again. "But I think it absorbed the contents of our minds. Will absorb. Has always absorbed. And must have decided to, you know . . . get its *fingers* out of our business. When it comes to our solar system, it must have decided to adopt a . . . *hands-off* policy."

Harrison couldn't help but smile. "You're really leaning into Lukas's fingertip analogy, aren't you?"

Mira's eyes twinkled. "Seven fingers. One hand. And now . . . it's finally letting go."

"Yes," agreed Lukas. "It's folded back into dimensions beyond human reach, leaving only the memory of connection in its wake. Its shadow is no longer visible to us because it turned in a different direction. Lifted its fingertips off our plane of existence, which made it seem to disappear. But it didn't. If we were able to look in the right direction, we'd still see it. But alas, human minds aren't yet equipped to see beyond the boring three dimensions we're accustomed to."

"Be that as it may," said Harrison, "the stars are back where they belong, their positions unchanged by the curvature of alien gravity. The universe had regained its apparent original geometry. And we just saved humanity, to boot."

"We're always saving humanity," said Mira. "We always did. And we always will. The past, present, and future are equally present at all times."

Wei Lin nodded sagely while Harrison shook his head. "Now you're beginning to give me a massive headache," said the colonel. "How about one mind-blowing concept at a time."

"The importance of what happened here can't be overstated," said Mira. "At the risk of blowing your mind even further, after our communication with the entity, I discovered something extraordinary."

She paused for effect. "The Nirolex was never injected."

"Come again," said Michael Torres in disbelief, while Lukas and Liu looked equally shocked.

"The Nirolex was never injected. You can see for yourself if you want."

"How can that be?" asked Lukas.

She shook her head. "It can't be. The system was absolutely foolproof. It *couldn't* have failed. Yet it did. I have no idea how." She raised her eyebrows. "But I think I know *why*."

No one even dared to breathe, hanging on her every word.

"It had to be the entity. Showing off, perhaps. But it wanted to send a clear message. We already knew the priests in Egypt were able to commune with it, without the use of Nirolex. But now we know it doesn't take 30 years of practice, either, like tukdam does. I think the entity wanted to make it clear that the encounter with a multidimensional being, the expansion of our consciousness, the communication beyond all known boundaries, didn't require outside chemicals. The potential was already within us, waiting to be awakened."

Lukas grinned. "Amazing. The message is clear. We were able to make contact with an extraterrestrial intelligence, not with our sophisticated inventions, but with the power of our consciousness. We need to focus on the hidden capabilities of the human mind at least as much as our technology. In fact, it's clear to me that human consciousness itself is a multidimensional phenomenon, a key to truths that our physics books can't possibly describe."

"I'm finding myself envious of your journey," said Harrison. "It was obviously a life-changing experience."

"To say the least," said Liu. "We found a form of consciousness that transcended every human conception of mind, thought, and perception. I was a blind man seeing for the first time."

"Yet its consciousness was also impossibly different than ours," said Mira. "It has no thoughts in the way we're used to perceiving thoughts. No inner voice wandering narratively through past and future. No emotionally colored memories rising up, or plans projected forward in time. Instead, it exists in a state of pure awareness that encompasses all possible states simultaneously."

Liu nodded. "In Buddhist philosophy, there is a concept called *rigpa*—the original awareness that lies beyond all conceptual constructs. I believe the entity lives in a permanent state of consciousness without subject-object separation, without temporal sequence, without the illusion of separate phenomena.

"Humans think sequentially," he continued. "One thought follows another, conclusions arise through logical chains. The entity, however, perceives all information *simultaneously*. When it looks at our solar system, it doesn't see Sun and planets in sequence. It perceives the entire system as a single, complex structure—all gravitational interactions, all possible orbits, all potential future states exist simultaneously in its perception."

"Exactly," said Mira, picking up the torch. "My understanding is that advanced practitioners of meditation can experience something similar for short periods. Linear perception of time disappears. Past and future become mere concepts, and the present expands into an eternal now. The entity lives permanently in this state."

She paused in thought. "Which is why its intelligence is also of a different order than ours," she continued. The entity doesn't solve problems. Because it doesn't *see* problems. All possible solutions already exist in its omniperspective perception. It doesn't plan because it already sees all possible future states simultaneously. It doesn't remember, because everything is occurring simultaneously."

"Another reason it didn't respond to our attempts to reach out," said Lukas. "From its perspective, we had *already* communicated. *Were* communicating. Would *always* communicate."

"For me," added Mira, "the take-home message is this: the fact that we were able to make contact at all suggests that the potential for expanded states of consciousness already exists within us, and that our species has unlimited potential to evolve it further."

She was about to continue when the long-delayed message from Earth finally arrived. "*Hope*, this is Starbase," said Director Patterson from the SpaceX Launch Control Center. His voice sounded both solemn and incredulous, and they could hear thunderous cheering in the background.

"We have incredible news. All 7 pyramid-shaped objects in the solar system have disappeared. *Completely*. No gravitational signatures, no electromagnetic emissions, nothing. They simply no longer exist. It worked! Mindmeld worked!"

Harrison activated the communication system, suddenly feeling a bit choked up. "Affirmative, Starbase," he said, struggling to keep the deep emotion from his voice. "We observed the disappearance here directly. What is the situation on Earth?"

Again, they waited what felt like an eternity for the answer to arrive.

"*Hope*, it's . . . it's hard to describe. The live feeds are just coming in. People are dancing in the streets. Spontaneous celebrations in every major city, in the villages, everywhere—spontaneous parties are breaking out everywhere. Humanity is celebrating the end of the apocalypse!"

Lukas closed his eyes and felt a wave of relief wash over his body, reaching deeper than any physical sensation. Somewhere in the depths of his expanded consciousness, he understood that they had gained more than just insight. They had enabled a transition, a transformation that had certainly changed him, but perhaps also humanity.

"And we also have great news on your end," the voice from Mission Control continued. "We've run the latest telemetry. The structural damage to the *Hope* is extensive, yes—the ion engines took a beating under the gravitational load. But the good news is that the anomalies cleared just in time. You won't have much fuel to spare, or much life-support to spare, for that matter, but you're going to make it home!"

The silence that followed wasn't empty, but electric. Harrison's eyes widened. Wei Lin let out a quiet laugh of disbelief. Lukas felt tears prick at the corners of his eyes—not from sadness, but from something larger.

"Starbase," said Harrison, voice steady but thick, "we copy that. We're coming home."

There was a brief rustling, then Carlos's cheerful voice burst through the speakers, sending a warm wave straight to Lukas's heart: "Oi, amigos! Every nation on Earth is already working on your welcome parade. You gave humanity back its future. Now we're giving you back yours."

The voice paused. "And there will be cold cervezas waiting for you all—plenty of them! Santiago's finest. Well, for most of you," added Carlos impishly. "For Lukas, I'll have that German swill he loves so much on hand. But I promise not to torture the rest of you with it."

Lukas grinned broadly. "I'll be counting the days, my friend," he said, feeling euphoric.

After a few more minutes, their connection with Starbase ended—until the next time.

Lukas gazed at the stars through the panoramic window of the *Hope*—those eternal beacons in the cosmic darkness. Each point of light was a star, possibly surrounded by worlds filled with life forms awakening to their own nature, recognizing their own connection to the whole.

The universe wasn't empty and cold, as he had once thought, but a vast playground of consciousness finding itself.

"Perhaps," he said quietly to his companions, "this is only the true beginning of our journey."

Mira reached out and squeezed his hand. Torres floated over and clapped Harrison on the shoulder. Wei Lin smiled—the first real, unguarded smile Lukas had seen from him.

They had saved humanity. They had glimpsed a towering consciousness that spanned the entire universe and every event within it. And now, against all odds, they were going home.

And now the four of them would have a new mission. A mission to convey to the world the deeper truths they had learned. Given all that had happened, humanity couldn't help but take their insights seriously. Behaviors and philosophies would change. Lukas had absolute faith that this event would be the catalyst that eventually led humanity into a new realm of consciousness, a new philosophy of the cosmos.

The *Hope* turned slowly, engines flaring to life. Ahead lay Earth—home, friends, the next chapter—while behind them stretched the stars, silent witnesses to the moment when four minds touched the infinite.

And the infinite had touched back.

DOUGLAS E. RICHARDS' DISCUSSION OF THE NOVEL

(WHAT'S REAL AND WHAT ISN'T)

Thanks so much for reading *Nexus*. We hope that it left you with a sense of wonder, a few new questions, and perhaps even a spark of hope for what humanity might become.

If you enjoyed the book, we'd be grateful if you'd help spread the word by recommending it to friends, sharing it on social media, and—if you have a moment—leaving a star-rating or review on Amazon. Even a quick "mind blown" or "loved the ending" makes a huge difference in helping new readers discover it.

The idea at the heart of this novel comes from Joshua, who has always been fascinated by the idea of a higher-dimensional being who can only be contacted by what lies beyond our experiential dimensions—the largely unexplored vastness of our consciousness.

For those of you who have read my novels, you'll note that I, too, have long been fascinated by higher dimensions. Since I was 15 years old, actually, and first read *Flatland* by Edwin Abbott.

Finally, Joshua has also been a practicing meditator for some time now. As for me? Well, let's just say that I've probably been practicing whatever is the exact *opposite* of meditation—whatever that may be ☺

As many of you know, I love closing novels with a section that unpacks which elements of each work are grounded in real science, which are speculative, and which are pure imagination. These notes seem to resonate with readers. I wrote this end section, but it reflects contributions from both Joshua and me.

So now, without further ado, I'll get right to it. I've listed the subjects I'll be covering below in order of appearance. Since research and interpretations can differ, I encourage you to explore these topics further to arrive at your own conclusions. And if you aren't interested in an early topic on this list, feel free to skip ahead to one that might interest you more.

- **Higher Dimensions**
- **Have We *Already* Communed With Higher-Dimensional Beings?**
- **The Timeless Nature of the Entity (Block Universe & Simultaneous Perception)**
- **The Pyramids of Giza Connection**
- **The Power of the Human Mind—Additional Mysteries and Possibilities**
    - **Tukdam: Meditation After Death—A Scientific Mystery**
    - **Meditation and Neuroscience: How the Mind Changes the Body**
    - **The Placebo and Nocebo Effects: The Mind as Healer and Harmer**
    - **Inedia and Breatharianism: Living Without Food?**
    - **Other Real Phenomena Highlighting the Mind's Power**
- **Rigpa and the Nature of Consciousness**
- **Fundamental/Primary Consciousness**
- **The Hard Problem of Consciousness**
- **Fictional Paper: Geometry of Consciousness**

Higher Dimensions: When I was a kid, I watched countless episodes of a show called *The Twilight Zone*. I'm an old guy, so we only had three black-and-white channels at the time, but even if I had unlimited choices, I'd have still watched every episode of this show.

The show always opened the same way, with a Rod Serling voiceover: *You're traveling through another dimension. A dimension not only of sight and sound but of mind. A journey into a wondrous land whose boundaries are that of imagination. That's the signpost up ahead—your next stop: the Twilight Zone!*

Really cool, right? *Traveling through another dimension.* But I had no idea what another dimension really was. I figured it was like a cool alternate universe, the Upside Down from *Stranger Things*. It never occurred to me that another *dimension* might actually have something—everything—to do with the boring, ordinary dimensions of length, height, and width. How could the coolest concept *ever* be tied to the most mundane?

Which is why, when I was finally exposed to *Flatland*, my mind was blown forever. For my longtime fans, you've read me waxing on about higher dimensions since my kids' novel, *The Prometheus Project: Stranded*, and have no need to read further. I write about this and the miracle of birth—how can an entire human, complete with billions of perfectly organized neurons, emerge from a single fertilized cell?—*a lot*. So often that you're probably sick of it, but I can't help myself, because I find both subjects so incredibly interesting.

In any event, I'll keep this short. It goes without saying, again, that the core idea of Nexus—that a higher-dimensional being could intersect our reality in ways that seem impossible—is inspired by real physics and mathematics. Edwin Abbott's *Flatland*, written all the way back in 1884, is an absolute classic. The five-fingers-on-a-plane analogy (five separate circles appearing to 2D beings) is straight from Abbott and has been used by physicists like Carl Sagan, Brian Greene, and Lisa Randall in popular science books.

Modern string theory and M-theory do require extra dimensions—usually 10 or 11—most of them "curled up" at tiny scales (Calabi-Yau manifolds). These extra dimensions are mathematical necessities to unify gravity with quantum mechanics, but they remain unproven experimentally.

The novel's 6D being is pure fiction, *I think*, although if you read the next section, you might not be too sure. Given my obsession with higher dimensions, it's a bit ironic that I didn't come up with this premise, but I'm glad that Joshua did.

Have We *Already* Communed With Higher-Dimensional Beings? I had thought that Joshua came up with a really cool, *purely fictional* idea for a novel. But as I did further research for these notes, I ran headlong into a drug that was uncannily similar to Nirolex.

And which yielded results that were uncannily similar to the results experienced by our stalwart crew.

In fact, I discovered an entire book about this drug, which eerily parallels Nirolex's role. It's called *DMT: The Spirit Molecule* by Rick Strassman, M.D. (2000). Diving into it to refine these notes left me stunned, as it hinted that *Nexus* may be much closer to the truth than I had imagined.

Strassman's book chronicles his groundbreaking clinical trials in the early 1990s, where he administered intravenous DMT (N,N-Dimethyltryptamine)—a potent, naturally occurring psychedelic—to over 60 volunteers in a controlled medical setting. DMT is found in trace amounts in the human body and plants, and is a key ingredient in brews used in shamanic rituals. What makes it the "spirit molecule," as Strassman calls it, is its ability to rocket users into hyperreal, otherworldly experiences in mere minutes, often feeling more vivid and meaningful than waking life.

The parallels to Nirolex are *insane*. In the novel, Nirolex is designed to facilitate direct contact with a higher-dimensional being, dissolving the crew's sense of self and opening a gateway to timeless, non-dual awareness. Strassman's volunteers reported something strikingly similar: breakthrough doses of DMT propelled them into alternate realms where they encountered intelligent, autonomous entities—often described as aliens, machine elves, insectoid beings, or spiritual guides. These weren't vague hallucinations; they felt like genuine interactions with external intelligences in multidimensional spaces.

One volunteer recounted meeting beings who imparted knowledge about the fabric of reality. Another described merging with a vast, loving consciousness that transcended time and space, much like the crew's experience in the story.

User reports from Strassman's studies (and countless anecdotal accounts since) paint a fascinating, consistent picture. DMT experiences often begin with a rapid "breakthrough"—a sensation of blasting through a membrane into hyperspace, accompanied by geometric fractals, vibrant colors, and a dissolution of the ego. Time collapses; past, present, and future blend into an eternal now. Entities frequently communicate telepathically, offering profound insights. Many users emerge transformed, with a deepened sense of interconnectedness, reduced fear of death, and a conviction that they've glimpsed a hidden layer of existence.

In *Nexus*, the pyramids are cross-sections of a single higher-dimensional entity, intersecting our reality like fingertips on a 2D plane. DMT users often describe their encounters in similar terms: beings from "higher dimensions" or parallel realities, defying 3D physics.

What fascinates me most is how *Nexus* inadvertently echoes these real reports while taking them a step further. In the novel, the crew's contact reveals that consciousness itself is multidimensional, a key to truths beyond physics textbooks. Strassman's volunteers often returned with the same epiphany. DMT isn't just scrambling the brain, it's tuning it to frequencies of reality we normally filter out. Advanced meditators achieve similar states without drugs (as in tukdam or rigpa), suggesting the potential is innate, just as *Nexus* ultimately reveals that Nirolex was a placebo—the crew communed with the entity through pure awareness.

Recent studies at Imperial College London and Johns Hopkins confirm DMT's role in inducing entity encounters and ego death, with brain scans showing reduced DMN activity and increased connectivity akin to deep meditation. Some physicists, inspired by string theory's extra dimensions, speculate that psychedelics might allow glimpses into these hidden realms.

Strassman's studies were groundbreaking. The first U.S. government-approved human research with psychedelics in about 20 years. In fact, they restarted a field that had been effectively shut down since the early 1970s. But the research stagnated again after this. The delay wasn't because DMT lacked intrigue—it was due to decades of legal/regulatory roadblocks and cultural stigma. Now that those barriers are slowly easing, DMT is finally getting the attention it deserves.

Imperial College London recently conducted proof-of-concept studies on DMT infusions (published in 2023), with participants reporting entity encounters and immersion in alternate realities. Researchers have discussed follow-up trials that could test whether these realms and entities are shared or objective, calling them potentially explosive, with implications rivaling alien disclosure.

Proposed designs include inter-participant communication tests, where isolated volunteers in simultaneous DMT states attempt to meet, exchange verifiable passwords, or describe shared layouts. Success could suggest a reality beyond individual brains. Participants might also query entities for novel, verifiable facts.

As of early 2026, these ambitious trials remain in planning, with no published results yet available.

The twist in Nexus was that Nirolex wasn't even needed—pure consciousness did the work. This reflects emerging evidence that the potential for expanded states is already latent within us, waiting to be accessed through practice. And the more we learn about the awesome and mysterious power of the human mind (see below) the more I'm convinced that the next leap in human understanding might be inward rather than just technological.

The Timeless Nature of the Entity (Block Universe & Simultaneous Perception): Einstein's block universe is real physics: in special and general relativity, time is treated as a fourth dimension, and all moments—past, present, and future— exist equally in a 4-dimensional "block." The entity's ability to perceive all timelines simultaneously is a logical extension: if it exists in higher dimensions, it could navigate time as easily as we move through space. Quantum mechanics adds further support with concepts like superposition (all possibilities existing until observed) and the many-worlds interpretation (all outcomes branching simultaneously).

The Pyramids of Giza Connection: The ancient pyramids of Giza were constructed around 4,500 years ago with astonishing precision (more about that below), and modern technologies like muon tomography and ground-penetrating radar are being used, and are revealing hidden chambers and corridors.

In *Nexus*, the entity only *inspires* the ancient Egyptians to undertake the monumental task of building the Giza pyramids, it doesn't do it for them. Still, the real-world achievements of the ancient builders remain one of humanity's most awe-inspiring engineering feats—and yes, they still spark plenty of healthy debate and wonder on their own.

The scale alone boggles the mind: the Great Pyramid of Giza required precisely placing about 2.3 *million* massive stone blocks—some weighing up to 80 tons—into a structure taller than a 40-story building. Its base is ridiculously close to a perfect square, with each side measuring about two city blocks long, and with the sides aligned to true north within a fraction of a degree. The precision is staggering: the base is level to within inches across its enormous footprint, and the blocks fit so tightly that you couldn't slide a razor blade between many joints.

Even with today's cranes, lasers, GPS, and heavy machinery, replicating this would be an immense challenge—requiring flawless surveying in harsh desert conditions, transporting and lifting colossal weights, and maintaining structural integrity over millennia without steel reinforcements or advanced modeling software. Many engineers today admit that while possible with unlimited resources, it would still push the limits of current technology, logistics, and human coordination, making the ancient accomplishment feel almost superhuman.

The bottom line is that if the Egyptians didn't have any help from aliens, they pulled off something truly extraordinary. While *Nexus* posits that they built it on their own, we can't rule out the possibility that run-of-the-mill 3D aliens—non-fictional ones—gave them a hand.

But that's for another novel . . . .

The Power of the Human Mind—Additional Mysteries and Possibilities: The human mind is far more powerful—and mysterious—than we can possibly imagine. In *Nexus*, the crew's ability to commune with a higher-dimensional entity without any external aid reflects a deep belief that consciousness itself holds untapped potential. This idea isn't just speculative fiction; it's inspired by real, documented phenomena that science is still struggling to fully explain. Here are a few examples:

Tukdam: Meditation After Death—A Scientific Mystery: Tukdam was something I first learned of from Joshua. Wow! Really? How could something like this be known to exist, yet so few people be aware of it? (I checked around, and I wasn't the only one who hadn't heard about it).

As you know from the novel, this is an extraordinary phenomenon in Tibetan Buddhist tradition—a state in which deceased monks show no signs of normal decomposition for days, weeks, or even longer after clinical death. Their bodies remain warm and flexible, their facial expressions peaceful, as if the meditator is still in deep contemplation.

Clinically, death has been confirmed (no heartbeat, no brain activity), yet biologically, something delays the usual processes. For Tibetan practitioners, the explanation is clear: consciousness has not yet fully departed the body.

Modern science is only beginning to investigate. Pilot studies have used EEG, thermal imaging, and other tools to document cases. This really happens! While results are preliminary, they suggest unusual stability in body temperature and tissue integrity—phenomena that challenge our current understanding of death.

Meditation and Neuroscience: How the Mind Changes the Body: Over the past two decades, meditation has become a serious field of neuroscience. Researchers like Dr. Richard J. Davidson (University of Wisconsin-Madison) and Dr. Antoine Lutz (Inserm, Lyon) have collaborated with long-term Buddhist practitioners to document measurable changes.

Key findings include:

- Increased gray matter density in the prefrontal cortex (attention, decision-making).
- Larger hippocampus (memory, emotion regulation).
- Altered connectivity in the default mode network (DMN)—the "self-referential" network active during mind-wandering.
- Increased gamma oscillations (30–100 Hz) during states of unity and clarity—a pattern seen in very experienced meditators.

On the physical side:

- Lower cortisol (stress hormone) levels.
- Improved immune function.
- Increased telomerase activity (delaying cellular aging—first shown in a 2009 study led by Nobel laureate Elizabeth Blackburn).

These changes show that sustained mental practice literally reshapes the brain and body—supporting the novel's idea that consciousness can access states far beyond ordinary perception.

The Placebo and Nocebo Effects: The Mind as Healer and Harmer: It has now been proven beyond a reasonable doubt that in many instances the mind is able to heal the body, using mechanisms that are not entirely clear.

The placebo effect is one of the most robust, reproducible phenomena in all of medicine—and it's growing stronger over time. Patients given sugar pills in clinical trials often improve dramatically, sometimes matching or exceeding the effects of real drugs. Studies have shown this in conditions ranging from pain and depression to Parkinson's disease and even surgery. In one famous trial of knee osteoarthritis patients, those who received sham surgery (incisions made but no actual repair) improved just as much as those who had real procedures.

The nocebo effect is the dark twin: negative expectations can cause real harm. Tell someone a pill will make them sick or impotent, and it often does—even if it's inert. The mind can trigger nausea, pain, erectile dysfunction, or tics purely through belief.

These effects aren't "just in the head" in a dismissive sense—they produce measurable physiological changes: inflammation, altered brain activity, changes in dopamine and endorphin levels. As someone who spent decades in biotech, I know this all too well: new drugs sometimes fail trials not because they don't work, but because the placebo response is so powerful that the drug can't outperform it.

In *Nexus*, the crew's consciousness expansion without Nirolex echoes this: when belief, expectation, and intention align, the mind can produce extraordinary change.

Inedia and Breatharianism: Living Without Food? Inedia and Breatharianism embody the idea that some people can live without food or water, sustained by prana, sunlight, or cosmic energy (which, in my novel, *Quantum Lens*, I proposed was the result of the quantum nature of consciousness being able to tap into zero-point energy from the quantum foam).

While most cases have been debunked, a few remain unexplained. The most famous is Prahlad Jani ("Mataji"), an Indian yogi who claimed decades without food or water. In 2003 and 2010, Indian military hospitals observed him under 24-hour surveillance for 10 and 15 days. He consumed nothing, showed no dehydration/starvation, and produced minimal waste—with normal vitals. Skeptics question the studies, but the cases have never been fully explained. Science says humans can't survive long without calories/hydration—yet these phenomena challenge assumptions about mind-body limits.

Other Real Phenomena Highlighting the Mind's Power

- Spontaneous Remission of Cancer: Hundreds of verified cases exist where advanced cancers disappear without treatment. Mechanisms are unknown, but many involve profound psychological or spiritual shifts.
- Extreme Meditation and Body Control: Tibetan monks practicing g-tummo can raise body temperature by up to 8.3°C (15°F) and dry wet sheets in freezing conditions—confirmed by Harvard studies (Benson et al., 1982).
- Hypnosis and Pain Control: Under hypnosis, people undergo surgery without anesthesia and report no pain—with reduced activity in brain pain-processing areas, showing the mind can override "hardwired" signals.

These real-world mysteries all point to the same idea: consciousness isn't just a passenger in the body. It can influence, modulate, and perhaps even transcend physical limits in ways we don't fully understand.

Rigpa and the Nature of Consciousness: Many spiritual traditions describe a fundamental awareness beyond thought, self, and duality. In Tibetan Buddhism (especially Dzogchen), this is called rigpa—the "original, pure awareness" that underlies all experience.

Modern neuroscience is beginning to explore similar states. Psychedelics and advanced meditation both reduce DMN activity, leading to ego dissolution and non-dual experiences. The novel's entity—a consciousness without sequential thought, without subject-object separation—is speculative, but it draws inspiration from these reports of pure, timeless awareness.

And we've already covered DMT, the so-called spirit molecule.

More and more scientists and philosophers are arguing that consciousness may be the fundamental reality—both primary and irreducible (which I'll explain more below). The novel's hopeful message—that humanity has untapped potential for expanded consciousness—reflects real scientific and experiential evidence that these states are accessible.

Fundamental/Primary Consciousness: The usual story modern science tells is that the universe is made of tiny physical bits like atoms, particles, and energy. Over billions of years, those bits bump together, form stars, planets, life, and brains. Eventually, consciousness pops out as a kind of side effect or "extra feature" from a very complicated brain.

But many are now arguing that consciousness comes first—it's the primary or fundamental thing. Everything else, the physical world we see, touch, and measure, is actually a kind of appearance or "display" inside consciousness. A good analogy is a dream. When we dream at night, the whole dream world—houses, people, physics, our bodies—feel completely real and solid. But none of it is made of "real" matter. It's all happening within our minds. The mind is the primary reality, and the dream stuff is just patterns or images inside that mind.

Philosophers like Bernardo Kastrup believe the waking universe is similar. That there's one big, universal consciousness (like a cosmic mind), and what we experience as separate physical things are like split-off or filtered parts of that bigger consciousness. So matter isn't the foundation—consciousness is. Support for this idea was given directly in the novel.

Near-death experiences (NDEs) were also mentioned in the novel. As a reminder of what I wrote: There are now highly credible documentaries and books on the subject. Accounts from numerous people who have been on the brink of death or clinically dead before resuscitation. And they share astonishing commonalities. Individuals report being able to observe their own bodies and events from above. Traveling toward a bright, welcoming light, and experiencing overwhelming feelings of peace, joy, and love. And so on. Many also report heightened awareness, altered perception of time, and a sense of entering another realm.

I then went on to detail the case of Pam Reynolds, which defies all reason.

In any event, NDEs also support Kastrup's views. Why? Because NDEs involve profound, expanded states of consciousness—like feelings of complete unity with everything and a reduced or absent sense of personal self—that many people report when brain activity is *severely reduced, flatlined, or absent.* This creates a puzzle for the standard physicalist view, which expects consciousness to fade or vanish when the brain shuts down dramatically.

In contrast, it fits naturally with Kastrup's idea that the brain acts like a filter or blockade that normally limits our access to a much broader universal consciousness. So, when brain function drops sharply, the filter weakens—allowing more of that vast, connected awareness to come through vividly, explaining why experiences can feel clearer and more intense precisely when the brain is *least* active.

I'll leave you with a few books on NDEs that are highly regarded, in case you have further interest:

Consciousness Beyond Life: The Science of the Near-Death Experience by Pim van Lommel (2010). Written by a Dutch cardiologist, this book draws on his landmark prospective study published in The Lancet of NDEs in cardiac arrest survivors across multiple hospitals. It presents strong evidence that consciousness can occur during periods of no brain activity and explores implications for mind-brain relationships. It's widely praised for its rigorous medical perspective and is considered one of the most scientifically robust books on the topic.

After: A Doctor Explores What Near-Death Experiences Reveal about Life and Beyond by Bruce Greyson (2021). Greyson, a psychiatrist and one of the world's leading NDE researchers, reflects on four decades of study. This memoir-style book combines personal insights with scientific analysis and is frequently highlighted as authoritative.

The Hard Problem of Consciousness: This was also touched upon in the novel. In fact, after I wrote this section of the notes, I liked my explanation so much, I used some of it in the body of the novel to match. So a bit of this you've read already, but there is also new material.

Much about the brain can be explained in purely physical terms—how neurons fire, how information moves around, how the brain controls behavior, solves problems, etc. Those are considered the "easy" questions, which doesn't mean they aren't impossibly hard to actually figure out.

But there's one thing we can't reduce or explain away with just physics: why does any of that brain activity feel like something from the inside? Why is there a subjective "what it's like" to see the color red, feel pain, taste chocolate, or be happy? That's the famous "hard problem."

Irreducible means one can't boil consciousness down to purely physical ingredients the way you can boil water down to H_2O molecules. No matter how detailed the description of brain chemistry, wiring, and electricity gets, it will never fully explain why there's an inner experience attached to it. An often-used analogy—which I've already used in this novel and in the notes of one of my earlier novels—is this: Imagine explaining to someone born blind what the color red "looks like." You could describe wavelengths of light, cone cells in the eye, brain areas lighting up, and so on, but you'd never convey the actual experience of *redness*. That inner quality doesn't reduce to the physical story—it's something extra and fundamental that exists alongside physics, not derived from it.

The bottom line is that these ideas challenge the view that we're just biological machines made of matter, with no deeper meaning. If consciousness is primary, we aren't stuck in a purely material world where everything is limited by physics and death. Instead, consciousness might be the deepest reality, and our everyday mind is just a narrow slice of something much bigger.

Science is starting to back this idea up with brain scans and studies showing these experiences are real and transformative, rather than just imaginary. Which offers real hope that humanity has a huge inner potential waiting to be explored.

FICTIONAL PAPER: Geometry of Consciousness: A Physical Model of Multidimensional Intelligence

The fictional paper provided below, 'authored' by Dr. Lukas Heuer, explores speculative physics inspired by the story. It's not real science but draws from concepts in M-theory and quantum consciousness. And this is all Joshua. Math was my best subject, but I was a molecular biology major so I stopped taking courses after calculus.

This is my long-winded way of saying that this math is beyond me, so thanks to Joshua for putting it together.

Geometry of Consciousness: A Physical Model of Multidimensional Intelligence

Dr. Lukas Heuer for the Journal of Theoretical Physics

Abstract: Based on direct observation during the *Hope* mission, we present a theoretical model of an intelligence operating in six spatial dimensions and possibly multiple temporal dimensions. Our analysis suggests that such entities manifest fundamental properties of M-theory and enable a new understanding of the relationship between consciousness and spacetime geometry.

Introduction: The encounter with the multidimensional entity during the *Hope* mission requires a radical reconceptualization of our understanding of intelligence and consciousness. The observed phenomena can only be understood if we consider the entity as a being operating in the additional dimensions postulated by M-theory.

Dimensional structure: The entity exists in a 6+1-dimensional spacetime continuum, with three dimensions overlapping with our known space and three more located in the compactified Calabi-Yau spaces of string theory. Its "physicality" manifests itself as a topological structure in this higher-dimensional space.

Mathematically, we can describe its existence as a closed 6-form in an 11-dimensional manifold:

$\Omega^6 = d\Theta^5$, where Θ^5 is a 5-form on the Calabi-Yau manifold.

The three pyramids we observed were 3-dimensional projections (hypercross-sections) of this 6-form into our familiar 3+1 spacetime.

Temporal perception: The most remarkable feature of the entity is its relationship to time. While we experience time as a dimension through which we can only move in one direction, the entity possesses what we must call "temporal navigability."

Consider the Minkowski metric of our 4-dimensional spacetime:

$ds^2 = -c^2dt^2 + dx^2 + dy^2 + dz^2$

For the entity, the extended metric appears as:

$ds^2 = -c^2dt_1{}^2 + dt_2{}^2 + dx^{(1)2} + dx^{(2)2} + dx^{(3)2} + dy^{(1)2} + dy^{(2)2} + dz^{(1)2}$

where t_2 represents a second, space-like time dimension that allows it to move orthogonally to our time direction.

Information processing: The entity does not process information sequentially, but holographically. Its "consciousness" can be understood as a quantum mechanical field that extends across all six spatial dimensions:

$\Psi(x_1,x_2,x_3,y_1,y_2,y_3,t_1,t_2) = \Sigma_n\ c_n\ \varphi_n(x_1,x_2,x_3,y_1,y_2,y_3)\ \exp(i\omega_n t_1 + i\kappa_n t_2)$

Each state φ_n represents a simultaneous state of information that appears in our space-time as separate, temporally distributed events.

Gravitational effects: The gravitational waves we measure are created by the projection of the entity's movements in higher-dimensional space into our 3+1 dimensions. These projections manifest as modulated gravitational waves with characteristic frequencies:

$$h_+(t) = A_+ \cos(\omega t + \varphi_+) \times \Pi(x^{(i)})$$

$$h_((t) = A_(\cos(\omega t + \varphi_() \times \Pi(x^{(i)})$$

where $\Pi(x^{(i)})$ is a projection function from the higher dimensions.

Causality and communication: The entity's apparent lack of response to our initial attempts at communication results from its fundamentally different relationship to causality. In its 6+2-dimensional reality, causal loops are possible, which appear in our spacetime as acausal correlations.

Communication did not take place through information transfer in the classical sense, but through quantum mechanical entanglement between our states of consciousness and the corresponding state vectors of the entity in the extended Hilbert space.

Geometry of the Consciousness: Our observations suggest that consciousness itself is a geometric property of spacetime. The entity exists in a state of maximum coherence across all available dimensions:

$$|\Psi\rangle = \int\int\int\int\int\int \psi(x_1,x_2,x_3,y_1,y_2,y_3)\,|x_1,x_2,x_3,y_1,y_2,y_3\rangle\, dx_1dx_2dx_3dy_1dy_2dy_3$$

This state corresponds to a complete superposition of all possible configurations in its space of existence.

Implications for the physics of consciousness: The fact that human consciousness—albeit only temporarily and under special circumstances—can interact with such a higher-dimensional system suggests that consciousness itself is not completely limited to three spatial dimensions.

It is possible that the quantum processes postulated by Penrose and Hameroff in the microtubules of neurons are actually projections of higher-dimensional consciousness processes into our 3-dimensional neural substrate.

Conclusion: The multidimensional entity represents a form of intelligence that is optimally adapted to the M-theoretical structure of reality. Its existence dramatically expands our understanding of both physics and the possible forms of consciousness.

The most important insight is that the universe may be populated by forms of intelligence so fundamentally different in structure from our own that we can only perceive them as forces of nature—until our own consciousness reaches the dimensionality required for direct encounter.

Correspondence: Dr. Lukas Heuer, Department of Theoretical Physics, Max Planck Institute for Gravitational Physics, Potsdam

That concludes our commentary on the novel. Thanks to those of you who decided to give this section a read, and thanks again for reading *Nexus*. Until the next time . . .

About the Authors

Douglas E. Richards is the *New York Times* and *USA Today* bestselling author of science-fiction thrillers that have sold more than three million copies (see list below). Richards has been celebrated for his gripping, thought-provoking works that blend cutting-edge scientific concepts with heart-pounding narratives.

Richards burst onto the literary scene with his debut novel, WIRED, published in 2010. The novel garnered widespread acclaim for its ingenious combination of scientific speculation and thrilling storytelling. This success set the stage for a series of bestselling novels, each marked by meticulous research, riveting plots, and characters that resonate with readers.

Known for his ability to translate complex scientific concepts into accessible and engaging narratives, Richards has become a go-to author for readers seeking an intellectually stimulating and adrenaline-fueled reading experience. His works delve deeply into the ethical dilemmas posed by scientific breakthroughs and the potential impact of technology on society.

A former Director of Biotechnology Licensing at Bristol Myers Squibb and a former biotechnology executive, Richards earned a BS in microbiology from the Ohio State University, a master's degree in genetic engineering from the University of Wisconsin—where he engineered mutant viruses now named after him—and an MBA from the University of Chicago.

The author has two grown children and lives in San Diego, California, with his wife and dog.

Richards loves hearing from readers, and always replies, so feel free to write to him at douglaserichards1@gmail.com and address him as "Doug". You can also Friend Richards on Facebook at Douglas E. Richards Author, or visit his website, where you can sign up to be notified of new releases.

SCIENCE FICTION THRILLERS BY DOUGLAS E. RICHARDS

<u>SERIES</u>

WIRED (Wired 1)
AMPED (Wired 2)

MIND'S EYE (Nick Hall 1)
BRAINWEB (Nick Hall 2)
MIND WAR (Nick Hall 3)
UNLEASHED (Nick Hall 4)

SPLIT SECOND (Split Second 1)
TIME FRAME (Split Second 2)

THE ENIGMA CUBE (Alien Artifact 1)
A PIVOT IN TIME (Alien Artifact 2)

<u>STANDALONE NOVELS</u>

QUANTUM LENS
GAME CHANGER

INFINITY BORN
SEEKER
VERACITY
ORACLE
THE IMMORTALITY CODE
UNIDENTIFIED
PORTALS
THE CURE
THE BREAKTHROUGH EFFECT

KIDS SCIENCE FICTION THRILLERS (9 and up, enjoyed by kids and adults alike)

TRAPPED (Prometheus Project 1)
CAPTURED (Prometheus Project 2)
STRANDED (Prometheus Project 3)

OUT OF THIS WORLD
DEVIL'S SWORD

Joshua T. Calvert is an award-winning author whose books have sold two million copies, reached the *USA Today* bestseller list and are currently available in English, German, Spanish, Italian and Russian. He is a regular speaker at universities, book fairs, and symposiums.

Printed in Dunstable, United Kingdom

81858032R00171